PASSION DENIED

"Tynan, you've shared your theory," Amara contended. "What I choose to do with it is my business. Now please leave before you embarrass us any more than you already have."

"What I really ought to do is take you out of that bed, sling you over my shoulder, and carry you back up to my suite."

"No!" Amara objected sharply. "Just say good night and go."

Rather than comply, Tynan pulled her into his arms and kissed her with soul-searching intensity. He felt her relax against his chest, compliant, seemingly eager for more, and he could not draw away until lack of breath demanded that he do so. Even then, he felt her reluctance to part. "Please come back to me," he whispered.

"No, I can't."

That wasn't the response he tasted in her kiss, and Tynan straightened up slowly. "You're lying. Why?"

CINNAMON BURKE

RAPTURE'S MIST

LEISURE BOOKS **NEW YORK CITY**

A LEISURE BOOK®

July 1993

Published by

Dorchester Publishing Co., Inc.
276 Fifth Avenue
New York, NY 10001

Rapture's Mist is gratefully dedicated to Julian J. Edney, whose suggestion we brainstorm in the Claretian Fathers' courtyard inspired its creation.

RAPTURE'S MIST

Chapter One

Lieutenant Amara Greer entered the office of the Secretary of Alado's Diplomatic Corps, crossed the gleaming black floor with three graceful strides, and upon reaching the ebony desk, greeted her superior with a seductive smile and a jaunty salute. Eager for a far more personal exchange, the tall blond man circled his desk and came forward to embrace the slender pilot. He nuzzled her neck, then tugged at her earlobe with a playful nibble.

"I've missed you," he whispered.

"The cease-fire must be holding," Amara replied. "I've not seen you this relaxed in weeks."

He stepped back, but left his hands resting lightly on the gentle curve of Amara's hips. They were both dressed in the iridescent gold uniforms of

11

the Diplomatic Corps, but her flightsuit had been spun to fit her lissome figure as snugly as a blush, while his jacket and slacks were more generously tailored to accommodate his superbly muscled build. Although of near equal height and with similar coloring, the intimacy of their gestures would have precluded anyone from ever mistaking them for brother and sister.

"It's holding," he assured her, "but only because I've arranged for Tynan Thorn, one of the most brilliant minds in the galaxy, to negotiate the peace, and when the treaty is signed, I intend to take full credit for it."

"As well you should." Amara slid her fingers through the tawny curls at his nape. "I was told you had an important assignment. Was that merely an excuse to see me?"

"No, of course not." He pulled her close for another lingering hug and didn't release her until he had had his fill of her luscious warmth. He then leaned back against his desk, folded his arms across his chest, and regarded her with a mischievous grin. "I'm making you responsible for Tynan Thorn's transportation. The Guardians are historians and have no spacecraft, so it will be your responsibility to see that he arrives at the conference site safely."

Stunned by the enormity of his request, Amara stared at the Secretary for a long moment before venting her exasperation. "I'd assumed he was already on his way there. How can you expect me to make the flight to Earth and back in time for the scheduled opening of the conference? It can't be done."

"Not in a diplomatic shuttle it can't, but I've arranged for a Starcruiser for you. If you leave now, you should be able to deliver Thorn to the Confederation base with at least fifteen minutes to spare."

His gaze had taken on a decidedly mocking gleam, and Amara grew wary. "Are you teasing me? The Guardians are one of the few exclusively male organizations. How is Thorn going to react? Will he merely be uncomfortable traveling with a woman, or will he be deeply insulted? How about giving me a male co-pilot?"

Unconcerned by her apprehensions, the Secretary, an accomplished diplomat, responded with a careless shrug. "I'll not allow whatever archaic sexist prejudices the Guardians may harbor to influence my choice of pilot. You're qualified; that's my only consideration." He straightened up, walked around his desk, and withdrew a large envelope from the top drawer. "You'll have no need for a co-pilot on such a routine flight.

"Here are all the necessary documents for the flight. You'll find your ship in docking bay eleven. Its library contains all of Thorn's writings. Familiarize yourself with his opinions so you'll understand him when you meet. I know I don't need to remind you of the importance of this mission. Without Thorn's participation, the other four corporations will boycott the conference. Peaceful exploration of space will be a thing of the past, and all the blame will fall on your pretty, freckled shoulders."

He paused, allowing a moment's contemplation to magnify his threat before he dismissed her abruptly. "Your gear has already been stowed aboard your new ship, and I know you've no one else to tell good-bye. I won't keep you any longer. You may go."

Amara had been the Secretary's personal pilot for three months and romantically involved with him for nearly as long, so she had had ample opportunity to observe his swiftly changing moods. He was a remarkably skilled lover who engaged in sex with the same artful concentration with which he undertook any challenge, but she did not appreciate this brusque reminder of the difference in their status. If not impossible, her assignment would certainly prove difficult, but he had not even wished her luck, let alone bid her the affectionate farewell she had expected from her lover. *Former lover,* she vowed silently.

Feeling betrayed, she watched him turn the golden dragon placed on the corner of his desk so that the crystal ball clutched tightly in the mythical beast's claws would better catch the light and throw a thousand brilliant rainbows against the room's pale gold walls. When he glanced up, and appeared to be surprised to see her still standing there, she could no longer control her temper. "I made a serious mistake in becoming personally involved with you, and it won't continue," she informed him with the same icy detachment he had just shown her. "After the conference, I'm going to request a transfer, and I'll expect a flawless performance evaluation."

Amused by her defiant demand, the Secretary again flashed a disarming grin. "As exciting as it would surely be, we've no time to quarrel and make up before you go. Besides, regardless of how we feel about each other, I want you to be confident about one thing—you'll not receive any kind of a recommendation, glowing or otherwise, unless Tynan Thorn attends the opening ceremony of the conference."

Amara was too angry to respond and didn't bother with another salute before she fled the elegant black and gold office. Devoted to her career, she had allowed few men the closeness she had shared with the Secretary, but he had just made it sickeningly clear that what mattered most to him was the success of the peace conference. The love conveyed by his abundant kisses had been no deeper than the highly polished sheen on his office floor. He had once described her as enchanting, but now she felt as though he merely regarded her as useful. She couldn't abide being used by anyone.

It was his smile that had been her undoing— that, and the incredible softness of his hands.

Annoyed with her own weakness as well as her ex-lover's insincere smiles, Amara forced all thought of him from her mind and hurried to one of the small, high-speed shuttles that connected the interior levels of the Fleet Command Base with the docking bays located on the outer ring. Built in the shape of a gigantic rotating wheel, its revolutions were timed to recreate the gravitational force of Earth. When she reached bay eleven, she found the newest Starcruiser in the fleet ready for take-off. Twice the size of a diplomatic shuttle, its sides were emblazoned with Alado's stylized wings—a pair of equilateral triangles bisected by a lightning bolt.

It wasn't the mere size of the ship that impressed Amara, however, but that it had, astonishingly, been outfitted with laser cannons. She ripped open the envelope she had been given and found her orders were specific in that regard. She was to defend Tynan Thorn with every means possible, which included not merely permission, but encouragement to fire on any vessel which exhibited threatening behavior. Clearly this was no "routine" flight!

Alarmed, Amara returned the mechanics' waves and hurriedly boarded the ship. Once seated in the cockpit, she re-read her orders, but there was no possible way they could be misunderstood. She was to guard Tynan Thorn's life with her own and not allow anything or anyone to prevent him from reaching the peace conference. In her opinion, such drastic action wouldn't be necessary. Fighting between the corporations had been confined to the uncolonized areas of the galaxy; no battles had been staged near Earth. Having an armed ship was a comfort, though, and pressed for time, Amara began her pre-flight preparations.

She still had reservations about the wisdom of sending a woman to fetch a man who cherished the cloistered life, but now that she had been given the opportunity to fly a Starcruiser, she wasn't going to complain about the mission. Her attention focused on the launch, it wasn't until she had left Fleet Command that she realized what the Secretary had done. He was the only diplomat she knew who excelled in provoking troublesome incidents merely to provide himself with challenges to overcome.

Sending her to get Tynan Thorn had been a monstrous practical joke, but she wasn't going to fall for it. She was going to provide the philosopher with the best escort imaginable so that he would have absolutely no reason to complain. Not only that, she would not merely produce him in time for the peace conference, but at least a day early. With that goal in mind, she ran the necessary calculations through the on-board computer, set the engines for the optimum speed, and sat back to enjoy the beginning of what she hoped would be a fast and smooth flight. There would be plenty of time to study Tynan Thorn's writings, but for now, all she wanted was a nap.

An only child, Amara Greer had the perfect temperament for a pilot and reveled in the isolation of space. By the time she reached Earth, she knew more about flying a Starcruiser than the engineers who had designed the ship. She also knew a great deal about Tynan Thorn. He wrote convincingly of peace and love as man's natural state, but there were no pictures of him in the files, and so little information about his personal life that she was most anxious to meet him. As she approached Norham Castle, she practiced what she wished to say and hoped Tynan would prove to be as charming a man as his writings made him sound.

Norham Castle had no landing facilities for spacecraft, forcing Amara to bring down the Starcruiser in an adjacent field. The castle was located atop a rocky cliff overhanging the Tweed River, and in the gathering dusk, the high walls and tower of the medieval fortress presented a forbidding silhouette. Restored from ancient ruins at the dawn of the twenty-first century, the original castle had once served as the residence of Edward I and claimed a long and glorious history during which possession had frequently passed between Scotland and England. No battles had been fought here in centuries, but despite knowing Tynan Thorn's pacifist views, Amara had the uncomfortable sensation that the Guardians still had the catapults loaded with boulders and were ready for a fight.

She opened the hatch and waited for a welcoming committee to appear, but when after fifteen minutes none had, she secured the vessel and trudged her own path across the deeply furrowed soil. Her gold leather boots came to mid-calf and didn't fill with dirt, but it still wasn't an enjoyable jaunt. When she reached the gravel road leading to the castle's immense gate, she again waited for someone to greet her. The Starcruiser was nearly silent in flight, but she could not believe her landing had gone unnoticed. She was positive Tynan Thorn was expecting Alado to send a ship for him, so why was her arrival being ignored?

Impatient to be on their way, she strode up to the tall wooden gate. A brass falcon attacking a fleeing rabbit served as the knocker and she grabbed the outstretched wing and sent the hawk's talons clanging against the rabbit's back. "What a charming touch," she murmured. She counted to ten slowly, then whammed on the knocker with brutal force. This time she heard someone scurrying to admit her. She stepped back, and when a small window cut into the door in the gate opened a crack, she smiled widely and introduced herself as Lieutenant Greer, Tynan Thorn's escort. Rather than being promptly admitted as she had expected, the window was hurriedly slammed shut before she had gotten even a brief glimpse of the man who had peered out, and the door remained closed.

The Starcruiser's emergency supplies contained climbing gear, but Amara hadn't thought she would have to scale the castle's walls to gain entrance. She grabbed the ornate knocker and this time thumped out three dots, three dashes, and three dots. It was a twentieth-century distress call, so she assumed the Guardians would recognize it, but she had to repeat the sequence several times before the small window was opened.

"Good evening," she tried again. "I didn't mean to disturb you. Please tell Tynan Thorn that his escort from Alado is here, and that we must leave immediately."

"Who are you?"

Shadows prevented Amara from seeing the man's face, but the suspicion in his voice wasn't encouraging. She tried not to sound sarcastic as she repeated her rank and name, but she was fast losing patience with the Guardians. She heard more scurrying feet, and while she couldn't make out their faces, she felt certain several Guardians were observing her now.

"I realize you don't entertain women here," she assured them, "but I don't plan to stay. Now where is Tynan Thorn?"

A muffled debate preceded the opening of the door, but when a hooded figure gestured for Amara to enter, she did. Four Guardians, their hoods drawn forward to shield their faces, regarded her for a long moment before again gesturing and leading her toward the massive tower that was the main structure of the Guardians' Keep. The path led across an inner courtyard, but long shadows hid the purpose of the small buildings clustered against the walls.

An outside staircase led to the second-floor entrance of the Keep, but once they had reached the small entry room, Amara's silent companions gestured toward a wooden bench and withdrew. She assumed they had gone to summon Tynan, but the philosopher did not appear nearly soon enough to suit her. Seizing the initiative, she rose and went to the door through which the Guardians had disappeared. When she found it locked, she swore under her breath and rather than return to the uncomfortable bench, began to pace the length of the small room. She counted the smooth rectangular stones in the floor, and with every step felt the wasted minutes draining away. When the door finally opened, she rushed forward so as not to be shut out again.

This man slipped the hood of his long robe down upon his shoulders and smiled warmly before he pulled the door closed behind him. Unlike her silent escort, he radiated a charming tranquility rather than a hostile gloom.

"Good afternoon, Lieutenant Greer. I'm Gregory Nash, the Director of the Guardians. I'm so sorry that you were kept waiting, but we have a bit of a problem here."

The Director was an attractive man in his fifties with curly gray hair and bright blue eyes, but Amara wasn't taken in by his fatherly manner. Unwilling to listen to any derogatory remarks directed at female pilots, she straightened her shoulders proudly. "Alado selects its flight crews with the utmost care. I'm the ranking pilot in the diplomatic corps, and that means I'm the best they could have sent. Now I would like to finally collect Tynan Thorn and be on my way."

While at first perplexed by her spirited defense of her qualifications, Gregory swiftly realized he was at fault. "Please forgive me if I offended you. The problem is not with you, lieutenant, but with Tynan. He frequently spends his afternoons in our gardens. I realize it was too late at the time of your arrival for you to have seen them clearly, but they are magnificent."

"Yes, I'm sure they are, but—"

Gregory raised his hand to plead for patience. "Please, lieutenant, let me finish. Tynan went out to meditate in the garden yesterday and unfortunately was stung by bees. That wouldn't be a problem for most men, but he had a severe allergic reaction and is now confined to his bed. I'm afraid he won't be able to leave here for several days."

He was obviously sincere, but Amara couldn't agree with him. "The peace conference begins in ten days. Perhaps you are unfamiliar with the times required for space travel, but we'll not arrive at the Confederation base for the opening ceremonies unless we leave within the hour."

"But Tynan is ill."

"I understand that, but he can recuperate on board my Starcruiser just as easily as he can here." Born on one of Alado's spaceships, Amara knew that she would be disparagingly described by the people of Earth as a Starchild. In her view, it was a ridiculous prejudice when they were all human.

"Now, may I please speak with him?" she continued. "I can't believe he would risk jeopardizing the conference for a few beestings."

She was being flippant, but Gregory excused it as evidence of her frustration and spoke with deliberate care. "You're the first woman ever to be allowed inside our walls. To provide you with full access to the Keep is completely out of the question. Go back to your ship. Contact Alado and instruct them to delay the conference for a week. Tynan will then be fully recovered, and arriving on time won't be a problem."

Anticipating the day when space travelers without a link to Earth would appear, all the members of the diplomatic corps were trained in telepathy, but Amara was still surprised to have the Director make such a blatant attempt to use the skill on her. His soft-spoken commands had been intended to pervade her thinking and create the illusion that they had come from her. She could not help but smile.

"You're very good, and I'm certain your suggestions are well received by the Guardians, but I've been trained to recognize thought control for what it is, and it won't work on me. The conference can't be delayed. If any of the corporations requested a postponement, it would be seen by the others as an attempt to seize more territory before negotiations begin, and war would break out immediately. I certainly don't want to take that risk, do you?"

Embarrassed that his attempt to influence her had been so transparent, Gregory gave his head a vigorous shake. "I was thinking only of Tynan's comfort."

"His is not the only life at stake."

"Yes, I realize that."

"My presence can be excused by the extraordinary circumstances. I've no wish to disrupt your routine or interfere in your historical research, but I really must see Tynan. I can't believe you think preserving the integrity of this male domain is more important than guaranteeing peace throughout the galaxy."

Amara's steady gaze conveyed a threat only hinted at in her words, and Gregory had no doubt that the determined young woman would go to any lengths to complete her mission. Realizing that the sooner she spoke with Tynan, the sooner she would leave, he moved to the door leading into the Keep. "We'll have to cross the great hall to reach the stairs to the private rooms on the third floor. I can't expect you not to be observant, but I must ask for your word that you'll never describe what you see to anyone."

"You have it." Intrigued, Amara took careful note of the vast chamber as they passed through. Lights placed in wall sconces provided only dim illumination, but it was enough for her to appreciate the high-beamed ceiling, arched windows, and the same stone floor she had paced in the anteroom. Colorful banners featuring dragons embroidered in golden thread were suspended overhead and provided the only touch of color to the gray stone interior. While impressed by its size, Amara didn't see anything particularly remarkable about the great hall. It was undoubtedly as faithful a reconstruction as the rest of Norham Castle, but if it held any secrets, they eluded her.

At the far end of the hall, three Guardians were setting long tables for supper. They paused in their work to look up at Amara and stare, but their hoods concealed the incredulous expressions she knew they had to wear. She couldn't resist waving to them but, apparently ashamed to have been caught staring, all three quickly turned away. The Guardians were known for their meticulous research and preservation of tradition rather than their hospitality, but Amara felt the chill of their chauvinist attitudes as deeply as the frosty nip in the air.

"Is it always this cold in here?" she whispered to Gregory.

"Unfortunately, yes. We've chosen our robes for warmth, not fashion."

Accustomed to living in a climate-controlled environment, Amara rubbed her arms briskly, but she was still shivering when they reached the stairs. Narrow and steep, they wound in a gradual curve to the third floor. She had to hurry to keep up with Gregory as he strode down the long hall. Tynan's room was at the very end, and as she followed Gregory inside, Amara realized that she had completely forgotten her carefully rehearsed greeting.

Stretched out on his bed, his face and hands heavily swathed in bandages, Tynan resembled an invisible man in monk's garb more than a learned philosopher. He already felt unwell, and Amara did not want to add to his misery. She stepped forward, hoping to inspire his faith in her and to convince him of the need for an immediate departure, but before she could speak, Tynan clutched his chest and uttered a painful gasp rather than any words of welcome.

Chapter Two

Gregory rushed to Tynan's side, felt the young man's thundering pulse, and turned to Amara. "He's suffered a relapse. Stay here with him while I go for our physician."

Amara scanned the small, sparsely furnished room. "You have no communications equipment in your rooms?"

"Certainly not," Gregory exclaimed on his way out the door. "It's a matter of respect for each other's privacy."

In Amara's view, respect for privacy was one thing and providing the necessary technology for summoning aid in an emergency quite another. She sat down on the edge of Tynan's narrow bed and took his bandaged right hand in hers. Unlike the Director, she doubted Tynan's sudden shortness of breath had anything to do with the beestings he had suffered. She thought the stress of negotiating peace was a far more likely cause for his distress. From his writings, she believed him to be a gentle soul who would be greatly pained should his attempts to reach an accord among the warring corporations fail. Surely her unexpected arrival in his room had brought on panic at the prospect of failure, not a renewed allergic reaction.

"Tynan," she whispered. "You mustn't be afraid. You'll be an excellent negotiator." She paused, knowing the Alado Corporation's high expectations for his success had to be a difficult burden and not wanting to worsen it. "Your beliefs shine with the beauty of truth. We do exist to help each other lead rich, rewarding lives, not to blindly follow destructive paths that bring only misery and death."

Amara continued to encourage the philosopher with words carefully chosen from his own writings until his breathing slowed. She saw the gleam of his dark eyes through his bandages and squeezed his hand lightly. "Are you feeling better?" she inquired. "I'm sorry if I startled you, but I had to speak with you about leaving here tonight. My ship was designed for comfort, and if need be, you can sleep all the way to the Confederation base. Do you think you can walk down the stairs? If not, I'm sure there are enough of us here to carry you."

The young woman's voice held a delicious sweetness that recalled the plaintive folk songs Tynan often listened to while he read. That she was familiar with his work was flattering, but it was exasperating to have been given a female pilot. If they had been introduced, he had forgotten her name, and he was grateful his bandages hid what he was certain was a blush as bright as the red roses he had been admiring when he was stung.

"I didn't hear your name," he admitted grudgingly.

While that wasn't the cooperation for which Amara had hoped, she nevertheless took it as a good sign. "I'm Lieutenant Amara Greer. I don't know why I wasn't given the assignment to be your escort much sooner, but with luck, we'll be able to arrive at the conference on time. Do you have your belongings packed? If not, I'll help you gather them, but we really must leave here tonight."

Before Tynan could reply, Gregory Nash returned with the physician, who observed Amara and Tynan conversing calmly and responded with a disapproving frown. Ignoring the lieutenant, he spoke to his patient. "Were you having trouble breathing again?" he asked.

Amara rose to make room for the doctor. He examined Tynan briefly, and apparently satisfied his patient required no further medication, he turned to her. "What he needs is rest, not visitors. You must go."

Amara would not even consider leaving the Guardian's Keep without Tynan Thorn. "No, I'm afraid that's impossible," she informed him calmly. "I'm Tynan's escort, and until I see him safely seated at the peace conference, I'll not let him out of my sight."

A thin, balding man, the physician raised a bony finger and pointed it at Gregory. "Your mistake was letting this woman inside the gate. Deal with her," he ordered gruffly, then grabbing his medical bag, he hurried from the room.

Gregory Nash looked embarrassed, and Amara hoped that Tynan was not equally upset by the doctor's rudeness. Wanting to put them at ease, she offered an excuse before they could. "He's an elderly man and deserves respect for his years, if not his views." She returned to her place at Tynan's side and again took his hand. "My ship is far more luxurious than this room, and I'm sure you'll be comfortable there. Come with me now."

Tynan found her presence in his room unsettling, but he was sufficiently recovered from the painful relapse to argue. "No, we must wait for the dawn."

Confused, Amara glanced toward Gregory. "That really won't be necessary. A Starcruiser doesn't require light to launch."

"Your ship isn't the concern," Gregory explained. "Guardians never begin any enterprise after sunset. It may seem a peculiar custom to you, but we've found the dawn is the best time for beginnings of all kinds."

Amara was positive she had made the reason for a swift departure abundantly clear, but she tried not to sound as angry as she felt. Had Tynan met her at the gate as she had expected, they would have been gone well before sunset and she would not be embroiled in such a ridiculous argument now. She could almost hear her boss laughing at her predicament, and that made her angrier still.

"Waiting for dawn may be customary for undertakings within these walls, but it certainly doesn't apply in this case," she stressed. "I can't allow your superstitions to jeopardize the success of the peace conference."

"There's a tremendous difference between tradition and superstition," Tynan replied.

Although still muffled by bandages, Tynan's voice had taken on a clear note of authority. Pleased that he now felt strong enough to argue with her, Amara began to smile. "We can debate that issue all the way to the conference, but we must leave here tonight."

Tynan withdrew his hand from hers and struggled to sit up. Still slightly dizzy, he needed a moment to compose himself before he spoke. "No. We'll wait for the dawn. No matter how tight your schedule, you must have allowed some time for dealing with emergencies. It will cover the delay."

Now that he was seated upright, Amara realized that Tynan was much taller than she had imagined. Charmed by the lyric beauty of his writing, she had mistakenly assumed he was a small, delicate man. Wondering if his expression would convey the same determination as his voice, she wished his face weren't so heavily bandaged. He was widely admired for seeking the truth, and she didn't even consider lying to him.

"Yes, my calculations have included a small amount of time for emergencies, but if we use it before our flight begins, we may come to bitterly regret it later. Let's not take that risk."

Tynan observed Amara closely as he considered her request. Her skin had a lovely, pale golden tan, and her sparkling blue-green eyes were framed with long, dark lashes. Her brows had a graceful arch, her nose a delicate perfection, and her lips an inviting fullness. Her golden blond hair was pulled atop her head in a small knot that failed to completely tame her lavish curls. If she had any physical flaws, Tynan couldn't find them, but her stubbornness certainly didn't please him.

"We'll leave at dawn," he repeated in a voice that brooked no further argument.

Amara took in a deep breath and let it out slowly. She had not thought it necessary to wear a laser pistol, and even if she had, she knew it would not be wise to make Tynan accompany her by force. She could scarcely kidnap a peace emissary and expect him to arrive at the conference in the proper mood to effectively argue Alado's case.

"All right," she was forced to agree. "We'll wait for the dawn and hope that no problems occur during flight."

Relieved to have the matter settled, Gregory gestured toward the door. "Thank you for being so reasonable, lieutenant. You may return to your ship. I'll give you my personal guarantee that Tynan will be aboard at dawn."

Amara remained seated on Tynan's bunk. "Apparently you misunderstood me, but I meant what I said earlier. I take my responsibilities as Tynan's escort very seriously, and if we aren't leaving now, then I'll have to stay here with him tonight."

Gregory looked aghast at her plan. "But we have no facilities here for female guests."

"I'm not one of your guests. I'm Tynan's escort, and I'll stay right here with him. They were setting the tables for supper as we came upstairs. Will you please ask the men in the kitchen to send something for me along with whatever they've prepared for Tynan?" She turned to the philosopher. "I'm

31

assuming you don't feel well enough to go downstairs to eat, but if you'd rather dine with the other Guardians, then I will too."

Tynan revised his opinion: Lieutenant Greer was not merely stubborn, she was downright aggressive, obstinate, and rude. While he felt far from well, he balked at the prospect of spending the entire evening alone with her. She might be marvelous to look at, but he doubted they would ever have a satisfactory conversation. "If you'll give me a hand, Gregory, I'll join the others."

"I really don't think you ought to exert yourself," the older man advised.

Tynan bumped Amara with his knee, and she got up to get out of his way. She offered him her hand, but he brushed it aside and reached for Gregory's instead. Offended, she moved to the door and waited for him there. While Tynan's steps were unsteady at first, he had released his hold on Gregory by the time he reached her side.

She had to look up at him, and although it was difficult to judge accurately with him wearing a hooded robe, she guessed his height at several inches above her own six feet. Sorry he had not proven to be the sweet, diminutive man she had envisioned, she preceded him down the hall, but she doubted she would taste a sip of the gruel or whatever insipid concoction the Guardians prepared for meals.

Tynan saw a shiver course down Amara's spine, and although he was astonished by the strength of his sympathetic reaction, he reached out to touch her shoulder. "Wait, you're cold. You'll have to borrow one of my robes."

Amara opened her mouth to argue, then thought better of it. She was cold, and donning the Guardian's garb for the evening meal would provide not only warmth, but a welcome anonymity as well. "Thank you. I believe I saw one hanging on the back of your door. Is that the one you're offering?"

"Yes, go back and get it. We'll wait here for you."

Tynan leaned against the wall to rest and watched her walk away. He swiftly decided that her figure was equally appealing from behind. "Are beautiful women usually so obnoxious?" he asked Gregory.

Gregory was also enjoying the view but caught himself before he replied. "Women's personalities are as different as men's. The lieutenant's manner is somewhat abrasive, but a great many men suffer from that same failing."

"Yes, that's true." Tynan had been dreading the trip, even before he had discovered that the pilot would be so difficult to abide. He had planned to read, perhaps write some, and listen to music to pass the time. He certainly didn't want to engage in a running argument the whole trip. "I hope the manning of the ship requires all her attention," he murmured.

"We've given you a superb classical education, Tynan, but in one significant way it's been incomplete. You might be wise to use the flight to study the lieutenant rather than avoid her."

Amara reappeared, still adjusting the length of the borrowed robe with the cord at her waist, and Tynan had no opportunity to tell his friend how little he appreciated his absurd suggestion. He had always been fascinated by ideas, but only mildly interested in his fellow Guardians and not at all intrigued by women. When Amara looked up at him and smiled, he was amazed to feel the heat of another blush flooding his cheeks.

There would be women attending the peace conference, and knowing he did not want to appear as uncomfortable in their presence as he was in Amara's, he grew determined not to allow her distracting appearance to bother him any longer. Still, even in a loose-fitting robe, she moved with a seductive feminine grace that made such a vow difficult to keep. He gestured for her to lead the way down the stairs, and when on the fourth step she tripped on the hem of her robe, he reached out to catch her. That exertion brought on a wave of dizziness that might have sent them both on a headlong plunge down the steep flight of stairs had Gregory not been alert and grabbed Tynan in time to save them.

"This is lunacy," Gregory scolded. "Come, let me help you back to your room."

Tynan now had a firm grip on Amara's arm with one hand and the oak railing with the other. His knees were weak and he felt miserable, but he still believed he would be better off in the great hall than in his room. "No, I'm fine. Be more careful, lieutenant. If you fall and I trip over you, neither of us will arrive at the conference on time."

Amara had never fallen down a flight of stairs and knew she would be in absolutely no danger of suffering such an embarrassing mishap now had she not had to wear a robe several sizes too large merely to avoid frostbite in the dank confines of the Keep. While Tynan had not called her clumsy, the sharpness of his tone had conveyed that insulting opinion, and she pulled free of his grasp.

"Let's avoid that danger then," she suggested with forced calm, and moved back up the stairs to now follow him.

Tynan hadn't wanted to give her the opportunity to observe how slowly he had to move and realized too late that he had just outsmarted himself by being so curt with her. Rather than speak, he nodded, and relying upon the rail for support, he continued on down the stairs. By the time they reached the landing, he was out of breath and had to stop and rest before entering the great hall. Ashamed of his lack of stamina, he turned to Gregory to cover it.

"We'll need a place set next to mine for Lieutenant Greer."

Looking as pained as Tynan felt, the Director went on ahead to arrange the change in seating. Some of the Guardians were already standing behind their chairs and missed seeing her, but those who did ceased talking and stared. Attempting to make the best of the situation, Amara smiled as though Tynan had begged her to join him for supper, but that only turned incredulous gapes to hostile sneers.

"It doesn't appear as though I'm welcome here," she whispered. "It's not too late for us to leave."

For a terrible moment, Tynan felt torn between the same protective instinct that had made him offer Amara a robe and later act quickly to prevent her fall, and the loyalty he owed his fellow Guardians and their traditions. He recognized the painful sensation, for it was the very same one he had experienced when he had been asked to speak for Alado at the peace conference. He had had not the slightest desire to accept such an honor, and yet in the interest of all mankind he had known he could not refuse.

Regarding Amara's presence as the natural consequence of that decision, he tried to think of it as merely part of an ordeal that would soon be over. "That matter has already been settled," he reminded her. "A few of the more conservative among us may walk out, but I can't believe you truly expected an enthusiastic response when you insisted upon joining us."

That rebuke had been unnecessary, but rather than tell him so, Amara simply straightened her shoulders and continued to smile as though she actually enjoyed dining with such backward and ignorant men. She made a quick count, and found they numbered slightly more than two hundred. Because she would be gone in the morning, she tried to convince herself she did not care what they thought of her.

Tynan watched Amara's gaze take on a decidedly defiant gleam and was forced to admire her courage. While she was definitely stubborn, she obviously had the strength of character to follow through on her decisions. That was such a commendable trait that in spite of his best intentions not to, he began to feel a grudging respect. "A little feminine company won't cause us any permanent harm. Come, let me show you to our seats."

As they started across the hall, the Guardians parted with unseemly haste, but Amara continued to display a regal posture and serene attitude. When they reached their table, she had only one question. "Do you always sit in the same places?"

"Always," Tynan revealed. "Tradition is what matters most to us."

"How could I have forgotten?" While there were ten places at the other tables, there were now eleven at Tynan's and Amara was grateful that she had not forced one of the Guardians to eat elsewhere when surely the sudden change in routine would have given him a terrible case of indigestion. As was their mealtime custom, the Guardians all lowered their hoods, and when Tynan brushed his back against his shoulders, Amara saw that his bandages did not completely cover his hair. She had wondered about his looks, and the glossy black locks curling down over his collar made her all the more curious.

Tynan introduced her to the others at the table, but they all simply nodded and quickly glanced away without offering a smile or a word of welcome, much less any show of interest in the journey she and Tynan would be taking. As a representative of the Alado Corporation's Diplomatic Corps, she was offended that the Director had chosen not to introduce her formally to everyone as she assumed important male guests were, but that was such a small slight compared with what she saw as the totally unnecessary delay in their departure that she kept the complaint to herself. She rested her hands on the back of her chair and, hungry, hoped the meal would soon be served. None of the Guardians had yet taken his seat, and she hoped they weren't waiting for her to be the first. Thinking that an absurd notion, she was about to ask Tynan what was causing the delay when he joined the others in chanting a blessing.

She recognized the language as Latin, and when sung by two hundred male voices, the effect proved deeply stirring. For an instant, the medieval castle and monk-like garb of the Guardians provided an eerie glimpse of a time long past when Gregorian chants filled monasteries with music that surely rivaled the songs of the angels. When the blessing came to a close and Tynan reached over to pull out her chair, she jumped in surprise.

"I meant to be polite rather than to startle you," he apologized.

Amara slipped into her chair and waited for him to take his. "The singing was so beautiful, I was simply lost in the moment."

"They don't sing in Alado's mess halls?"

"Occasionally they do, but never that type of song."

The evening meal arrived on large serving carts and platters were soon being passed around each table. A vegetarian, Amara refused the thick slice of roast beef Tynan offered and waited for the corn and green beans. There was a loaf of oatmeal bread that was especially good, but she didn't want to take more than her share.

"Is that all you usually eat?" Tynan asked.

"No, but this will be fine for tonight."

Taking her at her word, Tynan turned his attention to his own meal. He had managed to scoop the food off the platters and onto his plate, but his hands were too swollen for him to grasp a knife and fork firmly enough to cut his roast beef. Rather than ask for help from the nearest Guardian, he made such a request of Amara. "If you don't care for meat, would it offend you to cut mine into bites I can eat?"

When he raised his bandaged hands, Amara was sorry she hadn't thought to make such an offer first. "Of course not," she replied. "Your well-being is my responsibility, and if you can't eat, you'll arrive at the conference too weak to speak."

That she would regard helping him as part of her duties as his escort rather than common courtesy annoyed Tynan. "Do you view everything from a pilot's standpoint, lieutenant?" he asked.

Amara moved his plate closer to cut the roast beef. The ornate pattern of the sterling silver utensils recalled the elaborately embroidered court dress of the Middle Ages and seemed strangely appropriate for the stark castle setting. Again feeling terribly out of place, Amara was grateful to find that the knife had a surprisingly keen edge. She considered Tynan's question while she worked and didn't reply until she had reduced the roast beef to small bites and returned the plate to his place.

"Is that a trick question? How else would a pilot view things?"

"Simply as a person, a woman."

The doctor had wrapped Tynan's head loosely enough for him to eat without difficulty, but Amara again thought she could better judge his meaning if only she could see his expression. Before becoming involved with the Secretary, she had always kept her career and private life separate. Still disappointed with the way that relationship had turned out, she had vowed never again to allow her personal feelings to intrude upon her professional commitments.

"Escorting you to the conference is both an honor and a responsibility," she explained, "and while I've always enjoyed being a woman, my focus at present is on fulfilling my obligations as a pilot. Does that answer your question?"

Tynan wasn't certain that it had, but because he regarded his own career seriously, he could not fault her for doing the same. Eating proved to be so difficult a task that he dropped the effort at conversation and didn't speak again until fruit was served for dessert. Certain Amara must still be hungry, he thought and urged her to take several pieces. He watched as she peeled an orange; her hands were as lovely as the rest of her, her nails frosted with a delicate pink. Embarrassed to be staring, he looked away only to find the others at the table were equally fascinated with the care with which Amara handled the juicy fruit. When she raised her napkin to blot her lips, he was certain he heard a gasp of longing from several of his companions.

While he had been raised in the Keep, most of the Guardians had grown up in families with parents and a sibling or two. The majority were university graduates; many had had successful careers, married, and raised families of their own before they had abandoned the burdens of the outside world to enter the Keep. Divorced, widowers, lifelong bachelors, they had had ample opportunity to enjoy feminine companionship before renouncing the secular world for one devoted to preserving Earth's history.

That he alone was sharing a meal with a woman for the first time suddenly struck Tynan as a difference he hoped no one else would realize. Not only would they tease him unmercifully, but they would unknowingly remind him that he had never known a mother's love. That was not a point on which he wished to dwell, and the instant the meal was over, he pushed himself to his feet.

"Bring some fruit with you if you're still hungry, but I want to go back up to my room."

Having no desire to remain in the hall without him, Amara quickly left her chair and matched her pace to his as they crossed to the stairs. She glanced over her shoulder, and when she found every last Guardian observing her, she smiled and waved, but quickly turned away before any of them responded with gestures she feared would be more obscene than friendly.

"Do you need some help?" she inquired.

Tynan braced himself against the rail. "I hope not." He took care to move with slow, deliberate steps, and while it was a painstaking process, he finally arrived at the third floor without undue strain. He then had to pause to catch his breath before they walked to his room. When they reached the door, he hesitated to open it.

"You've seen enough to know I'm in absolutely no danger here, lieutenant. Why don't you go on back to your ship? I doubt that I'll get much sleep tonight, so I'll be awake in plenty of time for us to leave with the dawn."

While Tynan was more subtle than the Director, he had made several statements which could be properly described as commands, and Amara

41

felt certain he expected to be obeyed. She reached past him to open his door. "If you'd had as much difficulty coming this far as I have, you'd not leave either. It's still early—how do Guardians spend their evenings?"

Sorry she had not welcomed the chance to leave, Tynan followed her into his room and went straight to his bed. He sat down, and then summarized the activities available. "Some men play cards or chess. Others gather for group discussion of their studies. We have a complete library of twentieth-century films, and most of us never tire of those. There's art and music, of course, and a great many fine books to read. We have a gym, sports. We never run out of things to do here. How do Alado's pilots spend their free time?"

"With each other," Amara explained, without describing just how intimate those dealings might truly be. Looking around Tynan's Spartan quarters, she feared she was going to spend a long and uncomfortable night. She rested her hands on her hips and sighed softly.

"I've been studying your writings," she confided, "but I still don't understand why the Guardians aren't interested in anything that happened after the twentieth century. Why have you chosen such a narrow focus when the universe is ours to explore?"

"While the choice was made long before I was born, I've always shared the Guardians' preoccupation with the Earth's ancient history. It's a matter of personal preference, I suppose, the way a botanist chooses to study plants, or a linguist language. Initially, the Guardians were formed as a result of the men's movement which flourished in the closing decade of the twentieth century. Our area of expertise has always been Earth's history prior to the colonization of space. Rather than a narrow focus, that's an enormous amount of knowledge, lieutenant. No one man can master it all."

Amara began to pace the small room. "There was no biographical information included in the material I was given about you, so I hope you'll forgive me for being curious. How long have you been a member of the Guardians?"

Tynan punched up his pillow to form a backrest and settled himself more comfortably on his bed. Because everyone he knew was aware of his background, he was unaccustomed to recounting it and was hesitant at first. "I was orphaned as an infant. The Guardians took me in, and I've never had any desire to leave."

The thought of the sullen men she had seen at dinner successfully raising a child amazed Amara, and yet Tynan was undeniably a superbly talented human being, so they had obviously accomplished their task. "You have left here, though, haven't you? Perhaps to attend school, visit historic sites—simply to tour the Earth?"

Tynan looked down at the bandages covering his hands. "No," he admitted reluctantly, "but I've seen films and books which cover all of Earth's geographical features and societies. I've also talked with the men who come here on retreats about their homelands, but other than to help cultivate the fields where we raise our produce, I've not left the Keep."

43

Amara stopped pacing and turned to face him. "You've been here, with just the Guardians, your whole life?" she asked.

"It's no cause for shame," Tynan argued.

Sorry that she had upset him, Amara pulled one of the chairs from the table in the center of the room and sat down. "From what I understand, the Guardians are an entirely self-sufficient community, patterned after a monastery but with no religious ties. Is that correct?"

Tynan could see where their conversation was leading and was deeply embarrassed, but he could think of no way to redirect the inquisitive lieutenant's questions to a less personal area. "Yes, that's correct."

"There are no women here ever, are there?"

Tynan shook his head.

Amara sat back in her chair. "I knew this was going to be an awkward trip," she confessed, "but I'd no idea you'd not even seen a woman before we met."

"I've seen plenty of women," Tynan insisted, "in films, and books."

"Women who lived, loved, danced, and sang in the twentieth century, right?"

"Well, yes, that's true."

"A lot has happened in the last two hundred and fifty-seven years."

"We're not totally ignorant of the present, lieutenant. We merely prefer to study the past."

"And live in it," Amara murmured to herself. While she was far too considerate to ask him outright, Tynan Thorn had to be a thirty-three-year old virgin, but the intimacy imposed by the close confines of space travel made it unlikely that he would arrive at the conference in such an innocent state. Amara began to laugh at that prospect and couldn't stop. She tried, but the more she tried to stifle her giggles, the louder they became.

"Are you laughing at me?" Tynan asked.

"Oh no, please don't even think that," Amara assured him. "I'm just laughing at a trick my boss played on me. Don't you worry. We're going to have a marvelous trip."

As she continued to giggle, Tynan felt certain she had made him the butt of a joke he was too unsophisticated to understand, and he doubted a journey with her could be anything but taxing in the extreme.

Chapter Three

When Amara at last regained her composure, Tynan's dejected pose brought forth a heavy wave of guilt. "Really," she assured him, "I wasn't laughing at you. I'm the personal pilot for the Secretary of Alado's Diplomatic Corps—or at least I was until I received this assignment. I felt certain you'd feel more at ease with a male pilot, but he disagreed. He's forced us both into a difficult situation, and we'll simply have to make the best of it."

She reached over to position another chair for her feet and, stretched out between them, believed she was as comfortable as she was likely to get. Tynan's robe was whisper-soft and, enveloped in its comforting warmth, she no longer felt the Keep's chill. Like Tynan, she doubted she would get a wink of sleep, so the fact of such a makeshift bed didn't matter.

It took a few seconds for Amara's comments to fully register on Tynan, then he straightened up abruptly. "Won't you be the pilot on the return flight?" he asked.

Amara was certain he was more worried about getting home than missing out on her company. "I really can't say," she answered truthfully. "The Secretary and I didn't part on the best of terms, so there's a good chance I'll be replaced. But you needn't be concerned with your travel arrangements. You'll not be left stranded at the Confederation base regardless of how the peace conference turns out. Unlike some individuals, the Alado Corporation doesn't renege on its promises. You'll receive a safe escort home."

But no one could accurately predict how long the conference would last, or when he'd be returning home. Tynan was distracted from his concern by a tightening sensation in his chest. He took several deep breaths in a vain attempt to suppress the renewed allergic reaction.

Seeing his distress, Amara rolled off the chairs and came to his side. Again taking his hand, she spoke to him in a low, soothing tone. "I know this trip is going to be difficult for you, but you needn't give the flight home another thought. If it's not me, it will be another pilot who will take the responsibility for your safety as seriously as I do." She raised her other hand to his shoulder and exerted gentle pressure to create a steady rhythm. "Put your cares aside and breathe with me."

Tynan didn't know which was worse: the lingering effects of his allergy to bee venom, or having to travel with the impossibly helpful Lieutenant Greer. "It's the damn bees," he argued. "Please leave."

"No, I won't leave you here—or at the Confederation base," Amara promised, but he continued to struggle for air. Because she did not want to leave him to go in search of the physician, she made the only other vow she could. "Listen to me, Tynan. Regardless of how nasty things become between the Secretary and me, I'll arrange to be your pilot on the return flight. Does that ease your mind?"

"It's the beestings, not the trip," he reiterated irritably. "I'm just not fully recovered."

Wondering if she'd offended him, Amara didn't contradict Tynan but remained at his side until he exhibited no further problems in breathing. When she had come back for his robe, she had been delighted to find he had a private bathroom and she got up and went into it now. The fixtures were of quaint design, but fully functional and that was all she required. She splashed her face with cool water and tried to imagine how a man as intelligent as Tynan could possibly be content to live within the Guardians' Keep. It was so cold, with no human warmth to lend a much-needed heat. Considering it the most dismal place she had ever been, she was very anxious to leave.

Before she could again stretch out between the two chairs, a Guardian came to the door with a portable bed, but when Amara thanked him for his kindness, he hurried away without speaking— further evidence of the hearty dislike toward her that she had felt all evening. She rolled the bed into the room and, not wanting to crowd Tynan, placed it on the opposite side of the table from his bed. "We'll have to get up early," she reminded him. "I hope you won't mind if I go to bed now."

Relieved to be left alone, Tynan assured her that he wanted to go to sleep too. He doused the lights, struggled to remove his boots, flung off his robe, and got under the covers. He closed his eyes and tried to focus his thoughts on the upcoming peace conference. He soon discovered that Amara's image lingered in his mind with such fierce persistency that meditation was impossible. Thinking she hadn't had time to fall asleep, he called out to her.

"Lieutenant, you're a Starchild, aren't you?"

Surprised by his sudden interest, Amara rose up on one elbow. "Yes. My parents are geologists who study the composition of each of Alado's new acquisitions. I was born while they were en route from one colony to another, so the term Starchild is doubly appropriate in my case."

"Where do you call home then?"

"Right now, my quarters are at Fleet Command, but I'll probably be assigned elsewhere soon."

"No, I meant your real home," Tynan explained.

Touched by his attachment to the Keep, Amara strove not to insult him. "To a man who's spent his whole life in one place, it must seem as though I'm adrift on the solar winds, but home doesn't have to be a particular place. It can be wherever one's loved ones are."

"Mine are all here," Tynan admitted reluctantly.

"Yes, I know." Amara waited for him to say more, and when he didn't, she lay back down and closed her eyes. The room was very quiet, and without the constant low hum of the Starcruiser's instruments to lull her to sleep, she remained wide awake. Not one to waste a second of her time, she replotted their course in her mind and managed to squeeze an additional two hours out of their flight time.

Equally restless, Gregory's advice still echoing in his mind, Tynan supposed he was ignorant where women were concerned, but he couldn't use the trip to study Lieutenant Greer with the enthusiasm he would show a curious relic of ancient times. She was a person—surely not all that different from him.

"Lieutenant?" he whispered.

Amara was amused that he had become so talkative after they had said good night. "Yes?"

"I should have thanked you for your patience. I know you're eager to start our voyage."

"No thanks are needed," she insisted. "I really do admire your writing, Tynan, and I'll do my best to make your trip the easiest it can possibly be. I didn't think to bring references, but I've never received any complaints. At least—not yet."

When she laughed this time, Tynan was charmed rather than offended. He was trying to find a clever way to assure her he wouldn't complain as long as they made it safely to the conference and back, but a knock at the door interrupted him. "I'll get it this time," he quickly volunteered. There was only a narrow space between the end of the extra bed and his door, but Tynan managed to slide through it. When he found the Director waiting to speak with him, he was embarrassed that he hadn't taken the time to don his robe.

Amara recognized Gregory's voice, and thinking he might wish to speak with her, she sat up. Silhouetted against the light of the hall, Tynan's slim yet muscular build presented an appealing sight. In a close-fitting knit shirt and long pants, he looked more like a professional athlete than a philosopher, and she wasn't in the least disappointed. Leaning back on her hands, she wondered how long he would have to keep his face and hands bandaged.

Gregory was surprised to find Tynan already undressed for bed, and when he glanced past him, he was even more shocked to find Lieutenant Greer reclining in what he regarded as a provocative pose. While he had encouraged Tynan to enjoy his brief association with the attractive young woman, he had not thought it necessary to demand that he respect the Guardians' principles and wait until he had left the Keep to become more intimate with her. "I'm sorry to have disturbed you," he announced rather stiffly. "I merely wanted to make certain that the lieutenant has all she requires."

Amara left her bed and, ducking under Tynan's arm, greeted the Director with an innocent smile. "Thank you, but as you can see, I'm being well cared for."

At least she was still dressed in one of Tynan's robes, but Gregory felt certain she could remove it with a single, seductive tug. "You refused my suggestion that you return to your ship, but I hope I may depend on you not to abuse our hospitality," he said.

A slightly arched brow gave an unmistakable double meaning to his comment, and not appreciating being scolded like a naughty child when she had done absolutely nothing wrong, Amara instantly grew defensive. "I wouldn't think of it," she assured him. She then issued a challenge in the form of a gracious invitation. "Why don't you join us at dawn? I'll be happy to give you a brief tour of the Starcruiser."

Appalled, Gregory flinched slightly. "Thank you, but no. Space travel doesn't interest me. Good night."

As he turned away, Amara closed the door. "Most men would be thrilled by the opportunity to go on board a Starcruiser."

"Most men are not Guardians," Tynan reminded her.

Amara returned to her bed and pulled the light blanket up to her chin. "I can't tell you how thankful I am for that. Good night."

She had been laughing before Gregory appeared, and Tynan was disappointed by her change in mood. While he thought Gregory had been a bit curt with her, he understood the Director's point of view and didn't apologize for it. He went back to bed and this time, exhausted by the day, he fell into a deep slumber.

Amara had already showered and dressed in her uniform before Tynan stirred. She folded up the extra bed, rolled it out into the hall, and then woke him. Instantly alert, he showed no signs of having trouble breathing and made no excuses to delay their departure. After showering and dressing in clean underclothes, he donned his robe. He removed a small duffle bag from the closet, and with one last lingering glance around his room, announced that he was ready to go.

"I would like some hot chocolate first, though," he added.

That struck Amara as such a peculiar request that she feared he was again going to be difficult about leaving. "If it takes more than a minute to prepare, I'm afraid you'll have to leave without it."

"I'm not trying to stall."

"Good." Still wary, Amara opened the door for him, then hesitated. "I should have thought to ask yesterday if you have other clothes. I'm afraid your robe might prove cumbersome on board the ship."

"This is all I own."

He spoke with pride, and Amara understood that a Guardian's robe was all he cared to wear. At least she now knew he had on something under it. "I'm sure you'll be fine then." She reached for his bag, but he pulled away.

"I feel much better today. You needn't help me."

"Fine, I'm glad to hear it."

Amara was so eager to get under way that she nearly danced down the hall, and without the bother of a robe, she had no difficulty descending the stairs. She then had to wait for Tynan to reach the bottom. She had thought it too early for the other Guardians to be up, but they had all gathered in the great hall to bid Tynan farewell. The Director came forward first, and not wanting to bruise Tynan's swollen hands, he patted him on the back as he extended his good wishes. When Gregory failed to include her in either his glance or his words, Amara elected not to stand there while all the others snubbed her and instead went downstairs to wait for Tynan in the entryway. When he finally appeared, he was carrying two ceramic mugs of hot chocolate on a small pewter tray.

"I thought you might like some too," he offered.

Amara hadn't had any hot chocolate in years, but accepted it as though it were precisely what she wanted. While Tynan hadn't apologized for his friends' continued rudeness where she was concerned, she was grateful for this small kindness. "Thank you, this was very thoughtful of you. It was nice of your friends to see you off. I didn't expect it."

"Really? I did." Tynan set the tray aside and held the door open for her. They continued sipping their cocoa as they crossed the courtyard. The dawn had just broken, filling the sky with a soft golden glow. He turned to look back up at the Keep. "You see, this is the best hour of the day, the perfect time for our departure."

In the dimly illuminated interior of the Keep, Amara had believed the Guardians' robes were black, but with the sun coming up behind him, Tynan's was clearly an inky purple—not the garish color royalty had once favored, but aubergine with all its mysterious beauty. It was an elegant choice that in her mind transformed his appearance from that of a monk to a medieval wizard. Amused by the prospect of such a serious individual conjuring up magic spells, she began to giggle.

"You don't agree?"

"Yes, I most certainly do," she insisted rather than explain how far her thoughts had wandered. When they came to the gate, she reached out to stop him. "We'll have to leave the mugs here. Every article on board the Starcruiser is specially designed to fulfill a specific need, and there just isn't room to store these."

"I understand." Tynan finished the last of his hot chocolate in a long gulp, set his mug down by the door in the gate, and struggled to turn the key with his bandaged fingers.

"Here, let me do that." He stepped aside and Amara easily unlocked the door. "You don't post a guard?" she asked.

"No, we have no enemies."

"Let's hope you return without any either." Then, fearing that a discussion of the conference might be unsettling, she quickly changed the subject. "I'm afraid we have a bit of a walk to reach the ship, but I didn't want to put her down any closer to the Keep."

Tynan looked out over the barren field to the magnificent silver ship. Even perfectly still, its power seemed barely tamed. Triangular in shape, fuselage and wings were merged in a masterpiece of form and function. In spite of his best efforts not to, Tynan found himself regarding the vessel with unabashed awe.

"I didn't realize your ship would be so beautiful," he confessed.

Amara was moving over the newly plowed field with small steps so as not to tire him. "I'm glad you agree, but anything of beauty can transcend its form, and all of Alado's ships succeed in that regard."

"Are there many different kinds?"

Pleased by his interest, Amara hoped he would not recognize the laser cannons for what they were. They were so close to launch that she didn't want him to balk now, and she felt certain he would if he knew the ship as armed. "Yes," she exclaimed, attempting to distract him. "Each has its own specific purpose—exploration, colonization, transportation of people or cargo. I'll show you a description of the fleet if you like."

"Yes, would you please?"

"Of course." When they reached the Starcruiser, Amara pressed in the code and the hatch opened with a welcoming hiss. "Watch your head," she warned. "I don't want you to arrive more battered than you already are."

"I'm not especially battered, just swollen."

"Good." Amara took his bag, which was surprisingly heavy with what felt like several books in the bottom. She tossed it up the ladder and gestured for him to precede her. He hiked up his robe and climbed in. She followed and quickly secured the hatch before he had a chance to change his mind. She stowed his bag in a cargo compartment, then caught his hand and led him into the cockpit.

"Do Guardians type and use computers, or are you sworn to preserve the quill pen?"

That remark would have incensed Tynan the previous day, but he was fast growing used to the lieutenant's flippant manner and simply answered rather than complain. "We confine our studies to Earth's history, but that doesn't mean we can't use modern technology to do it."

Amara didn't care to debate the Guardians' procedures when for once they were helpful. She slid into the pilot's seat and motioned for Tynan to use the co-pilot's at her right. She went through a quick series of checks, then activated the navigational computer. "Fleet command programs my electronic co-pilot into whatever ship I'm assigned. "Good morning, Steve."

"Good morning, Lieutenant Greer," a male voice with a faintly metallic ring replied.

"This is Tynan Thorn. Imprint his voice and follow his commands as you would mine."

"Good morning, Tynan Thorn," Steve replied.

While they did have computers which responded to voice commands in the Keep, none was responsible for flying a spaceship, and Tynan wasn't certain he wanted Steve to follow his commands.

"Wait a minute," he begged. "I haven't the slightest idea what to tell him to do."

"Imprint complete," Steve responded.

Amara reached out to touch Tynan's sleeve. "Steve has already been programmed with our route. He uses the position of the stars, as well as the beacons from navigational satellites or space buoys. If anything should happen to me, you need only report it, and he will land the ship safely at Confederation base."

"What could happen to you?" Tynan asked.

Hearing his apprehension, Amara raised her hand to plead for patience and completed the sequence for launch. "We can talk about it once we're under way. Now fasten your seatbelt; lift off is always a jolt."

Annoyed that she hadn't answered his question, Tynan quickly became frustrated when he couldn't secure the buckle with his bandaged hands. Amara reached over to help him and adjusted the length of his belt. When her fingertips strayed across his lap, she felt him jump, but held captive now, he couldn't escape her unintentional caress.

"Sorry. You'll soon get used to our bumping into each other fairly often. It can't be helped in such close quarters. As soon as we're launched, I'll take you back to the passenger cabin. The Starcruiser is equipped with its own gravity device, so you'll be able to move around comfortably."

Tynan couldn't peel his tongue off the roof of his dry mouth to reply. He gripped the padded arms of his seat and shut his eyes. He heard Steve counting down the seconds to launch, not knowing what to expect but anticipating the worst. When the Starcruiser floated into the air, he relaxed slightly, thinking that spaceflight wasn't going to be so terrifying after all. In the next instant, the engines fired and the ship blasted through the clouds with a force that snapped his head back and imprisoned his body against the seat with a horrible pressure that threatened to crush him. It sickened him clear through and he tried to scream, but no sound escaped his lips.

When the Starcruiser at last escaped Earth's gravity and the wrenching sensation ceased, he opened his eyes to find nothing but endless blackness stretching out in front of them. For one terrible moment, he feared the void was the face of his own death. While he was not a deeply religious man, he had not expected to spend eternity in hell, but surely that was what this was. When Amara spoke, and he realized that they were both still very much alive, his fright swiftly turned to anger.

"As lauchings go, those from Earth aren't bad," Amara informed him. "The gravitational pull of the Confederation base isn't nearly as strong, so in the first few seconds of our flight, you've survived the worst you'll have to endure."

Even considering the vast difference in their experience, Tynan believed her description of the launch had been woefully inaccurate. "You call that a mere jolt? I felt as though I were being sucked back into the womb!"

"My, what a colorful way to put it." Even though she could not read his expression, his tone of voice made his outrage clear and as a member of the diplomatic corps, Amara strove to be diplomatic. "I'm sorry you found it so difficult, but I certainly didn't mean to mislead you. People frequently have different reactions to the same event, so while it's unfortunate, it's really not all that unusual for us to disagree on the severity of the launch. For the rest of the trip, I'll do my best to see you don't have any more unpleasant surprises."

Amara waited for an equally conciliatory gesture from Tynan, but a stony silence was the only response to her apology. He definitely had a temper, but she thought this a poor time to mention it. Instead, she asked Steve to check the new calculations she had made to shorten their flight, and he swiftly confirmed them. Pleased, she again turned to Tynan.

"Steve's capabilities make even unmanned flight possible in a Starcruiser, and I'm sure you'll soon learn to trust him. The cockpit is designed for a crew of one or two, depending on the need, and I'll welcome your company whenever you wish to join me. As for problems, none are projected for this flight, but the unexpected can always occur. It's possible, although highly unlikely, that I'll suffer some injury or incapacitating illness. If I do, just inform Steve. He'll notify Confederation base and assume total command of the ship. You'll be as safe with him as you are with me."

Still badly upset, Tynan didn't mince words. "I don't feel safe."

The last thing Amara wanted was to begin a ridiculous argument that might last the entire way to Confederation base. Rather than defend herself, she leaned forward slightly. "Steve, when was the last time a Starcruiser was lost or crashed?"

"No Starcruiser has ever crashed or been lost, lieutenant. The ship has a perfect safety record."

Tynan did not appear to be impressed, so Amara continued. "How many diplomatic shuttles have been lost or crashed?"

"The diplomatic shuttle also has a perfect safety record," Steve replied.

"How many interstellar passenger vessels has Alado lost?"

"None, lieutenant."

Amara looked over at Tynan. "Would you like me to continue?"

Tynan already knew the lieutenant was clever, and because he knew nothing about Alado's fleet, he would not put it past her to inquire only about the ships which had never met with tragedy. "How large is Alado's fleet, Steve?" he asked.

"At present the fleet contains six hundred and seventy six vessels."

"How many ships of any kind has Alado lost?"

"In what time frame?" Steve inquired.

Tynan saw no reason to ask about the corporation's safety record in its first two hundred years of operation. "The last ten years."

Steve printed his response on the screen in the co-pilot's console as he spoke. "Eight experimental craft were lost during unmanned test flights. Seventeen cargo transports were hijacked by pirates. Four Banshee scout ships were lost while on expeditionary flights, and two were destroyed during a dispute still under investigation."

"That dispute, as Steve calls it, is the reason we're on our way to a peace conference. Did his data provide the reassurance you seem to require?"

Tynan could understand experimental aircraft blowing up, or pilots disappearing on expeditionary flights—but pirates? He had not even known space pirates existed. "Why didn't you mention the danger posed by pirates? If they've taken seventeen ships, aren't they a threat to us?"

Amara unfastened her seat belt and tapped his screen. "They're interested in cargo vessels, not passenger ships."

In his teens, Tynan had made a lengthy study of sixteenth- and seventeenth-century pirates who had plagued the treasure-laden Spanish galleons sailing home from the New World. Merciless villains, they had frequently turned the azure waters of the Caribbean crimson with the blood of their innocent victims. To imagine such an evil crowd plying their trade in space made his skin crawl. "They must need fast ships to attack cargo vessels. Isn't this ship fast?"

"Very," Amara admitted, but she stopped short of revealing that they had the means to defend themselves.

"I should have been warned about pirates."

Amara considered this new worry of his absurd. "Would it have changed your decision? Would you have said, if there were even the remotest possibility that you might fall into the hands of pirates, you wouldn't serve as a negotiator? If the corporations can't solve their worst territorial dispute in a century, and nuclear war is the result, death will surely find you even in the Guardians' Keep, Tynan, can't you understand that? Pirates! Believe me, pirates are the least of our problems."

Thoroughly disgusted with him, Amara left her seat and went back to the passenger cabin, where she hoped Tynan would have the sense to stay the entire trip. When he didn't follow her immediately, she grew increasingly impatient before realizing that he must not be able to release the buckle on his seatbelt. Her mood as foul as when she had left him, she returned to the cockpit to provide the assistance she was sworn to give. Tynan had already ripped the bandages from his hands, however, enabling him to unfasten his seatbelt and stand.

He was facing her, and rather than being swollen as he had described, his hands looked perfectly normal to her. His skin was golden brown, his fingers long and slim. A poet's hands, she thought to herself—or a philosopher's.

"It looks as though the swelling has gone down. That's good. It will make everything a lot easier for you."

Tynan flexed his fingers to ease their stiffness. His hands were not too stiff to strangle her, but he swiftly swept that option aside, for the time being, as unnecessarily severe. He lowered his hood and began to unwrap his head. "You keep parceling out vital information in dreadful bits, lieutenant. I can't help but wonder what your next surprise will be."

Amara had thought she was too angry to care how Tynan looked, but when he yanked away the last bandage, it was her turn to gasp in surprise. Thick curls brushed his forehead, and his cheeks were shadowed by several days' growth of beard, but being unkempt didn't diminish his appeal one bit. His features, while definitely masculine, held a hint of the sensitivity she had expected him to display. She had known his eyes were brown, but not how intriguing his glance would be, and he had a mouth that instantly drew speculation as to how his kisses would taste. Ashamed that her thoughts had turned erotic, she forced herself to complete the task at hand.

"I've no surprises planned. Now let's go," she ordered brusquely. "I promised to show you the passenger cabin."

As she turned to lead the way, Tynan reached out to tap her shoulder. "Do I look that bad?" he asked.

"Of course not," Amara assured him. "Besides, by the time we reach the Confederation base, you'll undoubtedly look even better."

Amara provided the promised orientation, but the whole time she was thinking how small the Starcruiser was, and how delicious Tynan looked. Because seducing a peace emissary might jeopardize his mission, and would probably end her career, she had to keep reminding herself it was absolutely out of the question. It might have been an amusing possibility last night, but now she knew Tynan was not a man who could be dismissed after a brief affair. He was one who would steal not only her heart, but her very soul as well. After the briefest of tours of his quarters, she hurriedly excused herself and returned to the cockpit, where she distracted herself from thinking about her maddeningly attractive passenger by cursing her boss for ever giving her such an exasperating assignment.

"I'll pay you back for this, Orion, I swear I will," she vowed darkly. But she had no idea how.

Chapter Four

On his own in the passenger cabin, Tynan slumped down into one of the comfortably padded seats, stretched out his legs, and flexed his hands in hopes of relieving the lingering stiffness. When exercise didn't help, he leaned back and closed his eyes. Instantly the seat shifted to a reclining position to better support his back and legs. Amara had told him the seats adjusted automatically, but he was still startled and grabbed hold of the arm-rests to steady himself. That brought a fresh burst of pain to his hands, and stifling an agonized moan, he made a mental note not to move so quickly.

After all, he was used to the Keep, where he had lounged against stone walls and had had to shove the wooden chairs into place. If he approached the furnishings in the Starcruiser with equal vigor, he would probably rip them from their moorings rather than ensure his own comfort. It was going to take a sincere effort to adjust not merely to the idea of space travel, but also to the reality of it.

For the moment, however, he was comfortably seated, so it was his mental, not physical, state that needed attention. He had been taught to meditate as a child and had continued the practice, but deep breathing and the softly cushioned seat failed to bring about the relaxation he sought. Despite the unexpected beauty of the Starcruiser, nothing about it was familiar, heightening his sense of alienation.

"Damn," he swore softly.

"Is there something you require?" Steve responded.

Again startled, Tynan sat up, then lurched forward and nearly fell as the seat anticipated his motions and straightened up with him. He caught himself, but just barely and took out his anger on Steve rather than the beautifully designed seat.

"Do you constantly eavesdrop on everyone?" he asked.

"I do not eavesdrop," Steve contradicted. "That's listening in secret. I am programmed to monitor all requests in order to fill them. I have no malicious intent. You seem troubled. Would you care to listen to soothing music or have something warm to eat or drink?"

Too distracted to appreciate music or food, Tynan shook his head, then realized that Steve needed a verbal response. "No, thank you."

"Do you like to play games?" Steve inquired.

"What sort of games?"

"Anything you like. I play them all."

Tynan found talking with a disembodied voice disconcerting and made a quick search of the cabin to locate the speakers from which Steve's voice flowed. They were flush with the bulkheads forward and aft, providing a complete circle of sound. He assumed listening to music there would be like wearing earphones or sitting in an orchestra pit, but he was too restless to lie back and enjoy one of his favorite symphonies.

"Do you know Captain's Mistress?" Tynan asked, choosing the favorite game of the eighteenth-century English explorer, Captain Cook. It was a dare really, as he didn't expect Steve to know it.

"Certainly. Do you wish to be light or dark?"

Tynan stared in amazement as a viewing screen descended from overhead and displayed a wooden box similar to the one he had owned in the Keep. The box opened. The lid was divided into seven slots, or chutes, where the light and dark wooden balls, called rounds, would be stacked in the course of the game.

"Light—no wait, I ought to be preparing for the conference, not playing games. Guardians never indulge in games during the day."

"As you wish."

As quickly as it had appeared, the screen returned to the compartment above Tynan's seat. "You don't give a man much time to change his mind, do you?"

"You may change your mind as often as you wish. I fulfill requests, I don't judge them."

This time Tynan took more care as he sat back, and the seat's shift seemed far more gentle now that he was expecting it. "No, I need to think, not play games, thank you."

"Another time then."

"Yes." When Steve remained silent, Tynan was grateful. He often mumbled to himself, and he certainly didn't want his train of thought interrupted by a solicitous computer. "Steve?" he called.

"Yes, Tynan?"

"If I don't call you by name, then I'm not talking to you, and you needn't answer. Is that clear?"

"Yes, sir."

"Good." Relieved that he wouldn't again be distracted by Steve, Tynan closed his eyes and made a sincere effort to visualize the peace conference. The participants would be seated around a central table, ringed by their staffs, with analysts forming the next row, and he supposed spectators would be assigned the remaining seats according to their rank. Alado had offered a staff of whatever size he required, but he had refused. He had no experience in delegating authority. That simply wasn't the way the Keep was run, and this struck him as a particularly poor time to attempt to gain executive skills.

No, he would be on his own at the conference, just as he was now, and he had never been so horribly uncomfortable. For as long as he could remember, he had been content with his life. No, he suddenly corrected himself. He had only found true contentment after Orion Chaudet had left the Keep. He marveled at how swiftly he had purged his memory of the belligerent young man and wondered if Orion remembered him. Probably not, he decided, for Orion would have made so many enemies over the years that his obsession with torturing a twelve-year-old boy would surely have been forgotten.

Tynan struggled another ten minutes to achieve the proper frame of mind to contemplate peace before realizing that he was too preoccupied to accomplish anything worthwhile. Rather than risk another mishap with the adjustable seat, he stood slowly, and pleased with himself for mastering at least a small part of the spacecraft, he went forward into the cockpit.

Amara's thinking had been no more productive than Tynan's, and when he slipped into the co-pilot's seat, she greeted him with a nervous smile. She had always been drawn to men whose coloring was as fair as her own, but Tynan's dark good looks were incredibly attractive. Wrapped in his aubergine robe, he had a wonderfully mysterious appeal. *Forbidden fruit,* she chided herself and, feeling uncomfortably vulnerable, chose to be flippant.

"Bored already?" she asked.

"No, just too restless to be by myself. You said I'd be welcome here with you."

"Yes, and you are." Wanting desperately for their relationship to remain the professional one it had to be, Amara chose the most obvious topic to pursue. "I've studied your writings and believe you to be an excellent choice to represent Alado at the conference, but I can't help but worry about the other firms' delegates."

"But why? Peace is the only rational course to pursue. They'll have to be as eager to ensure it as I

69

am. We shouldn't have any great difficulty working together."

Amara turned toward Tynan. He had such a thoughtful, intelligent expression in his eyes, but there was also an undisguised innocence that alarmed her. "How much do you know about the other negotiators?"

Tynan shrugged slightly. "I was given comprehensive biographies on them all. I made a point of learning their names and faces so I won't have to waste time getting acquainted. I believe they all must know, or know of, each other. I'll be the only outsider at the conference."

Fully trained as a diplomat as well as a pilot, Amara grew increasingly disturbed. "Did the biographies you received also explain each corporation's position on the treaty?"

"Yes, but we can't allow petty disputes to prevent us from securing peace. It's too vital a goal."

"I agree, but if you weren't warned before you accepted the post as Alado's negotiator, I really must tell you now that none of the other negotiators regard their firm's demands as petty. Each intends to achieve peace on the most favorable terms to themselves."

"They can't really expect that. There will have to be compromise."

"Of course, but each will strive to make the other corporations concede more points than they do."

Dismayed by her comments, Tynan frowned unhappily. "Apparently you regard me as pathetically naïve, lieutenant, but I understand a negotiator's role. We are all expected to win concessions from the other corporations, but with continued peaceful exploration as a common goal, we'll be sure to reach a just accord."

Amara knew precisely why Tynan feared she thought him naïve, but her opinion had absolutely nothing to do with his lack of sexual experience. "Please, you mustn't misunderstand me. I know your commitment to peace is sincere, and so is Alado's, but to assume the other negotiators share your desire isn't merely naïve, it's dangerous."

Although meaning well, Amara had pushed Tynan too far, and his eyes blazed with a cold fury as he replied. "If you were as brilliant a diplomat as you seem to believe, lieutenant, then you would have been asked to serve as Alado's negotiator rather than I. The fact I was given the honor proves just how little your opinions are worth."

With that hostile retort, Tynan fled the cockpit with such haste that the cord on his robe caught on the handle of the hatch. Abruptly yanked backwards, he was jerked off his feet and fell against the bulkhead with a sickening thud. Dazed, he lay where he had fallen, not knowing quite what had happened, but feeling exceedingly foolish.

Absolutely horrified that she had provoked not only a temperamental outburst but also a painful mishap, Amara rushed to Tynan's aid. She knelt beside him and, without pausing to think, brushed his curls off his forehead. It was a spontaneous gesture, but the inviting warmth of his skin burnt her fingers with shame and she quickly pulled away.

"Wait a minute," she cautioned. "Don't try to get up just yet."

71

Sprawled in an awkward heap, Tynan wouldn't have waited an instant had Amara not been so close. She had shown him the affection a mother would shower on an injured child, but it had been so unexpected, he didn't know how to respond. Unused to tender expressions of concern, he ached with an unfamiliar longing for far more. Embarrassed by his clumsiness as well as by what he saw as a pitiful burst of desire, he refused to stay put.

"I don't usually trip over my own feet," he stressed as he struggled to rise. With his legs entangled in his robe and Amara so near, he had to grab hold of the hatch and pull himself to his feet. Then he offered her a hand to help her stand. He now had a throbbing headache in addition to his other complaints, but he tried to smile.

That gesture was so endearing that as Amara pulled her hand from his, it was all she could do not to slip her arms around his waist and hug him tightly. "It wasn't your fault," she assured him. "Your belt caught on the hatch. I know you didn't bring other clothes, but I'm so afraid your robe will get in your way here. Won't you please consider wearing one of Alado's flightsuits?" She gestured toward the passenger cabin, and Tynan went ahead of her.

Reluctant to abandon his familiar garb, Tynan refused. "No, thank you. Everything is strange here. I'll simply have to be more careful."

"Yes, and so will I." Amara watched as Tynan cast a fearful backward glance before taking a seat and readily understood how difficult their voyage was for him. Rather than take the seat opposite his, she again knelt at his side. "Let me begin again. I'd

72

like you to wear a flightsuit so that you'll be not only safe, but more comfortable. Aren't you too warm in that woolen robe?"

In truth, Tynan was, but he shook his head. "No, I'm fine." Clearly his Guardian's robe was far more than an article of clothing to Tynan, but even appreciating his fondness for it, Amara wouldn't give in. "Let's try an experiment. I'll provide a flightsuit for you to wear today. All you have to do is give it a try. If you find it uncomfortable in any way, you needn't wear it again. Will you at least give it a try for an hour or two?"

Her request was not only reasonable, but made in such an enticing tone that Tynan heard himself agreeing despite his initial stubborn refusal to do so. Amara left him briefly, then returned with a shimmering gold garment she laid across his lap. Accustomed to the generous cut of his robe, he feared he would feel naked in it. Nothing about space travel was proving easy, and he could no longer hide his frustration.

"You needn't help me. I know how to dress myself."

Amara had been waiting for a word of thanks, not a plea for assistance, and shocked by his sarcasm, she immediately withdrew to the cockpit. She feared she was proving to be a poor escort for Tynan—and doing an even worse job of guarding her own emotions.

Tynan was tall and well-built, a bright and respected individual who certainly didn't appeal to whatever maternal instincts she possessed, but to something far more carnal. Positive she was only compounding her problems by dwelling on him, she propped her elbows on her armrests and held her head in her hands. She then silently berated herself for growing careless. She'd not touch him again, unless he lost his footing in front of her, but she hoped another such mishap wouldn't occur.

Forcing herself to focus on the conference, Amara soon realized that being attracted to Tynan was merely a minor personal problem compared to the diplomatic challenge that lay ahead. She had had only a brief opportunity to observe the scholarly philosopher, but since he felt so out of place on a Starcruiser, she feared the peace conference would be extremely difficult for him. He had been selected because he was such an eloquent spokesman for peaceful exploration, but with so little personal information available on the man, she doubted his temperament had been taken into account.

If he lost his temper as easily during negotiations as he had with her, then Alado wouldn't be well-served. Tynan would constantly be on the defensive and easy prey for the representatives of the other corporations, who would relentlessly pursue their own aims. While Amara certainly didn't want to see Tynan humiliated, she was even more deeply concerned about the future of Alado.

Orion hadn't given her any orders concerning her passenger other than to make certain he arrived in time to attend the opening ceremonies, but that had been an unfortunate oversight. What Tynan really needed was a quick course in the art of effective negotiation, and she was the only one in a position to provide it. It would mean they would have to spend most of their time together, which would be exquisite torture, but with the future of Alado at stake, Amara truly felt she had no other choice.

When he had finally convinced himself to go along with Amara's request, Tynan removed his boots, then his robe. He slipped his legs into the flightsuit, then stood to pull the garment up over his torso and don the sleeves. The suit closed down the front with a light touch and left him fully covered, but still feeling undressed. The garment was more loose fitting than Amara's, as comfortable as his underwear, but he felt reduced rather than enhanced, as his robe had always made him feel.

He walked the length of the cabin to get the feel of it, then drew on his boots. They were a deep purple leather that matched his robe, but not having a perfectly coordinated outfit wasn't his main concern. His head ached, and rather than ask for something to stop the pain, he sat down again and let it wash through him. Gradually, he began to relax and, drained by worry, soon fell asleep.

When Tynan didn't come forward in a reasonable length of time, Amara went back to check on him. She was relieved to find him asleep, but at the same time sad that their voyage had gotten off to such a disastrous start. Intending to put it away, she folded his robe over her arm, but found herself reluctant to leave. She reached out, then stopped herself just short of caressing his ebony curls. She had always enjoyed the company of men, but she had never met another who affected her so strongly. Now she almost wished he had worn his bandages until they reached the Confederation base.

* * *

Two hours later, Tynan awoke and, completely disoriented, needed a moment to recall where he was. His headache was gone, but as he had not eaten breakfast, he was very hungry. Amara had shown him the galley, but because there were only the two of them on board, it struck him as rude not to invite her to join him for meals. He was still insulted by her doubts of his negotiating skills, but when he paused to contemplate the fact that Alado had gone outside its own diplomatic corps to select him, he realized why she might have misgivings about his abilities.

He had to laugh when he realized that he had shown himself to be more hot-tempered than deliberate, and that was no recommendation for the job. He smiled as he entered the cockpit. "I want to apologize for what I said earlier. I know you were trying to offer helpful advice, and I shouldn't have reacted angrily."

Amara looked up briefly, then pretended a rapt interest in the navigational chart she had been studying. His apology had provided precisely the opening she required, but she didn't want to appear too eager to tutor him. "I'm very sorry too."

Tynan waited for her to say more and was disappointed when she didn't. He hadn't wanted her to grovel, just to say something to help start a conversation. "You told me I could eat whenever I'm hungry, but if you schedule your meals at regular intervals, I'd prefer that we eat together."

Amara smiled to herself, for a relaxed conversation over a meal would provide the perfect opportunity to discuss the conference. Striving to be the considerate escort he deserved, she quickly left her seat. "Most pilots prefer to follow a strict routine during flights, as it helps to make the time pass more quickly. We've missed breakfast, but if there's something you prefer to eat for your first meal of the day, it can still be prepared."

Amara had been friendly earlier, and the switch to a strictly professional attitude wasn't lost on Tynan. Certain he was to blame, he took hold of her arm as she passed by him. "I'm also sorry for what I said about helping me dress. You didn't deserve that."

Even through the protective fabric of her flight-suit, Amara felt the heat of his touch. She hadn't anticipated the change in his attire making such a difference in his appearance, but no longer draped in several yards of wool, he was not only extraordinarily handsome, but temptingly accessible. Determined to cultivate an immunity to his appeal, she gave his hand a sisterly pat and moved on.

"I told you we'd get used to bumping into each other, but I should have also warned you how easily arguments are started in flight. Now let's just forget the morning and have something to eat."

Tynan wasn't satisfied with her response, but woefully ignorant where women were concerned, he followed her aft to the galley determined to enhance his expertise with this woman. He took care not to stand too close as she repeated the list of foodstuffs on board. Because she was a vegetarian, the majority of the items available were cereals, grains, pastas, vegetables, and fruits.

"I suppose bacon and eggs are out of the question?" he asked.

"Sorry, but I can prepare a sandwich if you'd like. There's meat from a commercially grown fowl which has a taste similar to the chicken found on Earth. It's available in a variety of flavors from highly spiced to a subtle wine sauce. I'll bet you'd like that, and there's a selection of juices to drink." Amara began to rummage through the freeze-dried packages for the necessary ingredients.

"What are you having?"

"I never eat much on flights, but I've perfected a blend of yogurt and fruit that's filling."

That wasn't at all appealing to Tynan, and he was greatly relieved to find that, with the addition of liquid and heat, the sandwich Amara offered was seasoned to perfection and absolutely delicious, while the orange juice he chose tasted freshly squeezed. They shared a table in the passenger cabin and, hungry, Tynan finished the sandwich in half a dozen bites. He then discovered that Amara hadn't taken more than a couple of spoonfuls of her lumpy pink concoction.

"Would you like something more?" she asked. "Just help yourself. You needn't wait for me."

Most of the Guardians had hearty appetites, and Tynan had never been embarrassed about his eating habits before, but he certainly was now. He watched Amara scoop a bite from her bowl with an easy, graceful motion that made him feel very awkward by comparison. His hands felt much better after his nap, but he still doubted he could reproduce her elegance with a spoon.

"The food bins look like there's a generous supply of meals, but I don't want to eat more than my share."

Amara was doing her damnedest to concentrate on her food rather than on her distracting companion, but when she glanced up, she found his expression painfully sincere. She was used to spending her time with pilots who displayed a confidence bordering on arrogance, and Tynan's reserved manner continually caught her off guard. "The flight to Confederation base has been programmed for ten days," she explained. "Alado always sends double the provisions required for a flight, plus emergency rations. You needn't worry about depleting our stores. Have another sandwich if you're still hungry. Have two."

Convinced that food was plentiful, Tynan returned to the galley. The directions on the packages were so clearly written that anyone could produce a tasty meal, but he was nonetheless pleased with himself for having done it. He carried his second sandwich back to their table and this time attempted to eat more slowly.

Amara waited until they had finished, and hoping Tynan's mood was sufficiently calm, she attempted to subtly broach the subject of the conference. First she folded away the table to remove the barrier between them, then crossed her legs to get more comfortable. "In some respects, the Confederation base has much in common with the Guardians' Keep. There will be the same people to deal with each day and the same adherence to routine. The facility is one of the largest space stations, but it has limited boundaries, as does the Keep. I hope we'll be able to make you comfortable there."

"I hadn't thought there would be any similarities with home. Thank you for pointing them out."

Cinnamon Burke

Pleased that he agreed with her assessment, Amara's voice softened, yet remained persuasive. "The Guardians' world obviously provided you with both physical security and intellectual challenge, but in an important aspect, their customs have also been inhibiting. The lack of diversity is terribly limiting."

Tynan felt certain she was referring to the exclusion of women, but that was an integral part of the Guardians' structure, so he merely nodded rather than debate an issue made policy centuries earlier.

Assuming Tynan was following her argument, Amara continued. "There are a host of differences, and not merely in attitude or custom, that the Guardians fail to encounter in their daily lives."

"That's certainly true, but we have chosen to stress harmony over diversity."

Amara sat forward slightly. "Yes, but it's the manner in which the Guardians achieve that harmony that's at fault. They provide a nurturing environment, which by the very element of its exclusiveness fosters a dreadful deficiency."

That the Guardians did not have feminine companionship was what a great many of the men liked most about the Keep. As for himself, he had certainly not missed it. "I think the word dreadful is overstating it a bit."

"Oh, but it isn't, Tynan. This is a significant problem that needs to be addressed immediately."

Although Tynan could understand her opposition to a tradition that excluded her sex, he had not really expected her to proposition him, but clearly that was precisely what she was doing. That he was about to have his first sexual experience with a woman in a spaceship, of all places, was certainly daunting, but he was definitely eager to give it a try.

"Take down your hair," he asked when she paused.

"I beg your pardon?"

Tynan leaned over and felt for the pins that secured the knot atop Amara's crown. He found two, removed them, and her curls spilled over her shoulders in stunning disarray. "You have such beautiful hair. You ought to wear it down all the time."

Amara's cheeks flooded with a bright blush. "Tynan, please. I'm trying my best to have a serious discussion with you."

Tynan sat back, but couldn't contain a wide grin. "If it's a serious discussion you want first, go ahead. As you've just pointed out, there's a lot I don't know—so please, go right ahead and teach me."

Amara felt the heat of her blush spreading over her breasts, while a tantalizing warmth crept down her legs. She uncrossed and crossed them, but that didn't help to dispel the erotic sensation she recognized all too well. Without even touching her, Tynan was provoking a stunning response, and Amara didn't understand how she had gotten so terribly distracted from the conversation she had intended to have.

She looked down, and then had to brush her hair off her face when she looked back up at him. He was grinning now, and nodded, obviously expecting her to continue. The problem was, they couldn't possibly be talking about the same thing or he wouldn't be watching her with an expression of such devilish glee.

"Just what is it you think we're discussing?" she asked.

Tynan leaned forward, and took her hand. "You needn't be coy. I've already admitted I've no experience with women, and since that's obviously a deficiency that bothers you, we ought to do all that we can to remedy the situation."

When Amara simply stared at him wide-eyed and appeared to be too dumbfounded to reply, Tynan continued in a playful tone, "Look, I don't expect promises of undying love. If our affair doesn't last any longer than the flight to Confederation base, it will still have served its purpose."

That he would propose an emotionless affair hurt Amara very badly, and she yanked her hand from his. "You've misunderstood me completely," she argued. "I was attempting to lead you into a discussion of how best to deal with the diverse personalities you'll encounter at the conference—not into an affair. I don't know what you've heard, or imagine to be true, but women do have feelings, Tynan. I've never engaged in casual affairs, and I most certainly wouldn't do it with you simply to complete your education."

Confused, Tynan sat back slightly. At first, he didn't see how he could have misunderstood her so completely. Then he knew. "There have been several occasions," he recalled, "when you've touched me and spoken as though you really cared about me. Your manner is very gentle then; you were doing it again just now. It's very inviting—or at least, I thought it was."

Amara's throat tightened with the threat of tears. She had seen the Guardians' Keep and understood that he had been raised in an emotional vacuum, but that didn't mean she ought to sacrifice her heart when he offered nothing in return. He reminded her of Orion then, for his gestures of affection had also been devoid of love. She hadn't realized that fact soon enough with Orion, but she saw Tynan's request for exactly what it was.

"Making love has to mean something," she whispered, "or at least to me it does. If all you want is instruction, you'll have to find someone else."

Amara looked hurt by the fact that he wanted her, but Tynan thought his desire ought to be taken as a compliment. "I realize a Guardian and a pilot have no hope of a shared future, but does that have to mean we can't enjoy the present?"

Amara had heard that same argument from too many pilots to appreciate the fact Tynan believed it to be an original thought. She struggled to project a calm she didn't feel. "That's a trap I won't even get near, now please, let's just drop this subject."

Tynan shook his head, then reached out to slip his fingers in her tawny curls to draw her close. He had seen passionate kisses only in films, but he doubted they were difficult to give, and when he felt the incredible softness of Amara's lips, he ceased to think at all. He simply felt an overpowering need to take more, and more, and more.

Amara wasn't at all surprised that Tynan's kiss was not only confident, but delicious as well. She had every intention of refusing the second, and then the third, but somehow she lost count, and when he pulled her across his lap, she was so lost in desire that she forgot the emphatic refusal she had just given him. Even if she were no more than an experiment to Tynan, being with him definitely meant something far more important to her. Yet even in the initial bliss, she felt the inevitable pain of parting.

Usually a thoughtful, deliberate individual, Tynan had not expected his emotions to betray him so swiftly, but he was as lost as Amara in the magical attraction that flowed between them. He slid his hand down her lithe figure, and pressing her close to his heart and unable to catch his breath between kisses, he wondered how anyone made love without passing out in the process. To hold her in his arms and feel her tongue slide over his was so much better than he had dreamed, he didn't want to ever let her go. Had Steve not called her name in an urgent tone, he wouldn't have.

"Lieutenant, I am receiving an erroneous signal from a navigational buoy," the computer announced. "Please confirm my findings."

Startled, Tynan scanned Amara's expression to judge the seriousness of Steve's report. "Are we in trouble?" he asked.

Amara reacted to the call of alarm with a low moan, closely followed by a sigh of relief, for she hadn't meant for things to get so badly out of hand. She broke away from Tynan's grasp and slid off his lap. "It's a minor navigational problem. It's nothing serious."

"How can it not be serious? Are we lost?"

Amara entered the cockpit without answering, but while she was confident that the ship was on course, she feared that she was definitely lost in the only way that mattered—and that a handsome philosopher was to blame.

Chapter Five

Tynan took the co-pilot's seat, but the wide array of instruments and blinking lights that provided Amara with vital information meant nothing to him, and he remained baffled by the nature of the problem which had called for her immediate attention. She deferred questions with a distracted wave, and because he feared their lives were at stake, he honored her request. But he wanted answers, and right now—not when it was convenient.

He sat back and held his tongue, but the news bulletin announcing his death while en route to the conference was far easier to imagine than their safe arrival. He had already made a significant contribution in the field of philosophy, but the sweetness of Amara's kisses had convinced him that this was no time for his life to end. He glanced toward her. Her expression was one of simple interest rather than stark terror, and he tried to mirror her confidence. After all, she was the pilot, and if she wasn't hysterical, maybe they weren't in such terrible trouble after all.

He wanted to ask Steve about the problem, but fearing that would only distract Amara, he didn't dare consult the computer. All he could do was sit and wait, and the delay was pure torture. It was only Amara's calm adherence to procedure that kept him from losing his composure, and when she finally sat back and smiled, his head ached from the strain.

The navigational problem solved, Amara faced another with Tynan. Because he was clearly worried, she wanted to speak in a soothing tone, but she certainly didn't want her purpose to again be misinterpreted. Despite his complaint, she knew she hadn't been openly seductive in their earlier conversations, but now she had to strive to keep all hint of concern out of her voice. When just looking at him prompted so much emotion, it was a difficult challenge indeed.

"When we first came on board, I explained that we use the position of the stars and satellites, or space buoys, for navigation. Sometimes the space buoys malfunction, but because Alado doesn't rely solely on them, it doesn't present a serious problem for us. Smaller, private craft, whose pilots do depend on the satellites, can experience difficulties if their signal isn't accurate, so I've notified Fleet Command, and the buoy will be reprogrammed. Until then, pilots will be advised to disregard its signal."

"We're in no danger then?"

"Absolutely none."

"I thought satellites performed their function for generations. What could have happened to this one?"

Amara drummed her fingertips on her armrest. "Which would you prefer, a scientific explanation or the most probable cause?"

"The truth."

"That's impossible to discern without examining the satellite."

Tynan couldn't help but feel she was leading him in circles, and he didn't like it one bit. "Just give me your best guess."

"All right. This close to Earth, I think someone deliberately tampered with the buoy."

"Pirates?"

Tynan had a marvelously expressive face, making his apprehension easy to read, but Amara thought again of how strongly that same openness would work against him at the conference. "No, it was undoubtedly one of the deliquent gangs everyone calls Corkscrews. Have you heard of them?"

Tynan shook his head. "I had no idea I was so insufferably ignorant until I began this voyage with you."

"You're not in the least ignorant. You're merely out of your field of expertise. Corkscrews get their name from the fanciful keys they use to decorate their belts. They're just pranksters, rather than pirates. They sometimes sabotage navigational buoys, then board a ship that's strayed off course for joy rides. They're certainly an unpleasant crowd, but they've never damaged a ship or caused anyone permanent harm."

"As far as you know."

88

"Well, yes, as far as I know. They're just a nuisance, not a real hazard."

Tynan was losing his temper again, and Amara tried to prevent it. "I wish you'd just relax and trust me to get us to the conference safely. I wouldn't have been sent as your escort if Alado didn't have every confidence in my ability to handle whatever difficulties we might encounter. My flight to Earth was uneventful. There's no reason to believe this flight will be any different."

It wasn't that Tynan didn't trust her; it was just that everything was so damn unfamiliar, and the emotional upheaval created by the recent emergency, which apparently hadn't been an emergency at all, erupted in anger. "In the Keep, the dangers are few and easily anticipated. I don't know what to expect here. You provided a tardy warning about pirates and dismiss the threat posed by Corkscrews, but I have a sinking feeling there are even worse dangers ahead. What else haven't you told me? Is there something else that might prevent us from reaching the conference on time?"

Amara cocked her head, unaware of how the slightest motion sent ripples of reflected light dancing along her curls. It was an entrancing gesture, completely unintentional, and at odds with her rapidly shifting mood. She had done her best to establish a rapport with Tynan, but his hostile frown was a clear indication that she had failed. Believing he had also failed her, she didn't mince words.

"It's unfortunate you didn't share my concern about a timely arrival when we were at the Keep, because by insisting we wait for the dawn, you cost us twelve precious hours I can't replace. That's what I was talking about as limiting, by the way. The isolation of the Guardians' Keep fosters traditions that are ridiculous when applied to anything other than your own peculiar habits.

"If a timely arrival has finally become one of your priorities, I suggest you don't distract me any further." Amara swung around to face the computer screen that displayed the navigational chart for their sector. She had no more need of it, but rather than switch it off, she gave it her full concentration.

Tynan stared at her profile as he attempted to come up with an equally sharp response, but when, after a few seconds, nothing appropriately stinging came to him, he got up and left. He was fast wearing a rut between the cockpit and the passenger cabin, but as soon as he had entered the central portion of the ship, he called to Steve.

"Yes, Tynan?"

"Tell me the truth about the Corkscrews."

"Corkscrews is a slang term for the groups of young men and women who have no respect for the laws which govern space travel. They create hazards to navigation and harass private travelers as a perverse form of amusement."

"But not Alado's ships?"

"No, sir, none of Alado's ships has ever been boarded by Corkscrews."

"We could always be the first." Steve didn't reply to that sarcastic prediction, leaving Tynan at the mercy of his own dark thoughts. He soon realized that his questioning of the helpful computer had been incomplete.

"Steve, in addition to Alado, there are four other corporations. How many of their ships have been boarded by Corkscrews?"

"My files contain statistics pertaining only to the Alado Corporation, Tynan."

Again stymied in his quest for information, Tynan wished he had known what questions to ask before he had left the Keep. He could have gotten all the answers he needed there, but now it was apparently impossible. Although the passenger cabin was wide and uncluttered, he felt trapped. "Steve?"

"Yes, Tynan."

"How do you keep from losing your mind cooped up in here?"

"I have no mind to lose, sir, but if you're bored, I can offer many entertainments."

"Damn it, I'm not bored!"

"If the close confines of the ship annoy you, I can provide scenery from any planet you choose."

"I'd prefer the Earth."

"As you wish."

A screen descended at the front of the cabin, the lights dimmed, and after a brief introduction, a seascape appeared. Ocean waves brushed against the sand, leaving foamy kisses to evaporate on the shore. There were haunting bird calls and lush natural sound effects rather than music, and thinking any activity preferable to being with Lieutenant Greer, who kissed him one minute and called his traditions ridiculous the next, Tynan sat down to watch.

He was completely unaware that the film contained subliminal messages designed to create a harmonious calm among passengers during space flight. He felt only a warming sense of relaxation that flowed through him with the ease of the tide illustrated on the screen. Thinking the film one of the most charming he had ever seen, he lay back and enjoyed every frame.

Amara would have avoided Tynan for the remainder of the flight had she not had to pass through the passenger cabin to reach the galley and lavatory. As it was, she waited as long as she could before going aft. Tynan was pacing the aisle, and she had to wait for him to turn and see her before she could proceed.

The first thing Tynan noticed was that Amara had again secured her hair in a tight bun atop her head. He had made the mistake of thinking of her as a woman, and a very desirable one at that, but clearly she was the consummate professional. No doubt she was superb—not merely Alado's premiere pilot, but the best in the galaxy.

"Steve verified your definition of the Corkscrews."

Amara wasn't surprised, merely disappointed that her word hadn't been enough to convince him. "Before you two become best friends, you ought to remember that Steve can be programmed to repeat whatever information I provide." Amara watched the confusion fill Tynan's eyes, but felt no surge of triumph for having gotten the better of him.

"I'm sorry, I shouldn't have said that. Steve's programming is done at Fleet Command, not on board. I've got much better things to do than rescript his responses."

Tynan approached her slowly. "Is that all he does, just repeat scripts?"

"Yes. He's prepared to fly the ship and look after the passengers' comfort—nothing more. Steve?"

"Yes, lieutenant?"

"Men and women sometimes have great difficulty getting along. Can you provide any advice in that area?"

"No, lieutenant, I have no files on interpersonal relationships."

Tynan was now no more than a few inches away from Amara. "It looks as though we're on our own, lieutenant. Let's agree to a truce and dispense with the insults."

Amara knew she had insulted him—and deliberately, which was even worse—but she had been sorely provoked. It was going to be a wretched ten days if they didn't declare a truce, however, and she offered her hand. "Agreed. We ought to be civil to each other, but anything more is completely out of the question."

Tynan took her hand, but then refused to release it. "I would have sworn you were comfortable on my lap. What would have happened had Steve not interrupted us?"

Embarrassed by that lapse in judgment, Amara looked away. "I'd have stopped you myself. I meant what I said, Tynan. I don't give lessons in love, and from the way you handled yourself, it's plain you don't need them. Now will you please move aside? I need to use the lavatory."

Tynan dropped her hand and stepped out of her way. She had certainly sounded sincere, but she hadn't been able to look at him while she had set the rules limiting their relationship, and he took that as a good sign. "Do you believe in omens?" he asked.

Amara glanced back over her shoulder to respond. "No, I'll leave the superstitions to you."

Clearly that was another insult, but it had been relayed in such a teasing manner that Tynan chose to laugh this time. He had thought Amara would appreciate a frank appeal for physical intimacy, but since she didn't, maybe she would be susceptible to a more romantic approach. "Steve?" he whispered.

"Yes, Tynan?"

"Are you certain there's nothing in your files about relationships?"

"Yes, but I can forward your request for information to Fleet Command."

Tynan could readily imagine the hilarious response should one of Alado's clerks receive a request for tips on accomplishing a seduction from a Guardian on his way to a peace conference. "No, that's unnecessary."

"As you wish."

"Wait a minute. What information do you have on Lieutenant Greer?"

"You wish the data from her personnel file?"

Tynan sent a hurried glance aft and hoped Amara would stay in the lavatory long enough for him to learn all about her. "Yes, please."

"Amara Greer is twenty-seven years old. She had a distinguished academic record throughout her schooling and graduated first in her class from Alado's Flight Academy. She has served as a pilot with the diplomatic corps for five years, maintaining a continuously superior evaluation. An only child, she is the daughter of the noted geologists, Julian and Lené Greer. She has never married, nor had a child."

"That's all very interesting, Steve, but rather dry. Do you know anything about her preferences in men?"

"Alado does not track its personnel when they are off duty, Tynan. That would be an invasion of privacy."

Tynan swore under his breath. "Well, she's on duty during a flight, so you must have collected some information about her. Which of your films and games does she like?"

"On voyages like this one, where she's the only crew, she uses neither."

"She must do something with her time."

"She studies navigational charts and plots future voyages."

"Wonderful." His suspicion that Amara was indeed all pilot confirmed, Tynan thanked Steve and went back to the galley. When Amara left the lavatory, he was waiting for her. "You said having a routine helps to pass the time. Are you ready for dinner?"

"Yes, I suppose so."

Tynan leaned back against the counter. "I understand your terms. We'll talk about the conference rather than anything personal. The sandwiches were delicious. What else do you recommend?"

Pleased that his change in attitude seemed sincere, Amara relaxed slightly. "The rice and vegetable casserole is good, as are any of the pasta dishes. Some have ingredients you might not recognize, but their taste is pleasing."

She began looking through the bins and tossing packages on the counter, but again she didn't glance toward him, confirming Tynan's earlier belief that she simply couldn't meet his eyes. He had summoned the courage to check his appearance in the lavatory mirror and didn't think he presented a particularly unpleasant sight, so it couldn't be his looks that bothered her.

It was an effective way to avoid him, though, and he didn't want to be avoided. He got out the utensils and set up the table while they waited the few minutes required to heat their meals. He had never particularly cared for vegetables, especially those he couldn't name, but resting on a bed of rice and covered with a thick layer of cheese, these didn't look too bad.

Amara appeared to be content to eat in silence, so Tynan kept still too. He made an effort to eat more slowly, however, and finished his last bite at the same time she did. "I've been thinking about what you said earlier," he then began.

"About what?"

"About the other negotiators. Omega Corporation is sending Lisha Drache. She's young, without much experience. How does she pose a threat to us?"

"Us?"

"Alado, then."

"Ah, yes. Alado." Amara set their plates aside and rested her arms on the edge of the table. "Lisha is virulently loyal to Omega. They're the smallest firm, and they desperately want more colonies. They can't compete on the same scale as the other corporations without concessions she'll be certain to demand. I expect her to delay every meeting by pressing for her own goals rather than for mutual accord."

Tynan nodded. "What about Europa's representative, Gallager McGrath? How do you see him?"

"He's somewhat difficult to describe. He's the eldest of the negotiators and likes to play the statesman, but rather than wisdom, he's noted for having a mean-spirited, perverse nature. You can count on him to block every constructive suggestion you make."

"I can't wait to meet him. The Serema Corporation is sending Tava Micenko. Is she a reasonable person?"

Amara frowned slightly. "She's lovely, but dangerous. She'll agree with you one minute and betray you the next."

Tynan wondered if Amara couldn't be described in the same manner, but decided to keep that thought to himself. "Sounds charming. That leaves only Peregrine's negotiator, Derrel Simmons. What's he like?"

"Peregrine has never been an overly ethical concern. In fact, there are some who insist they're no better than pirates. Derrel won't take anything seriously. He'll probably sidetrack every discussion and press for open exploration without any restrictions."

"Then we'd soon be right back where we are now, on the verge of war over which corporation was the first to claim new territory."

Amara chose her words with care. "That's what I tried to warn you about this morning, Tynan. Peregrine doesn't see war in a negative light. In fact, I think they're eager for it. They're the exact opposite of Alado, with Omega, Serema, and Europa lined up somewhere in between."

Tynan sat back, seeing his role in a new light. He shook his head sadly. "I think I'm finally beginning to appreciate why Alado asked me to be their negotiator rather than handing the job to one of their diplomats."

"Really? Why?"

"So that when I fail to get a comprehensive treaty, the blame will fall on me rather than on Alado."

Amara let the absurdity of that opinion play out in her mind before she replied. "No, you're wrong. There was great enthusiasm for your appointment to the negotiator's post. You're seen as having not only the commitment to peace, but the intelligence to make it a reality."

"That may be what the others at Alado say, but now that you know me, what do you think?"

"May I assume that you want the truth?"

"Of course."

"I think we're in very deep trouble."

"And why is that?"

"Because expressing your opinions in writing, where you have no opposition, and pressing for your point of view in a heated debate are two entirely different things. How often did you have to defend your views in the Keep?"

Tynan gestured helplessly. "Never. We're all committed to peace."

"As well you should be, but the Guardians have left you woefully unprepared to negotiate peace on Alado's terms. Now, we have nine days left to remedy that situation, or we can spend our time praying that the other negotiators have a sudden change of heart on their way to the conference."

Thinking they might be able to strike a bargain, Tynan began to smile. "You're very loyal to Alado, aren't you?"

"With good reason. It's a wonderful corporation that places the highest value on its employees' welfare. Any of our competitors would willingly sacrifice a pilot and crew to gain an inch of new territory. I wouldn't work for any of them."

What Tynan wanted was Amara in exchange for the work she clearly expected him to do on the voyage. He had already learned that she didn't like to be pushed, however, and he wanted her to be as willing for them to become lovers as he was. He could wait a day or two before broaching the subject again, and if she was as good at debate as she was at flying, he thought she just might provide him with the very weapons to beat her.

"Let's start tomorrow," he suggested. "How do you spend your evenings?"

Tired, Amara didn't argue his choice. "I like to read, but I left so suddenly I didn't have time to bring any reading matter along. Steve has stories in his files, but I've read them all."

"You never read anything twice?"

"No, I like adventure stories, and once you know everything will turn out all right, there's no point in it."

"I understand. There's no suspense."

"Exactly."

"Do you ever play any games?"

"Not by myself, but when there are several pilots

on board, we have endless tournaments of Banshee Quest—but I doubt you played that at the Keep."

"No, I'm sorry, I don't know it. Would you teach me how to play?"

Amara regarded him with a skeptical glance. "It's a game involving speed and skill rather than thoughtful contemplation."

If it interested Amara, then Tynan was determined to like it. "Look at it this way—speed and skill may be precisely what I need for the negotiations."

"All right. Let's give it a try then, but if it appalls you, please just say so and we'll stop."

"I know when to stop," Tynan assured her.

He was flirting with her, but Amara decided that was better than arguing and didn't complain. She requested the game, and Steve provided a screen. After removing their table, Amara pointed to the armrest on Tynan's seat. "The controls are inside, just flip the top open."

Tynan followed her directions and removed a small control panel complete with blinking lights, levers, and buttons. "This looks pretty complicated. What's the object of the game?"

"To destroy the opposition's ships before they can destroy you. It can be played at varying levels of difficulty, so we'll start at the lowest and work up. Do you want to be black or red?"

"Black."

"Fine, try the controls. You've got the black ship. See what you can make it do."

It took several minutes, but Tynan finally mastered the basic maneuvers of the game. "I'm ready. Let's play—and treat me like another pilot rather than someone who doesn't know what they're doing. Otherwise, I won't learn what I should."

"You don't really mean that."

"Yes, I do."

"Begin the game, Steve." Amara allowed Tynan to get his ship in the air, then targeted him with her laser cannon and blew him up.

Startled, Tynan watched the shimmering pieces of his ship fade from the screen. "That was fast. Have I lost already?"

"No, you have nine more ships at this level. This time try to keep an eye on my ship instead of just watching your own, and you'll be better able to defend yourself." Again Amara waited a moment to give Tynan the opportunity to practice, but then she again blew him off the screen.

Discouraged, Tynan was still determined to learn the game. He sat forward slightly. "Let's begin the next round."

"Are you sure? All this game requires is coordination, not brains."

"I'll have plenty of time to play intellectually challenging games when I get back to the Keep. Let's go."

"Good luck." Amara gave Tynan more time to practice flying his ship with each round, but they all ended the same way, and she began to feel somewhat ashamed of herself for even telling him about the game.

Tynan, however, found himself actually beginning to like Banshee Quest. It was certainly violent, but it required quick thinking in addition to coordination. Even if Amara didn't see it as an intellectual challenge, he did. "It may take me the whole way to Confederation base, but I'm going to beat you at this."

"Are you?" Amara responded with a throaty laugh. "I don't think so."

"What's so funny? Are you Alado's champion?"

"Yes, but it's only a game, Tynan, and being the champion player has no real significance."

"Well I say that it does."

He didn't look angry, merely intense, and Amara was very pleased. "That's it. That's precisely the tone you'll need at the conference. Not outrage, but gritty determination."

Tynan hadn't been acting a part. "No, I really meant what I said. Being the champion player at any game or sport brings respect. It also creates a certain amount of envy, if not outright jealousy. What about all the pilots you beat at Banshee Quest? Are they eager to become your lovers, or do they avoid you?"

Amara didn't understand how he had swung the conversation in such an unfortunate direction. "Whether or not I take lovers is no concern of yours, Tynan."

"We're not talking about your lovers," Tynan denied. "We're talking about the way the other pilots treat you. If you're the best in the diplomatic corps, surely some of the other pilots must envy you."

Amara slipped her control panel back into her armrest and rose to her feet. "A lot has happened in the last two hundred years that may have escaped your notice. Men and women can now compete on an equal footing in anything they choose. Men don't avoid women who excel at their careers—far from it. Successful women are admired, sought after, cherished. Alado has always encouraged all its employees, both men and women, to realize their potential. Don't the Guardians do the same?"

Tynan sensed criticism in her voice. He stood to face her. "We are encouraged to exceed the known boundaries in all we do. Excellence is the very minimum we accept, not the norm."

"Yes, the Guardians are known for extraordinary scholarship. I'll give you that, but because you retreat from rather than interact with the rest of the galaxy, your focus will always be restricted. Now if you'll excuse me, I need to make a last check of the instruments before putting Steve in command for the night.

"You'll find two of the seats make a comfortable bed. Sensors adjust the temperature for sleep, so no bedding is required. I prefer using the seats nearest the cockpit. Why don't you chose two near the galley so we won't disturb each other. I already know you don't snore, but neither of us is used to sharing our quarters, and I want us both to be comfortable."

"You're very thoughtful, lieutenant."

It was plain he meant the exact opposite, but Amara pretended not to understand. "Thank you. Good night."

As Amara retreated into the cockpit, she still presented an entrancing sight. Like most tall women, she had long legs and a graceful stride, but it was her subtle curves Tynan liked best. In his mind, he again freed her hair, then peeled away the close-fitting uniform and whatever scant undergarments she wore beneath. Judging from her lips, her skin would be incredibly soft and the same luscious pale golden shade all over. For a man who had never had much interest in women, he feared he was rapidly becoming obsessed with his attractive companion.

"No, she's merely someone to study, someone who can provide an experience I can't get at the Keep." That's all she was, he repeated as a mantra, but he knew that even debating the point with himself, he had lost.

Amara updated the Starcruiser's log, waited a sufficient time for Tynan to fall asleep, then remained in the cockpit a while longer. Their first day together had been anything but smooth, but she thought she had finally convinced him to keep his amorous impulses to himself. It was a shame really, when he was so appealing, but he had warned her himself that a pilot and a Guardian had no future together, and she had learned a long time ago to listen to what men actually said, rather than hoping for what she wished to hear.

"Nine more days, Tynan," she whispered to herself, and her promise to be his pilot on the return voyage to Earth conveniently forgotten, she vowed to make each one easier than the first. Her heart ached with longing for the love she had never found, but when it came, she wanted it to last forever, not merely a few joyous, but ultimately bittersweet, days.

Chapter Six

The next morning, Amara awoke before Tynan. She first relieved Steve of command, then went back to the lavatory to shower and change her uniform. Using a fine spray of water that was continuously reclaimed and refiltered, she shampooed her hair, and in a reflective mood watched the soapy bubbles slide over her breasts and drip down her legs. Like most of Alado's pilots, her body was adorned with her own personalized tattoo. She had chosen a sea motif, and the same artist who had applied her indelible lip color and eyeshadow had entwined a softly swirling wave pattern around her right leg, swept her torso with the cresting water, and splashed her breasts with a lacy filigree of iridescent foam.

In pale shades of green and aqua accented with lavender, the tattoo was not only an exquisite work of art, but also decorated her slender body with the erotic tenderness of a lover's caress. She smiled to herself as she imagined Tynan's shocked reaction to the tattoo, then just as quickly banished the thought, for she had no intention of providing him with an opportunity to appreciate it. She couldn't recall just when full-body tattooing had become a favored means of personal expression, but she was fairly certain it hadn't been widely practiced in the twentieth century, and that was where Tynan's expertise ended.

Angry with herself for letting her mind again stray to her passenger, she shut off the water and waited the moment required to dry off in a warm rush of air. She slipped on a one-piece undergarment, then her suit and boots. Her hair was still damp, so she left the flowing ringlets falling free and, trying not to wake Tynan, began to prepare a breakfast of yogurt and fruit.

A light sleeper under the best of circumstances, Tynan heard one of the food bins open and sat up. He had awakened repeatedly during the night and felt far from refreshed. Two seats did make a passable bed, but it wasn't the bed he was used to, and that had made all the difference.

"If you'll give me a few minutes, we can have breakfast together," he called.

Amara gripped the edge of the counter. "Fine. Take all the time you need." She didn't turn as Tynan went by her to the lavatory, but that didn't prevent her from feeling his presence more deeply than she had hoped. She placed her yogurt mixture and a fruit juice blend on the table they had begun using and paced anxiously while she waited for him to join her.

Used to a rigorous schedule, Tynan needed only a few minutes to shower and complete his grooming. He then brought over a bowl of hot cereal and some orange juice. "If we're going to spend the day practicing how to debate, should we tackle the conference issues or merely some point of disagreement between us?" Now clean shaven, he flashed what he hoped would be a charming grin.

A slight growth of beard had provided him with a faintly roguish appearance, but now, clean-shaven, Tynan was remarkably handsome. Amara considered the change in him, stared a moment too long, and then couldn't remember his question. "I'm sorry, what did you ask?"

Certain her mind wouldn't be wandering if his attempt to impress her had been successful, Tynan dropped the effort. Adopting a more serious mood, he tried again. "Not that I want to create animosity where none exists, but if it's just the dynamics of negotiations that you want to rehearse, we can use any topic."

Amara had just begun to reply when Steve spoke her name. "Yes, Steve?"

"We're being approached by three private vessels. They're not transmitting the required codes. Shall I make the standard request for identification?"

Tynan lifted one eyebrow, and Amara reached out to touch his hand to reassure him. "Come on up to the cockpit with me. It's probably nothing serious, but let's make certain before we finish our breakfast."

Tynan would have followed even without an invitation. He dropped into the co-pilot's seat, and when Amara tapped the bottom of his computer screen, he found the three ships in question. Even to an untrained eye, they appeared to be rapidly closing the distance between them.

"What are you going to do?" he asked.

"Nothing yet. They appear to be scout ships, perhaps surplus purchased from Peregrine or Europa and converted to private use. Can you confirm their design, Steve?"

"Europa Gauntlets, lieutenant. They were declared obsolete approximately ten years ago and sold to private individuals."

"I hope that doesn't include Corkscrews and pirates," Tynan mused aloud.

"The Gauntlet is only a two-man ship, so there's no demand for them among pirates. It's most Corkscrews' favorite craft, but the Gauntlet is a reliable ship, and others use them too." Apparently unperturbed, Amara continued to watch the screen. She had been authorized to protect Tynan at all costs, but Alado's usual policy forbade being the aggressor in any situation, and she wouldn't attack without proof of a clear danger. After all, if she began firing on every ship that came within range, Tynan might quickly decide Alado was not a firm he wished to represent. She would have accomplished nothing if he arrived safely at the conference but then refused to participate.

Tynan found it impossible to take his eyes off the co-pilot's screen. "They're flying in tight formation. What does that mean?"

"They may merely be practicing, in which case it means absolutely nothing, or it could indicate that they intend to attack."

"You told me Corkscrews haven't bothered Alado's vessels. What purpose could private citizens have for attacking one of Alado's Starcruisers?"

"None that I know. Broadcast a demand for identification on the civilian frequencies, Steve."

After a brief pause, the computer replied, "There's no response, lieutenant."

"Are they armed?"

"Yes."

Knowing the weapons a Gauntlet was capable of carrying, Amara had kept a careful note of the distance separating them. Were Tynan anyone but a peace negotiator, she would already have fired warning shots at the pursuing ships, but for his sake, she chose the nonviolent option. "Let's outrun them. Steve, take us up to maximum speed for a minute and a half."

Tynan grabbed his armrests as a sudden jolt jarred through the ship. Thinking it was the increase in power, he wasn't overly concerned until, having outdistanced the pursuing ships, Amara called for a damage report. "Damage? From what?" he asked.

"We were fired on just as we turned up the power." Now knowing she had made the wrong choice, Amara was furious with herself for erring on the side of caution, but she could scarcely explain her feelings to Tynan. "I'm sorry, I shouldn't have allowed that to happen. It wouldn't have, had those ships been carrying their standard armaments. Obviously they weren't. Note that for the log, Steve, and notify Fleet Command that we were struck by fire from private Gauntlets when we should still have been out of range. Calculate

109

the distance and reset the alarms so it won't happen again."

"Yes, lieutenant. Damage is confined to the starboard scanners. Minimal in nature, it presents no hazard to the function of this ship or its crew."

Amara pursed her lips thoughtfully. "We're blind on the starboard side, Steve. I consider that a hazard."

"Alado classifies only the forward and aft scanners as vital to the operation of this ship, lieutenant."

"Please include a protest of that assumption in the report I just asked you to forward."

"Yes, lieutenant."

Tynan kept glancing toward the screen, but there was no sign of the ships giving pursuit. "What happened to the Gauntlets?"

"We just put ourselves well ahead of them. You needn't worry any more about them."

Tynan had spent enough time with Amara to recognize when her manner was strained. It showed in her eyes, and her usually relaxed posture had stiffened noticeably. "You still look worried."

Amara nodded. "You're a perceptive man. You asked about omens. Do you ever rely on intuition?"

"I'm afraid I haven't any, or at least no sixth sense that provides me with adequate warnings. What about you?"

"Let's just say I've learned to trust my instincts, and the whole incident with the Gauntlets was odd. I can't imagine the Corkscrews daring to approach a Starcruiser. But whoever that was, they had the courage not only to approach, but to fire on us with modified weapons. That's well beyond the capabilities of your average Corkscrew."

Tynan was almost afraid to ask his next question. "Could they have been trying to stop me from reaching the conference?"

As reluctant to consider that scenario as he, Amara took a deep breath, then released it slowly. She didn't want to believe he was right, but she couldn't deny it was a possibility. "I hate to think anyone would wish to sabotage the conference by such despicable means, but just to be safe, let's assume such desperate individuals exist and act accordingly. That means we'll have to be on guard for another attack, and we'll need to have all our scanners functioning properly. Steve, where's the nearest maintenance facility? I'm not flying blind on the starboard side even if Alado says it can be done. It's just too great a risk in this case."

Amara was a lovely and desirable young woman, but when she turned toward him, Tynan saw dogged determination in her expression. If anyone could get him to Confederation base safely, he was confident it was her. "You're a fine pilot," he finally admitted, "and I trust whatever decision you make. Just let me know what you'd like me to do."

All she really needed was for him to stay out of her way, but when he had graciously offered his assistance, she couldn't give what he would undoubtedly take as a rude response. Instead, she extended her hand and he took it. "Thanks. If there's anything that Steve and I can't handle, I'll let you know. Right now, you might as well finish your breakfast."

"What about you?"

111

"I'll wait for Steve to locate a place for repairs first."

"Then I'll wait too."

Before Amara could argue, Steve made his report. "The closest facility for repairs is an asteroid owned by Dr. Risto Cortez. It's a scientific research station with the necessary docking and hangar facilities to accommodate a Starcruiser. Approximate flight time, one hour."

"I've never heard of him, Steve. What's the next possibility?"

"Alado Repair Station 381, but the detour to reach it will increase your flight time by ten hours."

Faced with another difficult choice, Amara again took the option best for Tynan. "Ordinarily, I'd wait for an Alado base, but ten hours is just too long to risk if we're really being pursued."

"I agree."

"Fine, it's a joint decision then. Steve, replot our course for Dr. Cortez's asteroid and signal him that we're on our way." Amara hesitated a moment, then consulted Tynan. "Because we've no idea what this man's politics might be, let's not provide advance notice that you're on board. Agreed?"

Sickened that anyone might wish him dead, Tynan nodded, but when they returned to the passenger cabin, he found it impossible to enjoy breakfast as though the morning hadn't been interrupted by unknown assailants. "How can you eat?" he asked.

Amara had to finish chewing before she replied. "Our bodies run on food, the same way this ship runs on fuel. If we don't eat, we may find ourselves running out of energy just when we need it most."

112

That was the last thing Tynan wanted to hear. "Is that the type of practical advice they give at Alado's Flight Academy?"

Amused, Amara nodded. "Among other things, but I'm solely responsible for this ship, so if you aren't feeling up to eating, don't."

Tynan took a sip of orange juice, but couldn't bring himself to reheat his cereal. "I'm sorry, I know I suggested we spend the day planning strategy for the conference, but I can't do it now."

"The episode with the Gauntlets was unsettling, I'll grant you, but there won't be any less tension at the conference, and the stakes will be just as high. If the idyllic life at the Keep hasn't prepared you for conflict, then maybe we should play Banshee Quest until you pick up a real zest for it."

A sly smile curled across Tynan's lips. "Even if I did poorly, I did enjoy the game."

"Good." Amara patted his shoulder as she returned their dishes to the galley. "Which do you want to be today, black or red?"

"I'll take red this time. I know I haven't mastered the first level, but at which level do the champions play?"

He had already folded away the table, and as soon as Amara returned to her seat, she took out a set of controls. "There's no upper limit to Banshee Quest. It was designed to multiply on itself, so that no matter how proficient the best players become, the game can always present another, and more challenging level. That's the beauty of it."

"Interesting, but I think you're avoiding my question. At what level do you play?"

"That was very good. When you ask a question at the conference, insist upon getting an answer before you go on."

Annoyed that she had again redirected what he considered a personal conversation toward business, Tynan had to fight to hold on to his temper. "I'll be sure to do that, but I'm talking with you right now, and I want a straight answer."

Pleased that he hadn't backed down, Amara complied. "Nineteen. Would you like to see it?"

"Yes, please." Tynan waited while Amara requested a screen, but when it filled with wildly pulsating graphics, he couldn't even find the black and red spaceships, let alone imagine how anyone tracked his opponent through the gyrating maze. "This is giving me a headache just looking at it."

"It is almost painfully distracting, isn't it? That forces a lot of people out of the game at lower levels. Would you like to hear the sound effects?"

"Not if they're as raucous as the artwork."

"They're worse." Rather than provide a sample, Amara requested level one, and the frantic patterns swirling across the screen dissolved into a plain sky blue. "There you are. Begin whenever you like."

Tynan took out his controls, sat forward, and with steadily mounting success, played until Steve announced their approach to Risto Cortez's asteroid. Exhilarated by the competition, he looked forward to their next chance to play. "How long did it take you to reach level nineteen?" he asked.

Amara turned away to hide her smile and replaced the controls in the armrest. She had deliberately reduced her usual reaction time to a point Tynan could match so as not to frustrate him, but she hadn't meant to mislead him into thinking he already showed the makings of a champion. "I could say a lifetime. Banshee Quest is nearly as old as Alado. I'm a Starchild, remember, and having spent as much time in space as on the planets my parents explored, I had plenty of opportunity to play while I was growing up. For as long as I can remember, it's been one of my passions."

They were standing in the aisle, and Tynan had only to whisper to be heard. "And what are your others?"

While it was plain he was hoping men topped her list, Amara just shook her head and brushed past him. "Come on, I want a look at this facility before we land." Fortunately, she was favorably impressed by the design of the domed structure, which had an adjoining observatory and telescope.

"Looks like Dr. Cortez is an astronomer." There were three docking bays, and Amara flew the Starcruiser into the center one, which had been opened for their use. When she cut the power, Tynan started to leave his seat, but she reached out to stop him.

"Wait a minute. The bay must be closed and repressurized before we disembark. Watch the lights on the far wall. When they turn green, we can leave to meet our host. But no matter how pleasant he proves to be, or what assistance he offers, I intend to do the repairs myself."

"Do you know how?"

Tynan looked merely surprised rather than insultingly incredulous, so Amara didn't take offense. "Yes, all of Alado's pilots are so well-trained, we can build a spacecraft from spare parts if the need arises. I hope to have us out of here within the hour."

Tynan was relieved that she didn't again remind him that his peculiar customs were responsible for their shortage of time. He leaned forward to search the docking bay for signs of trouble, but there were no armed guards rushing out to meet them and no machinery that looked out of the ordinary. "Do I dare admit who I am?"

"Dressed as you are, you won't arouse any suspicion. To be on the safe side, why don't you use another name?"

"All right, I'll call myself Gregory Nash. I'm sure the Guardians' director won't mind. There are the green lights, let's go."

Amara flipped the switch to open the hatch and followed Tynan out into the docking bay. The end of the cavernous structure held as full a complement of tool lockers as any of Alado's maintenance facilities, and relieved she had made a wise choice this time, she smiled at the heavyset man who came rushing forward to greet them. His hair and beard were a startlingly bright red, and he nearly danced as he approached them. He shook their hands and giggled with an unabashed glee she found touchingly sincere.

"I'm Dr. Risto Cortez, and I am delighted to welcome you to my home. I realize you have some repairs to make, but I hope you'll have time to tour my whole facility."

Amara provided her name, and the one Tynan had chosen, but declined Risto's invitation. "Unfortunately, we have a schedule to keep, so I'll have to remain with the ship—but Gregory, you might enjoy a tour."

Tynan didn't want to leave her, but their host seemed so desperately eager to entertain them that he hated to disappoint him. "It's not too much trouble?"

"Certainly not," Risto exclaimed. "Are you sure you won't join us, lieutenant? My crew is fully qualified to service your craft, and they'd welcome the opportunity to work on a Starcruiser. They're performing routine maintenance in the first bay. Allow me to summon them."

"Thank you, but that won't be necessary. We've only a minor problem that I should be able to repair myself with the tools I have on board."

"If you insist. I'll send refreshments to you." Risto took Tynan's arm and directed him toward the door beneath the signal lights, which still glowed a bright green. "I have a magnificent telescope you really must see. I'm engaged in research on a variety of projects, but planetary orbits are of special interest to me."

Tynan looked back toward Amara and found she had already climbed out on the hull to examine the damaged scanners. She didn't even look up to wave as Risto escorted him into the facility of which he was so proud, leaving Tynan with a dismal sense of abandonment he fought to hide. Just as Amara had predicted, clad in an Alado flightsuit, he had been mistaken for one of Amara's crew rather than a passenger. To carry out the ruse, as he listened to Risto provide a brief synopsis of his research, he nodded as though he were as familiar with space as the scientist was. His mind wandered, however,

117

and he soon found himself concentrating on his host's bizarre mannerisms rather than his words.

Risto frequently placed his hands behind his back, then leaned forward on his toes until he reached the angle at which he had to catch himself to keep from toppling over. More than once, Tynan felt compelled to grab the scientist's shoulder to help him return to upright, but Risto continued to describe his work in such an animated fashion that he seemed totally unaware of how frequently he skirted calamity. When he was not leaning forward precariously, he was often spinning and gesturing in a convulsive dance as he pointed out the modifications to his telescope.

"Remarkable," Tynan murmured, confident the word conveyed the appropriate awe without revealing just how little he understood.

"My interest at present is in Jupiter, or rather its moons."

Tynan couldn't recall how many the planet had and provided another noncommittal response. "Is that a fact?"

"Come, let me show you my most recent photographs. They're truly spectacular." Risto reached out to take Tynan's arm and hurried him toward a central courtyard which not only served as a lovely indoor garden, but also contained large acrylic partitions for display of Risto's work. "Here you see all sixteen of the planet's moons. I've done a comprehensive study of each one, but the seventh and eighth, Ganymede and Callisto, are the largest and therefore deserve the most attention."

Truly impressed by the clarity of Risto's work, Tynan complimented him, then accepted his offer of refreshments. A tiny, white-haired gentleman, bent with age, soon appeared with a serving cart filled with delectable treats. Tynan was as amazed by the splendid array of desserts as he was by the frailty of the man serving them, but never having had many sweets, he was only mildly tempted and took a small fruit tart.

"You must try my punch," Risto insisted. "It's made from the juice of fruits grown in this very garden." He waved to the elderly servant, who filled two tall glasses with shaved ice, then added a pale blue liquid from a waiting pitcher. He handed them to Tynan and Risto, then, with a discreet bow, left the garden.

The men sat down at a conveniently placed table, and Tynan took a bite from the tart. Freshly baked, it was still warm, and though flavored with a spice he hadn't tasted at the Keep, it was as delicious as it looked. "This is very good. You obviously employ an excellent chef."

"Thank you. I like to think I've gathered the finest staff in the galaxy—but of course, Alado also has the highest standards."

"Yes, we do," Tynan agreed, and as he thought of Amara, he couldn't help but smile. "Just how many people do you employ here?"

"The number varies according to the project, but never more than one hundred." Risto had helped himself to an apple wrapped in puffed pastry, and as he popped the last bite into his mouth, he got up to get himself another. "More punch?" he asked.

Tynan hadn't taken a sip as yet. "No, thank you." He then strove to keep the scientist talking about things he could understand. Surrounded by vividly colored tropical blossoms, he was nearly overcome by the sickly-sweet fragrance filling the humid air and loosened the neck of his flightsuit slightly. "You must need several people just to maintain this beautiful garden."

"Oh yes, indeed I do."

Tynan wondered where they were. Other than the man who had brought the refreshments, they hadn't encountered any of Risto's staff. Tynan had no idea how long he had been sitting in the courtyard. Still, he thought they ought to have seen another scientist or two if a hundred were employed there. Then he realized that Risto had merely said he never employed more than that number, not that there were that many in residence at present. He reached for his glass of punch and took a tentative sip. Finding it too sweet for his taste, he set it aside and hoped Amara would soon complete the repairs.

Amara waved her appreciation and dismissed the man who appeared with a cart bearing refreshments, but she didn't leave the Starcruiser's hull to sample them. It had been a while since she had worked on scanners, and although these were similar in design to those she had replaced on diplomatic shuttles, a laser's blast had melted their components into an unrecognizable glob. Rather than easily unplugging for replacement, they had to be pried out, and Amara was soon cursing the fact she hadn't fired on the Gauntlets when Steve had first announced their presence.

"A disastrous mistake," she mumbled under her breath. The work was taking longer than she had anticipated, and thinking it would go faster if she had a tool not carried on board, she climbed down and searched through those contained in the bay's lockers. Finding a disappointing assortment, she assumed the mechanics working in the adjoining bay would have what she needed. It was surprising they hadn't come in to take a look at the Starcruiser, but she thought they might be working under the pressure of a deadline too.

She hit the button to open the door between the bays, then gasped when she found the number one bay empty. Not only were there no mechanics in sight, there were no ships moored there either. The bay had a faintly metallic odor, one she recognized as belonging to new machinery, and she doubted that it had ever been used.

"Well, Risto, where's this expert crew of yours?"

Not really caring why the eccentric scientist had lied, Amara again opened the tool lockers, but found these empty. She hurried back through the bay holding the Starcruiser and peered into number three. Relieved to find a Gauntlet housed there, she called out, but there were no mechanics at work on it and her voice echoed off the high ceiling with a hollow ring. Uneasy, she crossed to the tool lockers, and the first drawer she opened held precisely the tool she needed—along with a key whose fantastic design instantly identified it as belonging to a Corkscrew.

Badly frightened, she slammed the door shut, and after a quick glance assured her that there was no one in the bay, she returned to the

Starcruiser, gathered up the tools she had been using, and returned them to the ship's tool locker. She then entered the cockpit and summoned Steve. "Include this in the ship's log," she began. "I've found what appears to be a Corkscrew base, and we may very well have been fired upon to herd us toward it. The mere possibility that Dr. Cortez works in league with the Corkscrews is provocation enough for our immediate departure. I'll have to collect Tynan Thorn, but have the ship ready for launch as soon as we return."

"Shall I activate emergency procedures?"

"Not yet, but while I'm away, access the power and turn the ship toward the bay doors. Can you open them, or will I have to use the manual switch outside?"

"I noted the codes when we entered, lieutenant. I will repeat them on your command."

Amara sat back for a moment and, after thoughtful contemplation, decided she wasn't overreacting. While it was possible the key she had found could have been a souvenir picked up by one of Risto's unseen mechanics years ago, it was far more likely that it had fallen off a Corkscrew's belt within the last week. Increasing their speed had outdistanced the Gauntlets, but if they carried Corkscrews who were on their way to Dr. Cortez's base, they would soon arrive.

"Steve, I want the laser cannons operational." After giving that ominous command, she left the ship confident that Steve would have it fully ready for flight upon their return. She passed through the door she had seen Dr. Cortez and Tynan use, and almost immediately ran into the little man who had delivered the refreshment cart.

She smiled as though nothing were amiss. "I've completed our repairs. Will you please direct me to Dr. Cortez?"

Rather than respond in words, he gestured for her to follow him. Relieved that he did not want to converse, Amara followed him down the corridor. She noted a turn to the right and one to the left so that she could reverse their path at a run, but she hoped her apprehensions would prove ridiculous and that nothing was truly amiss. She thought it odd they didn't pass anyone else, for a facility of this size required a large staff to maintain it. But she had no time to question her guide before they reached the garden courtyard.

She strode up to Tynan and Dr. Cortez, and in a bold move she hoped he would understand, she leaned down, placed her hands on his shoulders, and gave the startled Guardian a lingering kiss. Forceful, insistent, the passionate exchange left them both gasping for breath. Amara swayed slightly as she straightened up, but her eyes never left Tynan's befuddled expression.

"I'm sorry to interrupt the party, Greg, but we're ready to go."

Tynan could not imagine why Amara had given him such an affectionate greeting unless it had been for Risto's benefit. Because the enthusiastic scientist seemed like an almost pathetically lonely soul, he thought it was rather mean of her—to say nothing of what it had done to him. After she had repeatedly rebuffed his advances, he didn't appreciate her carrying their act to such a ridiculous extreme.

It wasn't until Amara reached for his hand and dug her fingernails into his palm that he realized just how badly she wanted him to say good-bye.

Chapter Seven

Nonplussed by the nature of her summons, but now appreciating its urgency, Tynan rose to his feet. "Thank you for the tour and the delicious refreshments, Dr. Cortez. I doubt that we'll be by this way again, but your hospitality won't be forgotten."

Risto left his chair with an astonishingly agile leap. "But you've just arrived. I've so much more to show you, and the lieutenant hasn't seen anything."

Amara again took Tynan's hand and tugged as she started away. "Our flight is already overdue, Dr. Cortez. Please excuse us."

His quaint charm vanishing in an instant, Risto bounded ahead of them to block their way on the garden path. "There is, of course, the matter of a rental fee for the use of my docking bay. In the past, Alado's crews have always left vouchers so that I can receive the proper payment. Did you think I offered my facilities gratis to whoever requests their use?"

"In emergencies such as ours, I certainly hope that you do, but I'll be happy to provide a voucher in whatever amount you require. Come with us to our ship and I'll give you one."

Risto folded his arms over his ample chest. "I would also like a commendation from Alado's Fleet Command."

Certain he was stalling for time, Amara didn't argue the point. "Yes, you've an excellent facility here, and I'll be glad to make such a recommendation." She attempted to lead Tynan around him, but again Risto barred the way. "Dr. Cortez, please. We really have to go."

Now dreadfully sorry that she hadn't strapped on a laser pistol, Amara felt each of her miscalculations compounding to leave them in a truly desperate situation. She glanced toward Tynan. He had a muscular build, but she had no hope that he knew how to defend himself. She then favored the demanding scientist with an enticing smile and sent a thought command designed to win his cooperation.

For an instant, Risto's belligerent expression softened, and he appeared to be confused, but then he recovered and wagged his finger at Amara. "Mind control, lieutenant? You should be ashamed of yourself. My studies have left me impervious to such childish games."

Tynan could actually feel Amara's frustration, and assuming Risto was merely lonely, he made a hurried decision. "Gregory Nash is a friend of mine. I'm actually Tynan Thorn, and we're en route to the peace conference at the Confederation base. A commendation from the Confederation will be far more impressive than one from Alado. If you'll just wish us luck on our venture, I'll see that you receive the recognition you deserve."

Risto's face lit with a warm glow of admiration. "Tynan Thorn? Why, I'd no idea I had such a distinguished visitor. I've read your work and would have discussed it with you had I only known who you really were. It was very wrong of you not to tell me."

"Forgive me, now we really must go." Tynan pulled Amara along with him as he sought to pass Risto on the right, but the wily astronomer again used his bulk to thwart them. Not understanding the man's stubborn refusal to let them by, Tynan frowned in puzzlement. "Just what is it you're trying to accomplish, Dr. Cortez? The lieutenant and I won't be kept here against our wills. Don't make us resort to force."

"Force?" Risto burst into a wave of deep, rumbling laughter, then stroked his beard as he studied the Guardian with a mischievous gaze. "The foremost advocate of peaceful coexistence wishes to threaten me with force? Your reputation as a brilliant philosopher won't last longer than the time it takes that news to become public knowledge. You disappoint me, Tynan. I really expected better of you."

Tynan pulled Amara closer to his side. "Get out of our way," he ordered, "or what will become common knowledge is the fact that you're nothing more than this pitifully small asteroid's petty dictator."

Before Risto could move or respond, the door leading into the garden slid open and in strode two women and four men. The whimsically designed keys dangling from their belts rattled with a metallic cadence as they drew near. Even without being introduced, Tynan recognized them from Amara's description as Corkscrews. She hadn't mentioned that they tattooed their faces, however, and when a young woman whose eyes were masked with an elaborate leopard design pushed to the lead, he wondered just what else she had forgotten.

Determined not to make another costly mistake, Amara drew Tynan back toward the area where he and Risto had been seated. It offered the room they would need if they had to fight their way out of the astronomer's complex. She was prepared to do just that if a more reasonable approach continued to fail. It was obvious that the leopard-faced woman would be a tough opponent, for she was well over six feet in height and walked with her hips thrust forward in an aggressive swagger. Dressed in a burgundy flightsuit that exactly matched the color of her wild mop of hair, she dismissed Amara with a threatening smirk, but as she eyed Tynan, she licked her lips as though savoring a delicious morsel.

Next came a thin, dark-haired young man. He was dressed in black, as were the three other men. He did a credible imitation of the leader's walk and stance, but failed to project her aura of authority. A petite girl dressed in a fluorescent chartreuse fightsuit followed, a thick mass of brown ringlets partially obscuring her vision.

A slow-moving young man with the same heavy, thick-waisted build as Risto was close behind her. The last two men, despite their dark, masculine attire, were handsome in a soft, feminine way. One had wavy auburn hair tied at his nape, while the other's flowing blond locks gave him what Amara was certain was a deceptively angelic appearance.

In a valiant attempt to adjust the odds in her favor, Amara divided the Corkscrews into two groups—those upon whom she would have to use physical force, and those who would be targets for thought control. How much help Tynan could provide was still an unknown factor. That he had at least threatened to use force was encouraging, but when pressed, did he have the necessary skills to follow through?

"I was impressed by your work, Dr. Cortez," Tynan continued. "I can't believe you harbor Corkscrews here, when your rightful companions are the best minds in the galaxy."

Again placing his hands behind his back and leaning forward on his toes, Risto puffed out his lower lip in an indignant pout. "Such transparent flattery will get you nowhere, Tynan. Throughout the ages all truly visionary scientists have been scorned, and until recently, I was reconciled to suffering a similar fate. Then it occurred to me— all I need do is tamper with an orbit or two to demonstrate how greatly I ought to be admired."

"My God," Amara gasped. "You can't be serious. The orbits of the planets and their moons are in as delicate a balance as the workings of an antique clock. If even one were to shift its path, all the others would be affected."

Risto shrugged. "Precisely, lieutenant. But rather than create a catastrophe, I mean to merely give Jupiter's seventh moon a nudge toward the eighth. Jupiter has the mass to withstand a slight deviation in the paths of its moons, so while the change will be noted, it's doubtful any real harm will come of it. I'm a scientist after all, not a madman."

"But you can't be certain of your results," Amara cautioned.

"Like any experiment, it may prove to have unforeseen consequences, but once I discovered a means to change a moon's orbit, I couldn't very well not try it, now could I?"

The Corkscrews had followed Risto, Amara, and Tynan back into the central courtyard, but they looked bored with the discussion, and the petite brunette strolled over to the dessert-laden cart, swiped her finger across a fruit tart, and licked off the dollop of filling she had scooped up. "You want anything, Cid?"

The heavy-set youth joined her and took one of the apple-filled pastries. Amara hoped the pair would continue to eat and focused her attention on the others as she addressed Risto. "You had your colorful pets disable our ship so we'd stop here—but why? Alado knows we're here, and as I said, we're already overdue. They'll investigate our delay, and soon."

"Ah yes, a regrettable complication, but unfortunately unavoidable. You see, I needed an engine of sufficient size to accomplish what I've set out to do, and the Starcruiser's power can be boosted easily enough." He paused to gesture toward the

Corkscrews standing behind him. "My crew of talented mechanics will disassemble your ship and have the necessary components ready to be moved within the hour. When Alado arrives, and I do believe they will, they'll find no trace of you or your ship, lieutenant. I didn't expect Tynan Thorn to fall into my little trap, but now that he's here, he'll be able to observe my experiment first-hand."

"You needn't carry out your plan to gain the recognition you deserve," Tynan argued. "All you need do is present your findings at the next major scientific conference. For now, the peace conference should be your most vital concern. If I'm not there when it opens next week, and war results, the risk to mankind will be so great that no one will care in the slightest about your theories. You need peaceful cooperation as badly as everyone else, Dr. Cortez. Now let us go, and we'll see that Alado provides the support you need for your research."

Risto glanced toward his motley assortment of mechanics. "Did you hear that? I've just been offered a bribe!"

Obviously amused, the tall woman with the exotic tattoo stepped forward. She placed her hands on her hips and tossed her unruly burgundy mane. "I've never heard of you, Mr. Thorn," she bragged in a throaty whisper, "but you and I are going to become real well acquainted. You'll want him watched, Risto, so I'll take him upstairs to my room. He can spend his time tied to my bed, while the others give the lieutenant a farewell party."

Exasperated by her suggestion, Risto rocked back on his heels. "That's enough, Riva. You'll have to keep your salacious appetites in check until after

Cinnamon Burke

you've dismantled the Starcruiser."

Facing Riva, Cortez unwittingly provided Amara with the only moment of inattention she was likely to get. Seizing it, she gave Tynan's hand one last squeeze and then kicked the dessert cart into the curly-haired girl and Cid. The rich desserts went flying, and stepping on a meringue-topped custard, Cid slipped and fell, taking his girlfriend down with him. Next Amara sent a violent wave of nightmarish visions toward the pair of effeminate young men. Watching her, they were caught by the full force of the evil scenes, clutched their heads, and began to scream in fright.

Eager for a fight, Riva made a flying leap for Amara, but the lithe blonde was ready. Amara grabbed Riva's outstretched arm and used the brazen woman's forward momentum to hurl her right into the overturned dessert cart. Like Cid and the girl, she lost her footing on the cream-filled pastries and fell in a dazed and gooey heap. Amara went after the last Corkscrew standing, and out of the corner of her eye, she saw Tynan send a vicious chop into the side of Risto's neck. The scientist's knees buckled, and before she could utter an encouraging shout, Tynan struck Risto such a fierce blow on the chin that he went flopping over backwards into the tropical shrubbery.

Intent upon doing his share, Tynan brushed Amara aside and, with one well-placed punch, knocked out the last Corkscrew. He then grabbed her hand and, pulling her along behind him, made a dash for the door. He pounded on the control button, and when the door slid open he drew her through it just as Riva, Cid, and the little brunette lurched to their feet. Slowed by the widely strewn desserts, they started after them, but by the time they had opened the door, Tynan and Amara were already out of sight.

"Which way?" Tynan yelled.

Having memorized the route to the garden, Amara took the lead and led him back toward the docking bay. But as they rounded the last corner, they nearly ran into the ancient servant, who stood barring their way with a laser pistol he had to hold steady with both hands.

"Leaving so soon?" he taunted in a hoarse rasp. "I don't believe I heard Risto give you permission to go."

Amara raised her hands as though giving up, but after wiggling her fingers to distract him, she lashed out with a wild kick that knocked the laser pistol out of the astonished servant's bony hands and sent it clattering across the floor. She scooped it up, and again taking Tynan's hand, sprinted past the feeble guard toward the docking bay door. When it slid open, Tynan dove through it. Just then, Riva and her band came barreling into the corridor. Amara turned back, took careful aim, and fired a blast at Riva's feet. She then swept the hall with a blanket of fire, sending up a debris-laden dust cloud before following Tynan into the bay.

He was already at the ship, but waited for her before bounding up the ladder. After scrambling up behind him, Amara tossed him the laser pistol, sealed the hatch, and shouted the order for Steve to open the bay doors on her way to the cockpit. Responding to his transmission, the lights at the end of the bay turned red, and the wide doors at the opposite end began to slowly slide open.

Tynan buckled the co-pilot's seatbelt and watched as the rear scanners projected the scene at the end of the bay onto his screen. Presumably, Risto and one of the Corkscrews still lay unconscious in the garden, but Riva and the four others had followed them into the bay and were now being sucked forward as it began to depressurize. They grabbed for the tool lockers and each other, but it was plain they wouldn't survive for more than a few seconds once the outside doors had opened wide and the vacuum of space beckoned.

"Wait," Tynan called. "They're going to be killed!"

Amara sent him an incredulous glance. "Do you honestly believe they deserve to live?"

"Yes! Give them a chance to reach safety before you launch."

Amara weighed the danger of granting his request against the possibility of alienating him and, praying she was not making another costly error, spoke to the computer. "Close the doors for ten seconds, Steve, then open them again."

Amara watched the screen as the Corkscrews fought to hold on, the strain in their anguished faces pitiful to observe. When the bay doors slammed shut, they continued to shove and claw but now their efforts were in a frantic rush to flee. The last of them had just whipped through the door into the safety of Risto's facility when the bay doors again began to slide open.

"The rescue effort was a success," Amara reported calmly. She flew the Starcruiser out into space, then began a slow banking turn. "Close the bay doors, Steve, and give me a grid to target the cannon."

"What cannon?" Tynan cried. "This is a peace mission!"

"Don't panic. I'm just going to blast the bay doors so they can't pursue us. There shouldn't be any loss of life involved." Then, with methodical precision, Amara fired on the three bays, blasting away the doors so the interiors could not be pressurized and used. She also hit the Gauntlets moored in bay three. Their fuel tanks nearly empty, they created only a moderate explosion as they burst into flames.

Pleased that she had finally done something right, Amara circled the observatory and explained how finding one of the Corkscrew's keys while making repairs had prompted her to ask him to leave. "Please forgive me for the kiss, but I had hoped we could get off the asteroid before the Corkscrews arrived."

Shaken by the unexpected display of firepower, Tynan had nearly forgotten the kiss. "I won't deny that I was startled," he admitted, "but at least now I know your code. Do all of Alado's pilots recognize a kiss as a distress signal?"

"No, as far as I know I was the first to have to resort to it. Now help me look. Risto couldn't have planned to carry a Starcruiser engine with a Gauntlet, so there has to be another ship based here."

With his assistance, she searched the asteroid's barren terrain, and they soon found another well-camouflaged docking bay. She again blasted away the doors and the transport ship moored inside.

"That should keep Dr. Cortez and his friends at home until Confederation forces arrive." Greatly relieved, she turned toward Tynan and was disappointed to find him watching her with a frown. "I'm sorry not to have disclosed our weapons capability earlier. I was hoping we'd not have to use them, but I'm not willing to leave Risto with the ability to either pursue us or escape punishment."

"Why were arms thought necessary for a peace mission?" Tynan asked.

Amara thought she had just demonstrated why and had difficulty not being sarcastic. "To provide for any eventuality, and I'm very glad after what we just went through. You seem disappointed, though. Were you looking forward to being tied to Riva's bed?"

Disgusted, Tynan looked away. "How could you even ask such a question?"

"Easy. Your reaction to our escape prompted it. Thank you for your help. I wasn't certain you were serious when you threatened force, but I'm very glad that you were. Why didn't you tell me that you were proficient in martial arts?"

"There was no reason, and it's just one of the sports we practice at the Keep. Do you think I'm proud of having to resort to such brutal tactics?"

"I certainly hope so, because you could just as easily have convinced a stone to cooperate as Risto Cortez. You've no need to be ashamed. We did what was right."

Tynan shook his head. "No, I should have been able to influence him solely with verbal arguments. Instead, I handled things very badly." He leaned forward, meaning to unfasten his seat belt and rise, but growing dizzy, he fell back into his seat. "Inexcusable," he moaned softly.

At first, Amara thought Tynan was merely suffering under a heavy burden of regret, but then she realized that something was seriously wrong. "Tynan, look at me!"

Tynan turned his head toward her, but then his chin bounced off his chest, and he slumped over. He tried to grasp the armrests to straighten up, but there was so little strength in his arms that he failed. Had his seatbelt not been buckled, he would have slid right out of his seat.

Leaving her seat, Amara grasped Tynan's face between her hands. His eyes were open, but his gaze was alarmingly vacant. "Tynan, listen to me. You thanked Risto for the refreshments. What did you have?"

The whole cockpit was swirling around him in a dizzying kaleidoscope of images, and Tynan had to close his eyes in order to concentrate. "A little pie. Blue juice."

"Blue? Oh dear God, what did he give you?"

Tynan began to giggle. "I couldn't drink the juice. It tasted awful."

"What about the pie? How did it taste?"

"Strange."

"Think, Tynan. How was it strange? Was it too sweet, too sour? What was wrong with it?"

Tynan opened one eye, but Amara's features looked all twisted and contorted. Frightened, he shut it again. "Strange," he mumbled. "Like that leopard tattoo, very strange."

Amara left the cockpit to search through the medical supplies. The kit contained antidotes for poisons in tiny injection canisters, but not knowing what Tynan had been given, she didn't know what to use or in what dosage. Thinking it far more likely he had merely been drugged, she returned to his side.

"Do you feel sick to your stomach?" she asked.

Tynan tried to shake his head, but he lacked the necessary muscle control and it just rolled from side to side. "Everything has a magical sparkle, even you."

Amara rested her forehead against his. She had been frightened back at Risto's, but she was terrified now. She placed her fingertips on his wrist, and was encouraged when she found his pulse strong and steady. Calling upon Steve, she enumerated Tynan's symptoms.

"A hallucinogen is the most probable cause," the computer replied. "Did he ingest a great deal?"

Amara held Tynan's chin to force him to look up at her. "You said you ate a little pie. Can you show me what size it was?"

Tynan raised his hands and, shaking badly, put his fingertips together to form a circle the size of the tart. "Tiny," he mumbled.

"Risto didn't stop the Corkscrews from eating any of the desserts, so I'll bet it was the punch, or more specifically your glass of punch, that was laced with a drug. Are you sure you didn't have more than a sip?"

"Very sure," Tynan enunciated with exaggerated care, and then he began to sing, his words slurred and the tune unrecognizable.

In spite of her fears, Amara couldn't help but laugh. Tynan had a marvelous voice, but this was no time to compliment his singing. "Steve, I managed to replace three of the nine damaged scanners before I ran into trouble. While that isn't as many as I would have liked, it should enable us to reach Confederation base without further trouble. Now I'm giving you command of the ship while I tend to our passenger. Summon me immediately if there's even the slightest need."

"Yes, lieutenant."

Amara brushed Tynan's curls off his forehead and caressed his cheek. "Come on, hero, we're going to put you in the shower. Maybe that will help you to see things more clearly."

She unbuckled his seat belt, and hauled him to his feet, but he was almost limp and it was a real struggle to get him out of the cockpit. They stumbled and lurched into the passenger cabin, and when Tynan grabbed hold of the back of the first seat, Amara tumbled with him into the second, their arms and legs entwined in a comical jumble. The harder she tried to pull free, the more tightly he held on. He was laughing the whole time, as though she were as eager to wrestle as he.

"Tynan, stop that this instant!"

"Stop, stop," he begged in a giddy falsetto, but he didn't slacken his clumsy hold on her. He tousled her curls with a lazy caress, nuzzled her neck, and kept her sprawled across his lap in a confining bear hug.

Grateful that he didn't appear to be suffering from anything more severe than a drug-induced stupor, Amara rested her hands on his. "It's a good thing I didn't sample any of Risto's provisions, because I certainly wouldn't want to see both of us behaving in such a ridiculous fashion. Now come on, a shower and a long nap should be all you need to return to normal."

"All I need is you."

"Well, I'm not one of the options. Let go so that I can stand." When Tynan made no move to grant her demand, Amara sent him such a stern mental message that even in his dazed state, he complied. She stood in the aisle waiting for him to follow her, but he seemed incapable of doing so. Had whatever drug he had been given become effective a few minutes earlier, they never would have gotten off Risto's asteroid. Frightened by how narrow their escape had been, Amara urged Tynan gently to his feet.

She kept a firm grip on his waist, while dodging the kisses he was intent upon giving her. Rolling along, careening off the backs of the seats, she was nearly as exhausted as he by the time they reached the lavatory. She tried to prop him up as she opened the door, but he slipped through her grasp and slid to the floor. Amara would have complained bitterly had she not realized that it would be far easier to remove his boots with him seated. She knelt at his feet and tugged on the left boot.

"These are beautiful boots, Tynan. Do the Guardians make them?"

Tynan leaned forward, laced his fingers in her hair, and pulled her close for a deep, lingering kiss. The gesture was as dazed as he was, but Amara still had difficulty pushing him away. "That's enough, lover. Now come on, let me have your other boot."

"Boots," Tynan finally responded.

"Yes, you don't want to wear your boots in the shower. Or that flightsuit either." Tossing his second boot aside, Amara began to peel away the shiny gold garment she had lent him. She was relieved to find that he was wearing his long underwear, but it was still a chore to undress him. Because he was nearly impossible to control dressed, she had no intention of stripping him nude. He giggled and twisted, providing no help at all, and rather than stand, he finally crawled into the shower.

"I'm only going to leave you in there a minute, so there's no danger you'll drown," Amara assured him. She adjusted the controls, turned on the soapy spray and, leaving him to enjoy the warm, liquid massage, slid the shower door closed. She crossed to the galley to get a drink of water and waited the brief time she had promised before returning to the lavatory and turning off the spray.

His damp curls clinging to his head, Tynan was still laughing when he looked up at her. "You forgot the rest of my clothes. People don't shower in their clothes." He struggled to pull off his undershirt, then handed it to her, displaying a chest and arms that were the same warm bronze shade as his face and hands. Intent upon shedding his wet garments, he pulled himself upright, and before Amara could stop him, he tugged off the bottom half of his underwear.

That Tynan had the same magnificent tan all over either meant he sunbathed in the nude, which Amara doubted, or he had a Hispanic or Indian heritage not indicated by his name. Tracing his family tree was not one of Amara's priorities at present, however. Because warm air was used to dry off, the lavatory had no towels. Tynan was undeniably a handsome man, dressed or nude, but Amara didn't want him parading around in his natural state while he was in such an amorous mood. Gathering up his soggy underwear, she tossed it into the compartment which served to both wash and dry garments during flight.

Tynan grabbed hold of the lavatory door and smiled down at her. "You should have come in with me," he insisted in a slow drawl.

Amara focused her attention on his face rather than the rest of his superb physique, but it was difficult to prevent her gaze from straying to far more intriguing parts of his anatomy. She had seen quite a few men nude, perhaps too many. Each was uniquely fascinating in his own way, but she couldn't remember any of them now.

"The only place I'm going is to get your robe. Stay where you are."

As she turned to go, Tynan reached out to stop her. "No, stay with me."

"Tynan, I really must—"

Amara's protest was smothered by another enthusiastic kiss. Warm and damp, Tynan molded his body to hers in an erotic, living sculpture that swayed and throbbed in time with the beat of his heart. She placed her hands on his arms, then his shoulders, then slid her fingertips down his back. A smooth golden bronze, his skin hummed with life beneath her touch, calling to her with as compelling an invitation as his luscious kiss. He turned, bent slightly, his every move enticing, seductive, alluring, but a mere prelude to deeper pleasures.

Pulling free of his embrace took as much courage as fighting the Corkscrews, but after savoring a half dozen delicious kisses, Amara broke away. Despite their earlier conversation on the subject, Tynan was blatantly attempting to take advantage of her. Amara could forgive his behavior by blaming whatever drug he had been given, but she had absolutely no way to excuse the depth of her response. Ashamed that she could want him so badly, she wiped away the hint of tears that blurred her vision and pushed the two seats he had used the previous night into place for his bed.

She took his hand and led him toward it. "Go to sleep, Tynan, and this whole sorry episode will be forgotten by morning."

Tynan made another grab for Amara, but this time she anticipated his move and blocked it. "No," she stated forcefully. "What you want is impossible. Go to sleep." She left him to fetch his robe, and when she returned, he was stretched out across the seats, sound asleep. Unable to help herself, Amara bent down and placed a light kiss on the cool curve of his hip. Straightening up, she draped the soft woolen robe over him, and determined to finally concentrate on her duties, she entered the cockpit and recorded the details of their adventure with Risto Cortez in the log.

She was very careful, however, to note only that Tynan had been drugged, and not how badly each of them had wanted the other.

"There are times when I envy you, Steve," she confided sadly.

"Why? The advantages of being human far outweigh those of being a computer."

"Yes, but those advantages can sometimes be a burden."

"How?"

"We get unbearably lonely at times, so desperate for a friend that we'll converse at length with a charming computer."

"Thank you, but I do not believe charm is included among my programs."

"Perhaps not," Amara mused. "But you listen, and maybe that's all I need. I'm going to rest now. Wake me every two hours, please. I want to make certain Tynan is asleep rather than unconscious."

"Yes, lieutenant. Sweet dreams."

Amara patted the console as she left the cockpit. "Sweet dreams," she repeated, but since she couldn't have Tynan, she doubted Steve's wish for her would come true.

Chapter Eight

Tynan's drug-induced dreams were filled with wild, haunting images of leopard-skinned creatures with wickedly sharp talons and webbed wings. They ripped the air with their shrill cries as they dove and swooped in repeated attempts to pluck him off the Keep's battlements. Each pass brought them closer, and armed only with his wits, Tynan ran and dodged, stalling while he waited for the help he feared might never come.

He sent a beseeching gaze skyward, and in answer to his prayers a gleaming silver space-ship appeared. Certain Amara was the pilot, he stood to cheer—and lost his robe to the next winged demon who swept by in a blur of spotted fur. Laser fire caught the beast in mid-flight, killing it instantly. Its limp wings entangled in the folds of the deep purple garment, it drifted to earth in a lumbering spiral.

For an instant, Tynan felt the exhilaration he had

known playing Banshee Quest, for the battle surrounding him held all the thrills of the challenging game. The flying monsters scattered, but the pilot's aim was deadly, and in a matter of seconds all had been slain. Elated, Tynan continued to cheer, but rather than land, the spaceship circled the Keep one last time in a silent salute and then vanished against the sun.

He was deserted, just when he wanted so badly to celebrate. Tynan ran from the Keep and out across the fields, but the ship was gone, and his frantic calls went unanswered. Devastated, he awakened to find he was inside the very ship he had been chasing. The lights were dim in the passenger cabin, and still suffering from the effects of the hallucinogen, Tynan saw his surroundings through an iridescent lavender mist. The haze brushed his bare skin with a seductive warmth, and suddenly he felt as desperate to find Amara as he had been in his dream. Slowly he got up to search for her.

Amara had again made her bed near the cockpit and was sleeping soundly when Tynan stretched out beside her and pulled her into his arms. She responded with a sleepy smile and cuddled against him. He combed her curls off her face and kissed her cheek. Right now, he wanted only to hold her, to make her stay with him forever. Content for the moment, he drifted back to sleep.

"It's time, lieutenant," Steve announced later.

"Hmm," Amara moaned. She had gotten up twice to check on Tynan, but now she couldn't recall why she had asked Steve to wake her.

"Lieutenant," he repeated in a louder tone.

"Yes, I heard you." Amara sighed dreamily, and in the next instant felt the weight of Tynan's arm wrapped around her waist. Startled, she tried to sit up, but he tightened his hold to keep her back pressed firmly against his chest. His breathing was slow and even, and except for his grip on her waist, he was relaxed, lying on his side.

Amara tried to slide out of his grasp, but Tynan just snuggled against her all the more closely. Cradled in his arms, she felt precious, and though she was certain Tynan was sleeping too soundly to name the woman in his embrace, she wished that he really cared for her. It was foolish, she knew, but savoring the moment to the fullest, she came up with several plausible excuses for not waking him.

That the feeling of being cherished, no matter how fleeting, should mean so much to her brought tears to her eyes, and knowing her affectionate passenger wouldn't notice, she let them roll down her cheeks and soak into the sleeve of her flightsuit. She had met Tynan first through his magical prose and had mistakenly assumed he was an older gentleman who lived only for the pleasure of intellectual pursuits. When she had discovered he was a handsome young man, it hadn't dimmed her admiration for his ideas one bit. Overwhelmed with sorrow that they were such an unlikely pair and would be together all too briefly, she rested in his arms and waited for the night to end.

Tynan had never shared a bed, and when his first stretch of the morning met with resistance,

147

he reacted with a startled jerk. The cabin lights were still low, but they no longer held a hint of lavender, and he had no difficulty recognizing the woman who shared what he assumed was his bed. That she was still dressed while he wasn't made no sense to him, but if she had finally agreed to sleep with him, he wasn't going to argue about how she chose to do it.

He propped his head on his hand and might have watched her for hours had she not already been awake. "Good morning," he whispered, before leaning down to nibble her earlobe.

"Please don't."

Surprised by that response, Tynan turned her toward him. "What do you mean, 'don't'? Isn't it a bit late for that?"

Amara had meant to get up before he awakened— truly she had—but she had put off their inevitable parting a moment too long. Tynan's suggestive question was a clear indication that he believed something had taken place between them, and she almost hated to disillusion him. "I put you to bed last night to sleep off whatever drug Dr. Cortez gave you. When you climbed in with me, you were more asleep than awake, and I let you stay. So you see, nothing happened, and nothing ever will either."

Doubting her story, Tynan sat up slightly to look around and was chagrined to find they were indeed lying across her makeshift bed rather than his. "Do you generally allow naked men to crawl into bed with you?" he asked.

"Never."

"No, not 'never'. You did last night."

His sly grin annoyed Amara no end. "You've no reason to smirk, Tynan. Absolutely nothing happened."

Tynan studied her expression, again noting elements of strain around her mouth and eyes, and came to a different conclusion. "Frankly, I can't recall a thing after showering in my underwear, so I'm forced to rely on your account. But just for the record, I think you're lying."

"Lying?" Insulted, Amara would have rolled off the bed, but anticipating her move, Tynan rose to capture her between outstretched arms. "Get out of my way," she demanded sharply.

"Is that any way to speak to the peace negotiator you've sworn to protect?"

"If you continue to display such a revolting lack of manners, yes!"

Tynan leaned down to kiss her forehead. "I'm sorry if I disappointed you last night. I'm sure to do better with practice."

Positive that Tynan would never be a disappointment, Amara felt a bright blush flood her cheeks. To pay him such a flattering compliment would only encourage the affection she was determined to refuse, however. "It isn't practice you need, Tynan, just another woman."

Tynan raised a hand to brush a curl away from her eyes. "I didn't disappoint you then?" he asked in a husky whisper.

His smile was utterly charming now, but his question absurd. "Nothing happened," Amara stressed. "You were drugged and walking in your sleep. Don't let your imagination lead you astray. I simply took pity on you, nothing more."

Tynan leaned down to kiss her, and caught by surprise, Amara responded in a way that wasn't at all condescending. "This doesn't taste like pity."

Amara was certain her kiss was flavored with desire, but she wouldn't admit it. Instead, she turned her face away and closed her eyes. Since Tynan wouldn't listen to reason, she had no choice but to ignore him.

It was the hint of moisture on her lashes that stopped Tynan from pressing for more. He might know damn little about women, but he was positive Amara wasn't weeping for joy. "I didn't mean to make you cry," he apologized hurriedly, and embarrassed by the failure of his attempt to continue the bliss he had imagined they had shared during the night, he quickly left her bed and went into the lavatory. The flightsuit Amara had provided was hanging from a hook, as was his freshly laundered underwear. He looked into the mirror. Unshaven, he looked rather menacing. Perhaps it would be a good idea to grow a beard.

Once dressed, he had to wait for Amara to shower, but he spent the time making what he hoped was the fruit and yogurt mixture she liked. "I fixed your breakfast," he announced when she joined him. "Let me know how it tastes."

"I'm sure it will be fine. Thank you."

Amara set up their table and sat down, but she still looked near tears. Tynan didn't know what else to do. Grabbing his cereal, he joined her and did his best to improve the situation. "I know you're worried that I won't be able to represent Alado well—"

"That's not true!"

"All right, you're not worried about me, just the fierceness of the other negotiators. Is that better?"

Amara nodded and continued to eat her breakfast. Tynan hadn't gotten the right proportion of yogurt to fruit, but no other man had ever tried to prepare her meals, and she was so touched she would never have complained.

"The Guardians haven't always been the harmonious group they are now. When I was growing up, I had constant fights with another of the boys who'd been raised there." Tynan found it difficult to describe Orion Chaudet without sneering. "He was six years older than I and took a fiendish delight in tormenting me. If I was given a task, he'd wait until I'd finished, and then find a way to undo it, or ruin it, or in some way make it appear that I just hadn't bothered to do my chores. Then I'd be punished, and he'd laugh and encourage the other boys to make fun of me too."

"What about the Director? Didn't he realize what was happening?"

"Gregory Nash didn't hold that post then, and I'm sorry to say the man who did was completely taken in by my nemesis. He was very blond and could strike a convincingly angelic pose whenever the merest shadow of blame fell near him. We absolutely despised each other, but because he was six years my senior, I was at a serious disadvantage. It wasn't until I was twelve that I finally felt I had the strength to put an end to his mistreatment."

Involved in his tale, Amara set her yogurt aside. "What did you do?"

"I challenged him to a fight in the yard. There were too many witnesses for him to refuse without looking like a coward, and I did my best to make him pay for all the years he'd abused me."

"Did you beat him badly?"

Tynan laughed, although the memory was still painful. "No, he was eighteen and outweighed me by at least fifty pounds. He put me in the infirmary with three broken ribs, but when I got out, he was gone, and from that day to this, I've never backed away from a fight. It doesn't matter who the opponent is, or whether we're sparring in the gym or arguing some point of philosophy others might find trivial.

"I do sincerely believe in peace, Amara, but that doesn't mean I'll sacrifice my integrity or anything else to achieve it. However, if I grow a beard, wear my hood pulled forward, and drop my voice as low as I can, I should present a sufficiently intimidating image to enable me to achieve Alado's aims. I'll still welcome your advice on how to deal with the other negotiators, though. Will you help me?"

"It was presumptuous of me to offer help in the first place." Embarrassed, Amara pretended a rapt interest in the last of her yogurt. "I'm sure you'll fulfill Alado's expectations beautifully."

"I'd rather fulfill yours."

When Amara found the courage to meet his gaze, she saw no trace of the suggestive grin he had worn earlier. He looked completely sincere, as though pleasing her were every bit as important as securing lasting peace for the galaxy. Her eyes filled with tears. She wiped them away on her sleeve as she stood.

"Thank you, but that's impossible. Thank you for the yogurt too. It was very good." Rather than return her dish to the galley, which would force her to walk by him again, she left it on the table and headed toward the cockpit.

Tynan sat back and watched her go, but he felt as unhappy as she had looked. He had had ample evidence that Amara was a capable young woman who could handle minor difficulties and dangerous situations with equal aplomb, so why did offers of affection leave her in tears? There had to be a reason for such a peculiar response, but it certainly didn't look as though Amara would ever reveal it.

"Damn it, Steve! You ought to know a whole lot more about your pilot than you do."

"She is fully qualified, Tynan. No other information is required."

"Maybe not for you, but I don't know her nearly well enough."

"Then learn."

Tynan considered that suggestion for a long moment, then began to chuckle. "You're right. I don't know the lieutenant well enough to understand her, and I'm supposed to be the expert at insightful negotiations." Tynan finished eating his breakfast, then waited a while longer before joining Amara in the cockpit. One glance told him that she was worried, and he didn't think it could still be about him.

"What's wrong?"

Amara shook her head. "Nothing major. It's just that I didn't get all the scanners repaired before I discovered we were at a Corkscrew base, and now

153

one of the three I did manage to fix isn't working properly. Risto had his Corkscrews out searching for a Starcruiser, and any Starcruiser would have suited him, but even knowing that we weren't a specific target, and that he can't bother us again, I can't shake the feeling that we might still be in danger."

"What about that Alado maintenance facility you considered. Do you want to stop there?"

"We're way past it now, and with time being so short, I hate to detour to reach another."

"I'm afraid all my complaining about safety has upset you. I apologize for it. It was just that I'd never even flown in an airplane, let alone spacecraft and—"

Amara waved aside his excuses. "Your apprehensions were natural, Tynan, and believe me, they were only mildly annoying and didn't upset me in the least." Still preoccupied, Amara ran another test, with the same result—only two of the starboard scanners were working properly. "We're not completely blind on the starboard side, but close." Depressed, she sat back in her seat, but rather than speculate on how much trouble they might encounter because of the nonfunctioning scanners, she kept still.

"Is there something we ought to be doing?" Tynan asked.

"Just be on guard, that's all."

Tynan had hoped to raise her spirits with a game of Banshee Quest, but now that seemed like much too frivolous a suggestion. "Would it distract you to discuss the conference?"

"No—or rather yes, but I'd welcome it."

"Good. In the materials I was given, I have the issues Alado wants brought forth listed in their order of importance to the corporation." He counted them off on his fingers. "Continued peaceful exploration, of course, then colonization rights, environmental protection, exportation of natural resources, and shared use of space stations. I had the impression, or perhaps misconception, that the other four corporations would rank these same goals in a similar order. After talking with you, I've begun to believe I was wrong. What is Peregrine's primary goal?"

Grateful to have a neutral, although vital subject to discuss, Amara curled up in a more comfortable pose. "Their main interest is in natural resources—and not merely their exportation, but their exploitation. Wait a minute. Steve, give us a five-line, five-section grid so we can plot the corporations' goals."

Tynan gave a low whistle of admiration as the graphics Amara had requested appeared in five colors. With another command, the computer listed Alado, Peregrine, Europa, Serema, and Omega across the top and exploration, colonization, environment, resources, and space stations along the side to form the beginnings of a useful graph. "What about Europa?"

Amara frowned slightly. "I think they'd join Alado in wanting peaceful exploration."

"Serema?"

"They've never been strong in technology, so I expect them to make sharing space stations a priority."

"You mentioned that, as the smallest, Omega wants more colonies. Shall we count that as their foremost goal?"

"Yes."

Amara and Tynan listed each corporation's probable goals, and while they discovered some agreement here and there, there was no clear consensus on any of them. Tynan studied their chart at length and then asked Steve to save it. "You've been a great help," he complimented her. "I've read the prepared statements the other corporations have provided, but most are so vague it was difficult to discern any difference between them. Your insights are far more helpful."

"They'll prove helpful only if they're accurate, Tynan, and it's possible that one or more of the corporations will arrive at the conference with a different set of priorities than they have displayed in the past."

Tynan reached over to pat her hand. "If that happens, we'll rely on their past performance rather than rhetoric. In fact, we might even expect some to start the negotiations with issues they don't really consider vital in an attempt to simply learn how the group operates before they press for their primary goals."

"That's not a bad strategy."

"No, it isn't, but we've got to recognize the tactic for what it is." Tynan paused a moment, and then had what he considered a truly brilliant idea. "Alado promised me a staff of whatever size I required, but I'm so used to working alone that I refused their offer. Now I think I made a mistake. Will you work with me during the negotiations?"

Amara knew she had to refuse. "I'm a pilot," she reminded him. "That wouldn't be fair to the men and women whose primary function is diplomacy. I'm sure the Secretary can suggest people with far more experience than I possess. They'd be a real asset to you. I wouldn't."

"Nonsense. You're far too modest. And besides, I've already been promised whomever I want, and I want you."

Amara shook her head. "Just because I'm the only woman you know doesn't mean I'd be any good, Tynan. Besides, as soon as we reach Confederation base, you might meet someone with whom you'd much rather work."

Tynan regarded her with a skeptical stare. She ought to have referred to herself as the only person he knew outside the Keep, but she had said woman. That slip told him a great deal. "The first time I saw you, I simply dismissed you as a terrible distraction, and I'm embarrassed by how rudely I treated you. Now that we've had the opportunity to get to know each other, I think we make an excellent team. Please reconsider and say you'll work with me."

Torn by desire—and fear of eventual pain— Amara tried to delay having to reply. "Right now, it will take all my talents to get you to the conference site on time. Let's not make any decisions about your staff until after we arrive."

She was toying absently with the buckle on her seat belt, and certain he had just learned something important, Tynan reached out and took her hand. "I don't care how many women there are at the Confederation base, Amara. I'll still want you. You're bright, very beautiful, and wonderful fun. Before we met, I didn't laugh nearly enough. I'm ashamed of the way I asked you to sleep with me. You were right to refuse. Making love ought to be an expression of feelings, rather than merely pleasurable exercise.

"I've come to care for you, but I can understand why you'd be more comfortable with another Starchild. There's so much that occurs between men and women—courting rituals, if you will— and I don't know any of them. The Guardians provided me with an abundance of father figures, but not having had a mother or sisters, or any women in my life, seems like a tragedy now that I've met you. You were right, you see. The Keep is limiting, and perhaps none of us who were raised there is fully human. If I hadn't left, I would never have known."

When Amara pulled her hand from his, Tynan feared his confession had merely embarrassed her, and he hurriedly left the cockpit rather than force her to state that she had no feelings for him. He paced the passenger cabin, knowing full well that he was no adolescent youth suffering from his first crush, but feeling just as foolish. He supposed men must eventually learn how to react when they said they cared for a woman and she didn't share those feelings, but he was positive it would always hurt. Somehow, it was a familiar pain.

He stopped then and grabbed the back of a seat to steady himself. Even as a tiny baby, he must have felt the separation from his mother as acutely as he felt the loss of what would never be with Amara. The memory was long forgotten, but not the feeling. It swelled within his chest, and he knew he must have cried for days while men in aubergine robes tried to make him feel welcome in the Keep. They had eventually succeeded, and from that day to this, he had not missed the love he had lost.

Although stunned by Tynan's remarks, Amara didn't need long to consider them before she realized that although they might have only a few brief weeks together, the love they shared would be real. That someone as fascinatingly complex as Tynan Thorn could actually care for her was a bit overwhelming, but she trusted him to speak the truth. He had said that he cared for her, and suddenly that was all that mattered.

"Steve, take command. If the scanners pick up another ship, I don't care how distant, call me at once."

"Yes, lieutenant."

Amara was actually shaking as she left the cockpit, but it wasn't from fear. She was simply excited. When she found Tynan standing in the aisle, apparently lost in thought, she didn't know quite how to approach him. Then he turned and saw her, and it was too late to compose any eloquent speeches.

"I wish I had other clothes on board. I'm afraid my flightsuit isn't all that appealing."

Uncertain just why her clothes were a concern, Tynan shrugged. "No, you're wrong. It's very flattering."

Amara walked up to him and slipped her arms around his waist. "I had the advantage of reading your work before we met, so I knew your thoughts,

Cinnamon Burke

and I was as deeply impressed by their truths as is everyone else who reads them. The mental image I had of you wasn't at all accurate, though. I thought it must have taken a lifetime to acquire your wisdom and expected a saintly man with a wispy white beard. I never expected you to be as attractive as your beliefs, but I didn't want to be just an experience."

"I said I was sorry for that." Flustered that she had come so close, Tynan didn't know quite where to put his hands, but finally rested them lightly on her waist.

"I've only known you four days—"

"Yes, I realize now I was much too forward."

Amara couldn't recall another man ever apologizing for that failing. Tynan's philosophy had a timeless beauty, but in so many ways, he was like meeting a visitor from the past. That he held such old-fashioned views about men and women was endearing, however. He made the brash young pilots she had known seem insufferably shallow, and there was absolutely no comparison between him and Orion Chaudet.

She touched his lips to silence him. "No, wait, let me finish. While I haven't known you very long, I know you well enough to want us to share as much as we possibly can. I would like very much to make love to you, and with Steve fully capable of piloting the ship, there's nothing to stop us."

Amazed, Tynan kissed her fingertips, then her palm before sliding her hand down his chest as he unfastened his flightsuit. "You're right," he agreed. "These flightsuits aren't in the least bit attractive. Let's get rid of them."

160

Tynan swiftly peeled off his along with his boots and undershirt, but Amara hesitated to remove more than her gold boots. "What do you think of tattoos, Tynan?"

"Like the one Riva had across her face? I think they're hideous. Why?"

"Then we'd better dim the lights."

"No, I want to be able to see every delectable centimeter of you." Impatient, Tynan reached for the tab at her collar and opened her suit down the front. She had on a scarlet, lace-trimmed undergarment that inspired a wicked grin. "You couldn't have known I'd see your lingerie. Is it all this seductive?"

"Every bit of it," Amara admitted proudly.

"Good." Tynan continued to peel away the flightsuit, but it wasn't until she had stepped out of it that he caught a glimpse of the tattooed wave that began at her right ankle. Her figure was so stunning, he didn't think she needed additional decoration, but that was before she turned in his arms and he saw that the wave appeared to move with the rhythm of the sea.

"How far does that go?" he asked in an awestruck whisper.

"Does it bother you?"

Tynan chose his words with care. "Yes, but not in the way you mean." He reached for the narrow straps on the red undergarment and slid them off her shoulders. "I've never undressed a woman," he mumbled, "but you already knew that."

"There's no need to rush." To prove her point, Amara gave him a lingering kiss that she didn't

161

end until they had both begun to grow dizzy. She then outlined the shape of his lips with the tip of her tongue, and he made the next kiss very much his own. Leaning back against a seat, Tynan soon found the aisle far too confining, and wanting her to share his bed, he took Amara's hand and led her back to the seats he used. Now adept at creating a bed, he did so, and pulled Amara down beside him.

He savored her next kiss, but found the one following even better. Amara ran her fingers through his curls, then down his back in a gentle massage that mirrored the slow, lazy, curling thrusts of her tongue. Drowning in sensation, Tynan now considered the exotic wave tattoo the perfect complement to the young woman's talents.

Amara wasn't too lost in Tynan to remember that this would be his first experience with lovemaking, and she wanted it to be truly memorable. She gradually eased out of his arms, and after making certain he was lying comfortably across the bed, she spread a teasing spray of kisses across his chest. She licked his leathery nipples, then traced the hard planes of his abdomen with her tongue. When she reached his underpants, she sat up to tug them off and tossed them aside.

Tynan sat up slightly as Amara curled herself around his thigh. "Just what is it you're doing?"

"Just getting comfortable."

Tynan held his breath. "For what?"

Rather than describe what she intended to do, Amara showed him. She raked her nails up his inner thighs, encircled his hardened shaft in an expert grasp, and used her lips and tongue to bestow a series of wildly pleasurable kisses. Shocked, but thrilled to find her such a wanton partner, Tynan wove his fingers in her curls, pressing her face closer still, but she paused to keep the rapture she was creating from cresting too soon. She took him time and again to the brink of ecstasy, only to draw away and allow his emotions to float freely before renewing her tender assault on his senses.

Considerate as well as adept, Amara knew just when to stop her exquisite teasing. When she at last coaxed his release from him, she knew she had given him a taste of paradise. Having satisfied him so completely, she curled up beside him, rested her head upon his shoulder, and waited for him to regain the strength to repay the favor.

Chapter Nine

Nothing Tynan had ever experienced compared in intensity to the volcanic sensation Amara created. Even after it overflowed its peak, the explosive joy continued to radiate through him with a delicious heat and left him too gratified to move, let alone speak, for longer than he feared was polite. The best he could do was to fondle Amara's curls with a lazy caress, but while his mind provided a variety of imaginative ways to reward her for her lavish affection, he wondered if he would ever be able to carry them out.

Feeling perfectly at home in his arms, Amara closed her eyes, and having gotten only intermittent rest during the night, she was soon fast asleep. When Tynan later woke her with feather-light kisses, she responded with a graceful stretch and an apology. "I'm sorry, I didn't mean to abandon you, but I didn't sleep well last night."

"You can abandon me like that any time you wish."

Amara had expected him to be appreciative and rose slightly to kiss him. "I must warn you now that it's addictive. Perhaps you ought to stop while you still can."

Tynan knew she was only teasing, but still thought the danger was real. "I think it's already too late. Does what you were doing have a name?"

"Yes, that's an ancient Chinese technique called the Jade Flute. I think you can understand why it's survived to this day."

Tynan rested his forehead against hers momentarily, then drew away. "I can't help but wonder where you learned it."

He wore an enchanting smile rather than a jealous scowl, but Amara knew better than to satisfy his curiosity as well as his physical cravings. "Sorry, but I never discuss one lover with another. That may be frustrating now, but at least you'll be certain that whatever happens between us will go no further."

Tynan had assumed there had been other men in her life, but until she mentioned lovers, they hadn't been real to him. Now he wanted to know everything about them. Most important—why had they given up such a treasure?

"They all must have been fools."

Amara tried to sound indignant. "Are you insinuating that I have poor judgment when it comes to men?"

Tynan laughed. "No, you're sharing my bed so I think you have excellent taste where men are concerned. I just can't imagine why you're not with

165

your first love. He must have been a great fool to have lost you."

Amara studied Tynan's expression with a lingering glance. He was her first brown-eyed lover, and he was so wonderfully unique in all respects that she swore to herself that she would never take another. "You are my first love," she confided with unmistakable sincerity.

Although Tynan knew that couldn't possibly be true, he wished that it were. That he would one day have to tell her good-bye was too painful an eventuality to accept, let alone admit aloud. "And you are mine," he said instead. He kissed Amara then, his silent vow of devotion more eloquent than any of the flowery promises she had heard from others.

When he could bear to break away, he called to Steve. "You offered music once. Do you have anything romantic?"

Steve responded with a soloist plucking the modern equivalent of a harp with an almost unbearable sweetness, but the selection was touched with a melancholy strain that conjured up feelings of a painful good-bye rather than seduction. "Perhaps romantic was the wrong term, Steve. What I want is something pretty but not mournful."

Steve provided chimes that rang with sparkling clarity, but again the music struck Tynan as far too wistful. "Not sad, Steve, romantic," he chided. When next the rhythmic strumming of a talented guitar duo filled the passenger cabin, Tynan thought their tune a great improvement and thanked the computer.

Amara reached up to comb Tynan's ebony curls.

"Romance is often sad. In fact, all the great romantic stories are tragedies."

There was no hint of tears in her beautiful aqua eyes, but Tynan recognized her sorrow. He wanted to plumb its depths and dispel it for all time, but at the moment he felt compelled to concentrate on her slender body rather than her soul. He moved off the bed and, taking her hand, pulled her up beside him. This time, when he reached for her lingerie straps, he did not stop at merely slipping them off her shoulders.

Amara had lovely full breasts, which would have captivated him in themselves, but the addition of the foamy tattooed spray greatly enhanced their appeal. Fascinated with the living artwork, Tynan peeled away the scarlet garment and tossed it on top of the heap of their discarded clothes. He turned Amara then, and entranced with the waves scrolled around her body, he could not help but wonder aloud.

"The artist who did this certainly must have enjoyed himself."

"Yes, she did, but because the artwork was an enjoyable challenge, rather than for the reason you assumed."

Tynan recognized his question for the jealous one it was and apologized. "I'm sorry, I know so little about tattoos, it didn't even occur to me that the artist wouldn't have been male."

Amara moved close and rubbed against him. "I'd say you know a great deal about one tattoo at least."

"No, there's much left unexplored." Tynan sat her down on the edge of the bed, and knelt between

167

her knees. Holding her waist, he licked the lacy design curling over her breasts, then drew a pale pink nipple into his mouth. Amara leaned against him, draped her arms around his neck, and with soft murmurs of delight, urged him on. Her tattoo was so detailed, he had expected her to taste salty, but her skin was as sweet as her kisses.

"You taste good," he whispered before sampling her other breast.

"So do you," Amara replied.

Tynan leaned back slightly, found her smile genuine rather than teasing, and took her comment as the compliment she had meant it to be. When she leaned back on her elbows, he continued to trace the graceful wave down her ribs and across the gentle plane of her stomach. The tip of his tongue filled her navel, making her giggle, and he sat back on his heels to enjoy the sound before planting his next kiss on her knee.

The wave that flowed up her right leg caught his attention first, but then the natural peach tones of her left leg became equally appealing. He raked his stubbled chin up her thigh, felt her flinch, and decided it might not be a good idea to grow a beard now after all. This, however, was definitely not the time to excuse himself and go shave. He ran his hands up her thighs, but she was already completely open to him, and his adorning kisses hadn't provoked even a hint of shyness.

Of course, this was nothing new to her. He was ashamed to be jealous of men she would never name and he would probably never meet, but such feelings, no matter how unworthy, could not be controlled with logic. He wanted her all to himself, and forcing away his unseen rivals, he nuzzled the blond curls between her legs and inhaled her body's tantalizing perfume. To taste her essence was as natural as suckling at her breast, and lured on by her softly moaned encouragement, he lapped up his fill.

He could feel her trembling with delicious anticipation, but did not want to send her into pleasure's realm alone. He stood to draw her across the bed, and then, following the instinct which had led him this far, he joined her, molding the lean planes of his body to the soft swells of hers. They were near equals in height, and as he shifted slightly, she guided him so that his first thrust wasn't tentative, but deep. She arched her back to meet him, and while he was eager to move, he forced himself to lie still and savor her inner heat. For the moment, he was the only man in her life, and that he at last knew her completely was as great a thrill as the earlier joy she had given him.

She wrapped her legs over his to hold him in place and with a subtle nudge moved upward, then urged him to carry the downward motion. Trusting her lead, Tynan followed the pattern that soon created an intense mutual need. He nibbled her lower lip, then began an exchange of deep kisses to make their union complete.

Awash in exotic sensations, he felt her release begin with rippling contractions that lured him into her bliss. Exalting in the rapture that flowed between them with such perfect ease, he thrust more deeply, plunging to her core, until he finally came to rest, too content to move from her arms. Gregory Nash might have encouraged him to learn what he could about women from Amara, but Tynan had never expected her lessons to be so profound. As a lover, she would surpass any man's dreams, but more than mere technique, what Tynan truly felt was a warm bond of love.

Enjoying an equally delectable sense of satisfaction, Amara drew her nails up Tynan's back in a languid caress. She felt certain she had fulfilled whatever obligation she had had to initiate him into the mysteries of lovemaking, but she certainly hoped his curiosity was far from satisfied. Serenaded by guitars, she could easily imagine herself back on Earth, in some softly lit bedroom where the air would be scented with the lush perfume of the surrounding gardens. It was a pleasant daydream, but she feared that all too soon, the lure of the stars would call her home.

Clinging to the beauty of the moment, she forced away all thought of the future and continued to hold Tynan in an adoring embrace.

Without withdrawing, Tynan rose on his elbows. "Am I crushing you?"

"Not at all. We can stay this way all day if you like. Some recommend it as a position for meditation. That's another ancient custom, I believe."

"I don't think I could think of anything but you," Tynan readily confessed.

"I certainly won't complain if you don't."

"Is this just something you've heard, or have you actually tried it?"

Amara reached up to tousle his curls. "You have beautiful hair. With your golden skin, you might have Indian blood, but I've never seen an Indian with curly hair, so that seems unlikely."

Tynan didn't understand why she had changed the subject so abruptly, especially to a discussion of his heritage, which he was completely unable to trace. Then he realized that she must have thought he was again questioning the habits of her previous lovers. "I wasn't trying to trick you into telling me something you didn't wish to admit. I just wondered if you'd tried it." He kissed her rather than apologize any further.

"I don't want any barriers between us," he explained when he realized that a thousand kisses would still not be enough.

Amara tickled his ribs. "There's nothing separating us now."

Tynan had a philosopher's desire to explore the question more deeply, but Amara's teasing comment was a clear warning that she did not. Her past was a forbidden subject, and while he could understand her reasoning, he didn't like being excluded from any facet of her life. "You know all there is to know about me," he argued, "and I know so little about you."

Amara rose to kiss him. "You already know the most important things about me, and we have another seven days before we reach Confederation base. It's impossible to predict how long the conference will last, but you'll surely have plenty of time to pick up interesting little details."

"Did you just agree to work with me?"

Tynan's delighted smile was so wide that Amara was pained he had misunderstood. "No, I didn't, but for as long as the conference lasts, it will be the focus of the diplomatic corps' efforts, and I should be able to see you often. As for working together,

I still want to wait on that decision."

Not pleased that she wasn't as enthusiastic about the possibility of being his sole staff member as he, Tynan opened his mouth to argue. But unwilling to waste what little time they did have, he kissed Amara instead. He withdrew only slightly, and felt himself again growing hard. He wrapped his arms around her and rolled over to bring her up on top of him. "Show me how to do it this way, so I can watch you as well as feel you."

Amara rested her hands lightly on his chest. "Is it only my tattoo that interests you?" she purred.

Tynan pretended to need time to consider her question, but then he began to laugh. "No, your charms aren't only skin deep."

Amara bent down to kiss him, then straightened up and with a slow, undulating rhythm made her tattooed waves swell with life. With admirable dedication, she presented a lesson in love until neither teacher nor pupil needed more to claim mastery.

"You must be hungry," Amara suggested before drawing Tynan's earlobe into her mouth.

"What time is it?"

"What difference does it make? We can eat or sleep whenever we please."

Filled with a lazy warmth, Tynan needed a moment to decide whether it would be worth the trouble to get up and prepare food. He gave Amara a hug and left his arms clasped around her waist. "I suppose we really should stop to eat occasionally, otherwise we'll become too weak to make love."

"Yes, let's avoid that danger."

"I wish we had some real food in the supplies, something good like prime rib, or steak, or even lamb chops."

His anguished lament about the quality of Alado's meals prompted Amara to slip out of his arms. "Carnivore," she complained with a shake of her head. She bent over and fluffed out her curls, then straightened up. "When we get to Confederation base, you'll be able to order anything you like, but until then, you'll just have to suffer with the usual Starchild diet. It's extremely healthful, and we all think it's appetizing."

Tynan propped his head on his hand and watched her with a fond gaze as she gathered up their clothes. He had fast grown accustomed to her tattoo, and now he couldn't even imagine her supple body without it. "I think I've just been insulted."

"Nonsense. It's not your fault if the Guardians' diet was no more advanced than the cave dwellers' ".

Tynan was off his bed in an instant. He caught up with Amara as she started for the lavatory and swung her around to face him. "You can make fun of me all you want, but like your past lovers, the Guardians are not a subject for discussion. Understood?"

That she would lose Tynan all too soon to the Guardians was reason enough for Amara to disparage their habits every chance she got, and she raised her chin proudly, as though she had every right to do so. Ordinarily, she would have objected violently to his giving her orders, but because he had tied it to one of her own, she didn't dare.

"Of course." Holding an armful of laundry, she

felt at a disadvantage, especially when Tynan continued to stare at her after she had agreed to his conditions. He looked not only angry, but disappointed, and she couldn't tell whether it was because of her original remark, or for agreeing without giving him an argument. Disappointed in him, too, she pulled free, but she had just begun her shower when Steve summoned her.

Not bothering to don lingerie, Amara pulled on her flightsuit dripping wet and raced to the cockpit. Tynan, who had donned a clean pair of long underwear, again took the co-pilot's seat. "It's not more Corkscrews, is it?" he asked.

Amara studied the image on the screen. "No, but I asked Steve to notify me about all other ships, and it looks like we're about to overtake a private passenger vessel of some sort." She leaned forward to adjust the picture the scanners were transmitting and, recognizing the ship, began to smile. "I'll have to take you close to this one so you can get a good look at it. It's an absolute classic."

Tynan studied the jagged image on his screen. "In what way?"

"You'll see. When we come alongside, adjust our speed to match hers, Steve." That order given, Amara turned to Tynan. "The Rastafarians began in the twentieth century, didn't they?"

"Yes, but I didn't realize they had left Earth."

"They haven't established colonies elsewhere, but they run tours throughout the galaxy. Sort of space pilgrimages, if you will. They design their own ships with some of the most creative engineering you'll see anywhere. Because Alado never refuses aid to any traveler in need, I've met quite a few of their pilots. Let's see if I know this one."

Tynan leaned over to get a better view as they neared the passenger ship. The only similarity with the Starcruiser appeared to be the rear-mounted engines, and Tynan reacted with a low whistle. "It looks as though that's entirely built of spare parts. My God, there's actually printing across a section near the nose. Could it be from an old billboard?"

Amused by his question, Amara had to laugh, and their recent argument was forgotten. "It's probably a piece from an old high-speed rail car. They were built of a premium quality alloy, and when they're scraped, they make perfect material for the outer shell of space vehicles."

"Of course, but what caused all the dents?"

"Looks like damage from an asteroid shower. Like the rusted rivets and smoke-blackened hull, the dents look worse than they actually are. That ship's cruising at a speed some of Alado's passenger ship captains would envy. Here, I'll take us a little closer still."

Thinking they were already too close, Tynan frowned, but he didn't question Amara's action. Gradually, the blurs of red, yellow, and green clustered around the viewing ports became recognizable as brightly clothed passengers whose long dreadlocks bounced off their shoulders as they pointed toward the Starcruiser. What little he could see of the ship's interior appeared to be painted in bold patterns, and he thought they must have a very good time on their trips.

Amara transmitted a message to the captain, and he responded with an enthusiastic greeting. "It's Maubee. He's a friend."

Tynan listened as Maubee and Amara entered into a conversation that had meaning only to the two pilots. The man's voice was rich and deep, his conversation punctuated with frequent laughter, and Tynan couldn't help but wonder if he and Amara had ever been lovers. They would certainly have had more common interests than she shared with him, but ashamed of himself for having become so preoccupied with her past, he tried to accept the man as merely the friend she had described.

At the end of their conversation, Amara banked the Starcruiser toward starboard, and gradually increased their speed. After a few minutes, she again relinquished the controls to Steve. "Now I'm going to try and finish my shower. When you're ready, I promise to prepare something you'll find worth eating."

Tynan refused to touch that subject and led the way back to the passenger cabin. While Amara was fixing dinner, he showered and took the time to shave. "I decided I can look formidable without a beard," he announced when he rejoined her.

Assuming he wanted her opinion, Amara leaned against the galley counter and studied his appearance with an appreciative gaze. Finally she shrugged. "Frankly, I think you're far too handsome to inspire anything except awe."

Unused to compliments on his appearance, Tynan turned away and busied himself picking out their utensils. "Thank you. I've said that you're beautiful, haven't I?"

His pose hid the embarrassed blush that filled his cheeks, but Amara understood his shyness for what it was. She moved up behind him, and slid her arms around his waist. "Yes, you have. Thank you."

Tynan turned around to face her. "I'll bet you're tired of hearing it."

"No. Women, like men, never tire of compliments. Feel free to pay all you like."

"Give me a minute to compose something you haven't heard before." As soon as the words left his mouth, Tynan regretted them. Amara didn't scold him, she just backed away to complete the last of the dinner preparations. Grateful for an excuse to leave her, Tynan set up their table, put the utensils at their places, and poured the juice. When Amara carried in a steaming platter of pasta with what appeared to be a sauce filled with ground sausage, he was astonished.

"It tastes like sausage, and I hope you like it better than the vegetables and rice," Amara explained.

"I'm sure I will." Then, certain he had sounded much too keen, he tried to redeem himself. "What I mean to say is that the vegetables you fixed yesterday were very good. Really they were."

He had already made it plain that he hadn't cared for them, but Amara didn't press the issue. "I thought so."

Tynan waited for her to take the first bite, then scooped up a forkful of the pasta. He gave it a thoughtful chew and found whatever was masquerading as meat had not only the texture but also the highly spiced flavor of the sausage they had served at the Keep. "This is delicious."

"Thank you, but the only credit I can take is for knowing which packages to open."

"Well, it's greatly appreciated." Tynan was hungry, but thought he ought to make some effort at conversation. Never having taken a woman out on a date, he had no idea how to engage Amara in a playful banter. Instead, he again brought up the conference. "I think we ought to make a list of every demand any corporation could possibly have. I don't want to be caught off guard and have to request a recess to consider something that would have been obvious to a more experienced negotiator."

"Fine. We can do that later if you like."

Amara smiled, but Tynan wished he had something more entertaining to offer. They would make love again later—he was certain of that—but he wanted to involve her in his planning whenever possible so that she would want to continue being a helpful resource once the conference began. He paused to watch her take another tiny bite and suddenly realized that he had been preoccupied with her past, when the real question was whether or not she had another man in her present.

"I'm sorry," he began in a flustered rush, "but it didn't even occur to me that being on my staff might be difficult for you because of a previous involvement. Is there another man, someone who'll meet you when we arrive and expect to share all your free time?"

Jolted by unwanted thoughts of Orion Chaudet, Amara laid her fork aside and blotted her lips. Having been instrumental in arranging for Tynan's participation, Orion would be sure to greet them upon their arrival at the Confederation base. He and his staff would already be there overseeing the preparations for the conference and he would undoubtedly have planned a festive welcoming party for Tynan. She could not imagine anything more awkward than having to be in the same room with both men.

Tynan was far too sensitive not to realize that he had stumbled across another subject Amara didn't care to discuss. Now he didn't understand how he could have been so stupid as to assume all her lovers were in her past. Perhaps she took multiple lovers, and he would have several rivals vying for her time. Having been with her, he certainly couldn't blame them. It was no wonder she was reluctant to work with him during the conference. She probably wouldn't be able to work him into her schedule!

Fuming, he spat out his next request. "I understand your reluctance to name names. A simple yes or no will do."

"No, I don't believe so." At a loss for how to begin, Amara took a sip of juice and again blotted her lips. Knowing the truth was always best—especially so with a fine man like Tynan—she strove to make her explanation accurate but, out of necessity, vague. "Had I been involved with someone else, I wouldn't have encouraged your affection. I'm not promiscuous, Tynan. I've never been with a man I didn't care for, nor have I ever been unfaithful to a lover.

"Disease hasn't been an issue in a couple of centuries, and with contraception controlled with implants, an unplanned pregnancy isn't a risk, so we have unlimited sexual freedom. There are women, as well as men, who feel that any sort of morals are tedious relics of the past, but I can't agree. I believe people ought to be true to themselves—and to others." That much was easy to relate, and when Tynan nodded his agreement, she continued with the more difficult portion of her reply.

"As far as I'm concerned, I ended my last affair before accepting the assignment as your pilot. I doubt the man took me seriously, however. He's the type who's accustomed to getting his own way, and he may very well expect me to return to him. That's not an option I'll even consider. If he failed to understand me the first time I ended our relationship, I'll make sure he definitely will when next we meet."

Amara reached out to take Tynan's hand. "You needn't worry about my past romantic entanglements. I'll handle whatever problems appear myself, as I always have."

While Tynan was enormously relieved by her comments, her description of her last lover annoyed him. "He sounds like an arrogant bastard, and frankly, I'd welcome a fight. The conference will require such thoughtful deliberations, it might be just the sort of primitive diversion I'll need."

"You were more expert than primitive at Risto's, so that's not something I want to see," Amara replied, beginning to realize how much Tynan had changed from the reclusive Guardian she'd first met.

Tynan gave her fingers a squeeze before releasing her hand to finish eating. "You're very independent, aren't you?"

Hoping he didn't consider it a flaw, Amara waited for him to glance up before responding. "Independence is an asset not only for a pilot, but for a woman as well."

Tynan had had ample opportunity to observe her skills in both areas and had to agree. "You do believe that men and women need each other though, don't you?"

"Yes, of course, but two independent people make a far more successful couple than two pathetically dependent souls."

"Yes, I'm sure you must be right." For Tynan, the whole area of relationships between men and women was new, but when he considered how brief his liaison with Amara would necessarily be, he hated to open up the subject. Not that it wasn't a worthwhile endeavor; it would just be painfully irrelevant for a Guardian who would soon return to the Keep.

Amara watched Tynan's expression become increasingly serious and feared that, contrary to her best efforts, she had only increased his curiosity about her past. They needed to be able to create their own existence as a couple, but on board a Starcruiser their opportunities were severely limited, and when they reached the conference they would be just as restricted. Still, she felt she had to offer something more than sex that they could enjoy together.

"Banshee Quest isn't the only game in Steve's files. Is there something you play at the Keep that you'd like to teach me?"

Tynan immediately thought of Captain's Mistress, but just as quickly dismissed the game as being far too subtle to capture Amara's attention. "No, I want to keep playing Banshee Quest until I can be good competition for you."

"All right. Shall we begin a tournament as soon as we finish eating?"

Tynan considered her question and then shook his head. "Steve has a film about the sea, and I was fascinated by it even before I saw your tattoo. Let's make love while we watch it."

"What an intriguing idea. That's only one in a whole series of films. When we tire of the sea, we can move on to the rain forest, or the desert, or wherever you'd like to imagine us to be."

Tynan rose and took her hand. "It isn't my imagination I want to use."

Amara wound her arms around his neck, and when she pressed her hips against his, she found him already fully aroused. She slid one hand down between them to caress him. "Yes, I think I understand what you mean."

With that type of seductive encouragement, Tynan had her undressed and stretched across his bed before he remembered he had neglected to ask Steve to show the film. He quickly asked for it and had peeled off his own clothes by the time the first wave lapped the beach. Believing the man Amara had described would have been selfish rather than generous with his affection, he vowed to make certain he always pleased her.

He drew her into his arms and kissed her eyelids, earlobes, and then her mouth. "Show me what you like best," he whispered. "Tonight I'll be your slave."

Amara combed his curls off his forehead in a fond caress. "I've never had a slave. Why don't you just surprise me."

Tynan continued to kiss her, but at the same time sent a wandering caress over her breasts, across her stomach, and down between her legs. He rested his hand lightly on the delicate folds, feeling her heat before parting the petal-like lips and slipping his fingers inside. He shifted position slightly to tickle her nipple with the tip of his tongue, but he didn't stop his lazy perusal of her feminine core until his fingers were all slippery from her welcoming wetness.

His next kiss would have sampled that delectable treat, but first Steve called to her, and then the whole ship was jarred by a hard, metallic clang that reverberated all around them. Nearly thrown off the bed, Tynan grabbed protectively for Amara. "My God!" he cried. "What's happened?"

Amara's flushed face drained of color. Hurriedly escaping Tynan's grasp, she slid off the bed. Again dispensing with her colorful lingerie, she yanked on her flightsuit. Tynan's robe lay over an adjacent seat, and she flung it to him.

"Here, wear this. I should have known we'd need more than two starboard scanners, but I swear to you, I never thought we'd be boarded. We'll need God's own luck to get out of this alive, but I know you'll give it your best try."

Her curls flying wildly about her head, Amara looked terrified, and Tynan quickly grasped the reason. "Pirates?"

Amara could only nod, but when Tynan drew on his robe, he sent her such a defiant glance that she thought it just might be the pirates who were in mortal danger.

Chapter Ten

"What about the laser cannons?" Tynan asked.

Amara grabbed hold of her hair and, twisting it into a tight coil, secured it atop her head with pins from one of her pockets. "It's too late. With the ships joined, we would be shooting ourselves." She tipped the two seats they had been using for a bed back into place and told Steve to shut off the film.

"Depending on what equipment they have, it will take them anywhere from a few minutes to several hours to unscramble the code that opens the hatch. Steve will have already notified Fleet Command of our emergency, but help can't possibly arrive before we're boarded, so we're on our own.

"I want the pacification music on low, Steve." Amara bent down to pull on her boots. "We have subliminal messages on some of the films and tapes to enhance cooperation. I don't know if they will work on pirates, but it's worth a try."

Tynan had had no idea Alado engaged in such a practice, but this was no time to debate the issue of free will. "What about other weapons?"

"We've the laser pistol I took at Risto's, plus others in the emergency supplies, but with only two of us, and probably fifty or more of them, any armed confrontation can only end in their favor. Alado's policy is not to oppose pirates with force, unless ours is superior and clearly it isn't here. It must be the ship they want, and we'll have to convince them you're extremely valuable. That way they'll demand a high ransom rather than kill us."

Tynan pulled on his long underwear, adjusted the fit of his robe with the rope belt, and yanked on his boots. "We're both far too valuable to kill, Amara. Don't let them think otherwise."

Amara agreed with a distracted nod. "This is all my fault. I should have been in the cockpit keeping watch rather than—"

"Making love with me?" Tynan posed. "With several inoperable scanners, what could you have seen that Steve didn't?"

"Perhaps nothing, but still, all the blame for this disaster rightfully belongs with me, and I can only pray nothing happens to you because of my negligence."

Tynan pulled her into his arms and hugged her tightly. "You weren't negligent. The pirates have caused the trouble, not you. Now let's use whatever time we have to make our plans. Let's begin by citing the peaceful nature of this mission and demand to be released. If that fails, we can insist they ask a ransom for us. Then we'll bide our time and wait for rescue, but most importantly, we have to stay alive, by whatever means, until we're set free or help arrives. Agreed?"

Amara held on to him tightly. Inspired by his courage, she thought quickly. "Yes. They'll have to separate their ship from ours for the return flight to their base. We might be able to over-power whoever's guarding us then and get away. Pirates are a despicable sort, and if they are as careless as I've been, we should be able to outwit them."

Tynan put his hands on her shoulders and stepped back slightly. "Stop blaming yourself. It's not getting us anywhere. I saw you send two of the Corkscrews into screaming fits with thought control. There might be an opportunity for you to use it again."

The Guardians shared too great a respect to meddle in each other's thoughts, so he had no experience in the skill, but from what he had heard, all it required was a narrow stream of consciously focused thought. The trick was to clear the mind of all distraction and release its power with sufficient force to invade the thoughts of another. This would be a difficult time for Amara to attempt such a feat, but he didn't know what else to suggest.

Amara took a deep breath, but her voice still trembled with emotion when she spoke. "Pirates aren't as easy to manipulate as Corkscrews. They're the absolute bottom dwellers of society. Most have long criminal records. They're usually drunk or high, which renders thought control ineffective, but I'll give it my best effort if there's even the slightest chance it will work. Perhaps the pirates' own stupidity will work against them. There's a report of one who poisoned the tip of his knife to enable him to kill a man with a slight wound. Then he forgot, used the knife to cut his steak, and poisoned himself."

Amused in spite of the darkness of their situation, Tynan shook his head sadly. "I knew there was a good reason why we ought to have steaks on board, but even if poisoned meat is out, there has to be another way for us to defeat them. We ought to have a signal, so we don't inadvertently block each other's moves. I don't think a kiss will do in this case."

Amara quickly provided an alternative. "I'll call you Guardian, rather than use your name, and you refer to me as Lieutenant Greer, but this can't possibly be as easy as getting away from the Corkscrews, so don't be reckless."

Tynan shook his head. "If you think I'll let us be kidnapped by pirates without trying my best to foil their plans, then you don't know me very well. I realize they might not be receptive to cleverly worded arguments, but that's where I'll start. Then, we'll exploit whatever opportunity presents itself to escape."

"I'm afraid I'm forcing you to compromise your ideals."

While they could scarcely be worse off, Tynan couldn't help but laugh. "Not at all. I've no intention of becoming a martyr on the way to a peace conference. Is there any chance those subliminal tapes will influence us to cooperate with the pirates rather than the other way around?"

"No, because I've warned you the tapes are playing, and you're clever enough to block their message. Of course, pretending to be cooperative can't hurt us."

Before Tynan could reply, the hatch swung open. After a lengthy delay, during which they heard several men arguing heatedly about which one would be the first to enter the Starcruiser, a heavy-set individual, his bald head covered with a wool cap pulled down to his eyebrows, came barreling into the passenger cabin. He was dressed in ragged combat fatigues in shades of faded browns and oranges, and reeked of sweat.

Amara stepped forward to meet him. "You have illegally boarded an Alado vessel engaged in a vital diplomatic mission. That is an error which will have severe consequences for you and your crew. Summon your captain immediately, so that we can deal with this blunder before it becomes any worse."

Tynan knew just how terrified Amara was, yet there was no sign of fear in her manner now. He listened in amazed silence as she berated the pirate as though she were in control of the situation rather than he. She was displaying the same courageous attitude he had admired when she had walked into the great hall of the Keep for dinner, and he was doubly impressed now. Unfortunately, the pirate wasn't.

He held a laser pistol on Tynan and Amara while he searched for additional passengers. Finding none, called over his shoulder, "Come look what we've got here, Toes—a priest and a mouthy pilot to replace that whore Monro skewered last week."

Toes was as shabbily dressed as the first man, but his tastes ran to brilliant colors and his wool cap barely tamed his frizzy blond hair. Lean rather than corpulent, he held a metallic canister he shook like a maraca with every step. Following the tradition of an Indian shaman blessing a site with a sacred rattle, he walked all through the ship to the accompaniment of his own softly thudding rhythm before circling Amara and Tynan three times. Apparently satisfied that the pair provided no physical threat, he returned to the hatch and waved another man through.

This fellow entered the cockpit first, then joined the others in the passenger cabin. Short, he carried himself with a stiff-shouldered dodging gait as though he had spent so many years shadow boxing in a cell, he had forgotten any other way to move. He was dressed in splendid fashion in an elegantly tailored blue flightsuit accented with a long blue and green plaid scarf draped across his shoulders, but he was no cleaner than his mates, and his dark hair fell in greasy curls.

He lacked even one attractive feature. Thick brows met above heavy-lidded brown eyes, and a drooping mustache framed thin lips. In his right hand, he carried a gardenia branch bearing three deeply fragrant blossoms which he lifted to his large, hooked nose as he studied Amara and Tynan. When he spoke, the gap where his left central incisor should have been gave him a whistling lisp that made his speech difficult to understand.

"I am Mak Trumbo," he announced proudly, "and you are now my prisoners."

189

"I think not," Amara countered confidently. "This is a diplomatic mission, and your interference will cost you dearly unless you free us now."

Startled by that unexpectedly defiant retort, Mak frowned slightly, then shouted. "Monro!"

In answer to his call, a man wearing a worn and patched khaki flightsuit appeared. His red hair was braided in half a dozen haphazard pigtails that bounced this way and that as he came forward. Blind in one eye, he squinted for a better look at the captives. Tynan had thrown his hood forward to shadow his face, so Monro couldn't see much of him, but he broke into a wide grin when he focused his attention on Amara.

"Want me to look after the woman, captain?"

Unable to turn his head easily, Mak swung his whole body around to face Monro, then pivoted back to gaze at his captives. "You'd like that wouldn't you, Monro? We'll see, but for the moment, I'm more interested in the priest. Would you hear our confessions, father? I'm sure we could describe sins you didn't even know existed." Mak laughed at his own humor, and his men quickly joined while Toes kept time with his peculiar rattle.

Tynan towered above Mak, but deliberately kept his manner non-threatening as he explained just who he was and where he and Amara were bound. For him, peace held a mystical appeal, but knowing it could not be among a pirate's ideals, he presented a purely practical argument. "You've attempted to hijack the wrong vessel," he argued persuasively. "If I don't arrive at the peace conference on time, war may break out, and once Alado fully arms its fleet, pirates will be the first to die."

Mak took a step closer to Amara and gestured toward her companion. "What makes you two think you can threaten me?"

Amara had never heard of Mak Trumbo, but that did not mean that he wasn't dangerous. "What Tynan says is correct. If there's war, the usual treaties covering arrests and trials will be suspended. There will be huge rewards for killing pirates, and if we suffer even the slightest harm, every ship in Alado's fleet will be out searching for you. We protect our own."

Mak danced the gardenia sprig across Amara's cheek and laughed when she flinched. "If this man were half as important as he claims, he would be traveling with a private guard, and there would be Banshees flying escort." Apparently growing bored, Mak again inhaled the gardenias' perfume, then sank into the nearest seat. Relaxing completely, he stretched out his arms and legs.

"Yesterday, we hijacked a ship filled with botanical specimens. Its crew had a far more amusing story. Didn't they, men?"

Again, the three pirates laughed uproariously, but the mirth didn't extend to their eyes. They were all watching Amara with a hungry gaze that left no room for a merry sparkle. Monro raised his hand to wipe the drool from the corner of his mouth and winked at her with his good eye.

Disgusted by the trio's lewd glances, Tynan concentrated on their captain. "Should we fail to arrive at the Confederation base on time, the bounty on your head will be so high that your own men will turn you in to collect it. I doubt they'd bother handing you over alive either."

"Threats." Mak waved a lazy figure eight in the air with the gardenia branch. "I can't believe I'm hearing threats from people in no position to make them."

"If you choose to see the truth as a threat, that's your option. Or is it simply that you'd prefer to contribute to the start of a war in which you'll surely die rather than admit, in front of your crew, that you've made a grave error?"

Tynan had pushed Mak too far, and the pirate leaped from his seat. "It is you who've made the error!" he shouted up at him. "You've missed the entire point! The peace conference will never succeed. War is inevitable, and this Starcruiser is worth a fortune to Alado's competition."

"This ship will bring nothing compared to what you'll receive in ransom for Tynan Thorn," Amara was quick to interject. "Even the most ignorant pirate ought to appreciate his value as a hostage."

Losing patience with her as well, Mak stepped close. "You don't understand either," he accused her in his strange halting lisp. "I'm a businessman. My only concern is profit, and there's no profit in peace. You two bore me. Tie them up in the cockpit, Monro, and get some of the others to clean out the galley. We haven't had a good meal in weeks."

Monro grabbed for Amara. Pulling a length of cord from a pocket, he bound her hands behind her. Although she offered no resistance, he pulled her along with a bruising grasp. Rather than place her in her seat, he shoved her down into the narrow space behind it. After he had tied her ankles together, he gave her breasts a rude squeeze and then ran his hand over her legs. She stared at him coldly.

"You've got spirit," he complimented her. "Even after Mak finishes with you, there'll be enough left for me to tame." Toes brought Tynan into the cockpit then, and Monro had to move to get out of his way. "Put him in the co-pilot's seat and gag the bastard."

Toes shoved the canister he had been shaking under his arm while he tied Tynan to the seat with his rope belt, but he resumed rattling it while he and Monro searched for something to use as a gag. Neither of them could produce a piece of cloth, so Toes went and got one from Mak. When he returned, he dropped his homemade maraca in Tynan's lap while he twisted the cloth into a tight strip. Pushing back Tynan's hood, he wrapped it around his neck rather than over his mouth, and pulled it taut.

"I'd like to finish you off now," he whispered, "but Mak always makes us draw lots for kills. Maybe I'll be lucky later." He placed a slimy kiss on Tynan's ear, and then shook out the gag and covered the philosopher's mouth. "What about the bitch?" he asked. "Shouldn't we gag her too?"

"No, let's save ourselves the trouble of undoing it if we have a chance to sneak in here later. Now come on, let's hurry or we won't get the best of the food." Monro started to go, then turned back to Amara. "Don't worry, I'll give you something to eat later." He poked Toes in the ribs, and the men's ribald laughter made it plain what he had in mind.

Amara stared up at them with a disgusted glance, but she was sickened by the thought of what she

193

might have to do to stay alive. She waited until they had gone and called to Steve, but there was no answer. Mak Trumbo had been in the cockpit, and Amara's heart fell as she realized that he must have disconnected the computer. The emergency procedures had already been activated though, and the ship would still be transmitting a distress signal. She rested her head against the back of the pilot's seat and tried to think calmly.

"They made their first mistake putting us together," she whispered. "They're sure to make more."

Tynan turned his head, but the back of his seat blocked his view and he couldn't see her. He hadn't really expected Mak Trumbo to release them, but he was deeply disturbed by the pirate's comment that war was a foregone conclusion. Was Mak only assuming that one of Alado's rival corporations would be eager to gain a Starcruiser, or had one of them actually commissioned the pirate to hijack one? When he had agreed to serve as a negotiator, he had never imagined just how much intrigue might be involved.

Toes's rattle still lay in his lap and although Tynan expected him to return for it at any second, he began to pull against the rope that held him. The belt had been new, so he had no hope of finding a frayed spot that he could work on until it tore. He leaned forward in an effort to scrape off his gag against the ropes wound around his wrists, but his arms were so firmly pinned to the armrests, he couldn't lean over far enough to reach them.

Trapped, he began to wonder about the contents of Toes's maraca. Whatever they were, they made a dull, rumbling sound when shaken so the canister couldn't be filled with pebbles, beads, or beans. Attempting to imagine a pirate's life, and what objects he would come across, Tynan finally decided it might be filled with corks taken from looted wine bottles.

When the seatbelt buckle caught his eye, he put an abrupt end to such idle musings. It was lying against the armrest. Steadying it with pressure from his knee, he tried to move it into a position where he could rub the rope looped over his left wrist against its edge. It was an agonizingly slow process, and he glanced about the cockpit searching for another method of escape. But even if there had been knives and scissors lying about, he wouldn't have been able to reach them.

Sick with guilt as well as dread, Amara replayed the pirates' seizure of their ship again and again in her mind, and each time she came to the same sorry conclusion—an alert pilot would not have fallen victim to such a ridiculous band. She should have been in the cockpit, where she could have adjusted the Starcruiser's angle of flight every few minutes to compensate for the missing scanners. She could also have inverted the ship periodically so the fully functioning port scanners could sweep the starboard sector.

Thoroughly miserable, she was certain there must be a great many creative ways she could have handled the problem. She ought to have been able to protect not only her ship, but Tynan Thorn. It was failing him that caused her the most pain. When she had left Fleet Command, she had been so angry with Orion that she had promised herself she would never again blur the line separating her personal life and the performance of her job. She had never dreamed breaking that vow would cost her so dearly.

"I'm sorry, Tynan. We spent too much time talking about the conference, when I should have been concentrating all my efforts on just getting you there. You questioned whether I was more pilot than woman. Well, we have the answer, and it's been tragic for us both." Catching the scent of gardenias, and fearing Mak Trumbo would overhear, Amara fell silent.

Mak entered the cockpit, dismissed Tynan with a glance, and knelt down in front of Amara. "My men are a crude lot, but you needn't fear I'll let them near you. Unless, of course, you would prefer them to me. If so, I'll allow all forty-six of them to share you. Would you like that?" When Amara refused to look him in the eye, Mak grabbed her chin to force her.

"They have a delicious array of brutish perversions and would undoubtedly be inspired to develop a few more with someone so lovely as you. Unfortunately, our female captives never live long. I'm ashamed to admit some of my men have proven to be inept guards where women are concerned and have allowed more than one to take her own life, but I suspect they are the ones who actually prefer their women dead. Then there is Toes, who is satisfied with little bits and pieces of pretty girls."

Mak released her, rose, and tossed the gardenias into her lap. "Take your time to consider your choices."

"What choices did you give the botanists?"

Mak tugged on the end of his mustache. "They weren't nearly as attractive as you and had no choices at all. In fact, I didn't even ask them for their last requests." Again amused by his own humor, Mak laughed as he swung around to look at Tynan. Not having seen him without his hood earlier, he was shocked to find him such a handsome man and stopped to stare. He then leaned down and sniffed his robe.

"I mistook you for a holy man, but you reek of *her*." Obviously disgusted, he reached into one of his pockets and withdrew a jeweled knife. A flick of his wrist produced a razor-sharp blade, and he pressed the edge to Tynan's cheek. "I think I'll cut you each time I take her. It may be only a slight nick like this," he boasted, drawing blood. "Or, I might pluck out an eye or slice off an ear."

"Alado will pay a fortune for him in ransom!" Amara swore again. "You mustn't harm him."

"Just listen to her, Thorn," Mak urged in his distinctive whisper. He closed his knife and slipped it back into his pocket. "She'll do whatever I want to protect you. Isn't that touching? Would you like to watch? I once tied a captain to his bunk, then tossed his wife across him and raped her an astonishing number of times even for me. The poor soul was quite mad by the time I finished with them both, but it was wonderfully amusing while it lasted."

Savoring the memory, Mak closed his eyes for a moment. "There's nothing quite so satisfying as listening to a woman beg for her lover's life. The silly creatures have absolutely no shame. They'll promise anything with great, gurgling sobs, and I always make them keep their word." Mak broke into a hilarious giggle. "And then they actually expect me to keep mine!"

Sickened clear through, Tynan was convinced Mak wasn't making up his gruesome tales, but heartlessly boasting of actual atrocities. Glancing down at the rattle in his lap, he was now positive that rather than old corks, it contained a truly ghastly collection of withered souvenirs.

He had known that really evil people existed, but the harmony in the Keep certainly hadn't prepared him to meet one. The ageless quest for truth and beauty had no meaning for Mak Trumbo, and Tynan vowed to beat him in the violent arena in which pirates played. All he had to do was get loose.

Disappointed that Tynan had showed no more fear than Amara, Mak grew bored with taunting him. "I've transferred most of your rations to my ship, and I'll come back when we've finished enjoying them. Until then, my pretty pets, I'll leave you with your thoughts."

As soon as they were alone, Amara again spoke to Tynan. "Don't believe a word he says; he's just trying to frighten us."

The gag prevented Tynan from arguing, but he disagreed. He yanked on the ropes binding him, gained no slack, and went back to scraping the tightly woven cord against the buckle.

Despite her words of encouragement, Amara had believed Mak too. Fearing he might not have the sense to ransom them, she twisted her hands, tugged on the cord looped around her wrists, and was badly discouraged when it remained securely knotted. Monro certainly knew how to tie up a hostage. She hoped he wouldn't soon return to display some of his other undoubtedly odious skills. Seated beside the compartment containing the emergency supplies, she focused her attention on how to gain access to them. But what good would they do, she agonized, when she and Tynan were so badly outnumbered?

"Tynan? We can't break the connection between the two ships from this side, so that means we'll have to wait for the pirates to do it. Somehow we'll have to keep Mak from splitting us up before that happens. If he really does like to force men to watch him rape their women, then it will work in our favor. Oh, I know that sounds horrible, but we'll have to turn everything, no matter how dreadful, to our own advantage."

Tynan shut out the hideous mental images Amara's words inspired and kept grinding away on the rope. All he had to show for his efforts was a slight crease, but he regarded that as slow but steady progress. If he could break free, then the next time Mak entered the cockpit, they could take him hostage, force the pirates to return to their ship, break the connection, and use the laser cannons to blast them all to the lower rungs of hell.

There were two problems with that plan, however. First he had to succeed at cutting through the rope, and second, Mak Trumbo's men had to regard their captain's life highly enough to meet his and Amara's demands. At that thought, Tynan slumped back in his seat. They had met only three of Mak's crew, and none had impressed him as models of obedience and loyalty. They followed Mak's orders out of fear, and if the pirate captain were himself taken prisoner, he doubted they would care. Still, until he thought of a better plan, he would keep sawing away on the rope.

Praying Mak had an enormous appetite, Amara hoped he would be gone for several hours. But all too quickly he returned. He staggered slightly and reached out to grab the back of the co-pilot's seat to steady himself. As she looked up, she sent him Alado's telepathic message designed to create feelings of blissful harmony, but his only reaction was a slight shake of his head as though he were being troubled by an annoying insect. There were no intoxicating substances on board the Starcruiser, but he had apparently been liberally sampling his own supply.

Undaunted, Amara took another tack. "When you have such high hopes for selling this ship, it's a shame you're too drunk to fly it. Or am I giving you too much credit? Maybe you've no idea how to pilot any ship, let alone a Starcruiser."

Mak leaned down to pluck the spray of gardenias from her lap and promptly whacked her across the face, leaving a welt on her right cheek and dislodging one of the fragrant blossoms before waving it for emphasis. "I've never been boarded, lieutenant," he slurred. "I guess that proves who's the best pilot."

"True, I was careless, but that's not a failing shared by Alado's other pilots. A rescue force is on its way. If you haven't asked for a ransom, do so now."

Mak lurched around to face Tynan. "Is she always so demanding? Some men find that exciting in a woman, but I like my women eager to please. Was she eager to please you?"

Tynan would have gladly drawn Mak's attention to himself to spare Amara the pirate's abuse, but bound and gagged, he had no idea how to go about it. He would not have satisfied Mak's curiosity even if he had been able to speak, however, and he glanced away. At the same time, he raised his knee to conceal the buckle he had been using in the folds of his robe. In the process, Toes's canister rolled off his lap.

Insulted, Mak grabbed a handful of Tynan's hair and jerked his head around. "I'm talking to you!" he shouted. "Nod or shake your head, but you answer every question I ask or it will cost you your tongue!"

"Stop threatening him!" Amara implored.

"I will threaten whomever I please!" Mak continued to stare down at Tynan. "Now answer me. Is the lieutenant so eager to have a taste of you that she'd crawl right under that robe to get it?"

Tynan raised his brows as though such a passionate response were extremely doubtful, and Mak gave a deep roaring laugh. "You have to make them beg for it." He slurred his advice, but clearly believed it. "Take whatever you want, but make them beg for it."

"You can have any woman you want after you ransom us," Amara called out.

Mak winked at Tynan, then slapped him on the shoulder. "I already have the woman I want." He shoved off against the back of Tynan's seat, bent down to cut the cord binding Amara's ankles, and, barely able to stand himself, pulled her upright. He then raised his hands as though he had just remembered something.

"I almost forgot; I gave you a choice. Which is it? Me, or the other forty-six men?"

Amara's glance was filled with hatred. "You."

Mak grabbed hold of her arm, but paused to speak to Tynan. "You see? You have to make them beg for it." He pushed Amara ahead of him and shoved her into the passenger cabin.

Seething, Tynan could easily understand how another of Mak's victims had lost his mind watching his wife being abused, but rather than imagine that horror, he began mentally composing a list of possible ways to kill the pirate as soon as he broke free.

Chapter Eleven

In addition to the three pirates Amara had seen earlier, five more of Mak Trumbo's men were sprawled around the passenger cabin. Several were either asleep or passed out, while the others were arguing over the way the profits from the sale of the Starcruiser ought to be divided. The difference in opinion prompted one burly brute to swing a lazy punch at Toes, who easily ducked the blow and drew a knife.

"Enough!" Mak shouted, and his angry scowl prompted Toes to return the weapon to his pocket. "There'll be no profits to divide if we don't make delivery. Monro, you'll be in command of our ship. Toes and I will follow in the Starcruiser."

"And the woman?" Monro asked.

Mak had a tight grasp on Amara's arm, and for one terrible moment she feared he might shove her toward the pig-tailed brute. She held her breath and focused on Mak's ridiculous lisp, which rendered the word Starcruiser nearly incomprehensible. He was an absurd individual, but dangerous, and despite Tynan's attempts to convince her otherwise, she knew she had only herself to blame for their capture.

Mak tightened his grasp on Amara's arm until he knew she had to be suffering, but not even a glimmer of distress showed in her expression. His passions inflamed by her stubborn show of indifference, he flashed a taunting grin. "No, she stays here with us. Now go. We've already wasted far too much time."

The pirates who were still reasonably alert rousted their stuporous companions and dragged them out. Knowing it was important to be able to identify them, Amara memorized their faces. Their crimes showed in their numerous scars and devious gazes, and none would ever be mistaken for anything other than the lawless jackal he was. Toes secured the hatch behind the last man, then began to look around.

"Where's my shaker?" he asked.

"Cockpit," Mak replied. "Go get it and stay there until I call you."

Amara had never intentionally harmed anyone, but as soon as she felt the slightly jarring jolt signaling the break in the connection between her ship and Mak's, a strange exhilaration took hold. This would surely be Mak Trumbo's last flight. When he grabbed her hair and yanked her head back, she scarcely felt the pain.

Inside the cockpit, Toes spotted his canister lying at Tynan's feet and leaned across him to get it. Repulsed, Tynan pulled back, but when he recognized the outline of a knife in the man's hip pocket, he raised his legs to bump him off balance. Toes lurched forward, striking the instrument panel, and before he could steady himself, Tynan had slipped his left leg over the pirate's head to capture his neck in a powerful knee lock. He crossed his ankles to increase the pressure and watched Toes's frantic attempts to break free without the slightest feelings of pity.

The pirate tried to go for his knife, but with his arm pinned back against Tynan's chest, he couldn't reach it. His cries were choked off by lack of oxygen and smothered in the folds of Tynan's robe. Gradually, his agonized moans grew increasingly faint. Tynan had felt a vibration, less intense, but similar to the one that had pulsed through the Starcruiser when the pirates had overtaken them, and he hoped that meant they had broken the link. He understood Amara's reasons for waiting until the ship had been released to begin their fight, and he hoped he had not hampered their efforts by striking too soon. Knowing Amara was with Mak Trumbo was such excruciating torture, however, that he could not pass up what might be his only chance to rescue her.

Determined to succeed, he didn't relax the pressure on Toes's neck until after the pirate had gone limp. The next challenge was to jostle the body so that Tynan could reach the knife despite his bound wrists. That took almost as long as it had to render Toes unconscious. Once Tynan was able to grasp the knife and open it, he maneuvered the blade under the rope and, using short, upward jabs, sliced through it.

It was then a simple matter to free his left wrist. He rolled Toes off his lap and stood. His arms ached from lack of circulation, and his back and neck from the strain of trying to break free. He clenched his fists and shook his arms before bending down to check for a pulse at the base of Toes's neck. Tynan had meant to kill the pirate, but when he realized that he actually had, he felt sick. But there would be time later to deal with his feelings of remorse, and for now he left Toes in a heap where he had fallen.

Not knowing how many men would be in the passenger cabin with Amara, he steeled himself for the very worst, but when he moved into position to gain a clear view, he saw only Mak Trumbo. Mak had stripped off Amara's flightsuit and freed her hair of the confining coil, but even the wild disorder of her curls didn't disguise the damage that had been done to her face. Blackened, her eyes were too swollen to see Tynan over Mak's shoulder, and when Mak struck her again before forcing her face down over the nearest seat, she couldn't see anything at all. Eager to rape her, Mak fumbled to open the front of his flightsuit and also failed to note Tynan's approach.

Tynan still held Toes's knife, but he tossed it away and struck the pirate captain at the base of the skull with a vicious chop that snapped the vertebrae with an audible crack. His neck shattered, Trumbo's body quivered with convulsive jerks. He fell in a slow spiral, recognized his killer with his last conscious thought, then slid down Tynan's robe and lay dead across his boots. Tynan shoved his body aside with a disgusted kick and gathered up Amara in his arms.

It was the softness of Tynan's robe that finally assured her that she was safe. "I'm sorry," she whispered.

Tynan brushed her curls away from her face and was grateful she had suffered only two badly blackened eyes, but an apology was such an unlikely response that it struck him as incoherent. He reached out to recline two seats to provide them a much-needed bed. He joined her on it, intending only to offer soothing words and tender caresses. He kissed away her tears, but rather than relax, Amara writhed beneath him, her body silently singing to his with an ageless yearning.

Tynan ached with longing, but hesitated to express his desire until Amara sought his lips for what became a wildly rapturous exchange. That she would still want him after the abuse she had suffered dissolved his reserve and inspired him to renew the bond passion had forged between them. Unwilling to leave her embrace even to remove his robe, he simply drew it up out of his way. Frustrated by that brief delay, Amara called his name in an urgent gasp.

He gripped her left knee, wrapping her leg around him, and the warmth of her bare skin against the softness of his robe was almost painfully sweet. He eased forward carefully, and with exquisite tenderness sheathed himself in her inner heat. As that delicious fire burned away the last of his reason, he laced his fingers in hers, pushing her down into their bed as he thrust his hips slowly

207

at first, gently, adoringly, but gradually gathering momentum until he was keeping time with the thunderous beat of his heart. He wanted to drive so deep that they could never be parted.

Amara's head was turned, her bruises masked with golden curls, but her lips still beckoned with a honeyed sweetness. After sampling them, Tynan imagined the shores of paradise etched on her foam-kissed breasts. As she tilted her hips to draw him down, he could feel the splendor of the celestial tides cresting within him until they at last burst forth, drenching them both in a blinding spray of ecstasy.

Awash in that heavenly triumph, Tynan would have savored the delectable contentment that filled him, but all too soon Amara struggled to break free. "What's wrong? Have I hurt you?" he asked.

Struggling to stand, Amara clung to the back of the adjacent seat and tried to calm the dizzying waves inside her head. "Where's Toes?" she whispered.

"I killed him."

Amara nodded. That detail accounted for, she tried to walk to the lavatory, but when it became obvious to Tynan that she couldn't make it on her own, he rushed to her side. She clutched his robe and begged, "Help me."

"Anything. Just tell me what you need."

"I'm going to be sick."

Tynan swung her up into his arms and carried her to the lavatory. He held her as she vomited and then stripped off his clothes to join her in the shower. He pulled her back against his chest so she would be in no danger of falling while the fine spray washed away what he hoped was the memory of Mak's loathsome touch rather than his own caress. He waited with her until they were dry, then found the compartment containing her clothes and helped her into lilac lingerie and a clean flightsuit before donning a flightsuit of his own.

Her hair a mass of damp ringlets, Amara resembled a battered child rather than the fine pilot she was. "I can't see very well," she confessed. "You'll have to help me again."

"Of course. Tell me what to do."

"Let's go up to the cockpit."

Again, Tynan carried her. He stepped over Toes's body to place her in her seat, then dragged the pirate out into the passenger cabin. He picked up Toes's rattle, but not even tempted to examine its contents, he placed it in the dead man's hands. He then took the co-pilot's seat. "What's next?"

"You'll have to tell me how you got free later, but right now, we have to take care of the pirates before they get suspicious about who's flying this ship and board us again." She leaned forward, and after feeling around the control panel, finally tripped a switch. "Steve?"

"Yes, lieutenant?"

"You missed all the fun. Activate the laser cannons and give me a target grid."

Amara turned toward Tynan, but she could only make out the black blotch of his hair and the golden smear of his flightsuit. "I've been authorized to use deadly force to protect you," she explained in a halting whisper. "File a protest if you must, but I can't let Trumbo's men live to attack us again."

"I'm not going to protest; I'm going to cheer. Let's do it."

"Steve, bring us within range. I hope there's no more than one ship ahead."

"The scanners report only one, lieutenant, a PJC Tomahawk."

Tynan leaned forward to study the image on the screen. "My God, that thing's huge!"

"Wave it good-bye. This will be just like a real live game of Banshee Quest. Damn, but I wish I could see better! Target the engines, Steve."

Amara waited for the computer to lock in on the pirates' vessel and then fired the cannon in a series of repeated bursts that ripped through the Tomahawk's engines and blew the ship into a thousand flaming fragments that burned with an eerie glow and then faded into the blackness of space. "Dust to dust," she murmured. "Take us off emergency mode, Steve. Replot our course for the Confederation base and notify Fleet Command we've survived the boarding and will return with two of the pirates' bodies. I want whatever help they've sent to continue as our escort. I've been injured, possible concussion. This is your ship until I say otherwise."

"Do you require immediate medical assistance, lieutenant?"

"Let's hope not. We've been up all night and I'm going to sleep."

"Sleep is not advised with head injuries."

"Thank you, Steve. Good night."

Amara closed her eyes, and Tynan thought she might already have fallen asleep. He reached out and shook her arm. "He's right. Try and stay awake long enough for us to be certain you're not more seriously injured than we think."

Amara could only open one eye, and when that didn't really help her see, she closed it. "What medical training do you have?"

"None."

"Then if I'm going to die of head injuries, I might just as well do it in my sleep because there's nothing we can do to prevent it. Just leave me here. Steve will get you to the conference if I don't make it."

"No!" Tynan shouted with a force that reverberated in the instrument-laden cockpit with a lingering hum. "You're not going to die until you're a very old woman with hundreds of great-grandchildren." He scooped her up and carried her back to their bed and put her down. "Now just rest, but try and stay awake while I tend to the bodies."

As he turned away, Amara reached out to catch his sleeve. "There are body bags in the emergency supplies. Look in the locker behind the pilot's seat."

"Thank you." Tynan turned back to kiss her forehead and then went about his grisly chore, separating a few of the pirates' personal effects for clues to their identity. The instructions on the body bags indicated that once filled and sealed, they would preserve a corpse indefinitely, but Tynan would have much preferred to send Mak and Toes off into the void with their companions. He had heard Trumbo threaten Amara with a crew of forty-six. Counting Mak, that meant Amara and he had just sent forty-seven men to their deaths.

He could readily imagine a press release describing him as a noted pacifist, and then going on to detail how he had been responsible for the deaths of nearly fifty men on his way to the conference. He sat back and stared at the neatly packaged pirates. They had behaved like vermin rather than men, and that he and Amara had had to endure even a minute of their insufferable company sickened him thoroughly. He had truly expected to feel remorse when the danger was past, but he didn't, not a bit. He felt only relief.

A quick survey of the ship prompted him to deposit the bodies in an alcove behind the galley. Then, recalling that Mak had ordered his men to clean out the meals, he quickly opened the bins. In a surprising show of forethought, Mak had left enough food on board to provide rations for the four of them for a couple of days, but no more. Tynan laid the packages on the counter, arranged them in rows, then in possible combinations of meals, but it was plain they were going to be awfully hungry by the time they reached the Confederation base.

Not wanting to worry Amara, he didn't refer to their lack of provisions when he returned to her. She was curled up on her side, but answered when he knelt beside her and called her name. "How do you feel?" he asked.

"Past caring."

"At least you're still awake. That's got to be a good sign."

"Not when we've been up all night. I've made a miserable mess of this whole flight, Tynan. I know I promised to be your pilot on your return to Earth, but when my boss reviews the log, I'll probably be demoted to records clerk and never allowed to fly again."

Tynan gave her a slow, sweet kiss to silence her complaints. "Stop it. I intend to use whatever influence I have with Alado to see that you're commended for heroism. This voyage won't be your last."

Unwilling to hope for anything better than disgrace, Amara sighed sadly. She dimly recalled Tynan mentioning her great-grandchildren, but he had referred to them as hers, not theirs. She didn't feel brave. She felt small, weak, and very much alone. Tears welled up in her swollen eyes and spilled over her lashes.

Thinking she must be in pain, Tynan took her hand. "I found the medical supplies in the emergency equipment. What can you take for pain?"

Amara's head hurt so badly that even if her eyes hadn't been swollen shut she knew she wouldn't have been able to see. "I couldn't keep it down," she replied. There was no remedy for the sadness that gripped her soul, however, and she truly did believe that her once-splendid career was definitely over. Alado was a wonderfully generous corporation, but they had no tolerance for pilots who became so enamored of their passengers that they foolishly put their lives and an expensive ship at risk.

"At least we saved you, didn't we?"

Her question held such a wistful note that Tynan grew frightened. "Don't you dare die on me!"

"No, I'm not going to die. I'm not that lucky."

Certain she was incoherent now, Tynan again joined her on the bed and kept her talking until they were both so tired that sleep could no longer be delayed. When Tynan awoke hours later, he was sufficiently cheered by the steady rhythm of Amara's breathing to believe her injuries weren't life-threatening. She was cuddled against him, and he rubbed his hand up and down her back, content merely to touch her for the moment. She leaned into his caress, but didn't wake. Hoping she would sleep until she felt better, he got up to have something to eat.

The pirates had apparently shared his contempt for a vegetarian diet and had left the cereals, but the fruit and yogurt Amara ate were gone, as was most of the juice. Tynan had become deeply worried before he recalled Amara's mention of emergency rations. Hoping they hadn't been confiscated as well, he went up to the cockpit and opened the locker where he had found the body bags. He removed the medical supplies, two laser pistols, an inflatable raft complete with paddles, climbing gear, and in the rear of the compartment, containers of water and packages of high-energy protein bars.

Although discouraged that there wasn't anything more appetizing, he opened one, took a bite, and found it crunchy-sweet with the taste of honey and almonds. Or at least, he thought that's what it contained. It wasn't at all bad, until he considered they would soon be reduced to eating them three times a day. Ashamed for not simply being grateful for being alive, Tynan carried the emergency rations back to the galley and put them away. The water containers he left on the counter, and out of things to do, he paced the aisle, hoping the whole time that Amara's bruises would soon fade.

He wanted them to arrive at the Confederation base looking their best and able to concentrate on the deliberations, but he now expected the process to be far more difficult than he had first anticipated. With Amara's help, he now had a better idea of the other representatives' goals, but their adventuresome trip had provided him with far more valuable insights into himself.

Perhaps his worth as a negotiator had been irrevocably compromised when they had resorted to violence to win their freedom, first from Dr. Cortez, then from Mak Trumbo. Or, perhaps his position would be strengthened when their wild exploits became known. He certainly felt changed, and it wasn't as a result of the gradual accumulation of knowledge as it had been in the Keep, but from practical experience brought on by necessity.

Except, of course, for the part Amara had had in furthering his education. That delicious memory made him smile, and missing her very badly, he paused in his pacing to find her observing him. At least, she appeared to be trying to look up at him.

"How do you feel?"

Amara tried to sit up, then quickly lay back down. "Better," she lied.

"I've never taken care of anyone," Tynan confessed. "I've never even owned a pet. Please let me know if I'm forgetting something important. Do you need to use the lavatory? Are you thirsty, hungry?"

"I'm your escort, remember?"

Tynan knelt by her side. "I know, but now it's time for me to be yours."

Amara reached out to caress his cheek and felt the cut Mak had inflicted. "You were hurt?"

"It's only a scratch." Tynan kissed her palm, and his heart swelling with emotion, he kept hold of her hand. She had become so dear to him, and he couldn't keep his feelings secret. "You cautioned me before that we haven't known each other long, but so much has happened to us since we left the Keep that time no longer has any real significance. I love you, Amara, I really do."

Amara knew she must look every bit as wretched as she felt, but she was deeply touched by his words even if she didn't believe them. "I'm the only woman you know, Tynan."

"So what? I could meet a thousand women, and it wouldn't change how I feel about you."

"Sex is new to you, but you mustn't mistake physical pleasure for love," she warned.

Insulted, Tynan drew back slightly. "I can understand how sex and love can be separate, but they don't have to be."

"No, ideally they're one, but all too often people are heartbroken to discover what they regarded as love was only pleasurable sex to their partner." Amara had thought she had learned that painful lesson long ago, but Orion Chaudet had provided an unwanted refresher course. "Then they feel betrayed, and rightly so. I don't want that to happen to you."

"What are you saying—that you don't feel anything for me but desire? Were you teasing when you called me your first love?"

"No. I really do care for you, but right now, I don't feel anything other than sick. Could we

216

please discuss this another time?"

Tynan understood; she cared for him, and perhaps a great deal, but not enough to make promises. Bitterly disappointed, he dropped her hand and rose to his feet. "I'm sorry if I spoke too soon."

Amara heard the anguish in his voice and wanted to draw him down beside her, but instead she summoned what little will power she possessed where he was concerned, overruled her heart, and let him turn away.

Tynan remained attentive, but displayed a gentlemanly reserve for the rest of the day. In late afternoon, they were intercepted by two Starcruisers dispatched from Fleet Command, and he had to help Amara up to the cockpit to speak with their pilots. They were friends, Piper Giles and Glen Archer, who greeted her with anxious questions about her ordeal.

"We survived, but I'm sure glad to see you," she exclaimed, although she couldn't make out more than shadows on the computer screen. "We've lost some time, but if the Secretary gives a lengthy welcoming address, we'll still make the opening ceremonies on time."

"I'm sure he knows that you expect his best."

Seated right beside her, Amara knew Tynan could hear the sarcastic accent to that comment and put an immediate end to the teasing by reporting the inoperable scanners and asking for constant surveillance for their starboard sector. As soon as the request was acknowledged, she ended the transmission. "They'll provide an escort the rest of the way," she assured Tynan.

"I just wish they had been with us from the beginning."

"So do I. Is the Secretary a special friend of yours?"

Amara had been expecting that question, but that didn't make it any easier to answer. "Not anymore he isn't."

Amara spoke with such fervent conviction that Tynan didn't doubt her, and yet he couldn't seem to stop himself from making an issue of it. "Even with my limited experience, I know it's unwise to become romantically involved with a superior. It makes for all kinds of problems from simple jealousy among co-workers to charges of favoritism."

"That's true, and I have every intention of avoiding that danger in the future."

"Is that why you don't want to work with me?"

"No," Amara responded much too quickly.

Surprised, Tynan leaned closer. Amara was looking straight at him, but her gaze was blank. He didn't want to frighten her, but the possibility that Mak might have permanently damaged her vision terrified him. "How much can you see?" he asked.

"Not much. Everything's blurred—double vision I believe it's called. It should clear up soon."

"Well, if you don't have perfect vision, Alado won't let you fly, so you might just as well volunteer to work with me until you recover, since you won't have anything else to keep you busy."

Amara leaned back in her seat and closed her eyes. "I do believe you're the most tenacious person I've ever met, but I've asked you to wait, so please don't press me about it."

"What if we wait, and the Secretary refuses to allow you to work with me? Just because you're through with him doesn't mean he'll step out of your life graciously. What am I going to do if he objects and assigns me several male assistants rather than the woman I want?"

"I don't know whether it's this discussion, or being struck so many times, but I'm beginning to feel ill again."

"Just answer my question and I'll help you back to the lavatory. If your mind's already made up, and you don't want to see me again after we dock at Confederation base, just say so now. Don't let me go on hoping there's a chance we'll stay together if you already know that's not what you want. Lovers, even those who don't care all that much for each other, ought to be honest with each other. At least I think they should be."

Amara could have reflected upon the concept of honesty for days and not been prompted to confess that she wanted to stay with him forever, because that wasn't even a possibility. "I'm not going to be any help at all if I can't see well enough to read transcripts and make notes. An assistant you have to lead around wouldn't be any help at all."

"I disagree, but if you need medical treatment, that will have to be our first priority. I won't ask you to work with me if it will put your health at risk. You're right—I am tenacious, but that's a quality I ought to save for the conference rather than practice on you. Here, let me give you a hand."

"No, I can walk now. I'm sure I can." Holding on to the backs of the seats, Amara made her way very slowly to her bed, but not really comfortable resting again, she soon went back to the lavatory. She could remember bathing earlier, but didn't feel clean. Bracing herself against the shower, she removed her flightsuit and lingerie with agonizing tugs. She stepped into the shower, adjusted the spray, and hoped this time she could rinse away the terrible memories of Mak Trumbo's despicable boasts.

Tynan could remember Amara's graceful stride, and it hurt him badly to watch her tottering by like some malfunctioning android. Not that they had had any androids at the Keep, but her pace was so awkward that he knew she had to be in considerable pain. Sorry now that he hadn't respected her wishes to delay any plans until after they had reached Confederation base, he stripped off his clothes and joined her.

"I'm afraid you'll fall," he explained as he slipped into the shower behind her.

"No, you aren't."

Tynan wrapped his arms around her and cupped her breasts tenderly. "You see a great deal even without your eyes, don't you?"

For the moment, Amara just wanted to enjoy the luscious feel of his muscular body. Sensing that, he began a slow, considerate massage that caressed not simply her back this time, but her arms down to her fingertips and her legs clear to her toes. Still behind her, he straightened up, slid his hands around her hips and down over her stomach to gently separate her legs. Soapy, his fingertips sought the sensitive bud at the tip of her cleft, and with a slippery touch he made lazy circles that soon had her clinging to his arms. He

meant only to pleasure her, but when the first thrill
of a delicious release began to spread through her,
she turned in his arms and placed her hands on his
shoulders.

"Quickly, pick me up," she urged.

Tynan readily complied, and Amara wrapped
herself around him, ground her hips against his
to heighten her pleasure, and then relaxed for an
instant to allow him to enter her with a single deep
thrust. She wrapped her arms tightly around his
neck and constricted her inner muscles, gripping
him in rolling waves as she coaxed him to join her
in another rapturous rush.

To want only to give pleasure and to be repaid
with such joyous abandon brought a deep moan
from Tynan's lips, but it was one of satisfaction
rather than pain. The confines of the shower
made vigorous movement impossible, but the
intensity of Amara's contractions created more
than enough friction to bring him to completion
with her. Rocked clear to his soul, he held her
pressed close to his heart and knew that if this
wasn't love, then he would never have it.

Grabbing a handful of Amara's hair, he tilted her
head so that she had to look up at him. "You'd have
to be dead not to feel what I do," he swore darkly.
Then, recoiling in horror at the tears streaming
down her face, he shut off the water. Not waiting
for the gentle rush of drying air, he carried her
back to their bed, where he dried her off with
his robe. He then wrapped her in it and lay down
beside her.

Until he had seen her tears, he hadn't realized
there was a difference between inspiring love and

demanding it. Now it was painfully clear. "It's all right, Amara. Whatever you feel for me is enough."

Crushed in his embrace, Amara brushed her cheek against his aubergine robe and knew he was wrong. She already loved him too much.

Chapter Twelve

Thinking it a shame that it was impossible to transfer food between Starcruisers, Amara savored the last bite of a protein bar. Three days after Mak's beating, she finally felt well enough to think clearly, but her vision was still blurred. She squinted slightly, but that failed to bring Tynan's face into sharper focus. She hadn't forgotten how handsome he was, but she was tired of having to rely on memory.

"When Mak brought me in here the other night," she began, "his men were arguing about how they'd split the profits on the sale of this ship. He silenced them with the threat they'd make nothing if they didn't deliver it on time. I'd completely forgotten about it, but it's a vital piece of information. It means he wasn't just speculating that war would inspire heavy bidding on a Starcruiser. He must have already been commissioned to hijack one."

Other than to describe how he had dispatched Toes, Tynan hadn't referred to the pirates since they had defeated them, but Amara's comment brought back their brief captivity in all its horrendous detail. Sorry that she had been dwelling on the ghastly interlude, he shuddered with distaste. "Since Mak also boasted that Alado's competition would be eager to have the ship, can we assume one of them must have hired him?"

"What else could it be?"

"You tell me," Tynan encouraged. "Is the galaxy full of rogue scientists like Risto Cortez who covet Alado's technology to carry out their absurd experiments?"

"I certainly hope not." Amara licked the last traces of the honey-flavored bar from her fingertips. "But if one of our competitors hired Mak to seize a Starcruiser, it means they don't expect the peace talks to succeed."

"Let's take that one step further," Tynan suggested. "Their plans must have gone past mere expectation if they're dealing with pirates. They must intend to sabotage the talks. That's a very cunning trick—to agree to a peace conference while at the same time commissioning pirates to hijack ships to prepare for war. Am I being näive again, or is such a course of action merely wise?"

"What you're describing is duplicity rather than wisdom."

"And the Peregrine Corporation would be the most likely to deal with pirates?"

"They are pirates!" Amara swore.

"Well, if Peregrine has already decided to deliberately sabotage the conference, perhaps by adher-

Thrill to the most sensual, adventure-filled Historical Romances on the market today...

FROM LEISURE BOOKS

As a home subscriber to the Leisure Romance Book Cl you'll enjoy the best in today's BRAND-NEW Histori Romance fiction. For over twenty years, Leisure Bod has brought you the award-winning, high-quality auth you know and love to read. Each Leisure Histori Romance will sweep you away to a world of high adv ture...and intimate romance. Discover for yourself all passion and excitement millions of readers thrill to ea and every month.

Save $5.00 Each Time You Buy

Six times a year, the Leisure Romance Book Club brings you four brand-new titles from Leisure Books, America's foremost publisher of Historical Romances. EACH PACKAGE WILL SAVE YOU $5.00 FROM THE BOOKSTORE PRICE! And you'll never miss a new title with our convenient home delivery service.

Here's how we do it. Each package will carry a FREE 10-DAY EXAMINATION privilege. At the end of that time, if you decide to keep your books, simply pay the low invoice price of $14.96, no shipping or handling charges added. HOME DELIVERY IS ALWAYS FREE. With today's top Historical Romance novels selling for $4.99 and higher, our price SAVES YOU $5.00 with each shipment.

AND YOUR FIRST FOUR-BOOK SHIPMENT IS TOTALLY FR
IT'S A BARGAIN YOU CAN'T BEAT! A Super $19.96 Value!

LEISURE BOOKS *A Division of Dorchester Publishing Co., Inc.*

Get Four Books Totally FREE— A $19.96 Value!

▼ Tear Here and Mail Your FREE Book Card Today! ▼

PLEASE RUSH
MY FOUR FREE
BOOKS TO ME
RIGHT AWAY!

Leisure Romance Book Club
PO Box 1234
65 Commerce Road
Stamford CT 06920- 4563

AFFIX
STAMP
HERE

ing to intractable demands, there's no point in Alado's attending what can only be a frustrating charade."

Amara nodded thoughtfully. "On the other hand, Alado can't accuse Peregrine of negotiating in bad faith before the talks even begin. If we did, Peregrine would blame Alado for undermining the goals of the conference."

"True." Tynan got up to dispose of the protein bar wrappers. When he returned to his seat, he offered another theory. "If Peregrine generally has a poor reputation, then one of the other corporations might have hired Mak Trumbo knowing that if anything went wrong, Peregrine would undoubtedly be blamed."

"So we should suspect everyone, not simply Peregrine?"

"I like the way you used the word *we*."

"A mere slip of the tongue."

"I don't suppose you'd care to slip that tongue around me for a while?"

Amara shook her head. She hadn't bothered to pin her hair atop her head in days, and her bright curls danced on her shoulders. "I've corrupted you terribly," she revealed with mock horror. "You were a scholarly historian when you were entrusted to my care, and look what I've made of you."

Tynan left his seat and pushed hers back into recline as he crawled over her. "You haven't done anything to me that I didn't want," he insisted between teasing kisses. "At least, not yet, you haven't."

Amara raised her arms to encircle his neck and made his next kiss her own, but she brought it to

225

an abrupt end. "Wait a minute, did you search Mak's pockets?"

Tynan rested his forehead against hers. "No, I just stuffed him into the body bag as quickly as I could."

Amara placed her hands on his chest to push him away. "I hate to ask you to do this, but I can't see well enough to tell whether or not I've found anything."

Tynan winced. "You want me to search him now?"

"I think it's imperative that you do. The sooner we discover who hired Trumbo, the more time we'll have to formulate our plans—*your* plans," she hastily corrected.

Tynan sat back, but rested his hands on her thighs. "I'll make a bargain with you. If you agree to being my assistant at the conference, then I'll search both bodies. Otherwise, Alado's security personnel can search them when we reach the Confederation base."

"You don't understand," Amara warned. "At the Confederation base, the security personnel come from all five corporations. So if one of them wishes to tamper with evidence, they can easily arrange the opportunity."

"I didn't realize that," Tynan mused thoughtfully, "but that'll make your decision a lot easier. You can't very well refuse to work with me if it might enable Alado's enemies to gain the first access to the bodies."

In the last three days, Tynan hadn't made another reference to love, for which Amara was extremely grateful. She had begun their affair blissfully unaware of how close their shared passion would come to costing them their lives. Now she shuddered every time she thought of it. She had lost count of how many times they had made love, but even when she hadn't felt well, it had been glorious. Deeply flattered that he continued to want her company, she now had reason to believe the price might be too high.

"Tynan, the peace conference will require the best effort you've ever given anything. I let you distract me, and Mak Trumbo took advantage of it. Thank God we got away from him, but we don't dare risk letting the conference fail because I'm distracting you."

Amara looked absolutely tormented by that possibility, and Tynan reached out to caress her cheek. "You're definitely a distraction, but I won't be nearly as preoccupied with you if you're with me than if you're not. My goal is to prevent war, and I'm positive I can reach it much quicker with you on my side."

"You know I'm on your side."

"Then stay with me."

While she couldn't make out his expression clearly, the urgency in his voice was compelling. "I don't want to refuse you," she whispered.

"Then don't."

Resting her hands in her lap, Amara called upon her diplomatic training. "Because we don't know how long the conference will last, or what conflicts might arise with my assignment, I can only offer my help for the first few days. I can't promise to stay for weeks or months. I've already told you that."

Tynan could see that making any sort of a concession was difficult for her, but he pressed for a further advantage. "Well then, I guess we'll just have to let the Confederation personnel search the bodies."

"Tynan! You're being completely unreasonable."

"I disagree. I think I'm merely being prudent. We work together beautifully, and I don't want to begin the conference and then have to deal with the bother of training another assistant."

"Tynan Thorn, you arrogant—" Amara almost called him a bastard, but suddenly realizing how badly that epithet would hurt him, she swallowed the insult with a forced cough. "You haven't trained me!"

Tynan ran his fingers up her legs. He now knew just where to apply pressure with his thumbs, and knowing that too, Amara brushed his hands away. "Is that your answer?" he asked.

Amara crossed her arms over her chest and glared at him. "I'll just have to wait and hope that I can see well enough to search the bodies myself before we reach the Confederation base."

"My God, but you're one stubborn woman."

"I am not stubborn," Amara denied. "I'm principled."

"Yes, and so am I," Tynan assured her. "Well, if I don't have to search bodies, then I can search you." This time Tynan stretched out beside her and enveloped her in an affectionate embrace. "Where shall I begin?"

Torn between the desire his nearness created and real worries about the success of the conference, Amara placed her hands over his. "Tynan, please search the bodies."

Tynan drew back slightly. The swelling had gone down, and the bruises surrounding her eyes had begun to lighten, resulting in revolting shades of yellow green that only a deeply depressed artist might admire. To him though, she was still a beauty, and he wanted to please her. "All right, but let's keep whatever we find so that we can examine it later if we need to."

"That could be described as withholding evidence."

"I agree, but I'm going to do it anyway."

"Yes, we probably should. I want to come with you." Amara rolled out of his arms and stood. "The fact that I can't see well might be an advantage."

"Those two didn't smell good when they were fresh," Tynan reminded her. "I think it's your nose that ought to concern you."

"Let's just hurry." Amara placed her hand on his back and followed him into the galley. He dragged a body out into the passenger cabin and carefully opened the bag enclosing it. When he wasn't overwhelmed with a disgusting stench, he looked up. "These bags work as well as their instructions claim. Thank God. Now what are the odds Mak would have concealed anything in his boots?"

"Slight, but you'd better check."

"I was afraid you'd say that." Tynan slipped off the boots, shook them, found nothing and set them aside. Mak's flightsuit had so many pockets it took him several minutes to empty them all. The most interesting item he had carried was a series of pornographic photographs of a voluptuous young woman apparently enamored of a two-headed snake. Tynan sorted through them, checked the backs for notes, found none, and tossed them aside.

He picked up the jeweled knife Mak had pressed to his cheek and wondered how many other people he had sliced up with it. "There's nothing incriminating here, nothing that would tie him to anything or anyone."

Amara sank down on the edge of the nearest seat and cradled her head in her hands. "We should have known whoever inspired the hijacking would be too clever to provide Mak with a written contract. He would have just used it against them later for blackmail."

"Don't be discouraged. It may work to our advantage to suspect everyone."

"Yes, you're probably right."

"Of course, I'm right." Rather than replace Mak's boots, Tynan shoved them into the bag with his body and resealed it. He returned the cumbersome bag to the alcove and searched the man they knew only as Toes. Again, Tynan found an assortment of peculiar junk, but nothing of any particular interest, and he still couldn't bring himself to open the metal rattle. He gathered up the men's effects and stored them inside one of the large foil packages that had contained the high-protein bars. Putting Toes's body back with Mak's, he stopped in the galley to wash his hands, but he still didn't feel clean.

"I'm going to take a shower," he called.

Amara waited until he had had time to wash thoroughly before she cast off her clothes, entered the lavatory, and joined him in the fine spray.

"Thank you for doing what I asked," she said, and shamelessly turned his welcoming laughter to low moans of surrender.

Except for their highly spiced erotic interludes, the remainder of the voyage passed uneventfully. Amara had frequent conversations with Glen and Piper, who were flying escort, and Tynan soon began to think of them as his friends too. Their ships each had a crew of five and were fully prepared for the type of emergency Tynan and Amara had had to face alone. While no other trouble appeared, the ships' presence was still a comfort.

Amara couldn't see well enough to play Banshee Quest, but encouraged Tynan to practice without her and shared his elation when he mastered levels one and two. If the exciting game honed the skills Alado's pilots would need in the event of war, neither shared those fears aloud. Instead, they concentrated their energies on plans to ensure peace.

As they were about to begin the approach to the Confederation base, Tynan walked through the passenger cabin filled with a heady mixture of anticipation and regret not unlike the conflicting emotions that had plagued him on leaving the Keep. The Starcruiser was of a compact design, yet his fascinating companion had kept him from ever feeling confined. Here, the muted grays were metal and fabric rather than stone, but somehow, in the ten days they had shared the sleek vessel, it had become home. Amara had once compared the Confederation base to the Keep, and Tynan knew that if he had been comfortable in a Starcruiser, he would certainly be comfortable there—as long as she was with him.

Amara was bending over brushing out her curls, and Tynan walked up behind her and gave her bottom a playful swat. "I had hoped once you'd donned your robe, you'd remember how to behave," she cautioned.

"Don't worry. I'll be so discreet everyone will think I can barely tolerate you. Will that please you?"

Amara straightened up. "You needn't be rude." She started to coil her hair atop her head, but Tynan reached out to stop her.

"Wear your hair down."

Amara tapped her brush against her thigh. She had always taken pride in her professionalism, and an abundance of curls wouldn't create the proper impression. "I need to look like I know what I'm doing, even if I've already proven that I don't," she argued.

Tynan brushed her lips with a light kiss. "Do it for me."

Amara relaxed against him. "Well, just this once. Maybe it will help to camouflage the last of my bruises."

"They're nearly gone." It pained Tynan that Amara still couldn't see well enough to appreciate the steady improvement in her appearance. "You're as beautiful as ever."

"Unfortunately, pilots aren't promoted for their looks, Ty, and it's going to take every bit of my once considerable ability to just hold on to my job."

"Ty? No one's ever called me that. I like it coming from you."

Amara tossed her brush into the bag holding her gear and took his hand. "Come on up to the cockpit. Maybe seeing the base will help you focus on the task at hand."

Tynan was positive he already had his priorities straight. "Would you stop worrying? We're on time. Wasn't that all the Secretary demanded of you?"

Amara rolled her eyes. "Remind me to tell him that."

Once seated, she verified the coordinates of the Confederation base, and directed Steve to begin the docking sequence. "I still can't see well enough to bring us in safely, and I certainly don't want to kill us now."

Knowing she was being intentionally melodramatic, Tynan reached over and took her hand. At first, the base was no more than a pinpoint of light, but gradually he began to appreciate its tremendous size. A gigantic domed wheel, it spun in an endless rotation, maintaining its orbit and the gravity its residents required for comfort. Still, he couldn't really understand why anyone would want to live anywhere but on Earth.

His fingertips brushing Amara's wrist, he felt her pulse accelerating. "Why are you so frightened? Isn't Steve as capable as you claim?"

"It's not the landing that terrifies me; it's the reception we'll receive."

"After the way Mak Trumbo greeted us, how bad can it be?"

"Thank you. I'll try and look at it that way. Then anything short of a summary execution will seem mild."

"They won't dare execute my assistant. There, that gives you a real incentive to stay with me."

Amara tried to smile, but failed. Half an hour ago, their escort ships had veered off to allow them to dock first, and she felt very vulnerable and alone. She gripped Tynan's hand more tightly and, closing her eyes, held her breath while Steve produced a predictably perfect landing.

"Geronimo!" she then cried.

"What's he got to do with this?"

"That's what paratroopers used to yell before jumping into a war zone. I keep telling myself they couldn't possibly have found a guillotine, so the worst will soon be over."

Tynan knew she was scared, but he couldn't help but laugh. "I've always admired your courage. Did I ever mention that?"

"No, but let's hope I've got enough left to get me through the next hour."

Tynan drew his hood forward to shade his face. "I'm known here only by my reputation, but let's use that to our advantage. As far as I'm concerned, you're still Alado's premiere pilot, and I'm going to object strenuously to anyone who says otherwise."

"Thank you. Forgive me for agonizing over my own pathetic situation when your task is far more difficult and important. I won't have you worrying about me. Just concentrate on the conference."

"I certainly don't consider what I hope is your imagined predicament as trivial, and I'll worry about you all I like." He waited for the docking bay to be pressurized, then unbuckled his seatbelt. "Open the hatch."

Amara promptly obeyed, lowered the steps, and, navigating by touch, led the way. There were several men approaching, and she recognized Orion Chaudet and two of his assistants by their splendid gold attire. They were followed by half a dozen of the Confederation's security forces dressed in black and white uniforms. When Orion reached her, he brushed aside her curls, and appraising the last of her bruises, frowned unhappily.

"I have a medical team standing by in the hospital unit. I was afraid you wouldn't be able to walk." He dropped his hand to her shoulder and gave her an affectionate squeeze.

While that was a far more considerate greeting than she had expected, Amara didn't appreciate being fondled in public and shied away. She was also badly embarrassed that Orion would ignore Tynan Thorn to express his concern for her. Completing her duties as the Guardian's escort, she presented the Secretary of the Diplomatic Corps to the philosopher.

"We've already met," Orion explained. A sly grin lit his face as he noted Tynan's clear dismay. "What has it been, twenty years?"

"Twenty-one," Tynan replied through clenched teeth.

Although unable to read his expression with any accuracy, Amara had no difficulty identifying the scorn in Tynan's voice. "I'd no idea you two had met. Why didn't you tell me?" she asked.

Tynan was so angry that the fierce loathing he felt for Orion spilled over into his reply. "You never mentioned his name. Was that a deliberate omission?"

Stung by that bitter accusation, Amara shrugged helplessly. "No, I didn't realize I'd never used it."

"Forgive me if I've caused problems between you," Orion rushed to interject. "You've certainly fulfilled your boyhood promise, Tynan, and I like to believe that I've fulfilled mine." He signaled for the security troops to come forward. "These men will dispose of the pirates' bodies, and while I'll need to review your ship's log and take statements from you both, that can be done tomorrow. The other four negotiators have arrived, and the opening ceremonies will begin as scheduled in two hours. My assistants will show you to your suite, Tynan. I'm sure you'd like to rest after your trip and make your final preparations for the conference."

"No, I want to stay with Lieutenant Greer while she sees the doctor."

Orion moved close and dropped his arm around Amara's shoulders. "How thoughtful of you, but that's completely unnecessary. I've already arranged for the best of care for her."

For an instant, Amara didn't think there was anything special about the way Tynan had chosen to refer to her, but then recalling their prearranged signal, she again pulled away from Orion and reached out to take his arm. "Thank you, Orion, but Tynan really ought to see the doctor too, and we might just as well go together."

"I had no idea you'd also been injured," Orion exclaimed.

Tynan didn't consider the scratch on his cheek worth mentioning, but glad Amara had provided the perfect excuse for them to remain together, he nodded.

Orion turned to his assistants, who, attractive and fair-haired, bore a remarkably close resemblance to him. "See to their luggage, then report to the conference area." He then gestured for Tynan and Amara to accompany him. "The hospital unit is on the next level." He led the way to the end of the docking bay and along a wide corridor to the elevators. One opened at their approach, and Orion stepped aside to allow them to precede him.

"Is this your first elevator ride?" Orion asked.

Again, Tynan remained silent and responded with a nod.

"I'm so glad you accepted Alado's invitation to serve as our negotiator. I knew it would provide a variety of new experiences for you, as well as providing us with your considerable talents." He winked at Amara, and when she didn't respond with the impatient shake of her head he had expected, he realized that she couldn't see him. "How severely is your vision affected?"

"I can see," Amara insisted, "just not all that clearly."

"Then I'll have to have you removed from flight status immediately."

"Yes, I expected that."

The elevator doors opened onto another wide corridor, which led to the hospital unit. Orion paused at the desk to announce their names, and hearing Tynan's, a startled technician checked his roster, was flustered not to find it, and then, learning Amara was the original patient, led them to a treatment room. He then tarried in the doorway, his glance lingering over Tynan before he reluctantly slid the door closed.

"I'm surprised he didn't request an autograph," Orion said. "I've arranged to be available, or to have one of my assistants escort you wherever you care to go so you won't be bothered with people who wish to draw you into conversation. It would be flattering, I know, but needlessly tiring."

"I've no shortage of stamina," Tynan protested. "All I'll need is a map of the base, and I'm sure Amara and I will be able to find our way around."

Orion smiled with what appeared to be genuine pleasure. "I thought you two might have grown fond of one another. I assigned you to adjoining suites. I just hope you'll be well enough to use yours, Amara. It would be a great pity if you were confined to the hospital for any length of time."

Amara was appalled by that prediction. Having finally agreed to work with Tynan, she didn't want her health to prevent it. "I'm sure that won't be necessary," she replied.

"Perhaps not. Oh, by the way, Confederation forces picked up Risto Cortez, which wasn't all that easy considering the mess you'd made of his docking bays. He's denying any wrongdoing and swears his mechanics can testify to the fact he offered you the use of his docking facilities only to be repaid with the most brutal sort of vandalism. He's demanding an apology and payment for all necessary repairs."

"Vandalism! What an imagination. Tynan also witnessed what happened, and I think he'll be believed a lot sooner than the Corkscrews Cortez calls mechanics. If they hadn't fired on us in the first place, we never would have stopped at Cortez's asteroid."

"Well, if the case should go to trial," Orion mused, "that might present something of a problem. Perhaps you ought to explain the Guardians' view on becoming involved in litigation, Tynan."

Tynan slid his hood back on his shoulders. He had to admit that the intervening years had been kind to Orion. His hair was still a thick, golden blond, and his waistline admirably slender for a man of thirty-nine. He had also acquired a polished elegance that Tynan assumed must be considered ideal for the diplomatic corps. Still, the light in his blue eyes was cold, and Tynan couldn't really believe that he had changed. Just as Orion had excelled at doing more than twenty years earlier, he was attempting to make him look foolish, but now Tynan refused to take the bait.

"Historically, Guardians have not become involved in disputes occurring outside the Keep," Tynan explained. "None has ever testified in any court."

Amara rested her clenched fists on her hips. "Is that another of your inviolate traditions, or will you make an exception in this case since you were actively involved? After all, delaying the start of our voyage until dawn certainly didn't bring us good luck."

"That's a matter of conjecture," Tynan stressed. "I think we were very lucky."

"That's no answer. Will you testify in my behalf or not?"

Tynan could feel Orion smirking even before he glanced toward him. He didn't appreciate being put in a position where he had to choose between the traditions he had upheld his whole life and

Amara's welfare. For no more than a fraction of a second, he felt torn, and then he knew precisely what to say.

"Risto Cortez is a dangerous lunatic, and I'll do whatever I must to see he's not allowed to put anyone else's life at risk. So the answer is an emphatic yes. I'll be glad to corroborate your story."

Greatly relieved, Amara would have hugged him had the doctor not entered the room. Amara had seen Solana Diaz before, and recognizing her by her dramatic dark coloring and the sound of her voice, she introduced Tynan. "I didn't know you'd left Fleet Command," she then added.

"I haven't," Dr. Diaz replied. "Orion summoned me when he learned you'd been hurt. Now sit down and let me have a look at you, and gentlemen, we'd really rather not have an audience."

Amara was tempted to ask Tynan to stay, but fearing the doctor might have bad news, she didn't want him to hear it. "Tynan needs to see you too. He'll wait right outside."

Orion preceded him out into the hallway, and the instant they were alone, Tynan stepped forward. He was now taller than his old adversary, and that he could look down on Orion gave him a great deal of satisfaction. "I know you and Amara were lovers, but don't try and use her to play out our old resentments ever again."

Orion adopted an expression of astonished innocence. "What are you talking about? My mention of the Guardians' reluctance to participate in trials? That's the truth, Tynan. Surely you aren't afraid of that."

Tynan reached out and grabbed the front of

Orion's flashy gold uniform and yanked him close. "You wouldn't recognize the truth," he threatened darkly, "if it slapped you as hard as I'd like to! Now stay away from me, and more importantly, stay away from Amara Greer." When Orion failed to react with more than an incredulous stare, Tynan released him with a disgusted shove.

Orion promptly adjusted the fit of his jacket, then sent an anxious glance up and down the hall to make certain Tynan's fit of temper hadn't been observed. "It may surprise you to learn that I've followed your career with real pride," he then proclaimed. "I was the one who suggested you serve as our negotiator, and Alado's board of directors enthusiastically agreed with my choice. I really thought you would have put such childish animosities behind you long ago. That you're still so hot-tempered is indeed unfortunate.

"Alado can't gamble on the outcome of the conference. I need your immediate assurance that you'll display the same commitment to harmonious interaction that pervades your writing, or you'll be replaced as our representative and sent home within the hour. If you still feel you have a score to settle with me, we can attend to it before you go, but right now, the conference is the issue, and it's one of vital importance."

Had Tynan known Orion Chaudet had anything whatsoever at all to do with the peace conference, he wouldn't have agreed to come, but now that he had arrived, he couldn't abandon his responsibilities, or Amara, who he knew wouldn't be allowed to pilot him home should he choose to leave. "As long as you aren't one of the participants," he said, "I shouldn't have any trouble maintaining the proper attitude."

Convinced of his sincerity, Orion nodded slightly. "Good. Jealousy is a most unbecoming characteristic, Tynan, and believe me, it's misplaced in Amara's case. I wasn't her first lover, and you won't be her last. If you've acquired a taste for beautiful women, I can supply all you'd like to meet. You see, there's really no reason for us to remain enemies. We're both working for Alado now."

Seething, Tynan might have again gone for Orion's throat, but Amara opened the treatment room door and called to him. "I don't need anything from you," he swore softly before joining her. "Not advice or presents of any kind. Just stay out of my way."

Ignoring that threat, Orion glanced toward Amara. "There's a reception after the opening ceremonies. I've placed an appropriate gown in your suite so that you'll be able to attend with Tynan. I know you'll both enjoy it. We can finish our discussion of your flight first thing in the morning. We're up on the fourth level. You and Tynan have suites 417 and 419. I'm just across the hall in 420. Join me for breakfast at eight. I can speak to you later, Tynan."

As soon as Orion turned away, Tynan stifled the impulse to spit on the floor and entered the treatment room. "There's nothing wrong with me," he announced.

Solana took one look at the fiery light blazing in his dark eyes and reached for his wrist to take his pulse. "I disagree," she remarked. "You're highly agitated. If it's the strain of the conference, then I can prescribe a mild tranquilizer that won't impair your intellectual abilities."

"No, thank you, I'd rather rely on meditation. Now what about Amara? Will her vision return to normal soon?"

"Yes, I believe so. I've recommended bed rest." The doctor made a last notation on Amara's chart, and then looked up to smile. "Preferably alone."

Tynan's chest ached with the fury of his anger, but as he reached for Amara's hand, he swore not to take it out on her. He sent the attractive physician a parting glance that made it plain he considered her suggestion utterly absurd, and hurried Amara out the door.

"We're going to have a long talk," he informed her, "and this time I won't accept your refusal to discuss a past lover. Understood?"

Amara had already surmised from the blistering hostility of Tynan's conversation with Orion that the Secretary must have been Tynan's boyhood rival. Still, she was about to refuse his request until she remembered that he had offered to testify for her, and if he would break one of the Guardians' traditions for her, then she could not do any less for him.

"Understood," she agreed, but she was frightened all the same. She loved Tynan, yet Orion controlled her career. If they despised each other, how would she ever be able to avoid being crushed between them and losing everything she held dear?

Chapter Thirteen

Tynan ushered Amara into the elevator and pressed the button for the fourth level. He turned toward her, meaning to begin their talk, but the elevator completed its ascent and the doors opened before he had had a chance to speak. There was a desk located directly opposite the elevator, and a cheerful clerk dressed in the black and white of the Confederation greeted them enthusiastically.

"Mr. Thorn, Lieutenant Greer, you're the last of our conference guests to arrive. Here are your room codes."

Tynan took both cards as though he actually knew what to do with them, and taking Amara's arm, he quickly located their suites. He touched the numbered panel beneath his room number in the sequence listed on his card, and the door slid open with a welcoming hiss. A small foyer opened into a sitting room decorated in shades of pale beige and cream. An intricate weaving of natural fibers interlaced with gold streamers adorned one wall, and an abstract mural repeating the muted shades of the decor filled another, creating a harmonious, if subdued, desert-like environment.

The door to the left opened into Amara's suite, which was as beautifully decorated and furnished as his, but in shades of pale aqua with silver accents. Here the artwork flowed with the undulating rhythm of the sea. Sending no more than a quick glance into her quarters, Tynan crossed his sitting room and opened the door to the right, where he found a spacious bedroom and bath. His single piece of luggage sat on the floor at the end of the bed. He rejoined Amara in the sitting room.

"I didn't expect anything nearly this luxurious," he declared. "Who pays for all this?"

"The five corporations making up the Confederation all contribute to its support. Because Alado is the wealthiest, it pays the largest share. After the rigors of space travel, most people feel the luxury here is well-deserved. I hope it doesn't offend you."

"Oh, I'm offended all right, but not by these rooms." Tynan took her hand and led her to the low couch so she would have a comfortable place to sit while they talked, but he preferred to stand. "Tell me exactly what Orion told you when he assigned you the job as my pilot. Why did you say that he had played a trick on you?"

Retreating from what she feared might become a lengthy interrogation, Amara sank down into the comforting folds of the couch. The loosely woven fabric had a nubby texture she began to explore with her fingertips. "He handled it as a routine assignment. I was distressed about the shortness of time, and he expressed confidence in my ability to overcome that problem. He didn't admit that you two had ever met, let alone that he had once lived with the Guardians. He is the one you described as bullying you as a child, isn't he?"

Tynan snorted in disgust. "The very same. Now what was the trick?"

"I'm ashamed I ever said that."

"Tell me," Tynan ordered.

Amara hesitated a long moment, then rushed through a brief explanation. "The close confines of space travel tend to encourage physical intimacy, and I felt it had been unfair of him to put us together when you had no experience with women."

"Because you thought I'd soon be begging you to sleep with me?"

"Tynan, please."

"You needn't be embarrassed. That's exactly what happened, only Orion wasn't playing the trick on you. He sent you to play another of his devious tricks on me, and it worked. I was completely enchanted with you."

The *was* cut Amara to the bone. "I'll grant you that Orion may have put us together simply to torment us both, but if so, the ploy failed because we enjoyed more than mere sexual escapades. Or at least I thought we did."

Amara had been so reluctant to express her feelings for him since their brush with the pirates that Tynan was surprised by her admission. "Yes, so did I."

"Then why should Orion's motives matter? You haven't seen each other in twenty-one years. Can't you put aside your old rivalry? The opening ceremony begins soon. You can scarcely attend in a rage."

"Why not?"

"Because it's unworthy of you and the enterprise you came here to undertake."

Amara was looking down at her hands rather than up at him, and the humility of her pose touched Tynan as deeply as her words. She could not, however, ease the sickening pool of revulsion that lay fermenting in the pit of his stomach. "You don't understand. Orion Chaudet epitomizes everything I abhor. He has no respect for anyone or anything but his own selfish desires. I can't work with him. It nauseates me to be anywhere near him. Mak Trumbo would have made a better friend than Orion!"

Amara waited to make certain he had finished his bitter tirade before she spoke. "Tynan, you haven't seen him since you were twelve years old. Perhaps he did torment you unmercifully when you were a child, but you're a grown man now and so is he. Can't you even entertain the possibility that he might have changed?"

"No! He may have learned how to mask his baser instincts with the superficial charm he tried to ooze all over me when we arrived, but it's all an act. He's a totally unprincipled, manipulative demon from hell. That's what he was and all he could ever be."

"Well, you're certainly entitled to your opinion, but—"

Cinnamon Burke

"Opinion? That's fact!"

Tynan was merely an aubergine haze as he paced up and down in front of Amara, and she was actually grateful she couldn't see the hostility of his expression clearly. "He's not someone I admire any longer either," she readily admitted, "but he's had a distinguished career with Alado. As head of the diplomatic corps, he's generally considered the natural choice for the next opening on the board of directors. If he were as flawed an individual as you claim, he would never have attained the position he has, nor be so highly respected.

"Let it go, Tynan. You've got to walk into the opening ceremony with your goals for the conference so well in mind that you positively radiate tranquillity. To be consumed by resentments stemming from childhood might well cause you to sabotage the deliberations as we suspected Peregrine might. You mustn't let that happen."

Tynan had never believed he possessed any intuition, but Amara's warning sparked a blinding flash of insight, and he saw Orion's purpose clearly. Orion had already threatened to replace him, which would severely damage his credibility as an influential spokesman for peace no matter how many people were still moved by his writings. If he failed as a negotiator, who would replace him? Tynan asked himself. One name came immediately to mind: Orion Chaudet.

That was precisely the type of despicable brilliance Orion had shown as a youth, but rather than continue to argue his suspicions with Amara, who had once been Orion's lover, he made a request. "Because we can't prove Mak Trumbo had been commissioned to hijack a Starcruiser, let's keep that hypothesis to ourselves. When Orion questions you, don't repeat Mak's remarks in any detail."

"That might prove to be a dangerous mistake."

"We've no proof, Amara, and with tensions already high, we ought not to contribute to them."

That was the most reasonable thing Tynan had said since they'd arrived. Pleased, Amara agreed. She rose, made her way into her suite, and found the bathroom. She splashed her face with cold water and wished she had asked Dr. Diaz for something to end the pounding ache in her head. Of course, she hadn't been bothered with pain when she had spoken with Solana, but she certainly was now.

From what she had observed, Orion Chaudet did nothing capriciously, so he had undoubtedly known what Tynan's reaction to him would be. Tynan had been such an inspired choice for negotiator, however, that it seemed obvious to her that Orion had risen above their old rivalry. Why couldn't Tynan be equally magnanimous?

She dried her face, fluffed out her hair and, as ready as she was likely to be, hoped Tynan had composed himself. She didn't want to spend what little time they would have together arguing about Orion. That discord would spoil not only the present, but the beautiful memories which she had planned to savor. Hoping they wouldn't have another confrontation, she gathered her courage and returned to Tynan's suite, where he was still pacing.

"I don't suppose there's any way we can get something worth eating? Didn't it occur to anyone that we might be hungry?"

"I'm so sorry, that's undoubtedly my fault. I couldn't eat if I tried, but I should have asked the clerk to send something for you. Shall we see if there's still time?"

"No, I'm sure there isn't. Let's just hope there's music of some kind at the ceremony to drown out the noise my stomach's making. Do you know where we're supposed to be?"

"Yes, the upper level. The assembly hall is directly under the dome. The view's spectacular, and it's hoped it will inspire the best from everyone. God help us if it doesn't."

That fervent plea brought Tynan a much needed jolt toward the proper focus on their situation. Agreeing with a heartfelt sigh, he raised his hood and took Amara's hand as they left his room. When they reached the elevator, two pilots were waiting to greet them. They were smiling as though he ought to recognize them, and he did once he had read the names embroidered on their flightsuits.

"Piper Giles and Glen Archer," he announced for Amara's benefit. "Thank you for providing us with an escort."

Piper was an attractive brunette with large, fawn-like eyes and an ample mouth that was set in a wide grin. Her companion, Glen Archer, was an earnest young man who looked as though he took everything seriously. "We should have been with you the whole time," he offered regretfully.

"But now that we're here," Piper added, "we'd be honored to serve as part of your staff for as long as you need us."

"Thank you, but Amara will be the only staff I'll need."

Piper and Glen exchanged an incredulous glance. "Has your vision cleared?" she asked.

"No, but it soon will," Amara assured them. "Will you sit with me during the opening ceremony?"

"Aren't you going to be with me?" Tynan asked.

Amara heard not merely confusion, but apprehension in his question and gave his hand a sympathetic squeeze. "I don't believe that will be possible. Whenever the Confederation convenes, the proceedings begin with a formal ceremony. It's a tradition," she stressed, "and considered important to foster cooperation among the five corporations, which are by their very natures competitive. I'm assuming you'll be seated with the other dignitaries and that can't include room for each negotiator's staff."

Not pleased by that announcement, Tynan bowed his head slightly, and as he straightened up, he made a valiant effort to wrap himself in the tranquillity Amara had suggested he project. It was the pervasive feeling at the Keep, but he had only the most tenuous grasp on it now. "Shall we go?" he urged. "After overcoming so much just to get here, I don't want to be late."

Glen pressed the elevator button, and the four joined three passengers who had boarded at lower levels. One of them gazed fixedly at Tynan; then, seeming to recognize him, he moved closer to introduce himself. "Tynan, I'm Derrel Simmons, Peregrine's negotiator. We'll be formally introduced in a few minutes, but I'd much rather we met now."

Derrel was nearly as tall as Tynan. He wore his dark brown hair cropped short on top, but long curls brushed his nape. A ruggedly handsome man with bright blue eyes and a mischievous grin, he was dressed like all of Peregrine's forces in charcoal gray brightened with an abundance of scarlet piping. He offered his hand and seemed genuinely pleased when Tynan took it.

"I've read some of your writings, or at least tried to," he admitted with a laugh. "I'm hoping you'll be much easier to understand in person."

Because Tynan strove for a simplicity of expression that allowed his ideas to shine through undimmed by elaborately complicated language, no one had ever complained that his work was obscure. The only people who didn't understand his views were those who hadn't read them, and he recognized Derrel Simmons instantly as a liar. Amara had warned him Derrel wouldn't take anything seriously, and her assessment had just proved correct.

Tynan responded with deliberate care. "If I must use words of one syllable, or speak slowly, then I will, but believe me, Simmons, we will understand each other."

The elevator doors slid open, and stepping out first, Derrel turned back to face Tynan. "I like your robe. Do you wrap yourself in it at night and hang upside down like a bat?"

"No, I make much better use of a bed."

Derrel saw Amara take Tynan's arm as they left the elevator and broke into a taunting grin. "Obviously, you do." He turned and waved. "Good luck."

"The same to you."

Glen started to go after Derrel, but Piper grabbed his elbow and pulled him back. "This is a peace conference," she reminded him. "They won't allow brawling in the corridors. Besides, Tynan just made it plain he can take care of himself."

Glen shook off her hand. "He shouldn't have made that crack about a bat. That was just plain rude."

"Yes, it was," Tynan agreed. "But he just showed me what I can expect from him, and I appreciate the warning."

The corridor was filling rapidly. Many of those lining up to enter the assembly hall were dressed in Peregrine's charcoal and red uniforms, but just as many wore Alado's gold. As they neared the open doorway, one of Orion's assistants, who had met them in the docking bay, came forward and Amara moved aside to make room for him.

"I'm Ross Belding," he told Tynan, "and I've been waiting for you. The negotiators are meeting together before the ceremony. Please come with me."

Distracted by Ross, Tynan took his eyes off Amara for only an instant, but when he turned to look for her, she and her friends had already been caught in the crush at the door and been swept inside. Unused to being among strangers, let alone being buffeted by a crowd, Tynan was distinctly uncomfortable, but slid his hands into his sleeves and tried to affect a studious calm as he followed Ross.

Going against the flow of traffic, they moved slowly, and at first Tynan thought the people they passed were brushing up against him accidentally. Then he realized that they were deliberately reaching out to touch his robe. They weren't only Alado's personnel either, but people in a variety of garb representing all five corporations. Appalled to be treated with such open adoration, he was relieved when they reached the small anteroom where the other negotiators were already gathered.

As they turned toward him, Ross introduced them, but Tynan had already recognized them from the photographs Alado had provided. Omega's representative, Lisha Drache, was a petite African woman dressed in a bright orange-and-black print gown, complete with an artfully swirled turban. She had been arguing with Tava Micenko, Serema's negotiator. Interrupted by Tynan's entrance, she halted a short, choppy gesture in mid-stroke.

Scarcely intimidated by Lisha, Tava ended their conversation by moving toward Tynan with a languid dancer's grace. She was dressed in a severely tailored navy-blue uniform, but her long, auburn hair fell free to brush her hips. She had a redhead's translucent skin, heavily shadowed green eyes, a classic nose, and a generous mouth. Tynan supposed she was considered a great beauty, but there was a strangeness in the perfection of her features that he found disturbing. He took the hand she offered but, finding the coolness of her touch unsettling, dropped it quickly.

Gallager McGrath, Europa's negotiator, hung back with Lisha. A stocky gray-haired man, dressed in his corporation's forest green, he shoved his hands into his pockets and greeted Tynan with a grudging nod.

Derrel, who had arrived only minutes earlier, was fixing himself a drink from a refreshment cart. He took a sip and then raised it toward

Tynan. "Now that we're all here, perhaps we can overcome our first challenge." He gestured toward Lisha. "There seems to be some disagreement as to the order in which we enter the hall. Lisha wants to go first, for no particular reason, while Tava and Gallager each think they should. I'd be happy to draw lots myself. What do you say, Thorn?"

Tynan refrained from suggesting alphabetical order which, as Alado's delegate, would place him first. He turned to Ross. "How has this matter been dealt with in the past?" he asked.

Ross looked slightly flustered. "We've always used a set of computer generated lists ranking the five corporations in every possible combination, but because one with Omega in the lead slot has never been drawn, Ms. Drache has refused to consent to their use today."

Tynan was in no mood for petty bickering. "We ought to agree right now not to dissipate our energies in such absurd arguments. Why don't we line up according to height? That will put Ms. Drache first, then Ms. Micenko, Gallager McGrath, Derrel Simmons, and I'll be last, or we can reverse the order, and I'll lead."

Derrel laughed, then finished his drink. "That's either a brilliant idea or an utterly ridiculous one. I can't tell which."

Tava moved close enough to brush against Tynan's robe. "I rather like Tynan's plan myself. I'll grant you it's peculiar, but he's right. If we waste our time debating trivial issues, we won't bring our best to the actual negotiations. Will you

255

agree to using height, Gallager?"

Gallager McGrath yanked his hands out of his pockets and straightened up. "Wait just a minute, I don't recall electing Tynan Thorn the conference chairman. Why should we accept his plan without listening to any others?"

"That's an excellent point," Derrel agreed. "We ought to elect a chairman before we begin deliberating the entrance issue. I nominate Tynan Thorn." He turned back to the cart to mix himself another drink.

"Our first session isn't until tomorrow," Lisha cried.

"So what?" Tava replied. "Unlike the rest of us, Tynan Thorn is an independent individual unaligned with a particular corporation except for the duration of these negotiations. He's noted for his wisdom. I think he's the perfect choice for the position of chairman, and I second his nomination. Shall we vote?"

Derrel clapped his hands. "I'll vote with Tava. You'll vote for yourself, won't you, Thorn? That's a majority right there. What do you two say, shall we make it unanimous?"

Lisha looked anything but pleased. "We haven't even decided that a simple majority decides anything," she argued.

Gallager threw up his hands. "Enough. Tynan's right. If we waste our time arguing over such insignificant points, this conference will last a decade. He has my vote for chairman."

Derrel set his now empty glass aside and walked over to clap Tynan on the back. "Congratulations on your first victory. Now let's get ourselves into line and march right on into the hall. Lisha, you get to be first after all."

That she had gotten her way, but not in the manner she had wanted, frustrated Lisha no end, but she moved toward the door. She was wearing several strands of colorful glass beads around her neck and wrists which provided a faint musical accompaniment to each step.

Tynan stepped back to allow the others to arrange themselves in line. He had been away from the Keep for only ten days, but it was beginning to seem like forever. Bombarded with unfamiliar people, sights, and sounds, he understood that he was suffering from sensory overload, but he couldn't escape into meditation now to restore himself to calm. He looked up to find a Confederation officer summoning them from a door at the opposite end of the room.

The small procession began. Uncertain of what lay ahead, Tynan followed Derrel, who looked back over his shoulder to wink at him. "This reminds me of graduation from the Peregrine Academy," he whispered, "but we had a lot more pretty girls."

Tynan sent Derrel such a forbidding glance that he ceased trying to amuse him, turned around and, throwing back his shoulders, marched into the assembly hall with a proud swagger. At the negotiators' entrance, those gathered to view the ceremony stood, and Derrel waved to the Peregrine delegation, which cheered and waved in response, prompting murmurs of dismay from the members of the other four corporations. That the need for proper decorum in a serious situation so completely eluded the Peregrine Corporation

257

fit Amara's description of the group so perfectly that Tynan immediately began to search the crowd for her.

Even dressed in gold as were the other members of Alado's diplomatic corps, she was easy to find. Her blond curls framed her face like a halo, but her expression was troubled, not serene. Piper and Glen were standing to her right, but Orion Chaudet was at her left. Tynan tried not to blame Amara, for in a blur of gold uniforms how could she have known he was there? She couldn't have found him, so it was evident that he had made a point of taking the seat beside hers. He was still her supervisor, Tynan reminded himself, but that rationalization failed to soothe his mind.

Distracted, he nearly walked right past the seat assigned to him, but he caught himself just in time and took his place on the dias. He then tried to focus his attention anywhere but on the one person he wanted to see.

Beneath the transparent dome, the assembly hall had the ancient design of an amphitheater with a central stage surrounded by seats built into rising tiers. A small orchestra had been placed on the right of the stage, and the officials providing support services for the conference were on the left. As the spectators had filed into the auditorium, the orchestra had played a varied selection of tunes, but now with everyone standing, it began the Confederation anthem. The anthem had no lyrics because the corporations had never agreed on any of the words proposed.

Uneasy, Tynan shifted his weight from foot to foot as he waited for the lengthy number to end.

He had never seen the instruments featured in this orchestra. They were of tubular metal, but triangular in shape and strung like the Celtic harp he had once studied. Strummed like that instrument, they also had a reed mouthpiece and were being played as woodwinds by a portion of the musicians while still others held theirs aloft and tapped the gleaming frame like chimes to produce beautiful clear tones. A variation in size provided for a full range of sound in all three modes.

The conference was opened by Judd Griffith, a member of the Europa Corporation who had just begun a four-year term as Confederation Chairman. An imposing man with a resonant voice, he read a brief welcoming address and recited the Articles of Agreement which had established the Confederation of Populated Worlds. Another musical number followed, then the negotiators were introduced, each with a flattering biographical sketch highlighting his or her qualifications. Tynan was the only one who had not graduated from a corporation academy and excelled in corporate administration. After a final musical selection, Griffith declared the conference duly open and that negotiations would begin the following morning at ten.

Ready to leave, Amara started to rise with Piper and Glen, but Orion reached out to stop her and dismissed the pilots with a nod. He waited until the others in their row had filed out before he spoke. "What do you think of the gown I provided for you?"

"Gown? Oh, I'm sorry, there wasn't time to look at it. Not that I could see more than the color, but you have marvelous taste, so I'm certain it's lovely. You really ought not to have bought it, though."

"I enjoy buying you presents," Orion confided. "Besides, I didn't give you an adequate amount of time to prepare your wardrobe for this conference. So as I see it, it was my responsibility to supplement your uniforms."

Orion sounded sincere, but Amara wished she could see his expression. He frequently delivered serious comments with a teasing grin. "I'll reimburse you," she promised.

"There's no need."

"No, truly there is."

"I'd no idea Tynan would be such a jealous sort. Will he forbid you to wear anything I provide?"

Bristling at the word, Amara certainly hoped Tynan would know better than to forbid her to do anything, but she wouldn't admit that to Orion. "You should have told me that you two knew each other. It was a very unpleasant surprise for him to find you here."

Orion sighed. "I thought he would have grown up; I did. Like everyone, I was swayed by the intensity of his commitment to peace. It never even occurred to me that he would be so belligerent. I hope that he doesn't have to be replaced."

Alarmed, Amara gripped his arm. "Do you really think that might happen?"

"If he behaves as badly in the negotiations tomorrow as he did with me earlier today, yes. Alado can't afford to be at a disadvantage at this conference because we made the mistake of employing a vindictive negotiator. That would prove disastrous for us all. I think you can be a good influence on him. Will you at least try to convince him not to allow his regrettable distaste for me to color his work?"

"Yes, I already have tried, but he's in no mood to forgive and forget."

The majority of the spectators had already left the hall. Those that remained behind were clustered about, talking in small groups, so Orion was confident his remarks wouldn't be overheard. "Then perhaps I should replace him now, before the first negotiating session even begins."

"No—please, wait. I think he'll be able to do what's expected of him."

Orion hesitated a long moment. "All right, but I intend to review each day's transcripts. If I don't feel Alado is getting fair representation, I'll replace him with an alternate immediately." Orion covered her hand with his. "I'm sorry for the way we parted. I was flippant when it was obvious your feelings were hurt. Can you forgive me?"

Unlike Tynan, Amara didn't harbor grudges, and she quickly agreed. "Yes. I'm sorry too. Now I really must go. Tynan and I didn't have time to agree where to meet, and I—"

"He's waiting by the door, but rather than upset him any further, I'll say my good-bye here. I'll stay out of his way at tonight's reception too. It's in Suite A, right down the hall from your room."

Orion helped her from her seat and down the stairs, but left as promised by another exit rather than speak with Tynan. Ross Belding was standing with the Guardian, as were Piper and Glen. Amara smiled and prayed Tynan was smiling in return.

261

As she approached, Piper called out, "The nego-tiators have elected Tynan chairman. Isn't that wonderful? The conference has just begun, and he's already taking charge."

"Congratulations," Amara replied.

"Frankly, I don't believe it's an honor. Now could we find something to eat?" Not meaning to be rude, Tynan reached out to take Amara's hand, making it obvious that his invitation included only her.

As Amara moved toward him, she waved good-bye to the others. "We'll see you at the reception."

Piper and Glen went their own way, but Ross fell in step behind them. "I'll accompany you to your rooms," he said.

"That won't be necessary," Amara argued.

Ross lowered his voice. "Everyone attending the conference has a security clearance, but it's still felt that Mr. Thorn ought not to go about alone."

"He isn't alone," Amara replied. "I'm with him."

"Lieutenant, please. We could already have been up at your rooms by now." Ross gestured toward the elevators, then realized that she couldn't see him and led the way.

Not feeling the need for a guard, much less one working for Orion, Tynan dismissed Ross as soon as they reached the fourth-floor desk. He then asked the clerk about having food sent to their rooms. "We haven't had much to eat in days," he explained. "Can you find us some real meat?"

The clerk's eyes lit with glee. "But of course. The Confederation has an unlimited menu. Whatever you'd like can be delivered to your suite within minutes."

"I want the thickest steak you've got, and an assortment of vegetables. What would you like, Amara?"

"They'll have food at the reception. I can wait."

Once the clerk assured Tynan that he would place his order immediately, Tynan took Amara's arm. "I don't think you get nearly enough to eat."

"Please, Tynan, I don't want to argue with you about how much I consume. I've got an awful headache, and I really just want to lie down and rest before the reception."

Tynan provided the code and his door slid open. "Maybe we ought to call the doctor."

"No, really, I'll be fine. I just want to rest."

She started toward her suite, but Tynan scooped her up in his arms. "You're going in the wrong direction. My bed is this way."

"I wasn't going to use your bed."

Tynan had decided against mentioning the fact that he had seen her talking with Orion, but now he couldn't help himself. "What did Orion say to you? Did he tell you not to sleep with me unless I behaved?"

"We were discussing Alado business, not with whom I choose to sleep. I didn't mean to insult you, just to get some rest. Please put me down."

Despite her protests, Tynan walked into his bedroom and deposited her on his bed. "This is where you belong," he announced confidently. "Sleep as long as you like."

He closed the door as he left the room, leaving Amara filled with a curious mixture of defiance and delight. Being with Tynan was an endless thrill, but had she felt better, she would have flown right off his bed and told him that like her eating habits, where she slept was her own business. Unfortunately, she didn't feel up to asserting herself and just curled up on his bed and closed her eyes, confident she would feel well enough to make herself understood when she awoke.

Chapter Fourteen

Tynan's steak arrived promptly, as promised. The waiter placed his tray on the table and removed the cover to display the tempting meal. While it made Tynan's mouth water, he could not help but marvel at the pale apricot rose in the accompanying bud vase. It was deliciously fragrant.

"Do you choose a flower to match each room's decor?" he asked.

"Certainly, sir. Because you failed to specify a beverage, we added mineral water to your order. I hope that's satisfactory. Is there anything else you require?"

"Peace and quiet," Tynan murmured under his breath.

Treating the off-hand remark as a command, the waiter bowed and left the room. Tynan cut his steak, found it superbly prepared, and savored every bite until he had taken the edge off his hunger. Then, having grown accustomed to sharing

265

his meals with Amara, he grew lonely. For a man raised in a close community, it was a deeply disturbing sensation. He put down his knife and fork and let the feeling wash through him, just as he had the painful sense of loss which had assailed him on the Starcruiser.

He had thought his hopes for love would come to naught then, and yet Amara had been in his arms within minutes. Now she was merely asleep, not gone, yet he missed her terribly. He got up, peeked into the bedroom and, after making certain she was resting peacefully, returned to his meal comforted. He finished every bite. Then, keeping the single rose, he set the tray out in the hallway for room service to retrieve.

He glanced toward Orion's door, and wished he had been given a choice about where their rooms were located. He wouldn't have willingly accepted any within such close proximity. He frowned at Orion's door and closed his own. Then, seating himself comfortably on the floor, he proceeded to clear his mind of all thoughts save those of universal peace, harmony, and love. It wasn't until Ross came to the door to see if there was anything they needed before the reception began that he realized he had allowed Amara to oversleep. After promising that they could reach a party on their floor without an escort, he dismissed the conscientious young diplomat.

He then plucked the rose from the vase and used it to tickle Amara's cheek until she awakened. "Where did you get that?" she asked. Enjoying its fragrance, she put her hand over his to bring the bud close.

"It came with the steak. I don't know what I

expected—an android maybe, or a compartment in the room where food would magically appear—but it was a surprise to have a man deliver my order. Obsequious fellow too. I'm surprised he didn't knot the napkin around my neck."

Laughing, Amara sat up and gave him a kiss. "That certainly sounds like an android to me. What makes you think he was human?"

"Well, nothing really. I just assumed that he was."

"Ask him the next time you order something to eat. Androids can't lie."

"Perhaps not, but I'd hate to insult anyone with that question if they were human. I'm afraid I should have awakened you sooner. Ross has already been here to see if we're ready for the reception. Do I have to do anything other than attend?"

"No, that's all there is to it. Everyone wants to meet you, but this party is for Alado personnel only. We won't have to stay long, unless you're enjoying it."

Tynan took her hands to help her to her feet. "I was invited to a peace conference to stave off the imminent threat of war. Shouldn't the party be held after a treaty is signed, assuming we reach an accord?"

"There'll be parties then, too," Amara assured him. "I know tonight's gathering might seem frivolous, but it's meant to give you a proper greeting. I'm sure you can be gracious enough to accept it. How was your steak?"

That she would warn him to be polite and then abruptly change the subject amused Tynan. "Excellent."

"Good. Now come and tell me what you think of the gown I'm supposed to wear. I'll have to rely on your opinion."

Tynan took her hand, but as they passed through her suite, he hoped she would never have occasion to use it. He opened the bedroom closet, found several gold uniforms, a pair of gold sandals, and a white gown with an embroidered lace bodice which looked as though it provided shamefully little coverage. Shocked, he removed it from the closet, and held it aloft.

"I've no idea what women wear here—"

"Or anywhere else," Amara teased.

"True, but this can't possibly be acceptable. This has got to be another of Orion's tasteless jokes."

Amara fingered the silky fabric of the long skirt. "It feels wonderful. What's the matter with it?"

Tynan sighed unhappily. "Well, it's immodest."

Amara doubted it. "I'll call Piper and ask her to come have a look at it."

"You don't believe me?"

"Yes, of course I believe you, but I also think it's possible you know so little about women's fashions that it might seem immodest to you and not to anyone else."

"It doesn't take a couturier to see that with a top this flimsy you might just as well be wearing only a skirt!"

"Oh, is that the problem?" Amara pursed her lips thoughtfully. "That's the current style, Tynan. A great many women have full body tattoos the way I do, and they like to show them off. Tattooed skin never really looks bare."

That Orion had undoubtedly had ample opportunity to appreciate Amara's wave-kissed breasts and not simply to ogle them through a sheer gown pushed Tynan dangerously close to a murderous rage. His first impulse was to rip the white gown to shreds, cross the hall, and throw the tatters in Orion's face when he opened the door. Fortunately, an hour of meditation had left him sufficiently calm to deal with this crisis in a more mature manner.

Tynan replaced the gown in the closet. "Call Piper. I'll abide by her decision, as I would abide by yours if you were able to see well enough to make one."

"Fine. Where's the communications panel?"

"On the wall between our two rooms." He waited quietly while Amara spoke with her friend, but then grew curious. "Is it only women who have tattoos?"

"No, they're popular with men too, but men don't wear specially designed evening clothes to display them."

"Tell me about Orion's."

That was the last thing Amara wanted to do, but she made no attempt to dodge his question. "He has a dragon similar to the ones on the banners in the Keep. Because the beast can be rendered with a ferocious vigor as well as striking beauty, a lot of men choose it."

"Have you taken an extensive survey, or just kept a running tally of the ones you've seen?"

"Neither!" Amara protested. "Some things are common knowledge, especially among pilots."

"Orion's not a pilot."

Cinnamon Burke

Disgusted by his coolly superior attitude, Amara took the gown from the closet. "I absolutely refuse to argue with you about him. Now I'm going to shower and dress. When Piper arrives, please ask her to come in."

"You're not actually going to wear that."

Amara hesitated at the bathroom door. "Not if Piper says it's as scandalous as you think it is, but she can't judge from the hanger. Now excuse me. I have to hurry."

Tynan opened the door to his suite so that Piper could enter, then went to take a shower in his bathroom. Here, as on the Starcruiser, it consisted of a fine soapy spray and continuously recycled water. He shook out his wet curls, shaved, dressed in clean underwear, and again donned his robe. Designed for the drafty Keep, it was really too warm for the controlled temperature of the base, but he did not even consider requesting other clothes.

When he stepped out into the sitting room, he found Piper already conferring with Amara. The brunette's pale green gown was slit up the side to reveal a lengthy expanse of leg adorned with a swirling floral tattoo. He held his breath as she turned toward him, but while low-cut, the top of her gown was opaque and didn't reveal how far her tattoo extended.

Relieved on that account, he steeled himself as he glanced toward Amara. He focused his gaze on her gold sandals then let his eyes drift upward over her snowy white gown. When he discovered that the embroidery decorating the lace bodice had been strategically placed, ripples of delighted relief washed through him. Rather than boldly displaying her lush curves, the lace complimented her superb figure with a flowery, almost virginal sweetness. She had swept her curls off her face on one side and caught them with a pin holding the apricot rosebud. The total effect was one of stunning ethereal beauty and not in the least bit indecent.

A glance at Tynan's awed expression prompted Piper to announce his decision. "It's obvious he approves. I'm glad. I think the gown is gorgeous. Will you let me borrow it sometime?"

"Did you ever return the blue one?" Amara asked.

Piper flushed with embarrassment. "I'm sorry; I'd forgotten just whose it was. Is it yours?"

"Yes, but you might as well keep it now, and no, you can't borrow this one." Amara turned around slowly. "Do you really like it, Ty?"

Despite the fact it had been a gift from Orion, he really did. "Yes. Now shall we go?"

He came forward to take her hand, and with Piper leading, they made their way down the hall to the reception. The door was open, and welcoming music and laughter spilled out around them. "I still say this is inappropriate," he whispered in Amara's ear.

Amara raised her hand to caress his cheek. "Think of it as an attempt to ease tensions and make more thoughtful deliberations possible tomorrow."

"It will be a challenge, but I'll try."

Amara paused before entering the reception room. "This is your party," she stressed. "I'll be here the whole time, but please let me stay in the background. It'll be best for both of us."

271

She followed Piper through the door before he could object, but Tynan again reached for her hand. He smiled as he drew her close, but his steady gaze provided an eloquent denial. She had once promised not to leave him, and he was holding her to that pledge now.

This suite was twice the size of the ones Tynan and Amara had been given. It was decorated in gold and white, with crystal vases holding delicate stems of white orchids on every available surface. Amara had mentioned food, but Tynan hadn't expected buffet tables laden with mountains of seafood, cheeses, thinly sliced meats, and bouquets of artfully arranged fresh vegetables, nor ice fountains dripping sparkling wine. There were perhaps fifty guests present, and all turned to either raise their glasses in a silent toast or applaud as they entered. Piper hurried over to join the crowd.

Orion approached them first and extended a formal greeting before gesturing toward the other guests. "I want to make certain everyone has the opportunity to meet you tonight," he began. "Then, if you need assistance later, you'll know whom to ask."

"Better yet," Tynan replied so softly that only Orion and Amara could hear, "I'll know whom not to ask."

Orion flashed a ready grin, as though Tynan had shared a humorous confidence, but Amara was mortified by that quip. Fearing that her presence added to the probability that the men's conversation might soon deteriorate to blows, she hurriedly extricated herself. "I already know everyone," she declared with an innocent smile. "Will you two please excuse me? I haven't eaten for hours, and I'd like to join Piper at the buffet."

After having complained that she did not eat nearly enough, Tynan could scarcely stop her, but he knew precisely what she was doing and it was difficult not to be provoked. "Of course," he managed to respond. "Bon appétit."

Then Orion began the introductions. There were among Alado's Diplomatic Corps people with expertise in a great many areas, and he took care to provide each with the recognition he deserved. Sensitive to Tynan's lack of regard for him, he then stepped back and allowed the guests to converse with Tynan on their own.

As they moved around the room, Tynan never lost sight of Amara. Despite her plea of hunger, she only nibbled an occasional zucchini spear. She sent frequent smiles his way, but for the most part appeared to be enjoying the company of her friends. That the majority were young and male didn't surprise him, but it still brought a smoldering resentment. That he could easily imagine cleverly designed dragons swirling around their muscular torsos only worsened his torment.

He nodded distractedly as a man identified as a legal consultant asked why he had chosen to study philosophy. "It chose me," he replied.

"Of course," the man observed, "like a calling."

"Precisely." No one present had ever met a Guardian, and Tynan was amazed by how easily their curiosity about the congregation of historians was satisfied. More than one guest had reached out to touch him, stroking his robe with a reverent caress. Often the denseness of the crowd made

273

it impossible for him to back away to avoid the overly familiar gesture, and not wanting to insult the people who were plainly impressed with him, he had to simply endure their fawning. A few referred to a particular piece of his writing as a favorite, which was immensely flattering, but it was clear that most knew his work only by reputation.

Attentive waiters continuously replenished the sparkling wine, and the noise level of conversation rose steadily. Feeling horribly out of place, Tynan grew increasingly warm, and in hopes of leaving promptly after shaking the last hand, he began keeping track of how many people he had yet to meet. He had refused all offers of refreshments, but when the introductions were finally complete, Orion pressed him again.

"I know the Guardians enjoy wine—are you certain you wouldn't like to sample ours? It's made from a hybrid grape grown in many of our colonies, and even the most critical of connoisseurs regards it as superior to the finest champagne produced on Earth."

"No, thank you." Hoping Orion had fulfilled his obligation as host, Tynan hastened to dismiss him. "Don't let me keep you from your other guests."

Orion would have turned away, but Solana Diaz walked up to them then and slipped her arm through his. She was dressed in a bright red gown which left one shoulder bare to display a colorfully tattooed spray of butterflies that Tynan could readily imagine dipped low over her breasts. It wasn't the only tattoo he had glimpsed that evening, but it was one of the prettiest.

"This is a marvelous party," Solana said enthusiastically. "I'm sorry to be late, but I swear, whenever I have a social engagement I can count on a patient turning up at the very last minute with a minor complaint they insist upon calling an emergency."

Orion patted her hand lightly. "You're not late at all, doctor. We're just getting started, and because Tynan has made it clear that he'd prefer anyone else's company to mine, I know he'll excuse us."

Masking his surprise that Orion had apparently lost no time in transferring his affections from Amara to the beautiful physician, Tynan nodded obligingly. What he craved most right now was solitude. He searched the crowd for Amara, saw her listening attentively to a story being told by yet another young man, and didn't interrupt them before slipping out the door. He stopped at the desk at the end of the hall, found there was a chapel on the fifth level, and made his way there.

As he passed through the chapel door, he was greeted by a feminine voice with the same faintly metallic ring that had flavored Steve's. "Welcome. How may we serve you?"

The lighting was dim, but as Tynan took another step forward, he was enveloped in a warm, golden light. Chimes sounded a celestial chord, and a cooling breeze stirred the hem of his robe. "I just want to be by myself," he replied.

The circle of light surrounding him enlarged to reveal a long, rectangular room containing twelve rows of thickly padded pews. The chapel was available to personnel of all faiths, and while there was a gleaming silver and clear acrylic altar at the

275

far end, no other religious paraphernalia of any kind was visible. The walls were a pale blue-gray, and in response to Tynan's reply, a light sprinkling of clouds was projected across them. The billowing images floated lazily toward the ceiling, then drifted low again, painting a serene, heavenly scene.

"Do you find this pleasing?" the voice asked.

"Yes, thank you." Thinking it unlikely that he would be disturbed that late in the evening, Tynan removed his robe and sat down in the last row.

"Do you have a preference as to music? We have the traditional hymns of all denominations, as well as ancient chants and modern instrumentals."

"The chants, please."

Immediately, the familiar sound of male voices filled the chapel. Relaxing, Tynan made himself comfortable. He raked his curls off his forehead and let out a wistful sigh. Although surrounded by soothing sights and sounds, he found it difficult to shake the stifling sense of alienation he had suffered during the reception. He had known it was a mistake to attend, and he was angry with himself for not following his instincts. Unused to being singled out for attention, he regarded the whole affair as an embarrassing error he would not repeat.

He had had a sample of what the negotiations were going to be like that afternoon, and to press for an agreement among such diverse personalities was going to tax every bit of intellectual and creative talent he possessed. Why had he allowed himself to be manipulated into attending something so draining and utterly pointless as a party honoring him before he had even begun the task he was expected to accomplish? He slumped down slightly as he realized why—Amara had asked it of him. Perhaps the members of the diplomatic corps were adept at balancing serious endeavors with social functions, but he wasn't a diplomat, nor had he ever had any desire to be one.

He inhaled deeply, noted faint traces of an exotic floral incense, and remembering how placid his life had been before Alado had plucked him from the Keep, he longed for the day he would return.

Amara laughed as Jeffrey Hart, a pilot she had known since their days at Alado's Flight Academy, gave a wickedly humorous slant to his account of a particularly grueling flight. He was a good friend she hadn't seen in some time, and she was delighted to hear about his recent adventures. Scarcely knowing where to begin, she had kept silent about her own. Just thinking about the debriefing Orion wished to hold in the morning made her head ache, and she raised her fingers to her temple to massage away the pain.

While she could not make out individual faces, she was having no trouble recognizing the people who came close enough to speak with her. In his aubergine robe, Tynan was easy to find, and she glanced around the room, again looking for him. When she didn't immediately locate him, she reached out to grip Jeff's arm. "As Tynan Thorn's pilot, I feel responsible for him, and I don't see him. Do you?"

Annoyed that Amara hadn't been so fascinated with him that she had forgotten the Guardian had ever existed, Jeff surveyed the room with a desultory glance. "No," he finally reported. "Neither do I."

Alarmed, Amara asked for his help again. "Is Orion still here?"

"Yes, he's filling Dr. Diaz's glass from the last fountain."

Amara offered a breathless word of thanks and, taking leave of Jeffrey Hart, made her way toward the couple. She had spoken with Solana earlier, and she had no trouble locating her red dress. "I'm sorry to bother you," she began. "But I can't find Tynan. Do you know where he is?"

Orion hurriedly scanned the crowd. "I just left him a few minutes ago. He can't have gone far. Perhaps he returned to his suite. Come, I'll go with you." Leaving Solana to sip her wine alone, Orion took Amara's hand and led her down the hall. He knocked lightly, but there was no response. "What's the code? Maybe he's in the bedroom and can't hear us."

"I've no idea what the code is, nor mine either."

"Wait here, I'll get it from the desk clerk."

When asked if he had seen Tynan Thorn, the clerk was eager to be of help to a diplomat of Orion Chaudet's stature. "Why yes, he stopped at my desk a short while ago to ask directions to the chapel. Shall I have him paged?"

"No, I don't want to disturb him, but Lieutenant Greer needs her room code. I'll take it to her."

The clerk had only to glance down the hall to see Amara standing outside her door, and he readily provided Orion with her code. "Would you care to leave a message for Mr. Thorn?" he then asked.

"No, I'm sure to see him later. In fact, when he returns, you needn't mention that I was looking for him."

Keeping Tynan's whereabouts to himself, Orion returned to Amara, used the access code to open her door, and followed her into her suite. He then led the way into Tynan's, conducted a brief search, and appeared to be as confused as she when they found it empty.

"I don't understand where he could have gone," Amara agonized. "This is all my fault. I shouldn't have left him."

Orion ran his hands up her arms in a soothing caress. "Don't blame yourself; you were in the same room with him. He's the one who's disappeared."

"Well, yes, I know but—"

Orion interrupted her protest with a kiss, but broke away when she failed to respond. "Don't tell me you've actually grown fond of Tynan? How touching."

"Of course I'm fond of him. He's an extraordinary man."

"Yes, and completely devoted to his career. You mustn't forget that, Amara. Tynan is the ultimate Guardian, a man so superbly focused on his calling that nothing else will ever be anything more than a momentary distraction to him. He said as much to everyone at the party. Don't let him break your heart."

"The way you did?"

Orion pulled her close. "It isn't over between us. Perhaps I'll be the one who'll be left with the broken heart." He kissed her again, but very lightly, a

279

mere hint of what could still be, but again she drew away. Orion stepped back slightly. "That gown is as beautiful on you as I had imagined. I hope Tynan didn't object to your wearing it."

Unwilling to reveal Tynan's original opinion of the dress, Amara shook her head. "It's a lovely gown; why would he object?"

"Because it came from me."

"You must have treated him very badly, Orion."

"We were young, and Tynan was so sensitive to teasing that he brought it on himself. I certainly wish now that both of us had been more tolerant, but after twenty years, I think it's ridiculous of him to still harbor a grudge. He's far more charitable in his writings."

"Yes, he is. I was astonished to find him such a hot-tempered individual."

"You mean he's turned that nasty temper of his on you?"

Orion sounded sincerely outraged, and Amara was surprised. "I didn't realize you'd care."

Again Orion drew her near. "There's a great deal you didn't realize. Tynan won't be here long, and when he's gone, I'd like to try again."

His fingertips caressed her cheek before he tilted her chin slightly. His kiss was the warm, familiar tribute of an accomplished lover, and for just an instant, Amara truly enjoyed it. Unfortunately, Tynan chose that precise moment to walk through his door.

Sighting the couple, he halted abruptly. "Forgive me," he said. "I must be in the wrong room."

Fleeing Orion's embrace, Amara went toward him. "Where have you been? When I discovered you'd left the party, I couldn't imagine where you'd gone."

Tynan's menacing glance locked with Orion's wholly innocent stare, creating a bridge over the years they had been apart. For Tynan at least, they were back at the Keep, where no one had ever seen past Orion's angelic appearance to the evil, twisted beast that dwelled within. He nearly choked on the vile taste of hatred that welled up in his throat. He took a step toward Orion, but Amara blocked his way.

"Go out through my suite," Amara called to Orion.

"I'll not sneak away," Orion replied. "Tynan knows we were lovers, and I'm not ashamed to admit I still care for you. Unlike the historical times in which he revels, men no longer behave as though they own women. If I seize every opportunity to impress you, it shouldn't surprise you or him."

"Nothing you do surprises me," Tynan declared sarcastically.

"Orion, you're needed at the party. Please go," Amara begged.

Apparently unconcerned, Orion shrugged. "Yes, I suppose I am neglecting my guests. I'll see you tomorrow." He smiled as he left the room, but he didn't stray close enough for Tynan to reach out and strike him.

"I'm sorry," Amara continued. "I was worried about you and—"

Uninterested in hearing excuses when it was plain to him that she had not been worried at all, Tynan took her arm, led her over to the sofa, and with a gentle push, encouraged her to sit down.

He then knelt at her feet and removed her sandals. He slid her gown over her knees and ran his hands up her legs to separate them. "I should never have let you sleep alone this afternoon," he complained softly against her knee.

Thrilled by his touch, yet frightened by his mood, Amara again tried to explain, "Tynan, there's nothing between Orion and me—not anymore."

Tynan didn't glance up. He just kept pressing kisses on the cool smoothness of her inner thigh. He felt her shiver slightly, but knowing she couldn't possibly be chilled, he didn't stop. She was wearing lace panties, and after nuzzling the sheer fabric to breathe in her scent, he caught the waistband in his teeth and peeled them off, but he didn't touch her gown.

Amara knew Tynan was using sex to claim her, or reclaim her, as his own. She also knew she ought to object, and strenuously, to being treated with such commanding indifference rather than love, but when he parted the tender folds of her most feminine flesh and sent his tongue on a meandering journey through the delicate crevice, she clutched his ebony curls to hold him close. He sucked gently, then teased her with his thumbs, holding her open while he blew lightly across the swelling nub that threatened to burst with pleasure.

When the joy he gave was so intense, Amara was beyond caring why he wished to be intimate. She lay back and curled her hips to draw him down into the heart of her being. Hovering on the edge of a delicious release, she lunged into his next deeply satisfying kiss, pressing against his face. But suddenly he drew away. She moaned then in frustration rather than ecstasy.

"Do you know who I am?" Tynan asked. "Or better still, do you even care?"

Not waiting for an answer, he sloughed off his robe, shoved his underwear aside, grabbed her knees to yank her forward, and entered her with a jarring thrust. She was so wet that he slid deep and then, withdrawing slightly, plunged deeper still. "Am I as good at this as Orion? Or have there been so many men you can't remember how it felt with him?"

Tynan didn't break his rhythm as he spoke, and already poised on the brink of rapture, on his next stroke Amara rose to meet him. She wound her arms around his neck and, grinding against him, dove into a shattering climax that caught him by surprise. Whatever bitter lesson he may have been striving to teach was lost as wave after wave of delight washed through her. She clung to him, silently urging him to share that sublime thrill, and he fought her for no more than a fraction of a second before giving in to her spell.

Floating on a raft of euphoria, Amara was reluctant to release him, but as soon as his passion was spent, Tynan left her arms. He picked up his robe and hesitated only a moment before turning away. "Better use your own bedroom tonight. You don't dare risk disappointing Orion by being late in the morning."

Badly disappointed in him that night, Amara struggled to sit up. She straightened her now wrinkled gown, but didn't follow Tynan. He was a man of such rigid integrity that he apparently could not even imagine that the kiss she had given Orion didn't mean nearly as much as those she had given him.

"Don't let him break your heart," Orion had warned, but Amara was sadly afraid that she had broken Tynan's, and a man with his kind of pride was a stranger to forgiveness.

Chapter Fifteen

The next morning, Amara dressed in a gold Diplomatic Corps uniform consisting of a loosely fitted jacket and pants rather than a flightsuit, knotted her hair atop her head, and walked across the hall to Orion's suite a few minutes early. Decorated in a deep terra cotta with emerald furnishings, the sitting room conveyed the impression of tradition and wealth rather than the serenity of her rooms. Orion guided her to the table, where she found bowls of fresh fruit and yogurt, and as she served herself, she tried not to think of the morning Tynan had prepared her favorite breakfast for her. Her vision had continued to improve, and she felt encouraged that she was in better health, if nothing else. She tried to smile as Orion handed her a glass of juice.

His hand strayed across her shoulders in a sympathetic caress before he chose the chair opposite hers. "How did things go last night?" he asked.

Amara took a long sip of juice, then responded truthfully. "Miserably. What did you expect?"

Orion began to peel an apple, attempting to produce one lengthy coil which he spun slowly onto his plate. "I'm sorry. I thought you'd be able to calm Tynan after I left."

Amara was not even tempted to reveal how completely she had failed in that regard, or the savagely erotic scene which had followed. Uncomfortable talking about her relationship with Tynan, she reminded Orion of their purpose. "I thought you meant to discuss our flight from Earth."

Orion looked up to study her expression, found it as strained as the slight hoarseness of her voice, and nodded. "Yes, that is the subject of today's debriefing. I've studied your log, and frankly, I'm mystified by your actions. You were provided with clear orders to protect Tynan with whatever means necessary, but obviously you didn't.

"You allowed suspicious vessels to fire on you, causing damage that nearly led to your becoming prisoners of Risto Cortez. With impaired starboard scanners, you should have been on constant alert for further danger, but there's no evidence that you took any action, even defensive, to prevent Mak Trumbo from overtaking and boarding your ship. You're our best pilot, Amara, but if that was a fair sample of what Alado can expect from its flight crews, then we'll be in desperate trouble should this conference fail to prevent war."

Her appetite gone, Amara set her dish of yogurt aside. "I agree. I showed extremely poor judgment, and it nearly cost Tynan and me our lives."

Confused by her downcast mood, Orion grew

insistent. "That's unlike you. I don't want excuses, just an explanation." The apple successfully peeled, he sliced it into quarters, notched one to remove the seeds, and took a bite.

Amara tried to find a more comfortable pose, but failed and simply squirmed unhappily in her seat. "My first mistake was delaying the use of the laser cannon when we were approached by unidentified ships, but conscious of Tynan's pacifist views, I didn't want to risk offending him. I thought there was a real possibility he might refuse to attend the conference if I displayed a penchant for violence."

"But later you chose to do considerable damage to Dr. Cortez's installation."

"Yes, but at least Tynan understood the threat then and didn't object. Oh, he was appalled to find the ship armed with laser cannons, but he overcame his objection."

"All right, assuming that I understand your reasons for not wanting to take hostile action while ferrying a peace emissary, that still doesn't explain how you allowed your ship to be boarded by Mak Trumbo. What happened then?"

Badly embarrassed, Amara refused to describe how that catastrophe had come about. "I was inattentive."

"Inattentive?" Orion mimicked sarcastically. "Isn't negligent the correct term?"

Amara found it difficult to face him and glanced away. "Yes, I was negligent."

Not at all pleased by that admission, Orion also lost his appetite and moved his plate aside. "You're putting me in a very awkward position, Amara. Whatever our personal relationship happens to be, and I sincerely hope that it will continue to be a close one, I can't excuse professional misconduct. At the very least, I'll have to provide a reprimand and note it in your file. Unfortunately, there's a good possibility that because of the importance of your passenger, Alado's board will choose to review your conduct. If that happens, there won't be anything I can do to protect you. You may have an exemplary record, but in all probability the best you can hope for is to be demoted to flying supply runs to our most distant colonies, and that's only if you aren't terminated outright."

"Yes—and if there's no war."

Orion swore. "If there's war, you can brag about the fact that you destroyed a PJC Tomahawk with a crew of nearly fifty, but because of the peculiar circumstances you'll probably be deemed too unreliable to trust with a ship. If I use my influence, you might secure work in a munitions plant, though."

Amara had already been aware that her prospects were bleak, but she couldn't help but object to the righteousness of Orion's tone. This time she had no difficulty looking him in the eye. "If the board undertakes an investigation, I'll have to be candid in my opinions. You failed to warn me that you and Tynan were bitter enemies, but when you first gave me the assignment as his escort, I objected on the grounds that he might be offended by a female pilot.

"You brushed aside my concern, but when I later discovered that Tynan had no experience with women, I couldn't help but feel you had played a dreadful joke on us both. Wasn't it your intention to send Tynan a woman he'd find appealing? At the same time providing me with a passenger to whom I'd be attracted, but couldn't have? While I may not have conducted myself properly, you deserve part of the blame for deliberately manipulating our emotions."

Orion stared at her coldly. "What you're suggesting is preposterous. Neither women nor men are so weak that they succumb to sexual attraction at the risk of their lives. Female pilots have been traveling with male passengers for generations, so you won't gain the slightest sympathy with the ridiculous argument that Tynan distracted you so terribly that you couldn't do your job with the required professionalism. Don't even hint at that if you're questioned, or it might cost you even a supply run. After all, men make up the majority of passengers on those flights, and you'd constantly have to fight the temptation they'd provide."

Apparently disgusted with the absurdity of her comment, Orion sat back in his seat. "I can't believe you'd attempt to blame me for your mistakes—not after we've meant so much to each other."

Even without being able to see his expression clearly, Amara could imagine the disdain tugging at the corners of his mouth. "Why didn't you tell me you'd been raised by the Guardians?" she shot right back at him.

"I've never considered it a particularly interesting bit of information, but it's in my file. I've never made any secret of it."

"Why did you leave?"

"I outgrew them."

"After putting Tynan in the infirmary with three broken ribs?"

Genuinely amused, Orion threw back his head and laughed. "I'd forgotten all about that fight. It was really no more than a scuffle. Is that why Tynan thinks I left? Does he believe I was forced out? If so, he's wrong. I could have stayed, but I chose not to. I entered Alado's academy soon after, and here I am today. If I'm guilty of manipulating anyone, it was only in wanting Tynan to have an escort who would protect him. I'm as surprised as you were not to find him a quiet, introspective soul. I knew you'd look after him, but I really didn't expect you to form such a fierce attachment to each other. How could I have anticipated that?"

When he put it that way, Amara had to believe him. For a moment, she toyed with the idea of relating Mak Trumbo's plans for selling the Starcruiser, but because she had promised Tynan not to, she refrained from doing so. "It was a disastrous flight," she mused darkly, "rather than the routine venture you promised, but I did get Tynan here safely, so I completed my mission. If the Board wants to complain about the way I did it, fine, but they can't say I failed."

"No, and neither will I. I want to keep you with me, Amara. You threatened to demand a transfer before the flight to Earth. I hope you've reconsidered."

Feeling emotionally drained, Amara wasn't up to discussing her career. "Until I can return to flight status, it's rather a moot point."

"True, but you must still have some thoughts on the matter."

Relaxing slightly, Amara leaned back in her chair. "None other than having high hopes for the conference. Until we know how it concludes, there's no point in making plans for anything."

"I agree, but I still need your help. I intend to stay out of Tynan's way, but it's obvious he needs your company. If you'll just continue to be a calming influence on him, you'll be of great value to Alado. I know you'll want to help him anyway, but should there be an inquiry into your conduct, it will be to your advantage to show you've been instrumental in Tynan's success. After all, the Board can scarcely punish you if you assist Tynan in reaching an accord on Alado's terms. I know you'd do it anyway, perhaps out of a sense of duty to all humankind, but remember that whatever influence you have on Tynan will ultimately be of tremendous benefit to your own career."

In Amara's view, Orion was advising her to think first of herself, no matter what the situation, and she knew that was precisely how he lived his life. He might attribute his success to that self-serving attitude, but she had no desire to emulate it. "After last night," she confessed, "I'm afraid my influence with Tynan is nil."

Looking alarmed, Orion rose and helped her to her feet, but rather than release her hand then, he caressed her palm lightly with his thumb. "The negotiations are too important to allow a lovers' quarrel to interfere. Sit in the gallery today. After a full day of talks, I can promise you that Tynan will be eager for your company tonight. I'll reserve one of the private dining rooms. Take him there, order his favorite meal, and be the charming companion I know you to be."

Orion brushed her cheek with a kiss. "Seduce

him, Amara. I know you can do it as easily as you did me."

That wasn't the way Amara recalled their affair, but believing Orion was again slanting the facts to suit his own purposes, she left rather than remind him that he was the one who had aggressively pursued her.

The assembly hall was the site of the deliberations, and today an elegantly designed ebony conference table and matching chairs sat on the stage. The sessions were to be recorded and transcripts prepared, but all the technical equipment had been discreetly placed out of sight. Access to the deliberations was limited to the members of the representatives' staffs, and they sat together in tight clusters along the tiered seats.

Omega's contingent, dressed in the same bright prints as Lisha Drache, was the most colorful, but all wore expressions of fierce determination. Gallager McGrath's assistants wore Europa's subdued forest green—and worried frowns. Serema's members were clad in navy blue and appeared to be as supremely confident as their leader, Tava Micenko. Seated nearby, the Peregrine staff were slouched in their seats, their charcoal and red uniforms worn with a careless élan.

When Amara reached the doorway, she was relieved to find her name among those Alado had authorized to attend. Orion's name led the list, but she took him at his word that he would not be present. She slid into the row with Ross Belding and half a dozen others from the diplomatic corps. She had purposely not returned to her suite after her meeting with Orion, in order to avoid another confrontation with Tynan, and it was difficult for her to look at him now as he took his place at the end of the table.

When he glanced toward her, she thought for a heart-stopping instant that he was going to wave, and her whole body flooded with the warmth of anticipation, but just as quickly he refocused his attention on the other delegates, effectively shutting her out of his mind. "We are in deep trouble," she whispered.

Overhearing her, Ross leaned close. "I disagree. Tynan Thorn will prove his worth before the day is out. Just watch."

Amara hadn't been referring to the conference, but she didn't explain her comment to Ross, whom she knew only casually. She had brought along a notebook, but unable to take notes like the other spectators, she scribbled crosshatched designs along the margins to keep herself occupied. She and Tynan had discussed the other negotiators at length, but by the time the morning session adjourned for lunch, she was still amazed by how closely each had clung to his or her own agenda. She had warned Tynan that would happen and was pleased by the way he had kept skillfully redirecting the discussion to their primary mission of securing mutual accord and a lasting peace.

Not hungry, Tynan returned to the tranquil refuge of his suite to collect his thoughts during the noon recess, and when the conference reconvened, he felt refreshed. As he had that morning, he continued to concentrate on his role as chairman and tactfully guided the talks while silently studying the other negotiators' styles. Lisha Drache showed herself to be as rigid and demanding as though she felt personally cheated by the Confederation's current policies. Omega had been the last corporation to join the Confederation—hence its name—and she fought hard to raise her firm's status while Gallager McGrath took a vicious delight in shouting her down in order to put forth Europa's concerns. Ignoring that unfortunate interplay, Tava Micenko was coolly consistent and repeatedly stressed the need for cooperation and the sharing of technology.

Derrel Simmons kept up a running commentary denigrating everyone else's suggestions while he offered no constructive ideas of his own. Mentally, Tynan kept comparing him to Mak Trumbo and wondering what links, if any, had existed between the Peregrine Corporation and the pirate. Clearly, what Derrel was doing was a form of sabotage, for in ridiculing the others, he prevented even good ideas from being taken seriously.

Finally Tynan had had enough. Deciding to use whatever power he had as chairman, he rose to his feet. "The prospect of war is abhorrent to me, but I won't waste another minute of our time continuing the ridiculous farce we've carried on today. Alado is fully committed to peaceful exploration, but if there is no agreement that such a goal is even desirable among the rest of you, then I'm prepared to walk out now and not return."

While those seated at the table were too stunned to respond, a murmur of surprised alarm swept the gallery. Even knowing Tynan was sincerely dedicated to peace, Amara feared he had gone too far by using such a dramatic ploy so early in the talks. She sat forward to see how the other corporations' representatives would react. Finally, Derrel Simmons began to laugh.

"That threat won't work with Peregrine," he boasted. "It was a clash between our ships and Alado's that brought us here. We're fully capable of holding the new territories we claim, but if it takes a war to prove it, then it might as well begin."

"No!" Lisha cried, desperately eager to protect what few interests the tiny Omega Corporation had. "War is unthinkable!"

"I agree," Tava was quick to add. "What do you say, Gallager? Will you stand with the three of us—or Peregrine?"

Caught completely by surprise at the sudden serious turn of the discussion, Gallager looked first at Derrel's obnoxious smirk and then at Tynan's deeply troubled frown. Europa was a conservative firm which owed its success to thoughtful management, and he knew his board would never sanction an alliance with the renegades who ran Peregrine. "Europa will side with the majority," he announced.

Tynan waited a long moment to make certain Derrel fully appreciated the tenuousness of his position. Then he spoke directly to him. "You wanted war," he pointed out, "but Peregrine has no chance of succeeding when pitted against the four of us. Either you leave now, and let us get on with our plans to defeat you, or you stay and begin contributing something worthwhile for a change."

Derrel regarded Tynan with a darkly furious stare, but he had only to take a brief glimpse at the horrified expressions of the Peregrine spectators to know he had pushed the Guardian too far. Although slightly smaller in size, he truly believed Peregrine had a chance to defeat Alado's forces—but not if they were backed by the resources of Omega, Serema, and Europa. He shrugged helplessly. "We're not eager for war; I'll stay."

That concession won, Tynan resumed his seat. "We're agreed then, the talks will continue with a renewed emphasis on reaching an accord?"

The others at the table nodded in agreement, and an obviously shaken Gallager McGrath requested they recess for the day. Believing that was an excellent idea, Tynan voted with them for adjournment. Eager to discuss how the day had gone with Amara, he was disappointed when Ross Belding approached him alone. Tynan glanced past him, but the seat where Amara had been observing the deliberations was empty, and he was too proud to ask where she had gone.

After Ross had escorted him to his suite, Tynan was so anxious to rid himself of all memory of the day that he stripped off his clothes and stepped into the shower. Leaning back, he waited for the soapy spray to ease the day's tensions, but he was still far from calm when Amara appeared. She raised her hand to his lips to plead for silence. Then, with a smooth, sure touch, she gave him a light but deeply stirring massage. Combined with the delicious heat of the water, it would have been wonderfully relaxing, but nude, Amara was such an entrancing figure that it took all of Tynan's self-control not to reach out and grab her.

He shut his eyes, but found that only intensified the pleasure of her caresses. Jealousy had prompted him to send her away, but a sleepless night had taught him how stupid he had been in punishing himself as well as her by being vindictive. She had sworn Orion meant nothing to her, and as her fingertips moved up his inner thighs, her adoring touch made him increasingly inclined to believe her. Finally, he could no longer delay accepting what he certainly hoped she was offering.

He shut off the shower and, not waiting for the drying heat, took Amara's hand and led her to his bed. He pulled her down onto it and coaxed her to move astride him. Her wet ringlets dripped onto her breasts and sent tiny splashes careening across his stomach, but he liked her slippery wetness. It made her resemble a nymph cavorting in a Renaissance fountain, and he thrust up into her with a gentle lunge to begin what would become a long, slow journey toward the ultimate bliss.

Orion might have suggested that Amara seduce Tynan, but she was not merely following orders. She was doing it because she wanted him too badly to stay away. He had a superbly conditioned body, muscular and lean, and damp, his curls conveyed an appealing boyishness. Pleased by how easily he had accepted her affection, she pressed her knees against his sides and changed her rhythm to a more demanding cadence. When he gave a low moan of surrender, she felt his release throb deep within her and could at last abandon herself to the same stunning thrill. She stretched out on him, and aligning her body perfectly to his, drank in his pleasure with her own.

Content to hold Amara forever, Tynan kept her cradled in his arms until she chose to draw away. He looked up at her, his eyes glazed with a dreamy glow. Whatever anger he had felt the previous evening was gone, but he couldn't bring himself to apologize. When she smiled, he knew she didn't expect it. "Should we order something to eat?" he asked.

"No, we have reservations at one of the private dining rooms. It will be far more pleasant than staying here."

Tynan regarded her with an incredulous stare. "That's impossible."

"Wait and see. The dining rooms are all specially designed to create a particularly romantic mood, and they have marvelous cuisine."

"I'm already in a romantic mood," Tynan insisted, "and with your company, a crust of bread would taste sublime."

"Perhaps, but I know you'd rather have a steak."

"That's true."

Amara slid off the bed. "Get dressed, and we'll go."

Tynan propped himself up on one elbow. "Can you find other clothes for me? I doubt I'll be recognized if I'm not wearing my robe, and becoming anonymous is suddenly very appealing."

Amara paused at the doorway. "You're about Glen Archer's size. I'll call and see what he can lend you for tonight. Tomorrow, I'll have the Alado unit here provide additional clothing for you."

"Can you do that?"

Amara came back to kiss him. "Of course. Alado wants you to be happy."

Tynan grabbed her hand. "Only Alado?"

Amara ruffled his curls. "I think it's obvious that I want you to be happy—or at least, it certainly should be."

When she turned away this time, Tynan let her go, but he couldn't help but wonder what would happen if there were ever an occasion when Alado's and her interests weren't the same.

Glen Archer brought over a gold uniform that was close enough to Tynan's size to be comfortable, and he even had the presence of mind to include a pair of gold boots. Once dressed, Tynan glanced into the mirror on his bedroom wall, and somewhat surprised that he looked at home in the borrowed clothes, he asked Amara for her opinion. "Do you think I'll be recognized?"

"No, people expect to see you in a Guardian's robe, and they won't give you a second glance, except to note how handsome you are."

Amara was dressed in a loose-fitting long shirt and matching pants. The white fabric had a wavy texture that kept it from being transparent, but the shirt's single button was just above her navel creating a décolletage that allowed for a glimpse of seafoam-embellished breast. Because the abundant curls caressing her shoulders made her look so very pretty, he swallowed any complaint he might have wanted to make about the cut of her blouse. After all, just because he wasn't inured to feminine curves didn't mean the other men at the base weren't.

He took her hand, and after a brief elevator ride and a walk down a corridor lit with thousands of tiny, sparkling lights mimicking the stars, they reached the reservation desk for the private dining rooms. The clerk greeted them warmly, then handed Tynan a brochure listing the possibilities, which included not only Earth locales, but those from space colonies as well. There were tropical beaches, undersea gardens, snow-covered ski lodges, charming forest cottages, splendid castles, and eerie caves. No matter what a patron's tastes, the clerk promised it could be indulged.

Fascinated by the concept, Tynan read the entire list. "A tree house?" he finally asked. "You have a tree house?"

"Of course, it's one of our most popular choices. Would you like to try it?"

Tynan turned to Amara. "I'll let you decide."

"Yes, a tree house is perfect."

The clerk typed their selection into the computer, then handed them a room code. "Room eleven. Enjoy yourselves, and if you wish to remain for the night, please feel free to do so. Breakfast will be provided in the morning."

"Thank you." Amara took the code but relied on Tynan to locate their room and gain entry. The door slid open to reveal the wide plank floor of a tree house perched atop what appeared to be a gigantic oak. The walls of the room provided splendid views of a heavily wooded hillside bordered by a swiftly running stream whose bubbling harmonies sounded in the distance. The tree house was so perfectly fabricated, with windows and a spacious balcony, that Tynan remained staring in the doorway after Amara had entered.

"How do they do this?" he asked.

"If I explain, it will spoil the magic. Just believe that we're truly in a tree house, and we will be."

Tynan understood it was a clever illusion, a stage set and not real, but he could actually smell the woodsy odors of the forest and hear a mockingbird's melodic trills. As he stepped through the door, the tree's branches seemed to close around him, enfolding him in a private leafy world. "I always wanted to build a tree house," he murmured softly.

"Yes, a great many people missed out on that fun. That's why we choose to do it here." She patted the green cushion which could serve as either chairs or bed. "Come and sit down. We can enjoy the view while we decide what we want to eat."

Tynan adopted a cross-legged pose beside her. "What do kids take up to eat in a tree house?"

"That would depend on where the kids were from. Some might have fried chicken and biscuits, while others might have whatever delicacy was left over from dinner, or even fish they caught down there in the stream." Amara gestured toward a panel hidden in one of the limbs that supported the marvelous tree house. "Here's one of those magic compartments you mentioned. We place our order, and it appears without our ever having to be disturbed by servers."

Tynan thought only a minute. "I want to have a barbecue like the ones they used to have on Earth, with fried chicken, barbecued beef, ears of corn, and chocolate ice cream."

"That's perfect. What do you want to drink?"

"Orange soda. Do they have that here?"

"They have whatever we want." Amara tapped a button on the hidden panel, and the same voice Tynan had heard in the chapel responded.

"How may we serve you?"

Amara repeated Tynan's order, added a salad, and almost immediately the food began to appear, along with brightly colored plates, glasses, ice, utensils and a whole package of napkins.

"It looks as though they expect us to be messy," she complained.

"That's part of the fun." Tynan picked up a piece of fried chicken and took a bite. Piping hot, the crispy coating was delicately seasoned. "They've never prepared chicken this way at the Keep, and I've always wanted to try it."

While Amara didn't usually eat fowl, she made an exception and found it as delicious as Tynan had. "Say, this is good."

Involved in their fascinating game, Tynan forgot all about the conference for a while and felt genuinely happy. It wasn't until they had finished their ice cream that he realized the magic wasn't in the tree house, but in his lovely companion. He helped her clear away their dishes, then moved out on the balcony to take the best advantage of the view. The sights and sounds were gradually changing to create the illusion of sunset's approach.

"I think I may have appeared a little headstrong today," he admitted, "but I couldn't sit there another minute and let the talks go around and around rather than toward our goal. That would have been negligent, don't you think?"

This was the second time Amara had heard the word that day, and it gave her a moment's pause.

She hadn't been summoned to Orion's suite after the day's session, but she knew he would read the transcript and know precisely what had transpired. Then she would undoubtedly hear from him.

"To force a confrontation in which Derrel would have to back down was more audacious than headstrong, Tynan, but you got away with it, and that's really all that matters."

"Is it?"

"Some of Alado's diplomats may not be able to sleep tonight because they'll be so worried about what you might do tomorrow, but that can't be helped. You were asked to do a job, and you're doing it. Just keep following your instincts, and you can't go wrong."

"Come here." Tynan reached for her, and Amara went to sit beside him and rested her head on his shoulder. "Let's forget the conference for the night and just enjoy this tree house. It's very peaceful up here, isn't it, and I can smell the icy stream on the breeze."

So could Amara, but as they watched the shadows of the coming night fade the hillside's cool mauves to lavender, she was filled with a bittersweet longing to make everything real—and to make it last.

Chapter Sixteen

Amara had just taken her seat in the gallery when Orion tapped her on the shoulder. He motioned for her to accompany him, then realized that she couldn't see his gesture well enough to obey. "Come with me," he whispered.

Annoyed at having to miss the beginning of the morning's session, Amara followed him out of the assembly hall. "What's wrong?" she asked.

"Let's wait until we reach Alado's offices to discuss it."

Relieved that he hadn't suggested they talk in his suite, Amara nevertheless thought he sounded a bit stern and drew the most likely conclusion. "If it's about yesterday's session—"

"I said we'd wait!"

Insulted by that harsh command, Amara held her tongue until they had arrived at the level housing the offices of each corporation. She followed Orion through the maze of work stations where all of Alado's business interests involving the Confederation were handled and into a private office. Here, as at Fleet Command, the furnishings were of black and gold, but the familiar colors failed to give her any sense of comfort.

"Sit down," Orion ordered.

"I'd rather stand."

Orion shoved an ebony chair toward her. "Sit!" He paused while Amara reluctantly complied, then continued in a heated rush. "When I read yesterday's transcript, I was—how shall I put this?—perhaps *revolted* best expresses my reaction to Tynan's uncontrolled outburst. He's Alado's negotiator because we expected a brilliant yet subtle approach from him. We were all proud when we learned he had been chosen as chairman. We relied upon him to elevate the tone of the deliberations, to inspire the others to emulate the insightful method of problem solving he describes in his writing."

He scooped a copy of the transcript off the desk and slammed it down to make his point. "Instead, we got all the finesse of a lumbering pirate forcing his way through an overcrowded colony bar!"

Amara's vision was steadily improving, and although Orion's features still lacked accurate definition, she could see well enough to have no doubt that he was sincerely outraged. When he paused to draw a breath, she attempted to defuse his anger by agreeing with him. "You're absolutely right in your assessment. Tynan was surprisingly crude—but it was effective. Shouldn't a negotiator have a variety of styles? After yesterday, none of the others will mistakenly believe

305

he's too timid to fight for what he believes is right."

"It isn't merely our concern with how Tynan might be perceived that's at stake here, Amara. It's Alado's future!"

Obviously, she was having as little success influencing his mood as she had had with Tynan, and Amara ceased to try. "I don't believe we ought to be having this conversation without Tynan. Let's continue it when he's available." She started to rise, but Orion clamped his hand down on her shoulder to keep her in place.

"I haven't even begun to talk. Although you've flown only one mission in a Starcruiser, I'm assuming you understand all its capabilities."

Surprised by his sudden change of subject, Amara grew flustered. "Well, yes, I believe so."

"Then you know that when emergency procedures are begun, the flight recorder is activated. We have disks of everything that transpired while the pirates were on board your ship. It's unnecessary for me to question Tynan about his actions because I can document them all. That he murdered two men, and quite cold-bloodedly too, scarcely compares to *this*."

Orion pressed a button on the control panel on the desk, and a screen descended from the ceiling. Another button activated the laser disk which presented the scene in the passenger cabin immediately after Tynan had dispatched Mak Trumbo. In brilliant if blurry color, Amara could easily make out Tynan's deep purple robe and the peach tones of her bare shin. At their moment of triumph, it had been a wildly passionate celebration of life, but she was appalled to have to share it with Orion and looked away.

"Turn it off, please."

"I'll be happy to, just as soon as you assure me that Tynan will behave in a more responsible manner for the remainder of the conference. If not, I'll make certain copies of this disk become available to anyone who'll show them. I think you know what will happen to Tynan's reputation when it becomes common knowledge that the galaxy's foremost proponent of harmonious co-existence is a murdering rapist."

"That's not true! The pirates' deaths were justified, and I wasn't raped!"

"Really?" Orion stopped the disk, and replayed a crucial portion. "That's not how it looks to me, and with some clever editing, all the viewer will see is a badly beaten woman being ravaged by a Guardian who didn't even bother to remove his robe. It's a wonder you didn't smother. Tell me, do you actually prefer such abusive treatment to the far more gentle and tender loving we shared?"

Infuriated by his absurd insinuations, Amara could no longer be civil. "If you showed that disk to Tynan, he'd tear off your head and kick it around this office!"

Orion laughed. "My, what a grisly threat, but you've just proved my point. The man has so little self-restraint as to be a menace to anyone who holds an opposing view. I know he'd try to hurt me if I showed him this disk, but that doesn't mean he'd succeed. However, I've no intention of subjecting myself to the type of abuse you apparently enjoy."

"Tynan's not abusive!"

"That's a matter of opinion. Now, all I want is your word that you will exert your considerable influence to prevent Tynan from repeating any of yesterday's confrontational tactics. Or, as I said, you'll force me to share this marvelously entertaining disk with whoever would like to see it."

"Providing Alado's confidential material to unauthorized personnel is grounds for dismissal. I know you wouldn't jeopardize your career just to pursue a childhood vendetta, so stop threatening me with something you don't dare do."

Grabbing hold of her chair, Orion tipped it backwards slightly to trap her between his outstretched arms. "Don't make the mistake of underestimating me," he warned. "All I have to do is hand the disk over to the Confederation Security Forces—which, in the case of boardings and deaths, I am required to do. I haven't done it as yet, nor will I if Tynan behaves. But if he doesn't, the disk goes straight to Security, and I can guarantee it would be regarded as such a fascinating document that it would be duplicated and leaked by a dozen ambitious individuals within an hour's time. That Tynan's reputation was irrevocably damaged as a result could never be blamed on me. After all, in turning it over I'd only be complying with Confederation policy."

"Let me go!" Amara demanded.

Orion immediately released his hold on her chair and stepped back, allowing the front legs to drop to the floor with a jarring thud. "It's your choice, my dear. Cooperate with me for the good of Alado and your own career, or refuse and see your illustrious lover disgraced in what will surely be one of the most colorful scandals ever to touch the staid ranks of the Guardians. They'll take him back, of course, but even at the Keep there will be constant whispers about him."

He paused, then breathed almost silently, "Murderer."

When Amara refused to look at him, Orion took another tack. "Did he tell you that as an infant he was abandoned by his parents? With a little effort, I'll bet I could find out just who his people were. Do you think he'd like to know them, and why they threw their son away? They're probably still alive, and if so, I can arrange for introductions. Wouldn't that be a touching reunion scene? Of course, there's a strong possibility that they're the disreputable sort he'd be ashamed to meet."

Amara leapt from her chair so fast she grew dizzy and had to grab the back for support. "Stop it! To threaten to torture Tynan by producing the parents who abandoned him is positively diabolical. How can you even suggest such a despicable thing? Are there no depths to which you won't sink to hurt Tynan? Why do you despise him so?"

For an instant, it appeared as though Orion might actually satisfy her curiosity as to the cause of their feud, but this time he was the one to turn away. "You may go," he announced. "Tynan's probably missed you. Tell him we were talking about the Starcruiser's performance if he asks where you've been."

"I won't lie to him."

"Fine. Tell him I have evidence that will destroy him. The result is easily predictable. He'll come after me in what witnesses will surely testify was a totally unprovoked attack. That will ruin him even faster than the disk will."

Fearing Orion was right, Amara moved toward the door. "How do I know that once the peace treaty's signed, you won't use the disk to embarrass Tynan?"

Orion leaned back against the desk. "I've already explained why. I intend to take credit for his success. He'll be safe once the treaty's signed and he's returned to the Keep."

Even knowing that Orion always did what was best for himself, Amara still had doubts. "Why don't I believe you?"

Orion shrugged. "Tynan has contaminated your perceptions with twenty-year-old complaints. Trust what you know about me, Amara. Alado won't be well-served by a negotiator who throws temper tantrums. See that he maintains the blissful calm for which he's known, even if you have to satisfy his newly awakened sexual desires on the hour, and we'll both benefit."

"To say nothing of preventing war?"

"Diplomats seldom receive the proper credit for averting disaster, but believe me, I'll be more than happy to share whatever praise I receive with you. As soon as your vision returns to normal, you'll be my pilot again, and when Tynan leaves, we'll continue our personal relationship as well. The current turmoil is only temporary, but our liaison will survive."

Amara could not imagine a circumstance in which she would return to Orion's bed, but thought it might be useful to let him think otherwise. "Where does Solana Diaz fit into your plans?"

Pleased by her interest in his latest companion, Orion came forward. "She's no more than a fleeting diversion—the way Tynan is for you." He leaned forward to kiss her, but Amara eluded him by quickly slipping out the door.

Once she reached the elevators, she hesitated to return to the assembly hall. She was still shaking with bitter rage at Orion's demands, and she certainly couldn't encourage serenity in Tynan when she had none herself. The idea of returning to her suite held no appeal, but she recalled the spa from a previous visit to the base and, deciding exercise was precisely what she needed, went there. The spacious gym provided a variety of exercise equipment, both passive and active, as well as classes in which men and women could practice body toning routines to music.

Afraid she might become dizzy if she engaged in anything strenuous, Amara chose to go for a swim. She requested a bathing suit and towel and swam laps until she lost count. Tired, she finally felt more numb than anxious and stretched out by the pool to rest a moment before returning to the conference site. She yawned and, after a graceful stretch, fell asleep.

Tynan saw Amara leave with Orion and could not help but wonder what the pair had to discuss now. He could justify the summons by the fact that Amara worked for Orion, but when she wasn't able to fly, they couldn't be discussing travel plans. Orion had already questioned her about their flight, so that wasn't a possibility either. He supposed they could have some legitimate business of which he was unaware, but it was their personal relationship that worried him most.

That the only woman he had ever cared about had been with Orion first was unbearably painful. But then, if Amara hadn't been Orion's pilot, they might never have met. Tynan tried to think of Orion as useful in that regard, but it didn't assuage his lingering doubts over why they still needed to spend time together. If he knew Orion, and he believed he did, then the man was undoubtedly using Amara for some dark purpose.

Tynan had to remind himself that Amara didn't share his poor opinion of Orion, but that wasn't at all comforting. It meant she would probably believe her superior's explanations, rather than question his true purpose. He had to get her away from Orion—but how? How could he encourage her to request a change in assignment, when it would be obvious how badly he wanted her away from Orion's influence?

Lost in thought, Tynan jumped when Tava Micenko touched his sleeve. "I'm sorry," he said. "Would you please repeat your comment?"

Astonished, Tava looked at the others seated around the conference table. "Did any of the rest of you have difficulty following me?" she asked.

"None at all," Lisha assured her. "Your assessment of the situation is correct. It's the disparity in size between the corporations which causes all the friction. If part of Alado's and Peregrine's holdings were redistributed among Omega, Serema, and Europa, the resulting equality would bring peace."

Although ashamed to have been so inattentive, Tynan provided no excuses. "Forgive me for not understanding you," he began, "but the corporations were of approximately equal size at their founding, and there is absolutely nothing in the Confederation's charter which makes equality thereafter a goal. What incentive would there be for any of the corporations to aggressively pursue claiming new territory and founding colonies if their holdings were seized periodically to guarantee equality?"

Rather than being dismayed by Tynan's dismissal of her proposal, Tava's smile widened. "That's the beauty of my idea," she explained. "If holdings are adjusted at regular intervals, and wealth shared equally, there will be no need for disputes such as the one that brought us here. It will make absolutely no difference which corporation founds a colony if it may later belong to another firm, and the aggressive competition to seize new territory will cease."

"It will make a great deal of difference to the colonists," Derrel exclaimed. "What you're suggesting is a complete restructuring of the Confederation, which is way beyond the scope of this particular conference. If you had better leadership at Serema, you wouldn't be counting yourselves among the smaller firms. Now let's get on with the real business at hand, which is ensuring the continued peaceful exploration of space."

While amazed to find himself agreeing with Derrel on anything, Tynan was nonetheless grateful for his assistance in focusing on the issues. "Thank you, Mr. Simmons. Now I think we ought to concentrate on productive suggestions for avoiding conflict which don't require a complete reorganization of our corporations. Did you wish to say something, Mr. McGrath?"

"I most certainly do." Gaining the floor, Gallager proceeded to issue a blistering denouncement of Tava's suggestion. "Communism was a resounding failure in your country in the twentieth century, Tava. Don't try and foist it on us at this late date. As Europa's representative, I can assure you that our smaller size is no disadvantage whatsoever as we concentrate on founding quality installations rather than amassing numerous holdings of little value. It's not the number of colonies that matters," he exclaimed, "but the productivity of each one."

"But the smaller firms lack the opportunity to compete for new colonies," Lisha complained.

As Gallager refuted Lisha's claims, Tynan glanced over at Derrel, and the Peregrine representative winked at him. Two days earlier, he had been annoyed by the man's flippant attitude, but now he was beginning to think their firms had more in common than they had with the others. Borrowing one of Orion's tactics, he decided right then to befriend Derrel and discover all he could about Peregrine's link to Mak Trumbo. When the noon recess was called, and Amara still hadn't reappeared, he followed Derrel toward the door.

"I wonder if I might have a word with you?" he asked.

Startled, Derrel turned around to face him. "We don't dare make the others jealous," he replied with a ready grin.

"This isn't conference business."

"How will they know that?"

"They won't."

Impressed by Tynan's surprisingly defiant attitude, Derrel gestured toward the door. "Let's have lunch together. If we eat on the office level, so many people will see us no one will dare suggest we're plotting anything."

When Tynan agreed, Derrel led the way to the level Amara and Orion had visited earlier. A central cafeteria served the staffs of all five corporations, and while it was busy and crowded, the pair were recognized and treated with cordial deference. Tynan was relieved to find Derrel shared his appreciation of red meat, and at his suggestion he ordered a roast beef sandwich which was as deliciously prepared as everything he had been served at the base. He waited until Derrel had taken several bites before he casually mentioned pirates.

As far as he knew, it had not been announced that their ship had been boarded, so he chose not to share that fact. "I understand that transport ships are the preferred targets of pirates," he began.

"Indeed they are, and I don't mind telling you that the Confederation Security Forces haven't had much success in recovering stolen goods. It's probably a point we ought to add to the conference agenda, but I thought you didn't intend to discuss conference business."

Derrel had responded to his comment about pirates without the slightest hesitation, and expecting some hint of guilt if Peregrine had hired Mak Trumbo to seize a Starcruiser, Tynan pushed him a little harder. "As you just pointed out, pirates aren't on the agenda. Is cargo the only thing they're after, or do they sometimes hijack spaceships to steal their technology?"

Derrel continued to eat while forming his answer. When he looked up, he seemed completely sincere. "Most pirates are better engineers than any who work for the corporations. As soon as one of us has a new design, they're usually able to modify their ships to match it. That's what makes them so difficult to apprehend. They're always in the vanguard of technology. If only we could get the bastards to work with us instead of against us . . . but crime is as old as civilization, and it will probably never be completely eliminated."

Tynan had always been able to tell when Orion was lying. There was a special brightness about him at those moments, an almost lun.inous aura that others had never been able to perceive. As he listened to Derrel, he watched him closely, searching for a sign that he was also a stranger to the truth. But he detected none. Derrel was relaxed and, without his usual superficial charm, appeared genuinely perplexed about how to rid the galaxy of pirates.

"Have you ever heard of Mak Trumbo?" Tynan asked.

Derrel shook his head. "No. Who is he?"

"A pirate someone hired to hijack a Starcruiser."

"You're not serious!"

"Yes, I am."

"That's impossible. He might just as well have been hired to find the Holy Grail. A Starcruiser is too well-equipped and too fast to be forcibly boarded. It's a ship they'll try to clone, but they'd be wasting their time attempting to board one. Of course, if they can match its power, then there would be no need to hijack one."

"You're an expert on Starcruisers?"

Derrel shrugged. "Of course, and ask that pretty pilot of yours about our fleet if you want to know anything about Peregrine. I'll bet she knows more about our ships than we do. It's no secret that pilots like to brag, and a lot of technology is shared between them." Derrel paused to make certain none of the diners at the nearby tables was listening to them.

"That's how we got into the current mess, isn't it? Our scout ships, Alado's Banshee and the Peregrine Javelin, are remarkably similar. When our expeditionary forces enter the same sector, there's bound to be a violent difference of opinion over which ship was the first to reach and claim new territory."

"The other three corporations maintain expeditionary forces as well," Tynan reminded him.

"Yes, but they have fewer major tactical and reconnaissance vessels from which to launch scout ships, so we seldom have any disputes with them."

"I'd still like to know more about pirates. Let's say that someone actually did want to hire a pirate to hijack a Starcruiser—where would he go?"

Stunned by that question, Derrel stared as though Tynan were mad. "No one goes looking for pirates," he exclaimed. "No one. How can you make a deal with murdering thieves without running the risk that you'll end up dead too? You want to interview a pirate? Go out to one of the penal colonies and

Cinnamon Burke

speak to one who's already been captured and convicted. To look for any others would be just plain stupid, if it weren't outright suicide, and no one will ever convince me that the magnificent Tynan Thorn is stupid."

Tynan winced at the word magnificent. "Please, just plain Tynan will do."

"Fine, just promise me you won't go hunting for pirates. You might think that being the chairman of this conference is a thankless chore, but at least it isn't dangerous."

"You've had personal experience with pirates?"

"Only once, and I managed to outfly them. It's not something I'd recommend either. I've played Alado's Banshee Quest, and that's more than enough excitement for most people. I don't suppose you play?"

"I have a few times."

"Finish your sandwich, and I'll teach you the finer points of the game."

Derrel's eyes were alight with a familiar mischievous sparkle. Convinced he wasn't the culprit who had nearly gotten Amara and him killed, Tynan accepted his challenge, and the two played the demanding game until the time came for the afternoon session to begin.

Amara slept until early afternoon, awakened with a start, and was instantly furious with herself for wasting half the day. Remembering her promise to supplement Tynan's wardrobe, she ordered a gold diplomatic corps uniform, gold boots, and a generous supply of underwear. Then, thinking Tynan might have occasion to use it, she added the casual attire pilots wore off duty, when they preferred dark colors rather than gold. After asking to have the items delivered to Tynan's suite that afternoon, she made a very tardy return to the assembly hall.

Tynan had glanced toward the empty seat that should have held Amara so often that when he at last found her there, he had to hide his surprise. He had been working all afternoon toward simplifying each corporation's goals while at the same time stressing their many common concerns. The technique appeared to be working, and when they recessed for the day, he felt as though some progress had finally been made. He waited for Amara at the door, took her hand and, forcing himself not to pry into how she and Orion had spent most of the day, walked with her back to his suite.

Cold drinks and light refreshments had thoughtfully been placed on the table, and he poured himself some of the sparkling juice and handed a glass to Amara. "I missed you at noon, but rather than sulk, I ate with Derrel Simmons."

Amara opened her mouth to provide an excuse, but Tynan shook his head to show her it was unnecessary. "He'd never heard of Mak Trumbo, and he didn't even think it was possible for a Starcruiser to be boarded. If Peregrine were behind the plot to seize our ship, wouldn't he be aware of it?"

Shocked that Tynan had discussed the matter with Derrel, Amara needed a moment to reply. "Yes, he'd know, and if you asked him about it and he feigned ignorance, then he was lying. Did you really expect him to admit Peregrine was behind the hijacking of our ship?"

319

"No, but I'm positive I'd know if he were lying when he denied it."

"How could you tell?"

Tynan joined her on the sofa, setting his juice aside. "Even the most accomplished liars provide subtle hints when they aren't being truthful. Orion was always so blatant in his lies that he was believed, but it's precisely that arrogance that gives him away. Perhaps you've already noticed that yourself."

Orion was the last subject Amara wanted to discuss, and she looked down at her juice rather than up at Tynan.

"You, however, find it very difficult to lie. As you're doing now, you can't look me in the eye and say anything but the truth."

"I don't lie to you," Amara protested, making a concerted effort to look directly at him even though his features weren't perfectly clear.

"No, you just omit a great deal, the way you refuse to describe your feelings for me."

"I thought we were talking about pirates."

"You see, I've made you uncomfortable by mentioning feelings, and you've changed the subject."

"I thought the subject was pirates!"

Amused by her shyness to admit in words what she expressed so beautifully in bed, Tynan took her hand and placed an adoring kiss on her palm. "Yes, we are. We agreed not to confide in Orion, but did you tell him that Mak boasted he'd been hired to hijack a Starcruiser?"

Amara shook her head. Then, appalled by what she would have to explain, she swallowed hard before admitting how intricate the Starcruiser's systems were. "I'd forgotten, really I had, that the Starcruiser records not just cockpit activity, but what transpires throughout the ship once emergency procedures are activated. That's what Orion wanted to discuss with me this morning. He's viewed the laser disks of the boarding, and while he didn't touch upon Mak's mention of profits, he must have heard it."

Tynan watched Amara take a hasty sip of juice and then, realizing what else must be on the disks, he understood that she had good reason for her nervousness. "What does Orion intend to do with the disks? Will he show them at parties to amuse his friends at our expense? Providing, of course, that he actually has a few friends."

"No, of course not. You don't understand him, Ty. He's totally committed to the advancement of his career, and you're vital to his plans. If you achieve the excellent results Alado expects from you, then Orion's prestige will be greatly enhanced. He was the one who suggested your name to the board, and whatever success you have, he'll share."

Tynan was so disgusted by the prospect of Orion's benefiting from his efforts that he said the first thing that entered his mind. "Just like we share you."

That sarcastic retort was so unexpected, Amara gasped sharply. "I told you, I ended my relationship with Orion before we met, so you most certainly are not sharing me!"

Tynan watched her breasts heave as she defended herself. Her complexion brightened with a rosy tinge, and now that her bruises had faded, there was nothing to detract from the fiery brilliance of her green eyes. But even as he admired her spirited response, a truly insidious doubt began to take shape in his mind.

She was Orion's pilot, and while she might believe their affair was over, did he? Or was Orion confident she would soon return to him? Had Orion in fact sent her to the Keep with orders to win his confidence, seduce him, control him? Orion was definitely manipulative and clever enough to engineer such a plan. The real question was, how much was Amara like him?

"That was tactless," he admitted. "I'm sorry. I'll bet Orion was angry with me about yesterday, wasn't he? He must have complained that I wasn't behaving like the calm, reasonable philosopher he'd expected."

Amara slumped back into the couch. "He was livid."

"Why didn't he complain directly to me rather than to you?"

"You know why. He's certain your animosity for him will make it impossible for you to accept suggestions from him."

"He's right," Tynan agreed softly. "So he's using you as a lovely liaison who'll keep me in line with a more subtle approach. Is that how he describes it?"

"No, there's no requirement that I be subtle."

Tynan pushed himself to his feet and began to pace slowly in front of the sofa. Amara had just admitted that Orion had assigned her an important role to play. Was that the real reason she had been so reluctant to discuss her feelings? Maybe the simple truth was that she had none beyond the lavish enjoyment of the physical pleasure they shared. Tynan stopped and stared down at her. She had the same angelic coloring as Orion, and when she looked up at him, her expression held a remarkable innocence as well. How long had it taken her to master that sad, sweet smile—months, or mere days under Orion's skilled direction?

"If Orion expects to win a seat on the board, then playing a significant part in this conference greatly enhances his chances, but what will it do for you? What will your job be if Orion becomes part of Alado's board of directors?"

Sorry that Tynan believed her future lay with Orion rather than him, Amara shook her head. "It's really too soon to say. This conference has to be successful, and there has to be a vacancy on the board before Orion can fill it. There are too many uncertainties for me to correctly predict where I'll be a few months from now. If my vision doesn't return to normal, God knows what I'll do. I can't even catalog rocks with my parents if I can't see any better than this."

Rather than answer Tynan's question, Amara was talking all the way around it, and the noose of his suspicions tightened around her neck. "I'm going to ask you a question, and I want you to answer me truthfully. Will you give me your promise that you will?"

"What's the question?"

Another evasion, Tynan thought. "No, I must have your promise first."

Amara didn't like being pressured, but she could sense that this was important to Tynan. "All right. You have my promise."

"Thank you. Has Orion asked you to sleep with me?"

"Well, yes, but—"

That hesitant response pierced Tynan's heart like a thousand shards of jagged glass, but he understood everything now. Amara was merely doing a job for Orion, and to her credit, she *had* advised him to guard his feelings, warned him not to speak of love. While he should have thanked her for her consideration, he still felt badly betrayed. I should have known! he chastised himself. Anything and anyone tainted by Orion's evil touch wasn't what it seemed.

"Thank you for your honesty. Now I'd appreciate it if you'd just go."

"Go where?"

"I don't care—anywhere you like, off to be with Orion the way you were today. I just want you out of here, and out of my life!" Tynan crossed to the door connecting their suites and slammed his hand against the button to open it. "Go on, I know you're not too blind to make your way to your own room."

Amara set her glass of juice aside with badly shaking hands and struggled to her feet. "I don't understand what's wrong with you," she agonized. "It doesn't matter what Orion suggests, or orders, I've followed my heart with you."

"Don't make this any worse than it already is. Just go."

"Not while you're twisting my words to prove whatever ridiculous assumption you've made. I swear you don't even see me as a person, much less hear what I'm saying. You and Orion are just using me as a pawn in an absurd re-enactment of an old hatred. You're supposed to be grown men, not nasty little boys who'd rather die than make friends. It doesn't really surprise me coming from Orion, but I expected a far more enlightened attitude from you."

As Amara passed through the connecting door, she flung back, "You needn't worry about my straying in here again. You'd have to beg me on your knees before I'd tolerate your exasperating presence ever again!"

Chapter Seventeen

Within five minutes of leaving Tynan, Amara had gathered up her belongings and arrived at the medical unit. She asked to see Solana Diaz, and when the doctor appeared, she hurriedly explained her problem. "I overestimated my powers of recovery. I'm not feeling nearly as well as I should be by now, and if I may, I'd like to check in for a few days of complete rest."

Following Alado's standard procedure, Solana first ushered Amara into a treatment room to conduct a brief examination, during which she noted not only a slight improvement in the pilot's vision, but also the undisguised sorrow of her mood. That Amara had brought along a bulging flight bag tipped Solana to the desperation of her plea, for clearly she had no intention of returning to her suite. Thinking that perhaps a problem more severe than her visual complaint had brought her there, Solana attempted to delve deeper.

"You do look tired, lieutenant, and because I know you weren't following my orders about bed rest, I'm inclined to admit you; but first, is there something bothering you that you haven't reported?"

"Nothing that has anything to do with my health."

Solana leaned back against the examining table where Amara sat. "That's where you're wrong. Our feelings do indeed influence our physical well-being. Forget for a moment that I know Orion well and describe any problems you might have related to your work assignment."

That would be a real challenge, Amara mused darkly, but doubting that she could coherently untangle the painful mess that Tynan's misconceptions about her motives had caused, she refused even to begin. "No, although I am worried about future assignments if my vision doesn't correct itself soon."

"It will," Solana assured her. "What about Tynan Thorn? Have the demands of providing hospitality for him proved too taxing?"

"Hospitality," Amara repeated numbly, thinking it a peculiar euphemism for her involvement with the fascinating Guardian. Again evading Solana's question, she shook her head. "He'll be fine without me. Now will you please let me stay?"

That Amara had answered her question with a comment about Tynan rather than about herself made Solana suspect Amara was withholding an important truth. She considered the pilot's request as she reviewed her chart and reluctantly came to the conclusion that Amara's distorted vision did indeed justify her admittance. While it bothered Solana not to have gained more insight into her patient's emotional state, she hoped the next few days would provide such an opportunity.

"At present, we happen to be enjoying a period of extremely good health here, and with no shortage of beds, I've no reason not to grant your request. But please, you mustn't hesitate to confide in me if anything is troubling you."

Amara managed a wan smile, but there was too great a possibility that any confidence she shared with Solana would go straight to Orion. "The only thing troubling me is my vision," she replied.

"It's already improved; please be more patient. Let's go back to the desk and get you checked in. There are private rooms available. Do you have a preference as to theme?"

By the use of the same projection technique featured in the chapel, the hospital also had the capability of giving patients a choice between the soothing sight and sound of ocean rhythms, tranquil pastoral scenes of near heavenly perfection, or their favorite natural scenery from their home planet. Wanting something she couldn't possibly associate with Tynan, Amara asked for the constantly shifting sands of one of the outer colonies' blue deserts. Once in bed, however, the sight of the softly blurred sand dunes enveloped her in a cloud of despair, and she knew she had made an extremely poor choice. She had just reached toward the communications panel beside her bed to request a change when Orion strode through the door, followed by Solana Diaz.

"Did you really think you could avoid completing your assignment by hiding in here? If so, you were very badly mistaken. Now get up and get back to Tynan's suite where you belong."

Having apprised Orion of Amara's whereabouts, Solana was nonetheless shocked by his demands. "I advised bed rest when Lieutenant Greer first arrived, and she has now chosen to take advantage of our facility," the physician argued. "I don't tell you how to run the diplomatic corps, and I won't allow you to interfere in my patients' treatment."

There was something deeply satisfying about hearing another woman stand up to Orion. Enjoying the scene immensely, Amara had to force herself not to cheer as Solana demanded that Orion not return until he could speak in a civil tone, and then to do so only during visiting hours. Amara relaxed her arms and attempted to affect a gracefully pathetic pose. She closed her eyes for a moment, and while she would never have fallen asleep with such an entertaining argument going on at her bedside, she looked as though she had.

"Did you drug her?" Orion asked accusingly. He reached for Amara's hand and slapped it impatiently.

Amara opened her eyes and withdrew her hand from his. "No, I haven't been drugged. If you'll excuse us, doctor, I'd like to speak with Orion in private."

"Are you certain you feel up to it?" Solana asked.

"No, but I'll do it anyway."

Orion nodded, and while still obviously reluctant to go, Solana left the room. "You needn't shout at me," Amara began as soon as they were alone.

"Because I work for you, Tynan apparently can't tell where my assignment ends and my feelings begin, and he doesn't trust me anymore. If I were to return to his suite, he would just throw me out again, and that's not something I'd care to repeat, ever."

"He threw you out?"

"He didn't pick me up and toss me out bodily if that's what you mean, but he demanded that I leave, which amounts to the same thing."

"He's probably already reconsidered and is looking for you."

"Fine. I'll ask Solana to let him know the visiting hours too."

Frustrated by her indifference, Orion sat down on the side of her bed and this time took her hand in a gentle clasp. "I won't allow a misunderstanding to end your association with Tynan. It's much too valuable an alliance."

"Spoken like a true diplomat," Amara sighed wearily. "I gave it my best effort, and I'm sure Tynan has too, but under the circumstances perhaps he was right to end it. I plan to follow his example. You and I are no longer an effective team either, and I want a transfer to the Expeditionary Force."

Now crushing her hand in a bruising grip, Orion leaned close. "The answer to that ridiculous request is an absolute and unequivocal no. Do you understand me? You will remain on assignment as my personal pilot until such time as I decide you may go. At that time, I'll be the one to decide where you're reassigned, but since your performance on your last flight was negligent in the extreme, it may take me a long while to find any branch of Alado willing to accept you.

"Get all the rest you can tonight, because you're going to need it tomorrow. Then you'll have to find a way—I don't care how devious or perverted— to satisfy Tynan's desires. When he leaves for the Keep at the close of the conference, you'll be his pilot home. I'm certain that with such an able physician as Solana Diaz attending you, your vision will have returned to normal by then.

"Now, have I made myself clear? As long as Tynan Thorn is here at this base, you will be his adoring companion. If he's reluctant, then it will merely take more effort on your part, but I've not the slightest doubt that you can make him want you again. I certainly don't want any lewd behavior taking place on the conference floor, but when it comes to his suite, be as imaginative as you dare. Taunt him, abuse him savagely if you must, but make him so dependent on you for pleasure that he'll run the conference with an efficiency the others will all admire, never suspecting it's merely to allow him more time with you."

His message delivered, Orion kissed Amara's cheek. Then, releasing her hand, he left without waiting for her promise that she would obey. Caught between a demanding superior and a rejecting lover, Amara closed her eyes and searched for a way to avoid both. In but a moment, it came to her—she would convince Orion her best chance for recapturing Tynan's heart would be to remain in the medical unit until he missed her so badly that he sought her out. Then, when he begged her to return to him, she would do so on her own terms. Her arrogant boss would never have to know that her terms were in direct conflict with his.

Amara massaged her hand and swore that next time, she wasn't going to be the one left with the bruises. When Solana came to her door, she greeted her warily. "I'd like to change the room environment," she announced. "I'd prefer a bright red Martian desert."

Solana nodded, but remained in the doorway. "Does Orion always speak so harshly to you?" she asked.

Amara saw no reason to lie. "Not when he wants me to sleep with him, he doesn't."

Greatly intrigued, Solana came into the room and closed the door behind her. "He told me you'd had a brief involvement, but that it was over. Isn't that your understanding?"

"If you're worried about competition from me, you needn't. I don't even want to work with Orion, let alone make love with him. He uses people, and he's had his last chance to use me."

"Perhaps you're allowing hurt feelings to cloud your judgment."

"Not where he's concerned, I'm not," Amara insisted. "He's a skilled lover. By all means enjoy him, but there's no real emotion behind his affection, and his lavish compliments ring hollow. Now if you'll excuse me, I'd really like to get some rest."

Not pleased by Amara's description of Orion, Solana frowned unhappily, but again left without probing for more.

* * *

When Ross Belding arrived at Tynan's door and offered to accompany him to dinner, Tynan found it difficult not to shout an angry refusal. Then, remembering that Ross only followed Orion's orders, he reined in his temper and forced himself to say, "How thoughtful of you, but what made you think I'd be dining alone?"

Ross shrugged slightly and, obviously embarrassed, lowered his voice. "The Secretary told me you'd not be dining with Lieutenant Greer this evening, sir."

That Amara had gone back to Orion so quickly didn't surprise Tynan, but it still hurt, and badly. Had nothing she had ever said been true? "Thank you for asking, Ross, but I already have plans for the evening. Please tell the Secretary that I can arrange my meals without his help."

Tynan shut his door before Ross could do more than nod. In reality, he had no plans for the evening other than to curse the lovely young woman who had brightened his life all too briefly. He felt sick rather than hungry, and after flinging aside his robe, he stretched out on the sofa. Knowing he ought to concentrate on the conference, he tried to make plans for the next day's negotiations, but thoughts of Amara kept intruding. She had played her part with such masterful ease that it was a shame she had become a pilot rather than an actress. With the extraordinary talent she possessed, she would surely have had her pick of roles.

"Damn her!" he cried. Sitting up, he held his head in his hands until he finally convinced himself that he would have a lifetime to regret his folly where Amara was concerned and only a few more days, if all went well, to negotiate a peace treaty. In addition, there was still the question of who had hired the pirates. Thinking that was just the sort of puzzle to occupy his mind, he got out a notepad and began to make diagrams, charting the possibilities.

"If not Peregrine, then who?" he asked himself. Perhaps it hadn't been one of the competing corporations, if technical information passed as freely between pilots as Derrel Simmons claimed, but an individual—someone like Dr. Risto Cortez, but without a private army of Corkscrews. Lacking the means to track the infinite number of possibilities that supposition created, he grew frustrated, sat back, and stared at his confused drawing. Gradually, the eerie sensation that he was overlooking an important clue began to seep through his veins.

"What am I missing?" Half expecting Amara to answer, he glanced up, then remembered too late that she was gone. He closed his eyes, but unable to force away the sad sweetness of her smile, he replayed their encounter with the pirates in every excruciating detail. Unconsciously, his fingertips crept up to his cheek, tracing the faint scar left by Mak Trumbo's knife. Clearly, the pirate had meant to intimidate rather than cause him any serious harm. Perhaps he had intended all along to seek a ransom for Amara and him and hadn't dared to cut him up too badly.

Not that Mak had struck him as the type to analyze his actions all that carefully. No, the pirate had been a swaggering fool, and the other members of his crew were no better. "There's no profit in peace," Mak had said. What if he had been repeating the words of the man—or woman—who had offered to buy a Starcruiser? Who could possibly be so cold-blooded as to calculate the profit in war? A sudden shiver shot down Tynan's spine as a name came to mind: Orion Chaudet.

Stunned by the horror of that realization, Tynan sat back and drew a deep breath. What if he had been the pirates' real target, not the Starcruiser? What if Orion had paid to have him kidnapped merely to provide himself with the opportunity to negotiate his release? "My God," he whispered. Amara had freely admitted that Orion planned to take credit for whatever success he had as a negotiator, but wouldn't that credit be doubled if he had also won Tynan's release from pirates?

Tynan stood and began to pace the room. He knew from bitter experience that Orion was capable of treachery of the most despicable sort. He also knew that while Orion might claim to have outgrown their childhood hatred, the diplomat was completely lacking in the generosity to have done so. Once Orion had set his kidnapping plan in motion, it could have played out in any number of ways, with Tynan either surviving or dying a martyr's death, and Orion could still have manipulated the situation to make himself look like a hero.

And what about Amara? Tynan agonized. Had she been expendable? Had he not killed Toes and gotten free, Mak would not only have beaten her brutally, but raped her as well. Clearly, he had not been given orders to spare her pain. Orion had just thrown her away. Now terrified that he had sent Amara back to a man who might again

place her life in jeopardy, Tynan donned his robe
and rushed to the door between their rooms. He
pounded on it and called Amara's name, but there
was no response.

Putting good manners aside, Tynan hit the button to open the door, but it slid open on an empty
suite. He walked into the bedroom and, noticing
the closet door open, peered inside. It was obvious
that Amara had left. Certain he knew where she
had gone, he went right across the hall to Orion's
door. He hit it a near shattering blow, and Orion
swiftly appeared.

"Yes?" he asked with an untroubled smile. "Is
there something you need?"

Tynan pushed Orion back into his suite with a
forceful shove. "Yes, I need to speak with Amara.
Where is she? Amara!" he called.

Orion first adjusted the fit of his jacket. "I do
wish you'd at least try and speak to me with the
same courtesy you'd show a stranger."

"We aren't strangers, Orion, but bitter enemies.
Now where's Amara?"

Orion appeared perplexed. "I thought she had
told you herself."

"Obviously she didn't."

"Obviously. Well, she's exhausted and has
checked into the medical unit for some much-
needed rest. You really mustn't be so hard on
your women, Tynan. Just because men might be
able to tolerate your brutish ways doesn't mean
women can stand up to them."

Tynan stepped close, then smiled with satisfaction when Orion backed away. "Coward," he challenged. "Don't worry, I'll complete the work on

the treaty, but as soon as it's signed, I'm coming after you."

"I shall look forward to it," Orion vowed smugly. "Now if you hurry, you might just reach the medical unit before visiting hours end for the day. Amara's fond of roses. It's a pity you won't have time to find some."

Rather than dignify that suggestion with a response, Tynan turned and left. He had been to the medical unit, but that didn't mean he could find it again without stopping for directions at the desk. The clerk supplied them, and he arrived just as Orion had predicted, with several minutes of the visiting hours left to spare.

"I have to speak with Lieutenant Greer," he announced.

Pleased to see Tynan again, the clerk pointed the way. "She's in room twenty-eight, Mr. Thorn, but you'll have to leave in a few minutes."

Tynan had no intention of leaving before he had convinced Amara that Orion was dangerous, but rather than warn the clerk of his intentions, he nodded as though he would abide by the medical unit's rules. He strode down the hall, his robe whipping around his ankles, and entered her room at a near run. When he found her curled on her side sound asleep, he came to an abrupt halt. Suddenly feeling foolish, he closed and locked her door.

As he approached the bed, he found the strange red desert scene appearing on the walls a fortuitous coincidence, for it matched his mood perfectly. "Amara?" he coaxed gently. "Wake up."

Amara gave a lazy stretch, a wide yawn, and opened her eyes. She had hoped Tynan might eventually come to see her, but she had never expected him to arrive so soon. Startled, and not quite knowing how to respond, she sat up slowly. She was clad in a medical unit nightgown, and the cheery print was attractive, even if the oversized fit was not.

"I'm sorry you felt that you had to come here," Tynan began. "I hope it wasn't because of me."

"You already know I've no talent for lying, and I'd appreciate it if you didn't force me to be evasive."

"All right, so you are here because of me. Fine. You'll be safe here, and that's all that truly matters."

Having expected an apology, Amara was disappointed. "Safe? What are you talking about? I'm in no danger anywhere on this base."

Too excited to stand still or sit in one of the chairs provided for visitors, Tynan paced at her bedside. "Yes, you are. Now just listen. I've been thinking about the pirates."

"Really?" Amara was crushed. All she could think about was him, and he was preoccupied with pirates. "I think you'd better leave."

"Please just listen for a minute. Risto Cortez had his Corkscrews out searching for a Starcruiser, just any Starcruiser, but it's possible that while Mak Trumbo thought he was hijacking a Starcruiser, whoever hired him was really after us."

"You really mean you, don't you?"

"I wasn't traveling alone."

"No, but you could have been with any pilot. If someone wanted to stop you from reaching the conference, the pilot's identity wouldn't have mattered."

Tynan turned to face her. "You can accept the possibility, though, that we could have been boarded to take me as a hostage?"

Not really wanting to consider it, Amara shook out her hair, fidgeted nervously, and finally had to force herself to reply. "Yes, it's possible. The Peregrine Corporation has only the haziest concept of ethics, and they just might stoop to such a contemptible scheme."

"It wasn't Peregrine," Tynan swore boldly.

"Then who?"

"I once read that when detectives are faced with a crime, their first question is, who benefits? Now who would have benefited if I'd been taken hostage? Who would have arranged for my release and basked in the resulting glory? Or, God forbid, what if I'd been killed? Who would have taken my place at the conference and negotiated peace on Alado's terms? Who would have used my kidnapping or death to further his own ambitions? I can think of only one person that low. Can you name any others?"

Amara could scarcely believe her ears, yet Tynan's accusations made perfect sense. That didn't mean they were true, however. "I've known Orion to purposely create difficult situations simply to provide himself with an opportunity to practice his diplomacy. But what you're suggesting is way beyond the scope of anything he's ever tried."

"That doesn't mean he didn't do it."

"No, but it doesn't prove that he did, either. Besides, if you believe I'm merely Orion's puppet, why are you telling me your theory? Don't you expect me to go straight to him with it?"

Before Tynan could reply, a soft feminine voice coming from the communications panel announced the end of visiting hours. "I'm going to pretend I didn't hear that," he said. "I'm telling you because, whether or not you're Orion's woman, if he sent Mak Trumbo after us, it's obvious he was willing to sacrifice us both. Do you really want to work for a man who considers you expendable?"

Amara leaned back against her pillows. She knew Orion to be a master manipulator, but piracy, kidnapping, and the risk of complicity in murder? That was extremely difficult to believe of him. What was far easier to grasp was the fact that Tynan hadn't come there to apologize for doubting her, but to again rail against Orion. She was in exactly the same unenviable position she had occupied when he had asked her to leave his suite. His feud with Orion still meant more to him than she did.

Heartbroken by that realization, Amara replied slowly. "What you've described is merely a theory without proof, Tynan, and I know you haven't a shred of evidence to link Orion with Mak Trumbo. I believe you're allowing your hatred for Orion to spur your imagination, and that error has already caused me enough grief for one day. You're a man of superior intellect, but all you've given me is conjecture."

Disappointed in what he perceived as a stubborn refusal to see the truth, Tynan lowered his voice to an aggressive whisper. "I'm speaking from experience, Amara. Don't try to make it sound as though I'm hallucinating. We both know precisely what kind of man Orion is. You're his pilot; have you taken him anywhere in the last few months where he might have contacted pirates without your being aware of it?"

Dr. Diaz rapped lightly on the door. "I'm sorry, Mr. Thorn, but I must ask you to leave."

Tynan didn't bother to answer. "In your recent travels, can you recall an unusual or suspicious destination?"

"Orion travels a great deal," Amara explained. "We visited a number of colonies and several space stations. I seriously doubt that he was doing anything other than conducting routine business."

Exasperated, Tynan found it difficult to continue in a reasonable tone. "Maybe you'll think of something later—something that seemed insignificant at the time, but when analyzed now will convince you I'm right. If not, and you truly prefer Orion to me, fine, that's your choice. I couldn't have kept my suspicions to myself when they might cost you your life."

"Thank you. I appreciate your concern."

"Orion treats you like a whore he wouldn't miss, and all you can say is, 'I appreciate your concern'? What does it take to get through to you?"

Solana used her key to open Amara's door. "Don't make me call for Security," she begged.

"Call out every last man on the Confederation staff," Tynan responded angrily. "I'm not leaving here until I'm ready!"

Cinnamon Burke

"Tynan, you've shared your theory," Amara contended. "What I choose to do with it is my business. Now please leave before you embarrass us any more than you already have."

"What I really ought to do is take you out of that bed, sling you over my shoulder, and carry you back up to my suite."

"No!" Amara objected sharply. "Just say good night and go."

Rather than comply, Tynan pulled her into his arms and kissed her with soul-searing intensity. He felt her relax against his chest, compliant, seemingly eager for more, and he could not draw away until lack of breath demanded that he do so. Even then, he felt her reluctance to part. "Please come back to me," he whispered against her ear.

Amara desperately wanted to, but as long as his hatred of Orion colored his views on everything, especially her, she could not agree. "No, I can't."

That wasn't the response he had tasted in her kiss, and Tynan straightened up slowly. "You're lying. Why?"

While fascinated by the robed man, Solana refused to rescind her order. "I will call Security, Mr. Thorn. Don't make the mistake of believing you're above our regulations. No one is."

Still ignoring the physician, Tynan stared down at Amara. She looked so utterly forlorn that he knew she was as deeply hurt as he, but when she didn't give him any encouragement, he realized he was merely wasting his time. "I've always known you were stubborn, but I never thought you were stupid. I'll pray for you. You'll need it."

Tynan disappeared as quickly as he had arrived, and Amara had to fight back her tears. Solana Diaz, however, came to her bedside. She grasped Amara's wrist and took her pulse.

"You are an amazing woman, lieutenant. How have you managed to capture the interest of two of the most fascinating men on this, or any other, base?"

"Bad karma?"

"Really, I'm serious."

"So am I."

Giving up on ever getting any information out of her taciturn patient, Solana started for the door. "They'll bring your supper soon."

"Tell them I don't want it."

"No, you're already under the normal weight for your height, and rest alone won't help you recover your strength. You need a healthy diet as well."

Rebelling, Amara pulled the covers up to her chin and closed her eyes. Everyone had an opinion on how she should live her life, but all she wanted was to be left alone. When supper was sent to her room, she left it untouched.

Tynan returned to his suite, showered, and changed into a pair of the slacks Amara had provided. With one of the matching shirts, she had assured him that he would pass for one of Alado's personnel enjoying off-duty time and attract no notice whatsoever. He preferred his own deep purple boots to Alado's gold, however, and slipped them on. Intending to explore the entire base, he was annoyed when, just as he was about to leave, someone knocked at his door.

Tava Micenko smiled despite Tynan's frown. As usual, she was dressed in navy blue, but this time in a flattering, low-cut gown rather than a tailored uniform. "I wonder if I might have a word with you." She attempted to peer around him. "I hope I'm not interrupting something."

"I assume it's about the conference?"

"Of course."

The very last place Tynan wished to be with this aggressive woman was in his suite, but expecting some type of confidential disclosure, he beckoned for her to join him. She brushed close as she passed by, stopped to appreciate the suite's decor, and sat down on the sofa, where the side slit in her gown revealed a shapely pair of legs. She tossed her head, an apparently unconscious gesture which sent her long red hair across her shoulders in a graceful drape. For some reason, Tynan was reminded of a cobra's hood. He took the chair beside the sofa.

"What is it?" he prompted impatiently.

"It's plain you're new to the field of diplomacy," Tava surmised with a throaty laugh. "You should have offered me something to drink first."

"Would you like a glass of water?"

Startled that he had not taken her hint and offered something alcoholic, Tava shook her head. "No, thank you. I wished to speak with you privately. It seems that when all five corporations are represented, we inevitably become entangled in the petty rivalries that all too often have kept us from cooperating in the past."

When she paused, Tynan nodded. "That's certainly true," he agreed, "but although I'd like to foster a cooperative spirit, I'm not in favor of having the corporations share their profits equally as you suggested."

Tava shrugged slightly, a well-rehearsed provocative dip of her shoulders that deepened her cleavage. "My suggestion has a great deal of popularity at Serema, so I felt compelled to offer it, but I knew it had no chance of being accepted."

"I wish you hadn't wasted our time."

"Really, Tynan, you ought to make a more concerted effort to understand how the diplomatic community operates. All of us, with you as the possible exception, have come to the conference with proposals we'll make for any number of reasons, even though we have no hope of winning their approval. It's necessary for the art of compromise for each of us to offer something we're willing to sacrifice."

"Please, Tava, I don't require lessons in basic negotiation. Now what is it you really came here to say?"

Tava looked toward the door of Amara's suite. "I'm sorry, are you keeping someone waiting?"

Tynan didn't lie. "Only myself. Now, please continue."

Tava uncrossed and then recrossed her legs, adjusted the drape of her skirt, and looked up. "I think you and I might be able to reach an accord, and then sway the others to our point of view. It will be far easier for the two of us to court them one at a time than for you to hope the rest of us will gradually accept your point of view."

"Divide and conquer, is that your method?"

"Precisely," Tava agreed with a seductive smile. "I've always been clear on Alado's terms. Continued peaceful exploration depends not on a new set of rules, but simply on adherence to the original Confederation charter. Is Serema prepared to join us?"

"I'm prepared to work with you to make certain both of our interests are well served."

That wasn't the answer Tynan wanted to hear. "And just how do you propose that we work together?"

Tava rose and came to him. Standing between his legs, she licked her lips, pouted prettily, and then, resting her hands on his thighs, sank to her knees. "We'll be able to work together much more closely if we become better friends."

"And then, one by one, we bring the others into our bed?"

"My, what a delicious thought." Tava slid her hands up Tynan's thighs to his groin, but when she began to caress him appreciatively, he grabbed her wrists in a bruising grip and rose, forcing her to her feet.

"What is it you really want?" he asked. "A peace treaty, or me?"

Tava leaned close to tickle his lips as she spoke. "Can't I have both?"

Thoroughly disgusted, Tynan pulled her to his door and would have simply escorted her through it had Orion not chosen that moment to leave his suite.

"Good evening," Tynan greeted him with mock humor. "Tava's tastes don't suit mine, but I'm sure you'll find her incredibly appealing." With that taunt, he spun the redhead into Orion's arms and, leaving the flustered pair to disentangle themselves, went off to lose himself in the base's many entertainments.

Chapter Eighteen

Tynan's first stop was the desk at the end of the hall. "I need a map of the base. Do you have one?"

"I'll be happy to provide you with directions," the clerk replied. "Where did you wish to go?"

Something about the glint in the clerk's eye caught Tynan's attention. "Are there any androids deployed here?" he asked.

"Only in the maintenance department. Did you wish to see one?"

Tynan chose not to reveal that he knew he was speaking to one. "No, it was merely a point of idle curiosity. What I want is a map. If you don't have any, where can I find one?"

The clerk opened a drawer and removed a single sheet. "I can give you one of these, but most people find them more confusing than helpful."

Tynan thanked him and took the map, but rather than a simple floor plan of each level, it was an intricate diagram revealing all of the base's complex structure. He entered the elevator still not certain where he was bound and, not really caring, got off the first time the doors opened. He found himself on the corporate level. The cafeteria wasn't nearly as busy in the evening as it was during the day, but there were still enough people seated at the tables for him to remain anonymous among them. He ate a sandwich while he studied the design of the corporate floor and tried not to think of last night, when he and Amara had shared a picnic supper in the tree house.

He had known the tree house was a clever illusion, but he was not as sure of how true she was. How often had she advised him to trust his instincts? He had done exactly that where she was concerned and look what it had gotten him. Lost in his own misery, he stared out across the cafeteria, not really seeing the people moving past until a young woman approached him carrying a tray. She was petite and pretty and dressed in a gold flightsuit.

"You are new here?" she asked. "I haven't seen you before, so I thought perhaps you were. If you'd like some company, I'd be happy to sit with you and show you around later."

Unlike Tava, with her sultry smile and seductive gestures, this young woman exuded a wholesome warmth. Tynan found it impossible not to return her smile. "I wouldn't be very good company for you," he replied. "But I'm sure there must be a great many other men who'd be glad to accept your invitation." He turned and, spotting another young man dining alone, nodded toward him. "What about him?"

The friendly young woman rolled her eyes. "He's a navigator, and I'm a pilot. That's just not a good mix."

"It isn't? Why not?"

Thinking that she had succeeded in catching his attention, the young woman placed her tray on Tynan's table and sat down. "Pilots have a much more daring attitude. We're spontaneous and thrive on taking risks, while navigators are the exact opposite. They design programs for navigational computers, they don't fly, and they won't do anything unless they've made a careful plan."

Tynan gave the man in question another look. "Still, that combination of traits would create a couple with a wonderful symmetry—and he's very attractive."

"Yes, he is, and he's also insufferably opinionated and wouldn't date a pilot on a bet."

Tynan heard a note of frustration in her complaint. "Oh, now I see. He's the one, rather than you, who says you're a bad mix."

"Well, you might say that," she admitted. "But you must know how it is. It takes two to make anything happen, but only one to call it off."

"Yes, I know that only too well." Tynan looked down at the map. "Even if charts aren't your specialty, can you tell me what these columns are?"

The vivacious young woman turned the map toward her. "Sure, those are the ventilation ducts. They form a network between floors. Then you've got the power conduits and communications channels. They run along beside them. The maintenance people use these tunnels here, the ones marked in orange. They connect everything to the central core. Don't explore that maze without a ball of twine or you could be lost for days."

Tynan took back the map to associate her explanations with the illustration. He hadn't planned to do anything more than burn off energy strolling the halls where he was authorized to be, but the prospect of traveling around the base without being seen was immensely appealing. He folded the map, and slipped it into his pocket.

"Thank you." The young woman had begun eating her salad, and Tynan knew it would be rude to get up and leave after asking her help, but he really wanted to be on his way. "What's the navigator's name?" he asked.

"Fowler, and I'm Nita; I should have introduced myself before I sat down."

Tynan responded with his alias. "Gregory Nash. I appreciate your help with the map. What if I happened to pass by Fowler's table, and told him he was a fool for sitting by himself when he could be over here with you?"

"You wouldn't!" Nita tried to appear aghast, but began to giggle.

"It was nice meeting you, Nita. Now let me see what I can do." Tynan left their table and walked straight to Fowler's. "Nita speaks so highly of you, it's a shame you're both eating alone." He walked on then, but when he reached the exit and turned back, Fowler had already moved to Nita's table. She raised her hand to thank him, and he waved back, grateful to have solved at least one person's problems that night.

A sign pointing toward the corridor housing the Alado offices caught his attention, and he swung down it. There were names on some doors, but Orion's wasn't among them. Guessing that the door with an orange stripe at the end of the hall led to a maintenance area, Tynan hit the access button and was delighted when it slid open with a jerk and a hiss. He turned back to make certain no one was observing him before stepping into the narrow corridor beyond. The door slid shut behind him, and after an initial second of panic, Tynan took out the map.

Just as Nita had described, he stood at the entrance of a gigantic maze where the soft whir of the ventilation system vibrated through the perforated mesh flooring. Looking down, he could see the shadows of the levels below, and looking up, the levels above receded toward the dome. He really would need a way to mark his path if he did any serious exploring. But for now all he wanted to do was get a sense of the base, and how one might travel through it.

Surrounded by catwalks, steep metal ladders, and a forest of girders, Tynan entered an environment unlike any he had ever known. The sheer strangeness of it all made him grab for the handrail, and he wished with all his might for the firm footing of packed earth or solid stone beneath his feet. "Anything real," he murmured. Then, noticing the slight chill to the air, he closed his eyes and could readily imagine himself back in his room at the Keep. That calmed him somewhat, and he ventured a few steps, then a few more.

He had inched down the narrow walkway for perhaps half an hour before he noticed that the ventilation ducts had sliding panels at approximately ten-meter intervals. He opened one and, leaning inside, caught bits of a far off conversation. After consulting his detailed map again, he found where each room along Alado's corridor was connected to the massive ventilation system. By crawling through the ducts, one could listen to a conversation in any room on the base. It was certainly a crude form of surveillance, but when he thought of Orion, it had a definite appeal.

Unfortunately, he lacked the time to crawl around after Orion all day, and he seriously doubted the man would plot anything of major consequence on the base. Still, if he used the ducts to go from his room to Orion's, he might be able to find the incriminating disk Amara had told him about. Missing her terribly, he turned back. He listened at the maintenance door to make certain no one was in the outer corridor, then stepped out and walked away as though he had every right to go where he chose.

With the aid of the helpful map, he located the freight elevators and went to the level containing the medical unit. There was no reception desk here, only a storage room containing linens and other supplies. Enticing smells wafted from the unit's nearby kitchen, and he heard the laughter as a cook criticized the laziness of the breakfast shift.

The lights along the corridors were dim, and dressed in dark clothing, Tynan remained undetected in the shadows. He found Amara's room, quietly slipped through the door, and again locked it. A small light on the communications panel provided the only illumination and gave the sleeping pilot's golden hair a soft, burnished glow.

He longed to join her in the narrow bed, but she had made her feelings about that clear the last time he had visited her. Instead, he placed his hand on her shoulder and shook her slightly. She brushed his hand away and didn't awaken until he leaned down and kissed her.

Amara sat up, glanced around the darkened room, then up at Tynan. Unable to see more than a shadowy presence, she nevertheless recognized him by his scent. It was a deliciously musky aroma that recalled the times she had lain in his arms and tasted as well as smelled his splendidly masculine body. Those were precisely the types of memories she had come there to forget, and she reacted with a petulant impatience.

"Just what is it you think you're doing? I came here to rest, yet every time I fall asleep you wake me up. What's the matter with you? This afternoon you couldn't wait to get me out of your room, and now I can't keep you out of mine!"

"Please, keep your voice down," Tynan urged in a soothing whisper. "I've discovered how to use the maintenance tunnels to get around without being seen. Where would Orion have put that disk of us on board the Starcruiser? Would it be in one of the Alado offices, or in his room?"

Amara swept her hair out of her eyes. "What are you planning to do, steal it?"

"Steal doesn't really seem like the appropriate term, since we're the ones on it. I'd just like to know where it is. It's possible Orion might have other things, incriminating evidence, perhaps, stored with it."

"I want you out of this room right now, Tynan, and don't you dare come back until you're prepared to discuss something other than your obsession with Orion Chaudet. It has become tiresome in the extreme. Orion probably made copies of the disk and has them stashed all over the base. As for anything that would tie him to pirates, he's just too damn clever to keep it. Why don't you stop wasting your time—and mine—and get out of here."

Tynan took a deep breath. "I'm sorry, it's difficult not to think of us as a team."

"If we were ever a team," Amara pointed out, "you were the one who ended it. Now please go, or I'll call Security on you myself this time."

"No, you won't."

"Yes, I will!" Amara reached toward the communications panel, but Tynan caught her hand and brought it to his lips. After kissing her palm, he sucked lightly on each of her fingertips as though they were absolutely luscious.

"Only this afternoon you ordered me out of your life," she reminded him with a choked sob.

The pain in her voice forced Tynan to face how badly his contradictory behavior must have hurt her. He dropped her hand, sat down on the side of the bed, and pulled her into his arms. She rested her head on his shoulder, and he rubbed her back in lazy circles. He could feel her breathing evenly, and thinking she was calm enough to question, he opened his mouth to ask again about Orion, but caught himself just in time.

Finally understanding her anger, he kept still. There had to be other sources of information on the diplomat, and he vowed to find them on his own. "I shouldn't have bothered you," he said. "It's just that I know something's terribly wrong. I can feel its heat like an evil wind, and I don't want either of us to be caught up in it again." Leaning back, he smoothed her hair off her forehead and kissed her brow.

"Go back to sleep."

Amara huddled down into her pillow and sighed softly as Tynan closed the door on his way out. She had the same misgivings as he. The very same feeling of foreboding had plagued her since Orion had met them in the docking bay and the two men had first exchanged angry words. The only difference in their points of view was that Tynan blamed Orion, and Amara couldn't help but feel that he was also partly responsible. It was clear he took a perverse delight in baiting his old enemy.

As confused and frightened as when she had checked into the medical unit, Amara closed her eyes and hoped that when she opened them, she would be able to see more clearly than either of the men in her life.

Before leaving for the conference the next morning, Tynan stopped to speak with the desk clerk. "I'd like to send flowers, preferably roses, to Amara Greer's room in the medical unit. Can you arrange it for me?"

"Of course. I'll see they're delivered immediately. How do you wish the card to read?"

Tynan had never sent anyone flowers and had no idea what to say. It would require hours to compose a poem, but just a name suggested indifference. Finally he looked up at the clerk. "What do you advise?"

After a moment's contemplation, the clerk's face lit with enthusiasm. "The very finest of commercial roses are grown here in our hydroponic tanks. They're thornless, but perhaps we could make up a humorous pun with your name."

Tynan couldn't help but laugh. "No, I don't think that would be appropriate in this case. Better just use my name—no wait. I want the card to read, Love, Ty."

"As you wish, sir."

Tynan hoped that, unlike his visits, Amara would welcome the roses. With that thought he forced himself to concentrate on honing his skills as conference chairman. As the day wore on, he sought to find some way, short of handing Lisha Drache half of Alado's assets, that would put an end to her complaints about unfair competition. Tava Micenko refused even to look at him, while Gallager McGrath and Derrel Simmons twice nearly came to blows. All in all, it was their least productive day so far, and Tynan began to fear the conference really would last months at their current rate of progress.

When they adjourned in late afternoon, his first impulse was to visit Amara, but striving to respect her wishes, he decided against it. When he found Ross Belding waiting for him by the assembly hall doors, he greeted him with a warm smile. "I have some clothing I want to tie up in bundles," he

Cinnamon Burke

explained. "Could you find me a ball of twine?"

"A ball of twine, sir?" Ross appeared thoroughly confused.

"Yes, it's a heavyweight string."

"I know what it is. It's just that—well, it's an odd request and I'm not sure I can find any."

"Perhaps the laundry uses it?"

Ross's perplexed frown lightened. "Of course. I'll go there immediately."

After assuring the eager young man that he would be in his room, Tynan went down to the fourth floor, showered, and again changed into the dark shirt and slacks Amara had provided. He had just finished dressing when Ross arrived with a ball of twine so large he had to carry it with both hands. Tynan hoped he would not have to go to such great lengths before finding the evidence he needed.

"Thank you. I'll just cut off what I need and return this to you tomorrow. Why don't you come in for a minute, Ross."

"Is there something else you need, sir?" Ross asked, looking nonplussed at Tynan's sudden friendliness.

Ross's apprehension wasn't lost on Tynan, and he gestured for him to come forward and take a seat on the sofa. "No, I just have a question or two. How long have you been one of the Secretary's assistants?"

"Not quite a year, sir."

"I won't repeat this conversation to anyone; may I trust that you won't either?"

"No, sir—I mean, yes. I won't share a word with anyone." His curiosity piqued, the young man sat forward.

"I've known Orion Chaudet for some years," Tynan revealed with casual nonchalance. "Do you enjoy working for him?"

"Yes, I most certainly do. He's regarded as one of the most astute diplomats ever to serve Alado, and it's a great honor to be on his staff. I've learned more from him this past year than I would have working for five years with anyone else."

Tynan tried to smile. "Is that a fact?" He nodded as Ross continued to praise his boss with sickening sincerity. Obviously, he wouldn't discover anything of value from such an adoring associate. "Does the diplomatic corps have any interest in pirates?"

"No, they're handled, and many people claim ineffectively, by the Confederation Security Forces."

"So while you've worked with Orion, he's had no occasion to meet with pirates?"

"Never! They have no concept of honor, sir, and that is the heart of diplomacy."

Tynan nodded. "Is that one of the things you learned from Orion?"

"Yes, sir. He frequently mentions honor as vital. In fact, it was because he believed you to be a man of honor that he recommended you to the board."

"How flattering."

"It's true, sir. You're known for being a man of principle. Orion frequently complains that there aren't enough like you."

"I'll just bet he does. Well, thank you for the twine, and your time." Tynan walked Ross to the door, then appeared to have a sudden afterthought. "I believe Orion mentioned he'd be dining with someone tonight, but I've forgotten who."

Ross broke into a ready grin. "He's taking Dr. Diaz to one of the private dining rooms."

Tynan hid his own grin until after he had shut his door. Then he had to muffle a wild shout. He stood on a chair to study the grill covering the ventilation duct above his door and found that, rather than requiring tools to remove, the light-weight grid came off with a yank. It would be a tight fit, but Tynan was certain he could squeeze through, wiggle across the hall, and come out in Orion's suite. The man might not have anything of interest, but then again, he was so arrogant that he just might have kept a peculiar souvenir, no matter how dangerous, to remind him of his bargain with Mak Trumbo.

It was too early to begin exploring, so Tynan replaced the grill, ordered another steak, and enjoyed every succulent bite before deciding that enough time had elapsed to allow Orion to have left his suite to escort Solana to dinner. Just to make certain, Tynan read the instructions on the com-munications panel for contacting other rooms, and keyed in Orion's number. When the response was a recorded message, he ended the call. Doubting that he would need the twine to go such a short distance and return safely, Tynan nonetheless cut a generous length and stuffed it into his back pocket.

"A man of principle," he repeated to himself. He certainly was, and even if snooping through Orion's belongings might appear to be an unprinci-pled act, he was prepared to live with it.

Tynan's roses reached Amara's room just as she was eating breakfast. It was a lovely gesture, as innocent and sweet as the man himself, and she was genuinely touched. She placed the fragrant bouquet beside her bed and enjoyed the bright red roses throughout the day. She hadn't thought of how useful they were until Orion came by in the late afternoon.

"After our talk yesterday, I'm amazed to find you still here," he chided.

Amara fluffed up her pillow and faced him squarely. "I have a plan," she revealed, "and it's working. Tynan sent these superb roses, and he'll soon beg me to come back to him. Because he demanded I leave, he has to be the one to plead for me to return."

Orion started to object, then caught himself. "Today's session didn't go well, and it's plain to me that he needs you. By tomorrow or the next day, he should be willing to promise you anything. Whatever he offers, accept."

He paused to inhale the roses' lush perfume and smiled. "Tynan's allergic to beestings. I can remember chasing him through the garden once. He was looking back over his shoulder, not where he was going, and went barreling right into the roses. He was not only scratched badly by thorns, but stung several times. His face started to swell, and I thought that was going to be the end of him right there. Unfortunately, it wasn't."

" 'Unfortunately'? Did you really want him dead?"

"Of course. Children can be very cruel, but I'm now a grown man, and my choice of career proves I've become far more tolerant. How is your vision coming?"

"Much better, thank you. Solana was right; all I need is rest."

"Just don't malinger. Tynan needs you too badly. Do you miss him?"

Amara glanced away. "The way I would miss my soul if it were lost."

That Tynan could inspire such a devoted response annoyed Orion, and anger colored his reply. "Then hurry up and get out of this bed. You'd better enjoy him while you can. The conference will be over and he'll be gone before you realize it."

"I don't want to be his pilot home."

"Why not? You need the opportunity to redeem yourself in a Starcruiser, and it will allow for a prolonged farewell."

Wary of his mocking tone, Amara shook her head. "No, it would be much too sad. I won't do it."

"If I say you're his pilot, and I have, then you are. Why do you keep forgetting who's in charge here?"

"I haven't forgotten. I just won't take Tynan back to Earth. Send Glen Archer."

"Why not Piper Giles? Don't you think they'd enjoy the flight?"

"Not in the way you're suggesting."

"Come now, you don't really believe Tynan would be faithful to you, do you? Why give him the opportunity to expend his energies in another woman's arms?"

"That's enough, Orion."

Orion crossed to the door, but he couldn't agree. "You don't seem to understand that I'm serious, Amara, but I am. Either you pilot Tynan home, or you'll never fly for Alado again. The choice is yours."

Amara's glance was as cold as his. "The one I make may surprise you."

"I love surprises," Orion replied, and with a wicked laugh, he went on out the door.

"Bastard," Amara swore. How had she ever been so stupid as to accept the post as his pilot? Why hadn't she sensed what kind of man he was after her initial interview? "Because he's a master of diplomacy and masks his true character so well," she complained aloud.

She didn't even want to think about Tynan's leaving and pushed the whole troublesome subject out of her mind while she ate the supper she'd ordered. It was the same fried chicken they served in the private dining rooms, but without Tynan to share it, it didn't taste nearly as good.

Once she had eaten, she grew restless and wished she hadn't slept so much during the day. It would make falling asleep difficult now. She could finally see well enough to distinguish words, but reading would still be a strain. She had no interest in films and was too troubled to be entertained by her own thoughts. She wished Tynan would come by, but visiting hours were over, and it was too early for him to pay a late-night call.

Bored, she began to think about Tynan's preoccupation with pirates, and suddenly a remark Orion had made struck her as too important not to share. Thinking it might be hours before Tynan appeared, if he came at all, she left the bed and dressed in a flightsuit. Not wanting an argument as she passed by the front desk, she stole down the rear corridor and used the freight elevator to reach the fourth level.

She smiled at the night clerk. He was remarkably similar to the man who held the post during the day, a fellow of constant smiles and good cheer no matter what his guests' demands. "I've forgotten my room code again," she confided with such desperate remorse he promptly handed her another. Finally able to read it, she thanked him and hurried down the hall to her suite. Once inside, she immediately went to the door to Tynan's quarters and knocked impatiently. When he didn't immediately respond, she opened the door and glanced into his suite.

The chair and open duct provided clear evidence of where Tynan had gone. Appalled that he would go crawling through the ventilation system, she climbed right up and followed him. The tight metal corridor was lit from Orion's side. Using her elbows and knees, she scooted her way to his room, where she leaned out and called Tynan's name in a frantic whisper. He looked out of the bedroom, saw her, and came quickly to help her down.

"What are you doing here?" he asked, clearly dismayed.

"Oh, please. Isn't it obvious that I'm trying to keep you from getting caught burglarizing Orion's suite?"

"If Security catches us, they'll be sure to believe you're my accomplice, even if we both deny it."

"That smirk doesn't become you, Tynan. Now let's go."

"Smirk? Can you see well enough to describe my expression accurately?"

"I don't need perfect vision to recognize a smirk that wide. Now come on. I've remembered some-thing, but I won't discuss it here. Let's just replace the grill on the vent and go out through the door." Rather than wait for him to comply, Amara grabbed a chair, and replaced the grid herself. She had just started to swing the chair back into place when they heard laughter outside in the hallway.

Tynan recognized Orion's voice, and cursing under his breath, he grabbed Amara's hand and pulled her along with him into the bedroom. They had just cleared the doorway when Orion entered the suite with Solana Diaz. Thinking that they had had a remarkably brief dinner, or had not yet gone to eat, Tynan didn't want to hide in the closet on the off-chance they might use the bed. Keeping a tight hold on Amara's hand, he drew her into the bath-room, closed the door and turned on the light.

"Come on," he mouthed silently. "Let's get out of here." He stood on the toilet, yanked off the ventilation grill, and stepped down so Amara could precede him.

"Wait a minute, we can't just leave that grid on the floor. How are you going to replace it?"

Tynan tugged a length of twine from his pocket. "I'll pull it into place with this."

"Clever, but that means you'll have to back your way through the duct."

"I'll manage. Now go."

Amara pulled herself up with an agile stretch and slid into the duct, but she scooted only far enough down it to leave room for Tynan. After what seemed like a far too lengthy wait, his feet bumped into hers. His body now blocked the light from the bathroom, and she didn't like crawling through the dark. She continued to creep along, feeling her way, hoping for another vent so they could make good on their ridiculous escape, but all she felt was the slick, cool walls of the duct.

"I don't like this," she whispered.

"I don't either. Hurry up and find a way out."

"Why didn't you think to bring a light?"

"Let's argue later. Just get us out of here."

Amara kept wiggling along while she tried to form a mental picture of the layout of Orion's suite. The bathroom was off the bedroom, but on the opposite side from the hallway, so this duct was leading away from their suites rather than toward them. Cool air was flowing their way in a refreshing stream and helped her force back the fear of being so closely confined. She kept telling herself they would find a way out soon. Sure enough, several yards farther on, the duct opened out to the right and left where it met the central line.

"We've reached the main duct," she called back to Tynan. "If we go right, we should eventually come out in the maintenance area. If we go left, we should hit another duct to a bathroom, but Lord only knows whose it will be."

"You're the pilot."

Taking that as his assurance he would follow her lead, Amara entered the duct to her right and kept inching along as quickly as she could manage. She swept her fingertips along the sides frequently, feeling for grids she might miss in the dark, but there just didn't seem to be any. She had to force herself to breathe evenly, and think positive thoughts to keep the threat of hysteria at bay.

At last her fingertips brushed a seam that differed from the rest. She pushed against it, hoping to locate an opening, and all at once the section slid to the side. Blinded by the bright lights of the maintenance area, she turned away, but in the next instant she was rudely yanked out of the duct and placed on her feet by one of the androids whose province she had just invaded.

"Only maintenance personnel are allowed in this area," he announced without releasing her. "I will have to report you."

"I'm sure that won't be necessary," Amara replied.

"This area is dangerous. Unauthorized personnel are not permitted here."

Amara hoped Tynan would have the sense to stay put, then climb out and get away while she distracted the android, but almost immediately he joined them on the platform. The android turned toward him, then repeated the same message he had given her. "His orders are specific. I think we'd better do as he says," she suggested.

Tynan had thought an android would be so perfectly crafted as to be indistinguishable from its human counterpart, but this brawny fellow's physique and features were almost cartoon-like. Although clad in orange coveralls, a white hat, and thick gloves, no one could mistake him for anything other than an intricate machine.

"Good evening," Tynan greeted him warmly.

"You must come with me," the android responded.

"Fine," Tynan agreed, "but my friend doesn't see well. I'll hold her hand, and you lead the way."

Tynan reached for Amara's free hand, and after a slight hesitation, the android released her arm and turned away. He started down the walkway, his gait ponderous and slow. Tynan and Amara followed, but at an even more dawdling pace, allowing the distance between them to lengthen. When they came to a ladder, Tynan warned her to be silent, then sent her up it while he turned and ran back the way they had come. Hearing rapid footsteps, the android turned, saw Tynan running away, and set off in pursuit, but he lacked the speed to catch Tynan before he slipped through the door at the end of the hall.

Tynan didn't even think about ducking into his suite, but instead made straight for the elevators and went up a level. The clerk at this desk was a stranger, but he waved to him anyway, then sprinted to the end of the hallway and hit the button to open the maintenance door just as Amara reached it. He pulled her into his arms, certain they had escaped what would surely have been a wretched confrontation with whoever controlled the maintenance androids.

He was sadly disappointed when they turned and found half a dozen of the Confederation Security Force approaching. "I'm sorry," he sighed. "I sure hope whatever it was you wished to tell me is worth the trouble we're in."

Seeing the determined frowns on the guards' faces, Amara doubted that it was.

Chapter Nineteen

Instinctively becoming protective, Amara stepped in front of Tynan. "We're members of Alado's Diplomatic Corps," she announced confidently, "and as such claim diplomatic immunity, which begins with the right to refuse to respond to your questions. Please stand aside and allow us to pass."

Ignoring her command, the sergeant in charge of the security detail left his men to block the hallway, and came forward alone. Dressed in smart black and white uniforms, they were all unarmed in accordance with Confederation policy, but with their defensive postures and similarly intense gazes, they looked ready to use whatever physical force might be necessary to do their job. The sergeant was a surprisingly youthful man, who struck a belligerent pose and regarded Amara with a rueful stare, slowly taking in the smudges on the front of her uniform and her hair's wild disarray. After a brief glance, he dismissed Tynan, whose dark clothing hid the greasy streaks staining Amara's uniform, and extended his hand.

"Your credentials please, lieutenant."

Amara raised her chin proudly. "My name's embroidered on my suit. That's the only identification required."

"In other words, you aren't carrying your credentials." Not pleased, the sergeant motioned for Tynan to come forward. "Let's have a look at yours."

Tynan dimly recalled receiving an identification badge among the materials Alado had sent, but he had never seen any need to wear it. He slid his hands into his pockets, and shrugged when he came up empty. "I seem to have left mine in my room."

"So you're both claiming an immunity from questioning and detention which you cannot prove?"

"I'm Lieutenant Amara Greer, just as it says on my suit."

"That might be the name on the flightsuit you're wearing, but that doesn't mean you're Lieutenant Greer. From the looks of it, I'd say you stole that suit out of the laundry. Now I must ask you to come with us to verify your identities."

"That really isn't necessary," Amara insisted. "Restricted access to this base guarantees that there are no unauthorized personnel present."

While it would undoubtedly prove embarrassing to be taken in for questioning, Tynan didn't really understand why Amara was defending their right not to be detained so fiercely. Thinking it merely a matter of principle, he kept out of the discussion, but as her voice and the young sergeant's increased in volume, they began to attract the interest of the residents of the corridor. After the first couple of men appeared wearing Peregrine uniforms, Tynan called to one.

"Is Derrel Simmons on this level?"

"I'll ask the questions here," the sergeant ordered sharply.

When the man he had spoken to raised a brow, Tynan nodded, and the man slipped by the guards and rapped on a door. Derrel answered and immediately saw Tynan's predicament. "What's going on here?" he called as he walked toward them.

Recognizing Derrel as the Peregrine representative to the peace conference, the sergeant adopted a more cooperative attitude. "This is merely a routine detention, sir. You needn't become involved."

"That's where you're wrong. Believe me, you don't want to detain this pair. It would probably cost you your stripes, if not your job, and whatever problem they may have caused can't be worth the trouble reporting it would bring you."

Alarmed by Derrel's prediction, the sergeant turned his back on Amara and Tynan and whispered, "Can you vouch for them as Alado diplomatic personnel?"

Derrel looked past him to smile at the beleaguered pair. "It would be an honor. Now I'd like to make the further suggestion that there be no mention of this incident in the Security log. It was all an unfortunate misunderstanding."

The sergeant nodded and turned back to Amara and Tynan. "You may go." Then, looking neither to the right nor the left, he marched down the hallway, gathered his men, and made a hurried retreat. Thinking there was nothing more to see, the curious onlookers returned to their rooms, while Derrel joined Amara and Tynan.

"Have you been teaching Tynan how to do routine maintenance on a Starcruiser, lieutenant?"

Not fond of anyone connected with Peregrine, Amara wouldn't have bothered to reply, but because Derrel had been so helpful, she felt obligated to be civil. "Something like that. Thank you for dealing with Security for us."

"Come have a drink with me." Derrel gestured toward his suite.

Although reluctant, Amara preceded Tynan into Derrel's suite. As soon as she had crossed the threshold and saw Tava Micenko seated on the sofa, she drew to a halt. "I don't think we should be here. Let's go," she urged in a frantic whisper.

Tynan could readily understand her dismay, but seeing Tava's eyes widen in alarm, he realized that this was precisely where he wished to be. "Making the rounds, Tava?" he asked.

Tava's coldly menacing glance raked over him and Amara, and apparently regarding them both as beneath contempt, she failed to respond. She took a long sip of her drink, then smiled up at Derrel. "I was hoping we'd not be disturbed," she said with a poignant sigh.

"Don't be so impatient; we have all night," Derrel chided with a sly wink. "Come sit down. Tell us what you were doing to get so dirty. It's got to be an interesting story. What can I get you to drink?"

Derrel's suite was the same size as Tynan's, but the decor featured black mirrored walls that reflected the red furnishings. Amara would have considered it highly inappropriate for anyone other than a member of Peregrine's staff. For that rowdy crowd, and especially Derrel, the flamboyantly seductive room was perfect. She took the chair at the end of the sofa and was pleased when Tynan brought another over beside hers so they could sit together. She requested mineral water, and Tynan asked for the same.

"I was giving Tynan a tour of the base, and apparently we stumbled into a restricted area," she reported with a careless shrug. "But our story isn't nearly so intriguing as whatever you two must be plotting."

Derrel brought them their sparkling water in smoky tumblers, then sank down onto the sofa and slapped Tava on the knee. "We aren't plotting anything at all," he denied, "other than getting to know each other better."

Tynan stared at the pale-skinned redhead and couldn't suppress a shudder of revulsion. She was wearing the same alluring gown she had worn the previous evening. Though she was undeniably beautiful, he was surprised Derrel hadn't sent her on her way too. He leaned forward slightly.

"That's a damn lie," he offered boldly. "I know precisely why Tava's here, because she came to me first. I threw her out, and I'd advise you to do the same. Otherwise, I'll have to bring up this odd liaison at the morning session, and I believe the others will agree the goals of the conference have been irrevocably compromised."

Derrel scarcely seemed threatened. "First," he countered, "you'll have to prove we were doing more than merely enjoying a mutual passion, and that will be as impossible for you as it would be for us to accurately determine just what it was you two were up to tonight. Do you really think I'd have asked you in if Tava and I had been in the midst of a strategic discussion?"

"You might, so that you could claim this was no more than innocent hand-holding."

"There's nothing innocent about this," Derrel declared with a boisterous whoop of good cheer.

Revolted by that suggestive comment, Amara leaned forward. "I'd like to go," she announced firmly.

"So would I," Tynan agreed. He took Amara's glass and placed it with his on the nearby table. Then, taking her hand, he drew her to her feet. "Thanks again for your help, but don't overestimate my gratitude."

"I won't," Derrel assured him. He rose and walked them to the door, then followed them out into the hall. "I know exactly why Tava's here," he assured Tynan, "but that doesn't mean she'll get everything she's after—or that she won't get something she didn't expect." After giving them another wink, he returned to his suite.

"What a disgusting pair," Amara murmured. "If I hadn't already felt unclean, I certainly would now."

"Look at it this way—they just might deserve each other." He followed her around to the freight elevator, but balked when she pressed the button for the level that held the medical unit. "Let's go back to my suite."

Amara shook her head.

"Amara—" Tynan began, but he got no further before the doors opened and Amara stepped out.

"I'll walk you back to your room."

"I'd rather you didn't."

"I will anyway." He took her hand and led the way through the medical unit. When they reached her room, he followed her inside before she could protest. "Look, I know the mess we got into tonight was my fault, and I've already apologized, but you ought to remember that I didn't ask you to follow me into Orion's suite."

"No, of course not," Amara scoffed, "but I still feel responsible for you and I couldn't very well let you carry out such a stupid plan without trying to stop you. Right now, I just want to shower and go to bed. Please go."

Tynan drew one of the room's two chairs into the corner, sat down, stretched out his legs, and folded his arms over his chest. "Go ahead and clean up. I'll wait. After all, you had something important you wanted to tell me, and I still want to hear it."

The evening had gone so poorly that Amara just wanted it over. She placed her hands on her hips. "You don't seem to have any conception of how much trouble we were in tonight. That Security sergeant didn't look as though he had been out of the Confederation academy for more than a couple of weeks. That's why I tried the diplomatic immunity ploy on him. If we'd had some identification, it might have worked, even though diplomatic immunity isn't being honored during this conference."

"It isn't? Well, I was certainly impressed by your demand. It would have worked on me."

"Thank you, but that's really not the point." Even knowing that Tynan was completely out of his element at the base, Amara had a difficult time not losing patience with him. "If we'd been detained, just who do you think would have been summoned to identify us?"

Perplexed, Tynan needed a moment to consider the possibilities before he was struck by a horrible sense of the obvious. "Oh no," he moaned.

"Oh yes, Orion Chaudet, and he wouldn't have been pleased to find we'd been caught in a maintenance area. It would probably have taken him all of a minute to realize what we'd been up to."

Amara took a step toward him. "I've never wanted to be anything but a pilot, Ty, and Orion is doing his best to force me out of the only career I care to pursue. I can't afford to give him any more ammunition than he already has to prove I'm a reckless, incompetent, insubordinate liability rather than the excellent pilot I've always been considered before I began working for him. Or more correctly, before you two decided to renew your old rivalry, with me as the badly battered prize. Now just get out of here before I lose my temper completely and say something I shouldn't."

Tynan rose to his feet. "Is there anything you haven't said already?"

"I haven't even warmed up yet."

Her hair a mess and her flightsuit soiled, she did indeed look abused, but at the same time, she was still so incredibly appealing Tynan didn't want to leave. "First, tell me what it was you had to say?"

Amara exhaled slowly. "It's probably nothing."

"Come on, if it was worth leaving your bed to come find me, it's worth sharing."

"Then you'll go?"

"That's the last thing I want to promise, but yes, if you insist, I'll go."

"All right then. In one of my many recent conversations with Orion, none of which has gone particularly well, he criticized your behavior at the first day's session and compared it to a 'lumbering pirate forcing his way through an overcrowded colony bar.' I thought it no more than a colorful metaphor at the time, but tonight, it occurred to me that Mak Trumbo had an unusually stiff gait that could accurately be described as lumbering, and I flew Orion out to several of our colonies when I first began working for him."

"That was three months ago?"

"Closer to four now."

"That's about the time the conflict started, and I was first approached to mediate. I don't think Orion was just using an imaginative figure of speech, Amara. I think he carelessly dropped a vital clue. It may not be proof that a court would accept, but it's enough for me. I didn't find anything in his suite, by the way. You were right about his being too clever to keep incriminating evidence lying around, but the mention of a pirate in a colony bar is just the kind of slip I'd been hoping he'd make. Thank you, and I'm sorry about tonight."

Unmoved by his apology, Amara's lips remained set in a determined line. "Just don't do anything like that ever again. Neither of us can afford it."

"I won't. I didn't enjoy crawling through that drafty duct any more than you did. How do you suppose that Security detail got there so fast?"

Anxious for him to go, Amara moved toward the door. "Androids have an internal communications system, and the one we met undoubtedly called in an alarm when he first found us. The base has been put on full alert during the conference, but there's been no trouble, so Security must be eager to investigate any call. Now, please, let's call it a night."

Tynan was halfway out the door before he stopped and turned. "Aren't you curious about the visit Tava paid me?"

That the lithe redhead had approached Tynan didn't surprise Amara, but she didn't want to hear about it. "You must have been remarkably busy yesterday if you threw her out of your suite as well as me."

Hurt by that sarcastic barb, Tynan nevertheless felt it was deserved. "I made a serious mistake with you, but not her. She has the same predatory bent that makes Orion so objectionable, and I can't stand her." Softening his tone, he tried to smile. "It really doesn't matter who might have come to see me last night. I would have sent anyone but you away."

His dark eyes shone with touching sincerity. "I believe you."

"Good, but are you always so remarkably trusting where men are concerned?"

Amara turned away. "Not anymore I'm not. Good night."

She walked into the bathroom and closed the door, apparently trusting Tynan to go, but he couldn't. He stepped back into her room and waited until she turned on the shower. He remembered how her body felt all wet and slippery, how the swells and planes were decorated by the loveliest of subtle tattoos, and he ached to join her again. He closed his eyes, listening to her splash and at the same time remembering how bitter she had just sounded. He had only himself to blame for that too.

If his abortive foray into Orion's suite had ended up costing her her career with Alado, he would never have forgiven himself. She was far more than a mere pawn to him. Taking one of the red roses he had sent as a souvenir, he left, determined to find a way to prove it to her.

Amara stood in the warm, soapy spray, tears rolling down her cheeks as she recalled the times she and Tynan had showered together. She held her breath, hoping that he might join her again, and when he didn't, she slid to her knees and let the water spill over her tangled curls. She still wanted him, and badly, but clearly he was too lost in his dark desire to brand Orion a traitor to care.

When the negotiating session opened the next morning, Tava Micenko was in an even more subdued mood than she had been the previous day. They were well into the second hour of discussion before she spoke at all. Then she offered a surprising proposal.

"Every day that we sit here arguing," she complained, "is another day further exploration is delayed. While Alado and Peregrine won't suffer economically if they don't claim any new territories for months, perhaps even years, Serema will. Our expeditionary force is our most expensive contingent, and to have it idle has become an intolerable burden. I move that we draw up a treaty reaffirming the Confederation's commitment to peaceful exploration and promising a renewed dedication to that goal."

Derrel promptly seconded the motion, and an astonished Tynan asked for discussion. He had hoped they would reach this point on philosophical grounds, but he was certainly not going to argue if economic demands provided the necessary inducement to bring about lasting peace. He feared Lisha would lead them off on one of her usual inconsequential tangents, but she surprised him by slumping back in her chair and remaining silent while Gallager McGrath spoke.

"That is the most refreshingly welcome statement I've heard made at this conference," he declared. "The current truce is costing all of us a great deal of money, and I agree with Tava. Europa will sign an accord based on the original Confederation charter, but after all, we weren't the ones who precipitated the present dispute. Can Alado and Peregrine settle their differences over claims to new territory so that all five of the corporations can reach an accord?"

For once, Derrel Simmons' expression was truly thoughtful. "I don't wish to minimize the severity of the incident which brought us here. After all, lives were lost on both sides. Peregrine is willing, however, to turn the matter over to the Confederation court for a decision, provided Alado will abide by it. A settlement would clear the way for us to sign a new treaty."

Tynan turned to Lisha. "Ms. Drache? We are within reach of an accord. Will Omega join us?"

"Do you really expect me to refuse and declare war on the four of you?"

"No, of course not," Tynan assured her. "But I would like your opinion."

"Omega has never caused the Confederation a single problem, not one in all the years of its existence. Being the smallest firm, we have no choice but to go along. We can't stand alone against the rest of you."

"If only you would understand that size isn't what makes for a successful corporation!" Gallager said impatiently.

Tynan raised his hand to plead for silence. "This really isn't the time to extol the merits of Europa's corporate goals. I'm certain that if Omega Corporation wishes to hire you as a consultant later, it will. The only issue now is whether Omega will join us in signing a treaty."

Still defensive, Lisha nodded. "We shall have to."

Thinking that was all the cooperation they were likely to receive from Lisha, Tynan called for a vote on Tava's motion, and it was unanimously approved. All along he had herded the group toward a mutual accord. Now that it had arrived, however, he felt not the slightest sense of triumph, but only a deadening sorrow that what could well be the most extraordinary undertaking of his life had come to such an abrupt end. He glanced over to the seat Amara had once used, again found it empty, and thought it the perfect symbol for the vacuum he felt inside.

"It has been Alado's contention all along that peaceful exploration could be continued on the basis of our original treaty," he said. "Now that everyone agrees, let's recess for the rest of the morning to allow for consultation with our staffs and reconvene this afternoon at two to discuss the final details of the treaty." The session was adjourned, and Tynan stood back while the other delegates were surrounded by observers who couldn't wait to congratulate them. When Ross Belding and the members of Alado's diplomatic corps approached him, he motioned toward the door and led them out into the hallway.

"Let's not begin celebrating yet," he cautioned.

"I understand," Ross agreed. "It might jinx the treaty before it's even been written, but we can't help but feel that you've won a great victory for Alado."

"For peace," Tynan corrected him.

"Of course, for peace. The Secretary will want to see you immediately."

"He'll know where to find me." Tynan headed for the elevators and went down to the medical unit, but when he approached the desk, Solana Diaz came forward to meet him. "I need to see Amara, whether it's time for visitors or not."

"She's not here, Mr. Thorn. Her vision's returned to normal, and she's been released."

That Amara hadn't come straight to the assembly hall to observe the negotiations alarmed him. "Then where is she?"

"I've really no idea."

Tynan stared down at the doctor. "You must have some inkling of where she'd go."

Solana stepped back slightly. She found Tynan extremely attractive, and yet his flowing robe and contentious attitude gave him a menacing presence that had always been unsettling. "I'm not certain she wishes to be found."

"What did she do with my roses?"

"Your roses?" Solana smiled nervously. "She took them with her."

"Then they meant something to her, and she must still want to see me. Now where did she go?"

Solana debated with herself a brief moment, and then deciding Amara could definitely take care of herself, she offered what little information she had. "She mentioned something about playing Banshee Quest, so you might find her in one of the game rooms on the recreation level."

Tynan had been there once with Derrel, so he knew where they were. "Thank you." He started to turn away, then paused. "If I warned you that Orion's motives are never what they seem, would you believe me?"

Although startled by his remark, Solana shook her head. "Knowing you two aren't friends, I'm afraid I'd have to discount your opinion as prejudiced."

"What a shame." Having no more time to waste in giving unwanted advice, Tynan hurried away. He found the elevator full of people excitedly discussing the coming end of the conference and was forced to accept their good wishes, but he still felt it was much too soon to begin receiving congratulations. When he reached the recreation level, he found Amara seated alone in the third game room. A flight bag and his bouquet of roses sat by her side.

She was practicing her technique on a screen pulsating with weirdly gyrating images, while the strangest music Tynan had ever heard—indeed, he was not even certain the blaring sounds could be classified as music—played in the background. He slid into the seat beside hers and watched as she destroyed the last of the targets for that level.

"Very impressive!" he shouted over the jarring noise.

Instantly Amara shut off the game. "My timing is way off," she complained, "and that was only level fifteen."

"Well, you haven't played in a while."

"I've gotten clumsy and slow, and you needn't make excuses for me, Tynan. Now what are you doing here? Why aren't you at the negotiations?"

"They're over." Tynan watched a look of incredulous fear fill Amara's eyes. "Quite a surprise, isn't it? Somehow I think the major portion of the credit belongs to Derrel. Whatever happened between him and Tava last night inspired her to break the impasse this morning."

Amara listened in numb silence as Tynan summarized the morning's startling developments, but all she truly grasped was that if the conference was over, he'd be returning to the Keep and be lost to her forever. She knew she ought to congratulate him for chairing a successful conference, but she couldn't even manage a hoarse croak, let alone an eloquent speech. Her jaw began to ache, then the pain gathered in her throat, blocking a flood of anguished tears.

Tynan could not merely see her despair; he felt it as deeply as his own. "What are we going to do?" he whispered.

Unable to reply, Amara hit the control button to begin the next game, and the room was filled with the wild sights and sounds of Banshee Quest rather than the sobs that threatened to overwhelm her. Pitted against the game rather than an opponent, she missed the first target and then the second before tears blurred her newly regained vision and made even a pretense at play impossible.

Amara had no idea that Orion had stalked into the room until she heard his voice close behind her. "Shut that off!" he ordered. "This is no time for target practice."

When Amara didn't immediately obey, Tynan took the controls from her hand and shut off the game. He turned to face Orion, quickly decided he couldn't abide the man's triumphant smirk, and looked back toward the blank screen. "I got what Alado wanted. Isn't that what you expected?"

"Yes, but not nearly so soon. I must admit I didn't fully appreciate your methods until just now, but by forcing the issue of war at the outset, I think you paved the way for peace from the first day. By simply reaffirming the original Confederation charter, you've eliminated any possible disagreement this afternoon over specific articles. We should be able to go ahead, draft the treaty now, and have it ready to sign this evening."

"Guardians never begin any enterprise after sunset," Amara remarked softly.

Orion placed his hands on the back of her chair and leaned down to speak. "This is a space station, where daylight and darkness are programmed rather than natural phenomena, making such an objection absurd. I'll thank you not to remind me of the Guardians' customs."

Cinnamon Burke

"Apparently she has to," Tynan asserted. "I want the signing scheduled for tomorrow morning, and not before."

Exasperated, Orion walked around Amara's chair to face him. "There's always a danger that what sounded like an excellent idea to everyone today might strike them differently tomorrow," he warned. "Rather than permit a delay that might prove disastrous, I insist that the signing be scheduled immediately."

Feeling at a disadvantage, Tynan set the game controls aside and rose to his feet. "If the corporations are rushed into signing a treaty they don't truly want, then they won't feel bound to honor it. The next time Alado and Peregrine, or any of the others, come into conflict, the fighting might not be restricted to the loss of a couple of scout ships. It could well result in the all-out warfare we came here to avoid. I want to make certain that our work here has a significant and lasting effect. Another day will ensure that."

Orion raised his hands in mock surrender. "You're independent, of course, rather than under my command, so I can't order you to sign the treaty today, but I do believe I've made my reasons for doing so clear."

"Yes, you have, but I don't happen to agree."

"Why doesn't that surprise me?"

When neither Tynan nor Amara responded to that sarcastic query, Orion looked down at her and began to smile. "I can't tell you how relieved I am to learn your improved vision allows for your return to flight status. I do believe I've succeeded in keeping the details of your last flight sufficiently vague as to preclude an investigation, but I certainly hope your return flight to Earth won't be nearly so taxing as your voyage here. When would you like to leave, Tynan? I'll make certain Amara is cleared to take you."

Before Tynan could suggest a departure date, Amara spoke. "Let's discuss this again in private, Orion."

"But why?" Orion asked. "As I explained earlier, you either pilot Tynan home, or resign. Now which is it to be?"

"What's going on here?" Tynan was shocked to hear Orion present Amara with such dire consequences to force her to take him back to Earth. "You promised to escort me home, Amara. Doesn't your word mean anything?"

Amara swallowed hard. She couldn't bear the thought of a prolonged good-bye. "Of course it does, and I'd much rather discuss this privately with you too."

Orion couldn't help but laugh. "We seem to be on the same side again, Tynan, while Amara intends to defy us both. I really should have warned you not to become involved with a pilot. They're far more comfortable seated in a cockpit than they are astride a man's cock."

Tynan didn't need to hear another word. He went for Orion with both hands. Leaping up to stop him, Amara became entangled in his robe. Tripping over his feet, she knocked him off balance, and with a brutal shove from Orion, they both fell, and hard. Amara struck the back of her head on the floor, and her cry of pain brought Tynan to his senses. More concerned about her than with punishing

387

Orion for his foul mouth, he gathered her up in his arms.

Amara blinked away a fresh film of tears, then satisfied that her vision hadn't suffered, she struggled to escape Tynan's grasp. Seeing her difficulty, Orion reached down and helped her up, but the instant she was on her feet, she brushed his hands away. He was regarding her with the superior smirk she despised, while Tynan stared at her with a look of dark disappointment.

"This is a peace conference," she reminded them as she grabbed her flight bag and the bouquet. "It wouldn't enhance the reputation of either of you to show up at the signing ceremony tomorrow with blackened eyes and Lord knows what other evidence of your unending hatred. Alado deserves better, and so do I."

The men watched her walk out the door, then Orion gestured for Tynan to precede him. "She's right, I'm afraid. I don't dare leave you too badly hurt to attend tomorrow's signing, and I really don't want to settle for anything else."

"Neither do I," Tynan vowed through clenched teeth. It wasn't until they had reached the hallway that he realized there was something he had to know. "Tell me the truth if you can possibly manage it. Did Amara really refuse to be my pilot for the return voyage home?"

"Why would I lie about that?" When Tynan looked away in disgust, Orion continued. "Yes, she lodged a strenuous objection to the assignment. That's why I was forced to offer her the choice of resigning. I can't tolerate that type of insubordination from a member of my staff. Unless, of course, you'd care to request another pilot. Piper Giles, perhaps?"

Tynan absolutely despised Orion, but at that moment, he was livid with Amara too. "No," he answered, "make Amara choose." He turned away to hide his smile, but he knew Amara would never abandon flying just to spite him.

Chapter Twenty

Amara left the game room at a furious pace, went straight down to the docking bay level, and checked into the transient pilot's quarters. As expertly designed as the rest of the base, the Spartan cubicles served only as a place to sleep and dress; no one spent any time there. Amara slung her flight bag down on the bed and set the bouquet of roses on the shelf which served as both table and desk. She rearranged the still vibrant blooms to restore their artistic order and stepped back to admire her handiwork.

It wasn't until then that she noticed there were now only eleven roses in the vase rather than twelve. Certain she hadn't dropped one in her haste to leave Tynan and Orion, she came to the astonishing conclusion that Tynan must have helped himself to one before leaving her room last night. She sank down on the narrow bed and tried to understand why he had bothered. That he had wanted a memento of their brief affair was touching but didn't make loving him any less impossible, nor lessen the ache in her heart.

Hot, angry tears began to fill her eyes. Certain that crying wouldn't do her a damn bit of good, she went into the bathroom to wash the tears away. Her reflection had been fuzzy for so many days that, after drying her face, she was startled to look up and see herself clearly in the mirror. Drops would erase the redness from her eyes, but it was plain Solana was right about her being underweight, for her cheekbones weren't usually so sharply defined.

"You look as ghastly as you feel," she murmured. Too troubled to remain in such small accommodations, she hurriedly prepared to leave. She shook out her uniforms and placed them on the hooks attached to the door. She debated leaving the spectacular white gown in her flight bag, but finally pulled it out and hung it up too. Now that she could see well enough to fully appreciate its appeal, she was sorry it had been a present from the wrong man. Had it come from Tynan, it would have become a treasured keepsake. Now, she would probably let Piper borrow it, which was as good as giving it away.

Her unpacking complete, she left her cubicle to explore the docking bays. She doubted she would be flying a Starcruiser again, but she entered the bay where they had landed. The routine maintenance had already been completed on the magnificent ship's engines, but even deserted and shrouded in silence, it remained the embodiment of power and speed. It had been a joy to fly, but she was sadly afraid that her first flight in it had also been her last.

Checking on his own ship, which was moored nearby, Jeffrey Hart was delighted to come across Amara alone for a change. Not wanting to frighten her, he whistled from the end of the bay and waved when she turned toward him. "Planning another Earth run?" he called.

He was wearing a ready grin, but Amara had to struggle to find a faint smile for him. Along with Piper and Glen, Jeff Hart stood a good chance of being chosen to replace her as Orion's pilot. She envied the fact that his career hopes had suddenly grown far brighter than hers.

"No," she responded truthfully. "I'm just killing time."

"Until what?"

Amara shrugged. "Until the rest of my life begins, I suppose."

Intrigued, Jeff slipped his hands in his hip pockets. "Sounds ominous; tell me more."

Blond and blue-eyed, Jeff was definitely her type, but Amara felt only a painful numbness rather than any warm stirrings of physical attraction. "Another time, perhaps. Now if you'll excuse me—"

As she turned away, Jeff noted the sorrow that bowed her shoulders and reached out to stop her. "You look like you need a friend. Let's go get a drink, or maybe play some Banshee Quest."

Amara had spent countless afternoons, and enjoyable ones at that, with men like Jeff who were eager to entertain her. But recreation wasn't what she needed now. "I like you, Jeff, I really do, but I'd rather be by myself."

Her forlorn expression convinced him that solitude was the last thing she needed. Catching her off guard, he scooped her up into his arms and started toward the elevator. "Like hell you would," he argued. "I'm taking you to the spa and dropping you into one of the therapy tubs. That ought to relax you enough to be able to tell me what's wrong. Besides, you've got to get in the right mood for tonight's parties."

Too dispirited to argue, Amara looped her arms around his neck. "A lengthy session in a therapy tub would be nice, but I still won't feel up to sharing confidences or attending parties."

"Just wait and see. It looks as though the treaty will be signed tomorrow, but there's no reason not to start celebrating now. A party is precisely what you need—not another formal reception filled with staid diplomats, but a real bash given by Alado's flight crews."

Amara rested her head on Jeff's shoulder, but she had already made up her mind. She would spend the afternoon at the spa, but that night she definitely wanted to be alone.

Tynan also spent the evening alone. He ordered a steak dinner sent to his room and made every attempt to enjoy it despite the absence of his favorite companion. Once finished, he tried to read, but couldn't. Eager for any chore, he decided to shine his boots for the next day's ceremony. He reached into his bag for the special polish the Guardians made themselves, and as his fingertips brushed the packet filled with the items he had taken from Mak Trumbo and Toes a surge of revulsion swept through him.

Fighting back his sense of loathing, he emptied the pouch onto the bed, and slowly sorted through the pirates' few last effects. He again tried to find a link, no matter how remote, to Orion, but it just wasn't there.

The jeweled handle of Mak Trumbo's knife caught his attention. He opened it and tested the blade against his thumb. He didn't even like holding the evil man's blade, for it intensified the eerie feelings of impending doom he had suffered since his arrival at the base. Still, there was something darkly appealing about the pirate's weapon, and he set it aside, intending to carry it the next day. After all, Orion was as eager as he to give their old rivalry a definitive end, and he didn't trust him to fight fair.

He closed his eyes and probed his memory yet again. With meticulous calm, he sifted through each recollection until suddenly he realized that the clue had been right in front of him all along. Now he was ashamed to have missed it from the start.

Blaming herself, Amara had criticized her inattention so mercilessly for the pirates' boarding that Tynan had failed to consider any other possibility. Now he wondered why he hadn't previously analyzed the incident far more carefully. The pirates had approached the Starcruiser at the specific angle covered by the damaged scanners. Surely that hadn't been merely a fortuitous coincidence, but how had they known what course to set so they wouldn't trigger an alarm?

Amara had had to fly extremely close to the Rastafarians' ship before they could note specific details, so Mak couldn't have flown close enough to the Starcruiser to identify the damaged scanners without crossing the sectors monitored by the others. He had to have known most of the starboard scanners were out, but how? Amara had notified Fleet Command of the damage they had sustained. She was on a diplomatic mission, so it stood to reason that Fleet Command had informed Orion. Could he have passed that crucial bit of intelligence on to Mak Trumbo?

Tynan wished he could consult Amara, even though he feared she might call this another wild theory he couldn't prove. A summoning tone from the communications panel startled him, but hoping it would be her, he rushed to answer. He tried not to allow disappointment to deepen his voice when it proved to be Judd Griffith, the Confederation president. Embarrassed by the man's praise for his negotiating skills, Tynan tried to end the conversation gracefully, but Judd's next comment caught him completely by surprise.

"I'd like to offer you a post with the Confederation," Judd declared. "I know you might have believed your association with the Guardians to be a lifetime commitment, but you're a young man, and your circumstances might change."

"I sincerely doubt it," Tynan replied. "While I admire the Confederation's goals, my interest will continue to be philosophy."

Cinnamon Burke

"I'll wish you continued success then," Judd said, "but remember there'll always be a position for you with the Confederation should you ever change your mind."

"Thank you." Tynan disconnected the call. Somewhat confused by it, he wondered just what it was the Confederation thought he could do. If it was fostering a renewed sense of peaceful cooperation between the corporations, he thought Derrel Simmons might have been a better choice.

Feeling very much alone with his troubling conjecture, he realized just how little he knew about peaceful coexistence between men and women. Amara hadn't returned to her suite next door, and he knew better than to seek her out to discuss Orion. No, he would have to deal with Orion on his own. Then maybe he could finally convince her just how dear to him she truly was.

The next morning, the spectator section of the assembly hall was again filled to capacity for the formal signing of the treaty. Tynan and the other delegates entered in the same order, and for the second time the Peregrine forces greeted Derrel with boisterous enthusiasm. The orchestra repeated the Confederation anthem on their peculiar triangular instruments, and Judd Griffith once more praised the negotiators' dedication.

Almost afraid to look, Tynan forced himself to glance toward the section where Alado's personnel were located. When he saw Amara seated between Ross Belding and Orion Chaudet, he quickly turned away, but not before she had surprised him with a warm smile. He hadn't

396

heard anything about his travel arrangements from Orion. Perhaps the man didn't expect him to survive their long-delayed rematch and so hadn't bothered to force Amara into making a choice. Still, whatever the reason for her encouraging expression, he appreciated it. The next time he glanced her way, he saluted her with a subtle nod.

Once the ceremony's preliminaries were complete, Lisha Drache was the first to sign the new treaty. With obvious reluctance, she affixed her name to the document, then passed the pen to Tava Micenko. The Serema delegate appeared unusually subdued as she added her signature, but Gallager McGrath signed with a grateful flourish. Next, Derrel Simmons picked up the pen, and his face lit by a cocky grin, he inscribed his name in bold letters.

Now that it was his turn, Tynan could take little pride in this renewed commitment to the Confederation charter when he harbored the uneasy feeling that too many important issues had been left unresolved. Hesitant to sign, he rolled the pen between his palms. Looking up, he saw a beaming Orion Chaudet accepting congratulations from the diplomats seated around him. Sickened, Tynan knew that he had succeeded brilliantly in advancing his old enemy's career.

And anything Orion touched was tainted with evil.

With sudden insight, Tynan recognized the flawed treaty as merely part of a superbly orchestrated plan to win Orion a seat on Alado's board of directors. Once Orion had gained that position of power, no one would be able to control him.

Throughout history, there had been moments when tyrants could have been stopped, but all too often just men had failed to act. Sensing this was precisely such an opportunity, Tynan threw down the pen and, leaving the treaty unsigned, strode out of the assembly hall to a chorus of astonished gasps.

Outraged, Orion turned to Amara. "Did you know that he planned to walk out?"

As astounded as everyone else, Amara shook her head. "No, of course not."

Orion sent her a darkly threatening glance that made it plain he thought otherwise. Then, leaping from his seat, he followed Tynan at a run. Refusing to be left behind, Amara took off after him, while the rest of the spectators and stunned delegates looked on. As they reached the outer corridor, she caught a glimpse of Tynan's robe as he disappeared through a maintenance door. Rushing on, Orion hit the button to open the door, but it was Amara who slipped through it first.

"Tynan!" she yelled, her cry a frantic warning.

Having sought privacy to examine his dreadful realizations before having a final confrontation with Orion, Tynan had no need for company. Intending to send Amara away, he whirled on the catwalk, but seeing Orion lunge past her, he grasped the rails to steady himself and waited for his nemesis to draw near. "I won't sign your accursed treaty," he shouted. "It's as perverted as you are. Alado is already too powerful, and with you on the board, its future will surely be one of dark domination."

Orion came to an abrupt halt a few steps away. "What's led your thoughts in such a bizarre direction?" he countered. "I'm a diplomat, not a dictator, and if I'm someday elected to Alado's board, I'll work for peaceful cooperation as I always have."

"I don't doubt that you'll make a magnificent pretense of it, but at the same time you'll be in league with pirates and illegally expanding Alado's influence far and wide. I refuse to have any part of your diabolical schemes."

Orion laughed as though Tynan's prophecy were utterly absurd. "I asked you to keep an eye on Tynan for me, Amara," he scolded. "Why didn't you report that he's become completely unbalanced?"

While Amara wanted to defend Tynan, she was so shocked by his accusations that she didn't know where to begin. She looked down through the levels beneath them and had to fight off a wave of vertigo. "Please, let's find another place to talk this through."

Refusing her plea with a shake of his head, Tynan called to her. "Were our Starcruiser's transmissions to Fleet Command sent in code, or can anyone with communications equipment receive and understand them?"

Orion took another step forward. "Tynan, really—"

"Answer me!" Tynan yelled.

Not understanding his sudden interest in their flight, Amara shrugged helplessly. "All our transmissions were in code."

Tynan nodded. "Then someone had to have relayed the damage report to Mak Trumbo so that he could approach us undetected, and the

Cinnamon Burke

prime suspect is standing right here between us."

Orion glanced over his shoulder. "You can't believe a word he says, Amara. He's been obnoxiously argumentative the entire time he's been here, and he's making no sense at all now."

Amara had never seen so much as a glimmer of fear reflected in Orion's icy-blue gaze before that day, but clearly, he was terrified now. Clutching the rail, his knuckles were white, and she saw him shift his stance to cover a tremor that threatened to buckle his knees.

Facing them both, Tynan could see Orion fighting to maintain his usual stoic control over his emotions, while Amara's expression filled with disgust. "It's true, isn't it?" he taunted. "Trumbo was working for you, and probably not for the first time. How much of the profits from the cargos he hijacked wound up in your secret accounts?"

"The wilder your accusations become, the more insane you sound," Orion exclaimed. "You can't prove a thing."

"Can't I?" Tynan edged closer, and when Orion tried to back away, Amara blocked his retreat with her shoulder.

"Side with Tynan, and you'll never fly again!" the diplomat warned.

Tynan's question about coded transmissions had convinced Amara they had been betrayed. "Why would I want to fly for a man who tossed me to pirates? I knew you used people, but I never dreamed you would go this far!"

While Amara had Orion distracted, Tynan made a quick grab for the diplomat. Catching the front of his uniform, Tynan pulled him along the catwalk

400

toward a platform which provided sufficient room to fight. "Come on," he coaxed. "When you brought me to this conference, you must have been certain you could use me as easily as you had as a child. It's high time you paid for that mistake."

Orion hoped to find a maintenance android or a Security detail, but a hurried glance failed to locate any chance of rescue. This was neither the time nor the place of his choosing, but he resigned himself to fighting now. Straightening his shoulders proudly, he unbuttoned his jacket. "I'll fight you, and gladly, but first remove your robe. Your malicious claims dishonor everything the Guardians represent."

Outraged that Orion would issue such a righteous challenge, Tynan nevertheless was eager to be rid of the cumbersome garment. Hoping for a chance to fight Orion that day, he had worn a set of the off-duty clothes Amara had given him underneath. His eyes never left his old adversary as he untied his belt, but after hanging the cord over the railing, his vision was obscured momentarily as he drew his robe off over his head.

Orion shucked off his jacket, and, never one to abide by the rules of fairness, he immediately slammed his fist into Tynan's stomach. Then, grabbing for the thick folds of his robe, he twisted them around Tynan's head, forming a tight coil around his neck. Using the rail for leverage, he slammed Tynan into the corner and intensified his brutal attempt to strangle him.

That Orion would resort to such unprincipled tactics didn't surprise Amara, but unwilling to allow him to gain the advantage unfairly, she plucked

Tynan's rope belt from the rail, dropped a loop around Orion's neck, and yanked him backwards with a head-snapping jerk. Caught by surprise, Orion slipped on the perforated flooring of the platform and had to release Tynan to reach out for the rail. Athletic and fit, he not only managed to remain upright, but spun and slammed his fist into Amara's chin. Stunned by the blow, she staggered and fell back onto the catwalk.

Orion yanked the rope belt from around his neck and sent it sailing off the platform. "Stay out of this, bitch!" He would have accented his command with a spiteful kick had Tynan not caught his elbow.

Now that he had succeeded in sloughing off his robe, Tynan came at Orion with the full force of his long-repressed anger. He meant to punish him for all the suffering he had endured as a child, but still fueled by his inexplicable hatred, Orion was not easy to beat. Vanity might have kept him trim and fit, but he knew how to use every ounce of power he possessed and defended himself with hard-thrown blows.

Dazed, Amara struggled to sit up, but the men were hurling each other around the platform, sending vibrations echoing through the metal and jarring her so badly that she found it impossible to rise. In the distance she heard a faint shout and prayed that a Security unit was approaching.

Desperate to attract help, she made another attempt to stand and this time reached her knees. She flinched as Tynan opened a cut above Orion's right eye, sending a fine spray of blood across her sleeve. Sickened, she tried to look past him to search for whoever had shouted and saw one of the burly maintenance androids watching them on an adjacent catwalk. Apparently not programmed to respond in such an emergency, he was now doing no more than observing.

"Security!" Amara screamed. "Call for Security!" But the mechanical brute gave no indication he would obey.

Frightened by the ferocity of the fight, Amara pulled herself up and started to go to summon Security herself. Just then Orion slumped against the rail, and thinking the bout was nearly over, she stayed. Orion twisted his upper body slightly, blocking Tynan's line of sight as he reached into his back pocket and withdrew what looked like a tiny injection canister. Simple to use, these canisters were a part of all of Alado's emergency supplies. Pressed against the skin, they were an effective means to dispense drugs.

"Look out!" she called. "He's got something in his hand!"

Tynan pulled Mak's knife from his pocket. "If you prefer using weapons, why didn't you say so?" he asked and flicked open the blade.

"I've no weapon," Orion denied, but he clutched his stomach to hide the canister and stumbled forward.

Suspecting yet another underhanded trick, Tynan backed out onto the catwalk on the far side of the platform. "If you try to use anything on me, Orion, I swear I'll cut your throat with Mak's knife."

Pursuing him, Orion huddled against the rail. Blood from the cut in his brow dripped down into his eyes, and he was breathing heavily. "Enough," he gasped. "We're even."

"Even?" Amara repeated incredulously. "You nearly got us both killed. If Tynan doesn't want to slit your throat from ear to ear, then I certainly will!"

As she advanced, Orion feigned a step toward her, drawing Tynan in close, and when the Guardian was within reach, Orion stuck out his arm to shove Amara away. He then lashed out at Tynan with the injection canister, but his hoarse cry of triumph died in his throat when Tynan jabbed Mak's blade through his palm. The disposable syringe tumbled to his feet, and, cradling his torn hand, Orion made a dive for it, but Tynan was faster and kicked it away. Fearing it contained poison rather than a sedative, Amara snatched it up and discovered it bore none of the standard labels.

Certain it was the evidence they needed, she began to back away. Orion, however, wasn't ready to surrender. He came after her, and ripping and clawing with his one good hand, he succeeded in wrenching the canister from her grasp. Then, clamping his arm around her neck, he twisted her into position to serve as a shield.

"Drop the knife!" he shouted. "Or I'll use this on her."

Having no doubt that he would carry out his threat, Tynan closed Mak's knife and tossed it out on the catwalk behind him where it landed with a clatter. "Let her go," he demanded. "She's never been a part of this."

Even with his blood soaking her jacket, Orion didn't seem to be in any pain, and he flashed his usual mocking grin. "You're wrong," he insisted. "She's been working for me all along. Each time you've made love, it's been my words she's whispered in your ear."

"He's lying!" Amara screamed, and jabbing her elbow into Orion's solar plexus, she hurt him badly enough to wrench free of his grasp. Clearing the way for Tynan, she dove to the side and slid along the catwalk, coming dangerously close to careening off. She heard Orion laugh at her plight, but caught a strut with three fingers and hung on to save herself a headlong plunge into death.

Seeing how close Amara had come to falling, Tynan didn't waste the opening she had given him. He threw himself at Orion, and their fight continued in a wild, wrestling struggle for the canister. When at last he got a hold on it, Tynan shoved it into the torn flesh of Orion's bloody palm, releasing its contents with a sparkling hiss.

"Fool," Orion taunted in a hoarse rasp, "this won't work on me!" He managed to yank it out, but then a strange look of amazed confusion filled his eyes. Unable to maintain his balance, he lurched against the rail and, rolling backwards, would have toppled off the platform and fallen a dozen levels had Tynan not caught the front of his shirt to prevent it. Already torn, the fabric peeled away to show a tattooed dragon clawing its way up Orion's chest. Distracted by the design, Tynan might have lost hold of his longtime enemy, but going limp, Orion crumpled into his arms.

Rising on one shaking knee, Amara managed only a faint whisper. "Is he dead?"

Easing Orion down on the platform, Tynan didn't need to take his pulse before responding. "Very, but it's plain he expected whatever poison he used to work only on me. What could it have been?"

Unable to remain upright, Amara slumped down on the catwalk. "What does it matter? Orion's dead, and it might have been you."

"Yes, but it isn't." Unwilling to leave her, Tynan sat down beside her and pulled her into his arms. When a Security unit finally found them, Tynan looked up at the young sergeant they had encountered earlier, and doubting anything he said would make sense, he just shook his head.

Three hours later, things were no less confused. Alado had provided medical attention and sympathetic legal counsel, but seated in the office of Captain Harada, the Conferation's chief of security, Amara and Tynan were still being treated as murder suspects rather than Orion's near victims. They had answered the same questions put to them a dozen different ways, but always with the truth—Orion Chaudet had not been what he seemed, and when released, they would gather the necessary proof.

"We have never had a murder at this facility," the captain announced with obvious distaste. He had the compact build of a pit bull and an attitude to match. His dark eyes searched constantly for a glimmer of guilt on his prisoners' faces. "This incident, coming as it has in the midst of a peace conference, is most distressing."

"So was being boarded by pirates," Amara reminded him.

"Pirates!" Captain Harada threw up his hands in dismay. "According to you, Orion Chaudet was a master criminal, but pending a complete examination of his files at Fleet Command, there's no evidence to support your assertion."

"There was no murder," Tynan emphasized. "This was a case of self-defense."

"So you say." Harada picked up Mak Trumbo's jeweled knife and turned it in his hands. "The same sergeant who took you into custody today caught you two trespassing in a maintenance area night before last. You must admit that's a suspicious coincidence. Were you conducting a rehearsal for today?"

"No, of course not," Amara argued.

Tynan sat forward in his seat. "If you're going to press charges, file them against me and release Lieutenant Greer. She witnessed Orion's death, but had no part in it."

With Orion's blood splattered across her uniform, Amara doubted the captain would accept Tynan's suggestion. "We've been in this together from the start, Tynan, and I intend to see it through."

Before Tynan could reply, a lab technician entered the captain's office. He handed Harada his report, then clasping his hands behind his back, he issued a brief summary. "The injection canister found at the crime scene wasn't a commercial product, but the creation of a private party. Similar devices turn up occasionally in the colonies. They aren't difficult to make, and—"

"Please," Harada interrupted. "Just tell me what it contained."

"I was just getting to that, sir. It was an unusual concoction to say the least—the synthetic equivalent of the venom of honeybees."

"Honeybees?" the captain snorted. "Who would use that?"

Tynan reached out to take Amara's hand. "Someone who wished to kill a man who's as allergic to beestings as I am."

While the captain was clearly astounded, the technician nodded thoughtfully. "The venom was at such a high level of concentration that a scratch of the needle would have killed you. Apparently the victim didn't realize that he had created a dosage that would be lethal to himself as well."

Wearing a disgruntled frown, the captain laid the technician's report aside and topped it with Mak Trumbo's knife. "This case is obviously far more complex than it first appeared, but assuming you can prove the existence of an allergy—"

"Yes, it's documented in my medical records at the Keep," Tynan assured him.

"Well, then, I'm forced to accept your claim of self-defense. As for the rest of your story, I'll leave it up to Alado personnel to investigate Orion Chaudet's possible ties to pirates. It sounds preposterous to me, but I'm prepared to declare this portion of the investigation closed. You may go."

"Is there a back way out of here?" Amara asked.

Readily understanding her need to avoid the curious hordes undoubtedly waiting to interview them, Tynan rose and helped her to her feet. "A freight elevator is all we need."

"I would not recommend any more excursions through our maintenance areas."

"Come with me," the lab technician offered. "You won't be followed if you leave through the morgue."

Amara felt Tynan wince, but thinking the technician's suggestion a good one, she followed. "Come on, we don't dare go back to your suite, but you're welcome in mine."

Thrilled by her invitation, Tynan was sorry he had never felt less like making love. "Lead the way," he encouraged her, but with every step he shuddered at how easily he could have been the one lying in the morgue rather than Orion.

Chapter Twenty-One

Tynan hung his robe on the back of her door. "Aren't the closets in our suites larger than this room?"

"Almost, but throughout the galaxy there's a vast difference between the luxurious accommodations provided for important diplomats and the simple quarters assigned to lowly pilots. If you'd rather go back to your suite, just say so."

Not having meant to sound critical, Tynan pulled her into his arms. "On second thought, I like this room. You can't avoid me here."

Amara slipped her arms around his waist and hugged him tight. "We've had too many close calls, Ty."

Tynan stroked her curls and tipped her head slightly to meet her gaze. "The worst is over, and we're both alive—and together."

Amara bit her lower lip to keep from sniveling pathetically. "The worst hasn't even begun," she predicted darkly. "Orion had a great deal of influence, so there's sure to be a scandal when the violent nature of his death is made public. Malicious people will take an evil delight in making us the target of their cruel innuendos."

"We needn't pay any attention to their kind."

"Yes, I know, but unlike you, I'm not returning to a distant sanctuary where vicious rumors can simply be ignored. I'll be at Fleet Command, where the best way to silence suspicions will be to discover the truth about Orion. He always took meticulous care of details, so I know he had to have kept records and perhaps had long-range plans of what he hoped to accomplish when he was elected to Alado's board. As soon as I get back, I'll begin a thorough search of his files and bring every bit of incriminating evidence to light. I don't care if it's no more than a vague reference in his appointment calendar, I'll investigate everything."

Tynan stepped back slightly. "I can't help but admire your determination. I just want to go home and forget Orion ever existed."

Amara searched his expression for some small sign of regret that their time together was drawing to its inevitable close, but he merely looked relieved that he would soon be returning to the Keep. "What about me?" she whispered. "Will you forget me too?"

Appalled that she would ask such a question, Tynan pulled her back into a fervent embrace. "Never," he vowed, nearly crushing her in his arms. He wanted to hold her forever, and the impossibility of that desire brought a wrenching pain. It was only by turning his mind to practical matters that he succeeded in retaining his composure.

"We need to get out of these filthy clothes," he urged. "Do you have a shower?"

As emotionally drained as he, Amara moved away. "Yes, but I doubt it will accommodate us both."

Tynan unbuttoned his shirt. "Let's give it a try anyway."

Amara peeled off her uniform, rolled it into a rumpled ball, and shoved it into the trash receptacal in the wall. Seeing Tynan's startled expression, she shrugged slightly. "The laundry can remove the bloodstains, but it would be very bad luck to wear it again."

Sharing her superstition, Tynan stepped out of his clothes and tossed them away too. Then he took her hand, and with only a few seconds of careful maneuvering, they squeezed themselves into the shower. Amara then had to turn on the spray with a nudge of her shoulder, but awash in warm soapy bubbles, the horror of the morning gradually slipped away, leaving them refreshed in both body and spirit.

As soon as they were dry, Tynan pulled Amara down on the narrow bunk. He didn't miss their more spacious quarters and wide bed, for in whatever position they chose here, their bodies were snuggled together. "This is almost like being back on the Starcruiser," he said. Then, recalling that they still had a vital issue to settle, he sat up slightly.

"Were you really serious about not being my pilot home?"

Amara reached up to brush his curls off his forehead. "Yes. I know I promised that I would be, but please don't ask it of me. To take you home, and then have to leave without you, would be the worst torture I can imagine."

Tynan frowned slightly. "You've always known—"

Amara pulled him down into her arms and silenced his objection with a lingering kiss. "Yes, I have," she finally replied, "but that doesn't make saying good-bye any less painful."

Tynan didn't think he could even board a Starcruiser without her, but he wouldn't beg her to come with him if it would cause her the excruciating pain he was feeling now. He tried to speak, but found it impossible to give words to the tumultuous emotions seething inside him. He could have died that day, and yet he felt reborn in her arms. Drinking in her next kiss with grateful abandon, he lost himself in loving her.

He nuzzled, kissed, and licked every delectable swell, indentation, and curve of her lithe body, memorizing her intoxicating scent, and savoring her luscious taste. Tickling her with a rose from her bouquet, he found her fair skin every bit as soft as the crimson petals.

Occasionally the summoning tone would sound on the communications panel, but when Amara made no move to respond, Tynan ignored it too. No message could be more important than the unspoken promises they shared. A haze of pleasure blurred the hours, lengthening the afternoon into evening without his ever being aware of the passage of time. There was only the delicious present, and the fascinating woman he adored.

413

Grateful to again have clear vision, Amara studied Tynan with a loving gaze. She traced the shape of his ear with her fingertips and feathered the ebony curls at his nape. His face was bruised, but not badly, and she kissed his cheek before brushing her lips against his mouth.

"I can remember when you yanked off your bandages," she revealed. "You were furious with me, but I was so struck by how handsome you were, I don't think I put up much of a defense."

Embarrassed that he had been so short-tempered with her, Tynan chose to distract her with a seductive caress. "Let's talk about something else," he begged as he drew her knee over his hip. "Better yet, let's not talk at all."

Amara would have preferred an exchange of confidences, or simply intimate teasing that she could recall later, but because he did not, she ceased to reminisce. Instead, she pressed against his hand, silently coaxing him to deepen his erotic explorations until the fiery thrill he had stoked had to be cooled. Placing her hands on his shoulders, she pushed him onto his back, then moved astride him. She sat still for a long moment, savoring the hardness of him beneath her feminine crease. Then she eased against him with a subtle turn of her hips, sliding along his rigid shaft to create an exquisite friction until he was as eager to seek release as she.

Only then did she rise on her knees and guide him inside, relishing the rippling sensation as her inner core stretched to sheathe him deeply. She held still, waiting until Tynan's passion-drugged gaze inspired her to begin a slow, teasing motion that carried them to the outer reaches of paradise. Hovering there, she raked her fingernails down his chest, leaving pale trails as her inner heat singed his soul. When he pulled her down into his arms, she cried his name in a grateful gasp and he sent his last thrust plunging to her depths.

Becoming truly one in a sparkling burst of shared bliss, they lay in a satisfied heap until the fluttering longing to rejoin aroused them again. Sometimes teasing, always ardent, their loving play continued long into the night and at last, all their desires sated, they clung to each other in a deep, dreamless sleep.

It was the silence that awakened Tynan late the next morning—that, and the uncomfortable awareness of being alone in the bed. At first he thought Amara must be in the bathroom, but the door was ajar and he could see that she wasn't. Curious as to her whereabouts, he propped himself up on an elbow, yawned, and raked his fingers through his hair. Then he noticed his robe hanging alone on the back of the door, and the single rose lying where the bouquet had been.

"Oh God, Amara," he groaned. "Where have you gone now?"

It wasn't until he had gotten up and stretched lazily that he noticed the note beneath the rose. A chill of fear coursed down his spine. Even before reading it, he knew that this time she hadn't merely changed rooms, but had truly left him. After the dangers they had survived and the joys they had shared, he knew she would always live in his heart. To have lost her so suddenly was tragic. He had to sit back down on the bed to steady himself before he opened her brief note.

I can't bear to tell you good-bye.

Love always, Amara

Tynan didn't even try to stop the tears that filled his eyes. Inhaling the rose's heavy perfume, he let the full force of his sorrow wash through him. At the very least, he had thought they would have a few more days together. Each hour would have been as precious as last night. Why hadn't Amara craved more time too?

Heartbroken, yet furiously angry that she had not delayed her departure as long as possible, he looked for something to hurl, but the sparsely furnished room held nothing that would shatter with a satisfying crash, and he was forced to toss one of his boots against the back of the door. It landed with a dull thud, mocking his attempt to vent his rage. He rose, eager to leave too. The light on the communications panel lured him near, and thinking that if he couldn't have Amara, he could at least have her messages, he pressed the button to request them.

The first was from Jeffrey Hart, and while Tynan recalled the name as someone he had met, he couldn't place him. Jeff, however, obviously knew Amara well, for he begged her to contact him as though he had that right. The next call was from a tearful Solana Diaz, who said only that she was returning immediately to Fleet Command and would see Amara there. The next three calls were from Ross Belding, whose voice grew increasingly high-pitched and breathless as he pleaded for help in locating Tynan.

Feeling sorry for the conscientious young man, Tynan requested Ross's room number and reached him there. Relieved to hear from him, Ross greeted him with a rush of questions, but Tynan quickly interrupted to ask if Amara had already departed for Fleet Command. Once assured that she had, he slumped back against the wall.

"Calm down if you can," he advised, as much to himself as Ross. "I'll help salvage the peace talks. I owe Alado that, but I don't want to continue as their representative. With Orion dead, you must be in charge for the time being, so choose someone to succeed me. I'd like to suggest that he or she work toward a more equitable accord, perhaps by granting Omega and Serema loans for expansion."

Agreeing with his suggestion, Ross responded enthusiastically, but all Tynan truly wanted to discuss was how soon he could arrange a flight home. "I'll also need to leave a statement about Risto Cortez so I won't have to appear at his trial. Arrange that for me too, please." Promising to meet with Ross in an hour, Tynan ended the call.

As Tynan made his way back to his suite, he found that the very same people who had once moved close to touch him were now drawing away. Averted glances rather than smiles met him at every turn, and he hoped Amara wasn't suffering the same silent scorn. Reaching into his pocket for the rose she had left him, he was saddened to think that no matter how she was doing, he would never know.

Chapter Twenty-Two

Despite his hopes of returning home quickly, nearly a week passed before Tynan was able to leave for Earth. Glen Archer was assigned as his pilot, and the quiet young man proved to be surprisingly good company. Glen enjoyed discussing philosophy as much as he did playing Banshee Quest, and because the trip was nothing like Tynan's earlier voyage, he did not find it impossible to bear. The whole way he kept telling himself that once he had returned to the Keep, he would be able to pick up his life as though he had never been away. But as soon as he walked into his room, he realized how wrong he had been.

Although Amara had spent only one night there, when Tynan closed his eyes he could hear echoes of her sparkling laughter. She had sat on his bed to hold his hand, relaxed at his table, and slept near the door. He had not expected to feel her presence there so strongly. He was home, yet without her, it didn't feel like home anymore.

Having expected only good to come from Tynan's participation in the peace conference, Gregory Nash was distressed by the difficulties his protégé had encountered. Tynan had always relished the solitude necessary to pursue his studies, but now, rather than spending time in the Keep's magnificent library, he strolled the garden for hours on end. Respecting Tynan's privacy, Gregory had given him time to adjust to his return home, but the young man was no less morose than on his arrival.

When a message was transmitted from Alado's Fleet Command two weeks after Tynan's return, Gregory rushed outside to find him. He joined him on a bench in the garden and handed him the communique. "I hope this is good news," he offered, and thinking it just might prompt the confidences Tynan had yet to give, he waited for a report.

Tynan saw Alado's double triangle logo, and certain the dispatch had come from Amara, he hurriedly scanned it. Though it wasn't the warm personal message for which he had hoped, it did provide welcome news he was eager to share. "It's from Lieutenant Greer; I'm sure you remember her."

Gregory raised his brows slightly. "Of course."

"She's working with the team investigating Orion's activities. Apparently, he maintained extensive files, and a comparison of his coded notations shows a direct correlation with the dates of several hijackings. Alado lost only the transport ships carrying the most expensive cargoes, and it was generally believed that someone had to be alerting pirates to those valuable shipments. As Secretary of the diplomatic corps, Orion had unlimited access to Alado's communications equipment, permitting him to contact the pirates without drawing suspicion to himself. There's also a link between his visits to the outer colonies and the dates when sizable deposits were made into numbered bank accounts now identified as his."

Tynan summarized the final paragraph. "That's only what the initial inquiry has found; there's bound to be more."

Amazed by his former student's duplicity, Gregory shook his head sadly. "What could have possessed him to betray his own firm to pirates?"

Having given a great deal of thought to that puzzling question, Tynan felt certain he had the answer. "Orion had an insatiable lust for power. As a child, he was a mean-spirited bully, and as an adult he manipulated everything and everyone within his grasp. I'll bet he was in league with pirates merely because they must have been a challenge to control. I didn't mean to kill him the day we fought. I'd only intended to stop him from forcing a treaty that perpetuated a dangerous imbalance, and I'd hoped to block his election to Alado's board. I wanted people to see him for the tyrant he was sure to become."

Tynan turned to his old friend. "Orion and I were complete opposites, but why? We had the same upbringing here, were presented with the very same lessons about truth and responsibility to our fellow man. Why was I the only one to adopt the Guardians' high principles? My parents just threw me away, so I couldn't have come from better stock than he did. Why were we so different?"

Tynan looked so sincerely distressed by that question that Gregory found it impossible to provide a facile reply. Unable to meet the younger man's gaze, he looked down at the tips of his boots, then at the frayed ends of his belt. His conscience troubled him badly, and when he finally spoke, his voice held a hollow, fearful ring.

"There's something I should have told you a long time ago," he admitted reluctantly. "Perhaps it will help to answer your question. Come, take a walk with me, and I'll try to find the words for what must be said."

Greatly intrigued, Tynan folded the message from Amara and slipped it into his pocket. He would decide later whether or not he dared reply and risk renewing the feelings for her he had worked so diligently to suppress since they'd parted. He had expected Gregory to walk in the garden as they often had in the past, but the Director led him out the front gate and down the road bordering the fields. He and Amara had walked over plowed earth, but now the first of the summer's vegetable crops had sprouted, tinting the landscape a bright green.

Tynan's frequent sidelong glances made his impatience plain, and Gregory cleared his throat noisily. "I'm sorry to make you wait. It's just that I'm uncertain where to begin. Since you've been home, we've all noticed the change in you. You've become restless and easily distracted, which isn't like you at all. I hope you won't think I'm intruding, but I couldn't help but notice how glad you seemed to be to hear from Lieutenant Greer. Does she have anything to do with your melancholy mood?"

Disgusted, Tynan came to an abrupt halt. "Is this what you brought me way out here to say? Because if it is, I have no need of your advice. Whatever may have happened between Amara and me belongs to us, and I won't share it."

Gregory responded with a placating gesture. "Please, this is very difficult for me, and I don't want you to misunderstand. I was merely hoping that if you cared for her, you'd be more sympathetic to what I'm about to say."

Tynan wouldn't even make a pretense of not loving Amara, and he nodded. "Yes, I care about her. Now just what is it you have to say that's proving to be so damn difficult?"

Fearful of Tynan's response, Gregory focused his gaze on a distant oak tree and said a silent prayer for strength. He had attempted to gather his thoughts on their walk, but he still felt woefully unprepared. "Men become Guardians for a variety of reasons, and more than one has joined us because of a failed love affair. There was one man who loved his childhood sweetheart with all his heart and soul, but she was a high-spirited young woman who was determined to become a physician and wished to dedicate her life to serving wherever medical care was needed most. Eager to pursue her career, she refused the man's proposal, and knowing he would never want another woman for his wife, he came here.

"It wasn't until after she'd been killed in a senseless accident nearly nine months later that he learned he had a son just a few days old. Perhaps she would have told him—there's no way to know—

but her parents were too grief-stricken to raise the babe and brought him here. Only the father knew the truth about him. To everyone else, the child was an orphan placed in our care."

Because Gregory was a thoughtful man who did nothing without purpose, Tynan readily grasped the meaning of his tale. "You're talking about me, aren't you?" he asked. Unable to believe Gregory could actually name his parents, he grabbed his arm and nearly shook him. "You're right. This is a story you should have told me years ago, but you can't stop there. If my father's a Guardian, a man I've known my whole life, then tell me his name."

Gregory's eyes were blue rather than brown, but as they began to fill with tears, Tynan saw the truth the Director could not put into words. He stepped back and, clenching his fists at his sides, had a hard time not lashing out at his old friend. "What were you ashamed of—yourself, or me?"

Gregory wiped his eyes on his sleeve. "Neither," he swore. "I'll admit I was wrong, but I was afraid if you knew, I'd lose you. You're exactly like your mother, you see, and I thought if you knew about her, you'd want to live out her dream rather than mine."

Tynan could scarcely believe a man he had always regarded as generous and kind could have been so selfish. "What was her name?"

"Rafaella Castillo. Her parents were in their forties when she was born and didn't survive her long. My parents aren't living either, so we've only each other to call family."

"Who else knows I'm your son?"

423

"No one," Gregory assured him. "Although I think Orion may have sensed the truth. Although he'd only been here a few months when I came, when I was assigned to teach the youngest boys, he offered to show me around. He was a bright little fellow, very charming, and became quite attached to me. When you appeared, he was naturally jealous of the time I spent caring for you."

"And despised me to his last breath."

"Well, yes, apparently so. But like the others, I didn't realize how badly he had mistreated you until that awful day he broke your ribs in a fight he swore you had started."

"For once he was right; I did start it. He said that after that fight he left here of his own volition. Is that true?"

Gregory gestured toward the Keep, and Tynan fell in step beside him as he started back down the road. "No. He was expelled, and none of us knew what had become of him until his name appeared in the news bulletins from the conference." Lost in dark memories, Gregory remained silent until they reached the massive gate. "I have photographs of your mother. Would you like to see them?"

"Yes, but I needed to see them thirty years ago when I first learned there was such a thing as a mother and realized I didn't have one."

Gregory sighed unhappily. "I'm sorry. Please try to remember that I did what I thought was best."

"I would have been proud to know you were my father all those years when I needed one, but now that I'm a grown man, it's really too late."

"No, you're wrong," Gregory argued. "There are no time limits on love. I love your dear mother as much as ever, and I'll always regret not finding a way for us to be together. I should have been more persistent, gone with her, become a doctor too if need be. All three of us would have had vastly different lives if I had."

"Don't torture yourself; the past can't be changed."

"I know, but I've never stopped blaming myself for Rafaella's death. We were meant to be together, Tynan, and I never should have let her go. You have been a great comfort to me all these years, but perhaps I failed you as greatly as I did Rafaella by not allowing either of you the freedom to be yourselves."

Tynan began to back away. "This was a good life."

"Was?"

"I need time to think," Tynan confided. "Time to put things in perspective. Everything's changed since I got back—or perhaps it's only me."

"I've always been proud of you," Gregory replied, "and whatever you choose to do, I'll be proud still."

Unable to give an equally gracious response, Tynan just shook his head and walked back the way they had come.

That night, after everyone else had gone to bed, Tynan walked through the Keep alone. Carrying a lantern that cast a ghostly glow, he explored it all. He had always loved the cool, medieval feel of the place, and humming a chant he had learned as a child, he traversed the halls, climbed the stairs, and at last went out on the battlements. The overcast sky hid the stars, and gazing up at the darkened heavens, he saw his future devoid of light.

Sinking down in a drafty corner, he rested his arms on his knees and reviewed his life. Certain he would have loved philosophy regardless of where he had found it, he did not think his studies wasted, and he would pursue them still. Only now he knew how much more there was to life, and he was unwilling to settle for the narrow slice he had known.

He had gained a father that day, but while he had always admired Gregory Nash, he would not repeat his mistakes. At war with himself since his return to the Keep, he had felt torn between the loyalty he owed the Guardians and the love he felt for Amara. It had been a senseless battle, and he wished now that he had brought it to an end sooner.

The serenity of the Keep had lost its appeal. He didn't care how long it took, he was going to request transport to Fleet Command and convince Amara Greer to be his wife. As he stood, he recalled the faint memory of a drug-induced dream in which, like a winged goddess, Amara had appeared to rescue him from demons of his own making. This time, he was going to be the one to rescue her. Enjoying that thought, he broke into a ready grin, and feeling more like a knight than a philosopher, he looked forward to leaving the castle that had been his only home.

Chapter Twenty-Three

Jeffrey Hart leaned over to grab a copy of the transmission from the communications unit, saw Tynan Thorn's name, and winced. His first impulse was to destroy the brief message, but knowing Amara deserved better from him, he resigned himself to passing it along. "What do you make of this?" he asked.

Perusing one of Orion's files, Amara raised her hand in a silent plea for patience and read a moment longer before looking up. They had enough evidence to prove Orion dealt with pirates merely as a sideline; his real passion had been the gathering of intelligence. He had been a master at ferreting out the guilty secrets of Alado's executives and had hundreds of tantalizing indiscretions documented in his files, which he had clearly used to enhance his own position within the firm.

Sickened by how ruthlessly her former boss had preyed on others, Amara leaned back and reached out to accept the dispatch. Not expecting anything of particular interest, she gave it a cursory glance, but like Jeff, she was jolted by Tynan's name. Her heart firmly wedged in her throat, she struggled to draw a breath, but her cheeks glowed with a bright blush before she succeeded. They were working in Orion's office, but the elegance of the black-and-gold decor faded into a shadowy mist as memories of Tynan came alive with stunning clarity.

It became impossible for Amara to read as she heard him whispering her name, and she felt his gentle caress brush her curls. She saw him clothed in aubergine and, savoring the seductive softness of his robe, drank in his scent. His image was vivid, his presence so keenly felt that for a brief instant, she would have sworn Tynan was there with her. Catching herself before the daydream turned any more erotic, she focused her attention on the remainder of the message.

Her hands shaking now, she made a deliberate effort to hold steady. "Tynan wants to come here," she murmured numbly.

Jeff had been working closely with Amara in the month since their return to Fleet Command. During that time, he had admired the dedication she displayed while searching Orion's records, but he had continually cursed that same professionalism when she used it to maintain a maddening distance between them. He knew she had been more than a mere escort to Tynan Thorn, but the Guardian's message had caught her off guard, and this time she hadn't been able to conceal the depth of her feelings. Equally affected, Jeff finally saw his effort to win her love as a hopelessly lost cause.

"Then he's as good as here," he assured her. "The board members consider Tynan a hero for blocking Orion's rise to power, to say nothing of the brilliance of his suggestions for creating a new treaty. They'll give him whatever reward he wants. The only question," he emphasized, "is who's going to be his pilot?"

Amara stared his way without really seeing her handsome co-worker. "I don't think Tynan cares about rewards."

"I don't either. I think he's coming after you."

Unwilling to grasp at that faint hope, Amara shook her head. "That's absurd. He couldn't wait to get back to the tranquil life at the Keep, and there's no place for me there."

"If there were, would you go?"

Amara tossed the dispatch on the desk, where it fluttered onto the heap of other notes. "I know you don't mean to be needlessly cruel, Jeff, but there's no use pretending things could be any different than they are. I was the first woman ever admitted to the Keep, and the Guardians didn't hide their eagerness to have me gone."

Jeff nodded thoughtfully. "That may well be true, but there's something you're forgetting."

Not when her memories were so precious, Amara thought to herself. "I doubt it, but what?"

Jeff leaned forward to pluck the message off the desk and waved it as proof while he spoke. "The Guardians might succeed in shutting you out of their stronghold, but they obviously can't keep Tynan in."

A painfully sweet burst of joy swept through Amara, only to be swiftly smothered by abject despair. Tears spilled over her lashes, and horribly embarrassed, she hurried to wipe them away. "No, Tynan would never give up being a Guardian for me."

Jeff responded with a regretful smile. "Amara, he already has. Pack your gear and go get him."

Amara desperately wanted to believe Jeff's prediction, but if it weren't true, she doubted she would survive the disappointment.

Tynan received a terse confirmation of his request for a flight to Fleet Command, but no details other than an estimated arrival date. With nearly a week to wait, he had ample time to sort through a lifetime of belongings and pack away the things he didn't want to take along. He found the task far more difficult than he had first imagined. Space was at a premium on a Starcruiser, and certain that Amara's quarters would be limited at Fleet Command, he didn't want to bring so much that he would make her uncomfortable in her own home.

The thought of leaving behind his treasured collection of books pained him, but he had such high hopes for the life he and Amara would share that he decided that donating them to the Keep was a small price to pay. Finally choosing to include a few favorites, he rearranged the others on the bookshelves. Viewing the worn volumes with pride, he hoped the next person to occupy his room also enjoyed philosophy.

Turning to the mementos he had saved over the years, he came across few that had retained their meaning, but he set them all aside, thinking Gregory might want to keep some too. He had yet to call his old friend father and doubted that he ever would, but he did not begrudge him a souvenir or two of the child Tynan had once been. When viewed in that light, the assortment of trinkets seemed very sad indeed, but Tynan was too eager to embrace the future to dwell on the distant past.

Stretched out on his bed at night, he played out a dozen possible reunion scenes, each ending with Amara in his arms. He dared not hope that she would come for him herself, but he prayed she would be among those to greet him when he arrived at Fleet Command. If by some chance she had left for another assignment, then he would stay no longer than it took to find a way there. He didn't care if he appeared foolish now. His true mistake had been in not appreciating how empty his life would be without Amara's love.

When at last the day arrived for him to leave, he could see the sadness in his friends' downcast expressions, but he himself was filled with exhilaration. He didn't share their sorrow and promised only to send word of his travels. Anxious to be on his way, he paced the gardens and kept searching the sky for the first glimpse of a Starcruiser. When Gregory Nash joined him, he realized that in his eagerness to see Amara again, he had not thought how to tell him good-bye.

Gregory fell in beside him. "I've decided not to give your room to anyone else. It's not that I expect you to return. I don't, but yours is a place that can't be filled."

Touched, Tynan nodded thoughtfully. "Make it a museum if you must, but not a shrine."

"Oh no, a flattering tribute is all I intend. There's been a remarkable increase in the number of men seeking to join us since you participated in the peace conference. I'm hoping that's because of a sincere love for Earth's history rather than mere fascination with your exploits. All men are welcome to visit us for a retreat, of course, but perhaps after seeing your room, their curiosity will be satisfied, and we'll not hear from them again."

Tynan stopped in the middle of the path. Gregory was attempting to keep their conversation light, but it was obviously a strain. "You haven't lost me," he assured him. "My ties to the Keep are too strong. I'll come back, and perhaps more often than you'd wish."

"That's impossible, unless you intend to bring your pretty pilot along."

"Why not? I think she looks very good in one of my robes." For a brief instant, Tynan was tempted to describe Amara's tattoo, but at the last moment, he chose to keep the beautiful design, like the lovely young woman, all to himself. Again walking in step, he encouraged Gregory to talk of the Keep, but at the first sign of the Starcruiser, he bolted away.

Forgetting his carefully packed belongings, he stood at the gate to watch the silver ship land in the field. Then, unable to wait for the pilot to emerge, he ran out to meet it. When the hatch opened, he tore up the steps. A hurried glance into the cockpit failed to locate the pilot, but as he turned toward the passenger cabin, he saw her.

Amara had spent the whole voyage attempting to tame the wildly exciting expectations Jeffrey Hart had inspired. She had almost succeeded in convincing herself that Tynan merely wished to journey to Fleet Command to join in their research. But the happiness that lit his face mirrored the love in her heart too brightly for her to mistake his purpose.

"We have to talk," she stated firmly.

Eager to make love to her, Tynan shook his head. "Later."

He came toward her, but Amara raised both hands to stop him. Her memories had preserved his appearance in perfect detail, and the attraction she felt for him was stronger than ever. Still, she wanted to make certain the choice he was making was the correct one for them both.

"Now. Your request for transportation didn't provide even a hint as to why you wished to visit Fleet Command. Are you interested in Orion's files?"

Tynan couldn't help but laugh. "No, not at all."

"Something else then?"

She had worn her hair down, the way he liked it, and certain that had been a conscious choice, Tynan took another step forward. Amara tried to back away, but a seat blocked her way, and before she could turn down the aisle he caught her in his arms. He pulled her close and nuzzled her rose-scented curls.

"Why are you being so difficult?" he asked. "You must know how badly I've missed you."

If his seductive whisper and tender touch hadn't been her undoing, then the incredible softness of his robe would have. Amara couldn't bring herself to pull away and instead snuggled against him. She felt as at home in his arms as she always had, yet her emotions were still in turmoil.

"What do you want, Ty—for us to see each other whenever we can?"

Tynan ran his hands lightly down the back of her gold flightsuit before pressing her close. "No, that's not nearly enough. I want us to be together always."

Amara closed her eyes and tried to imagine never having to leave him. It was a glorious possibility, and yet, sadly, much too good to be true. "But the Keep is your home," she murmured softly.

"Not anymore. It's too small now, and much too barren for my tastes."

Amara looked up at him. "Do you really want to make such a drastic change in your life?"

Her expression was so serious that Tynan couldn't resist placing a light kiss on her forehead. "I don't blame you for doubting my sincerity when I used to be so stubborn in my defense of the Guardians' ways. But they've made me whatever I am, and I'll be the same person regardless of where I go. Are you worried that I'll change?"

"If the Keep no longer suits you, then you've already changed," Amara insisted.

"For the better?"

"I hope so."

When she turned shy and looked away, Tynan realized how inconsiderate he was being. "I'm sorry, but I thought you wanted us to be together. Do you feel as though I'm forcing you into something you don't want at all?"

Standing in his arms, it was difficult to remember to breathe, let alone respond to his question intelligently. "A classically educated philosopher and a pilot—what kind of life can we have?"

"A very good one, I hope. What worries you? I reached level six of Banshee Quest with Glen Archer, and with practice, I'm positive I can provide enough of a challenge to keep your interest."

Amara laughed at his teasing claim. "I don't care if you never master the game; I'll not lose interest in you."

"Nor I in you," Tynan promised. "You needn't worry about money either. I've donated the proceeds from my writing to the Keep in the past, but they'll provide sufficient income for us. I'd never ask you to stop flying, any more than you'd ask me to stop pursuing my interest in philosophy. Does the fact that I'm an orphan bother you? If so, I've found out who my parents were, and while it's a sad story, it isn't a scandalous one."

Tynan was doing a thorough job of eliminating the obvious problems, but he hadn't touched upon Amara's most compelling doubt. Afraid that he never would, she forced herself to step out of his embrace. "I can understand how a trip to the Confederation base would make you long for more excitement than you've known here. I can also appreciate how you'd miss the sex we shared because it was something new for you, but—"

"Oh no, you don't." Tynan reached out to grab her wrist. "You're not going to get away from me again. I've written about the beauty of love for years, but until I met you, I didn't really know how good it felt to love someone. I'm not just talking about making love either, but of the simple joy of being with you. If you don't love me, and doubt that you ever will, just say so, but don't insult me by insisting that just because you're the only woman I've ever loved, what I feel for you isn't real."

Impressed by the fierceness of his expression, Amara finally began to smile. She hadn't dared hope that he truly loved her, but if he did, then nothing else mattered. "Are you sure?"

"Sure of what, loving you? Yes, very sure. I love you, Lieutenant Greer, even if you're far too stubborn to admit that you love me."

"I wasn't being stubborn," Amara assured him as she stepped back into his arms. "I just love you too much to settle for anything less in return."

Thrilled by her delightful declaration, Tynan wove his fingers in her glossy curls to hold her close, and their first rapturous kiss blurred into a dozen. It wasn't that he had forgotten how good she tasted and felt, it was just that the sensation was ever so much better than relying on memory. He lifted her off her feet in a joyous hug.

"Close the hatch," he pleaded hoarsely.

Amara was so tightly wrapped around him that she didn't want to move. "Later," she begged. "I couldn't fly now if I tried."

"Don't worry," Tynan whispered. "We're not leaving until dawn."

"Dawn?" While Amara understood his reason, she couldn't hide her dismay. "I thought you'd left the Guardians. Are you still going to cling to their superstitions?"

"Only this one. I want our chaplain to marry us at sunrise, so the luck we take with us will last our whole lives."

Amara had never dreamed she could be as happy as he had made her feel, but she foresaw a problem even if he didn't. "Oh Tynan, that's a lovely thought, but since I'm the cause of your leaving, I doubt they'll let me back inside the Keep."

Recalling how she had stormed his room on her first visit, Tynan's grin grew wide. "They couldn't keep you out before, and now they won't even try. But that's not really the issue. I just asked you to marry me, and I believe I deserve the courtesy of a reply."

Laughter danced in his dark eyes, and there was only one answer Amara wished to give. Thrilled clear through, she couldn't express her joy in words. Instead, she threw her arms around his neck, and hugged him so tightly he could not mistake her response. He used his robe to dry her tears, then to cushion the weight of their bodies as they celebrated their reunion with all the passion their hearts could hold.

NOTE TO READERS

I hope that you enjoyed entering Amara and Tynan's futuristic world. Your comments on their adventuresome love story are most welcome. Please write to me in care of Leisure Books, 276 Fifth Avenue, New York, NY 10001.

LOVE SPELL

THE MAGIC OF ROMANCE
PAST, PRESENT, AND FUTURE....

Dorchester Publishing Co., Inc., the leader in romantic fiction, is pleased to unveil its newest line—Love Spell. Every month, beginning in August 1993, Love Spell will publish one book in each of four categories:

1) *Timeswept Romance*—Modern-day heroines travel to the past to find the men who fulfill their hearts' desires.

2) *Futuristic Romance*—Love on distant worlds where passion is the lifeblood of every man and woman.

3) *Historical Romance*—Full of desire, adventure and intrigue, these stories will thrill readers everywhere.

4) *Contemporary Romance*—With novels by Lori Copeland, Heather Graham, and Jayne Ann Krentz, Love Spell's line of contemporary romance is first-rate.

Exploding with soaring passion and fiery sensuality, Love Spell romances are destined to take you to dazzling new heights of ecstasy.

COMING IN AUGUST 1993

TIMESWEPT ROMANCE

A TIME TO LOVE AGAIN

Flora Speer
Bestselling Author of *Viking Passion*

While updating her computer files, India Baldwin accidentally backdates herself to the time of Charlemagne—and into the arms of a rugged warrior. Although there is no way a modern-day career woman can adjust to life in the barbaric eighth century, a passionate night of Theuderic's masterful caresses leaves India wondering if she'll ever want to return to the twentieth century.

_0-505-51900-3 $4.99 US/$5.99 CAN

FUTURISTIC ROMANCE

HEART OF THE WOLF

Saranne Dawson
Bestselling Author of *The Enchanted Land*

Long has Jocelyn heard of Daken's people and their magical power to assume the shape of wolves. If the legends prove true, the Kassid will be all the help the young princess needs to preserve her empire—unless Daken has designs on her kingdom as well as her love.

_0-505-51901-1 $4.99 US/$5.99 CAN

LEISURE BOOKS
ATTN: Order Department
276 5th Avenue, New York, NY 10001

Please add $1.50 for shipping and handling for the first book and $.35 for each book thereafter. PA., N.Y.S. and N.Y.C. residents, please add appropriate sales tax. No cash, stamps, or C.O.D.s. All orders shipped within 6 weeks via postal service book rate. Canadian orders require $2.00 extra postage and must be paid in U.S. dollars through a U.S. banking facility.

Name _____

Address _____

City _____ State _____ Zip _____

I have enclosed $_____in payment for the checked book(s).
Payment <u>must</u> accompany all orders.□ Please send a free catalog.

COMING IN AUGUST 1993
HISTORICAL ROMANCE
WILD SUMMER ROSE
Amy Elizabeth Saunders

Torn from her carefree rustic life to become a proper city lady, Victoria Larkin bristles at the hypocrisy of the arrogant French aristocrat who wants to seduce her. But Phillipe St. Sebastian is determined to have her at any cost—even the loss of his beloved ancestral home. And as the flames of revolution threaten their very lives, Victoria and Phillipe find strength in the healing power of love.

_0-505-51902-X $4.99 US/$5.99 CAN

CONTEMPORARY ROMANCE
TWO OF A KIND
Lori Copeland
Bestselling Author of *Promise Me Today*

When her lively widowed mother starts chasing around town with seventy-year-old motorcycle enthusiast Clyde Merrill, Courtney Spenser is confronted by Clyde's angry son. Sensual and overbearing, Graham Merrill quickly gets under Courtney's skin—and she's not at all displeased.

_0-505-51903-8 $3.99 US/$4.99 CAN

LEISURE BOOKS
ATTN: Order Department
276 5th Avenue, New York, NY 10001

Please add $1.50 for shipping and handling for the first book and $.35 for each book thereafter. PA., N.Y.S. and N.Y.C. residents, please add appropriate sales tax. No cash, stamps, or C.O.D.s. All orders shipped within 6 weeks via postal service book rate. Canadian orders require $2.00 extra postage and must be paid in U.S. dollars through a U.S. banking facility.

Name_____

Address_____

City _____ State_____ Zip_____

I have enclosed $_____in payment for the checked book(s).

Payment <u>must</u> accompany all orders.☐ Please send a free catalog.

COMING IN SEPTEMBER 1993
HISTORICAL ROMANCE
TEMPTATION
Jane Harrison

He broke her heart once before, but Shadoe Sinclair is a temptation that Lilly McFall cannot deny. And when he saunters back into the frontier town he left years earlier, Lilly will do whatever it takes to make the handsome rogue her own.

_0-505-51906-2 $4.99 US/$5.99 CAN

CONTEMPORARY ROMANCE
WHIRLWIND COURTSHIP
Jayne Ann Krentz writing as Jayne Taylor
Bestselling Author of *Family Man*

When Phoebe Hampton arrives by accident on Harlan Garand's doorstep, he's convinced she's another marriage-minded female sent by his matchmaking aunt. But a sudden snowstorm traps them together for a few days and shows Harlan there's a lot more to Phoebe than meets the eye.

_0-505-51907-0 $3.99 US/$4.99 CAN

LEISURE BOOKS
ATTN: Order Department
276 5th Avenue, New York, NY 10001

Please add $1.50 for shipping and handling for the first book and $.35 for each book thereafter. PA., N.Y.S. and N.Y.C. residents, please add appropriate sales tax. No cash, stamps, or C.O.D.s All orders shipped within 6 weeks via postal service book rate. Canadian orders require $2.00 extra postage and must be paid in U.S. dollars through a U.S. banking facility.

Name _____

Address _____

City _____ State _____ Zip _____

I have enclosed $_____ in payment for the checked book(s). Payment <u>must</u> accompany all orders.□ Please send a free catalog.